SENIOR SALES TAX PROJECT

**Provided by a
Union County
Senior Services
Grant**

D1367600

WILD RAN THE RIVERS

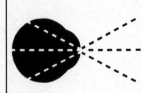

This Large Print Book carries the
Seal of Approval of N.A.V.H.

FIVE TRAILS WEST, BOOK I

WILD RAN THE RIVERS

ONE FAMILY'S WESTERN ODYSSEY

JAMES D. CROWNOVER

THORNDIKE PRESS
A part of Gale, Cengage Learning

GALE
CENGAGE Learning·

Farmington Hills, Mich • San Francisco • New York • Waterville, Maine
Meriden, Conn • Mason, Ohio • Chicago

GALE
CENGAGE Learning®

LIBRARY OF CONGRESS CATALOGING-IN-PUBLICATION DATA

Crownover, James D.
    Wild ran the rivers : one family's western odyssey / by James D. Crownover. — Large print edition.
        pages ; cm. — (Thorndike Press large print western) (Five trails west ; book 1)
    ISBN 978-1-4104-7696-8 (hardcover) — ISBN 1-4104-7696-0 (hardcover)
    1. Cherokee Indians—Fiction. 2. Indian families—Fiction. 3. United States—History—19th century—Fiction. 4. Large type books. I. Title.
PS3603.R765W55 2015
813'.6—dc23   2014042223

Printed in Mexico
1 2 3 4 5 6 7 19 18 17 16 15

To Penny, who nourished
the seed of an idea.

ACKNOWLEDGMENTS

In describing the New Madrid earthquake, I have relied heavily, but not exclusively, on the fine book written by James Lal Penick, Jr., *The New Madrid Earthquakes.* All the events described are as given by actual witnesses to the quakes and I have adapted and applied these events to the characters in my story.

Ruth Harris
Born: 1790
Place: Tennessee
Married: Tom Finn 1806
Married: Samuel Meeker 1815
Place: Village on the Middle Fork

Hiram Harris
Anglo-Saxon
Born: 1767
Place: South Carolina

Samuel Harris
Born: 1794

Sarah Fourkiller
Cherokee
Born: circa 1774
Place: Tennessee

Jerry Harris
Born: 1796
Place: Tennessee
Married: Kansas 1822

Joseph Harris
Born: 1805
Place: Tennessee

John (Pony) 1833
Jacob 1835
Luzina 1838
Parlee 1842
Zenas Leonard 1844

Jesse Meeker, nee Finn
Born: 1807
Place: Pirate's Island
Married: Amira Dreadfulwater 1831
Place: Chewey, Cherokee Nation

Born: 1844
Place: Arkansas
Married: Sophia
Maria Gomez 1876

Sarah Fourkiller Meeker
Born: 1816

PROLOGUE

Only a very small portion of the history of mankind has ever been written down and much of that lacks the ring of authenticity because it was not written contemporaneously with the events recorded or was seen through prejudiced eyes. History has been handed down from generation to generation verbally, often from tribal or clan historian to the next generation's designated historian, for thousands of years. These men and women practiced these stories over and over until they could relate them verbatim as they had been given, resulting in the verbal "recording" of history as accurate as any written word.

In our educated arrogance, we have divided man's time on this earth into "historic" and "prehistoric" times; prehistoric meaning the time before the written word and historic meaning when things were written down. In doing so and dismissing these legends as tales told around the fires, we miss a large portion of the history of man's struggles and accomplishments.

Even today and certainly in the late nineteenth and early twentieth centuries, there were and are those remarkable people who could remember the finest details of past events and could verbally pass them on with accuracy. By comparing them with the observations of other witnesses or participants of the same event, we may eventually gain a more complete picture of what occurred and its significance.

I first met Zenas Leonard Meeker while working for the Federal Writers' Project in 1937. We were collecting stories from the early settlers and someone said he had been around here an awful long time, so the next time I was near Pinetop, I detoured southwest down the Culp Mountain road. Mr. Meeker had a home on the west side of the Culp Mountain foothills above Culp Canyon.

On his porch overlooking the White Sands, I introduced myself and explained a little about our Writers' Project. "Wal, I reckon I *do* have a tale or two you might be interested in hearin', might even be worth writin' down," he said.

The screen door opened with a little

squeak and I rose to greet Mrs. Meeker, his wife of sixty-two years. She stood tall and erect for a woman of her age and her graying hair and fair skin bespoke of someone who had once been blonde or redheaded. She looked to be some years younger than her husband, but that was hard to tell. She smiled and handed me a tall glass of cool well water and visited with us a minute before excusing herself and retiring to the coolness of the adobe house.

Mr. Meeker, when he stood, was slim, erect and square shouldered, about five feet nine inches tall. He had a clear eye and firm grip when we shook. He still walked with a sure step though he occasionally carried a cane, "not because I need support, but so's I can keep the dogs out from under foot," he explained. His hair, though thinning, still held a lot of the black color it must have been in his younger days.

There were a couple of horses in the corral, a few chickens in a wire pen and I heard a pig squeal behind the barn. A milk cow grazed on the sparse grass nearby. "Sophie makes me keep a milk cow for cooking and the grandkids when they come by," he said with a smile. "And I like a little buttermilk with my corn bread, too."

Through a series of interviews with Mr.

Meeker, I gathered several stories of his experiences and the happenings in the Tularosa Basin and elsewhere. His memory was remarkable and I was able to verify its accuracy by comparing his versions of events with other accounts. In fact, as I gained confidence in him, I more often used his versions as the standard whereby other accounts might be compared. I also became aware that his was a remarkable story that went beyond the scope of the Federal Writers' Project. I therefore determined to talk to him about writing his biography, to which he readily agreed.

The story is about the westward migration of four generations of one family from the hills of Tennessee, ending with one descendant (Zenas Meeker) eventually settling in and around the Tularosa Basin in New Mexico Territory. Their trek, beginning in 1803, follows trails marked and unmarked across the country. Four of them were trails with names we know. One was the "paths" of the rivers, especially those east of the Mississippi, whose waters first opened the ways to the western wilderness.

The first named trail west of the big river is the Fallen Ash Trail. It probably first originated near the Falls of the White River at Flee's Settlement, an obscure place now lost in time which was near the present city of Batesville, Arkansas. From there it arced north and westward, through old Carrollton and terminated at Fort Smith. It was later expanded to the Mississippi River and called the Fallen Ash Military Road.

The third trail the family was involved with was the southern route to California as marked out by Captain Randolph Marcy. Originally called the California Road, it was later called the Southern Route.

The fourth trail the family followed was the Cherokee Trail established by the Cherokees in 1849. It began along the Arkansas–Indian Territory border and was the preferred trail for Arkansas drovers and Indian Nation travelers, having plenty of water and grass and avoiding the overgrazed trails to the north. A man named C. C. Seay took a herd of cattle, quite possibility white faced, over this trail from Cincinnati, Arkansas, to California in 1853.

And of course the most famous of all the westward trails was the Santa Fe, that grand highway to the provinces of northern Mexico.

Although some of the incidents of this story have been confirmed by other sources, other incidents related by Zenas Meeker have not. I say this not to bring the shadow of doubt on the veracity of our narrator but as a warning to the serious historian not to mistake this as a carefully researched document. Instead of time-consuming, exhaustive, and possibly futile research, this editor has chosen to write the stories as told and presents them here as being, if not entirely accurate, typical of the times. If nothing else, they are for the pleasure of the reader.

On the appointed day we were to begin, I drove out and took my customary seat on the porch, pencil poised over pad and he began "at the beginning," as he said. To my surprise, "the beginning" was before his father was born and in a place far removed from the basin! What began as a biography of one man became the story of three generations of his family. I was immediately confronted with the problem of how to present the story accurately and yet in a manner that would hold the interest of the reader. Ultimately, I decided to present the narrative as Zenas gave it to me. Hopefully, the result is something you will find readable and interesting. I have added some notes in the text where I thought an explanation was needed. I have annotated them with the initials "J.D."

James Daniels

CHAPTER 1
IN THE BEGINNING
1803

Zenas Leonard Meeker took a sip of hot black coffee brewed the old-time way, sat back in his chair rocking gently and composed his thoughts. "My grandpa was a pirate on the Mississip." My pencil froze in mid word and I caught his sidelong glance and grin as he watched my reaction. "My grandma was Ruth Fourkiller Harris, originally from the hills of Tennessee. Her pa, Hiram Harris, had married a Cherokee woman named Sarah Fourkiller and they had four children. Grandma was the eldest; then there was Samuel, Jerry and Joseph.

"Great-Grandpa Hiram heard about the land grants that the Spanish were offering to new settlers west of the Mississippi in what was then called Louisiana. So in the early spring of 1803 he traveled down the Cumberland River to the Ohio. At Paducah, he learned about the colony called New Madrid that Colonel George Morgan had established

some seventy miles below the mouth of the Ohio. Then late that summer came news of the Louisiana Purchase.

"He determined to go to the new territory, being assured that fertile lands were in plenty and available for immigrants. Returning home, he prepared to move his family to Louisiana. Having sold his land and what possessions he could not take with him, he packed the family in a wagon and started for the new land in the spring of 1806. At the Cumberland River, he traded his team and wagons for a flatboat and securing the services of an experienced river man, loaded the family and their possessions and began the float down the river to their new home. Grandma Ruth was sixteen when this happened and here is the way she told the story a hundred times, I guess."

We sold the wagon at Greenbriar, just above where the Harpeth flows into the Cumberland. Daddy hired a man who called himself Bill Wilson to guide the boat down the river. He was a big burly man, about thirty years old and full of fun and tales of the rivers. We all loved Uncle Billy, as the youngsters called him, and the trip seemed like a big lark, floating the river by day and tying up on the bank at night. In about ten days we reached the Ohio and the next day we pulled into Paducah for supplies. Pa bought staples for the kitchen and seed for planting. Ma bought some cloth and threads. Uncle Billy went uptown to inquire about the condition of the rivers. He came back stepping like a rooster wading the creek and singing loudly. He seemed especially jolly, but Pa said he would be grumpy in the morning.

We loosed from Paducah about sunup and made good time down the river. Uncle Billy was awful quiet and after a while, Pa gave him a pull from the jug. "Hair of the hound that bit him," Pa called it, and Billy cheered up some.

At the nooning, Billy told Pa that it looked like we would hit the Mississippi about sundown. "I don't favor navigatin' those currents 'cept in the light of day and there ain't no good dockin' places fer quite a spell, which means we would be well in the dark 'fore tiein' up. I know a good campin' place 'fore we gits to th' big river, we could make a short day of it today, rest up an' tighten th' cargo some and git a early start tomorry. Mayhap we could make Mad-rid in a couple of days if th' current's good."

Pa studied a minute. "Well, that sounds good with me, Bill, I guess we could use a little rest and I shore don't want any upsets this close to the end of the trip." Uncle Billy nodded and nothing more was said about it.

Along about mid afternoon, Billy pulled over near the south shore. "I'm lookin' for a slough, boys," he called. "First one to see it gits to shoot my gun."

Jerry and Sammy rushed to the front of the boat straining to be the first to see the opening to the slough Billy called Humpy Creek. After a while, Jerry, being the shorter of the two, climbed on top of the cabin to get a better view. They both spied the opening at about the same time and there was a big fuss about who was first.

Uncle Billy laughed and said, "I 'low it was a tie, boys, so maybe you both could take a shot." He steered the boat into the mouth of the slough and the speed of the river current was just enough to push the boat up to the gentle sloping bank. It was obvious this was a favorite camping spot. There was a place for a fire and wood enough left over from previous campers. Pa and Billy pulled the boat up tight to the bank and tied it up to a couple of stumps that had been cut for that purpose.

Sammy and Jerry set up a clamor to shoot, so Uncle Billy laughed and reached for his gun. "It's got a full load, so Sammy can shoot first. You see that knot on the end of that blowed-down tree across the crik? Thet's yore targit, now git down here ahind this stump 'an lay the barrel over the top 'an aim careful. Got 'er in yore sights? Good, now take a breath and hold it, squeeze the trigger slow and firm."

Boom! went the gun, and even resting on the stump, the kick knocked Sammy backwards. "I got it, I got it!" he yelled.

"Shore 'nough you knocked a chip off'n th' side." Billy squinted through the smoke. "We'll see if Jerry kin put a end to that ol' knob 'an we can git on about th' business of settin' up camp." He stoked a half load in the gun for Jerry and lined him up behind the stump. "Now do as I tole Sammy, line th' sights on th' knot. Got a good breath? Now squeeze th' trigger slow an' firm."

Boom! Even a half load kicked Jerry back some. "Did I git it?" Jerry was jumping up and down and waving away at the smoke.

"Durned if yo' didn skin t'other side of it." Billy was shaking with laughter. "Reckon that knot'll live to see another day, boys." He reloaded the gun and propped it up against a tree close to hand.

Pa busied about getting a fire going. He gathered some dried leaves and whittled off some shavings from a stick. Sammy brought a coal from the fire box on the boat and they soon had a fire going big enough for cooking. Ma got out the sourdough starter and made biscuits to set aside for rising.

"I heard a gobbler back up the river," Billy said, picking up his gun. "If I'm lucky, we could have turkey for supper." He slipped into the woods and that's the last we ever seen of him.

After a while, we heard a hail and looked up to see a couple of long canoes gliding into the slough. There were three men in the first boat and four in the second. "Howdy, folks," called a big rough-looking man from the front of the first canoe. "Mind if we join you? Name's Sam Mason Junior," he said as he jumped on the shore. The other canoe pulled up on the opposite side of our boat.

Pa reached for his gun as the men piled on to the bank. Ma was kneeling by the fire and I saw her fold the hatchet under her skirt. The boys both backed toward the woods with me. I was carrying little Joseph wrapped in his blanket asleep. As we reached the edge of the bushes, three or four men rushed out of them and grabbed us. Someone jerked my head back with my hair and I almost lost the baby. Sammy let out a yell and Pa raised his rifle and fired at the nearest man. He went down in a heap and Pa was clubbing his rifle at two others who were rushing him with pistols drawn. The first one fired and Pa stepped back with the impact of the bullet. He swung and I saw one man go down with the gun stock splintered over his head, then Pa crumpled with the sound of the second pistol.

At the same time, two men made a rush at Ma. She stepped back and, with a scream of defiance, crashed the hand ax into the skull of the foremost man. He fell lifeless across the fire. The second man was on her and she swung the ax again and slashed down his forearm to the bone. With a scream, he fell back and Sam Mason fired his pistol at Ma from across the clearing. I saw her head jerk and she sighed and crumpled into a heap. It must have been over in less than a minute. I was pushed roughly into the middle of the clearing, while one filthy man twisted Jerry's arm until he cried out and shoved him down at my feet. Joseph was crying.

"Where's Jobe with that other kid?" Mason asked. He was breathing hard and his eyes were white and flashing above his bearded face.

"I heard him thrashin' in the bushes over

there," one of the men said. He pushed the bushes aside enough to see the soles of two boots lying there. He grabbed the man's legs and began pulling him out of the bushes. "Don't tell me you lost that boy, Jobe." He was laughing. Then he swore and dropped the legs. Jobe lay there staring with lifeless eyes, a blue ringed hole just above his right eye. There was a trail of blood and gore where his head had dragged across the sand. Sammy was gone. Three men slipped into the woods after him.

"Looks like pore Jobe took a stray one," said Mason. "I swear, three men kilt and two maimed jist takin' a lil fambly like this. You fellers take the cake." He was really angry. "Roll Smitty out of that fire, he's stinkin' up th' place. Git everythin' on the boat and let's git out of here afore someone comes along!" Jerry and I were shoved on to the boat and the men loaded everything left on the ground. The man humped over his slashed arm wobbled onto the boat. His pants were soaked with blood to his knees and he was white as a sheet.

"What about Willie?" one called, bending over the man Pa had poled with the gun.

"If he's breathin', bring him with us." Sam Mason was still mad.

Two or three of the men picked up the

unconscious Willie and hauled him on board. After a short impatient wait, the three who had gone after Sammy came out of the woods empty handed. "Tracked him to the edge of the bayou up a ways but couldn't find hide nor hair," one of them said.

"Let him go, th' snakes and skeeters'll eat 'im," Sam Mason growled.

With that, they shoved off. They pushed out into the current with the canoes tied behind and we started downstream. I took a last look at the little clearing where Momma and Papa lay without even the dignity of burial. That vision is still in my mind after all this time. Jerry and I huddled under the lee of the cabin and sobbed quietly. Little Joseph slept some, but he was getting hungry and restless.

The eight pirates didn't say much, just went about their business steering and poling down the river. About the only sound from them was the low groaning of the man Mom wounded. Willie lay still as death. One of the men rummaged through our things and came up with a sheet he ripped up and bound the wounded arm. I took some comfort knowing Pa and Ma had put up such a good fight. With three dead and two bad wounded, what booty these pirates got was costly. It was growing dark, but we kept going. They must have known the rivers pretty good to navigate them in the dark. I got some blankets from the cabin and wrapped Jerry and the baby in them and we all slept.

Chapter 2
Pirate's Booty

Sometime 'way in the morning I felt the boat swing around a little and woke enough to realize we had pulled into the current of the bigger river. Just before daylight, we came upon an island over close to the west side of the river. The boat swung around on the east side and steered into a little cove near the downstream end. Two men with ropes jumped over the side and waded up under the overhanging brush to the shore. They pulled the boat up under the limbs until I couldn't see further than ten feet out into the river. We were practically invisible to anyone passing by.

The men hustled us off the boat. The man with the wounded arm looked very pale and weak and one of the men was helping him walk. I never saw Willie again after dark. I suppose he must have died and they rolled him over the side, though I wouldn't put it past any one of them rolling him overboard whether he was dead or not. It made more booty for them, such as it was.

The whole island was ringed at the water's edge with a heavy growth of brush, but when you got by the underbrush, there was a mature forest of hardwood trees and little undergrowth. Up under the trees were a dozen or more shanties and lean-to shelters. A small group of men and slatternly looking women and a few barefooted tykes in shirts or naked moved toward the boat. Jerry and I were shoved up the bank by one of the men, then he turned back to the boat where the men were unloading everything on it. No one paid us any attention. The women pitched in without a word spoken and making a bucket brigade line, they passed everything that was loose off the boat and up the bank into a big pile. One man dug out the fire box, throwing the coals into the water, then he pried up the frame and dug Pa's cash box out of the hiding place. It must have been a common place to hide valuables, 'cause it didn't fool *them* any.

While everyone was busy, I pulled a small trunk from the pile and got some clean clothes for little Joseph. Then I sat on the trunk making sure my skirts covered it so it wasn't visible. Joseph was crying with hunger and I couldn't do anything more than rock him. Momma had been nursing him and if we didn't get him some milk soon, he wasn't going to live long. A burly man in a black beard called, "Maudie, for Lord's sake, shut thet baby up 'fore he has every boat on th' river lookin' fer 'im!"

A large lady with dirty hands and clothes stepped up and reached for Joseph. "Let me have him, child, I've something here that will hush him up." Her smile gave me confidence that she meant no harm so I handed little Joseph to her. She lifted her blouse and offered the baby her breast and Joseph took it frantically. "*That* should hold her for a while." She smiled at me. "I'm sup-posin' you're not the mammy, child."

"*He's* my brother," I replied.

"So it's a boy, is it?" She smiled and rocked the suckling baby a little. "All I can have is girls, three of 'em to the present and Hi, my man, wants a boy awful bad. May-hap I found one for 'im!" I started to protest, but she was gone, pushing through the crowd to where her man was working. I watched her closely as she showed Joseph to Hi and spoke to him in undertones. The man gave me a glance and nodded curtly to the woman. "Goodness this child is hun-gry!" she exclaimed as she came back to where I sat. "He's got that side dry and I'm

29

gonna havta give him some from the other side." She deftly turned Joseph in her arms and he hungrily took the other breast. "My little Shawna is gonna be short some for her dinner. She's close to weanin' so I guess this will hurry her along to that."

Jerry looked at me, his face streaked with dirt and tears, his eyes swollen. "She ain't takin' Little Joe, is she, Ruthie, she cain't do that, can she?"

"Oh my heavens, child," Maudie interjected, "we're jist one big fambly here an' no one's gonna leave, not no times soon that is. Yore sister cain't feed him and keep him alive an' I've got a nice warm house for him. You'll have a home here close an' so will Sis. You can see Joe anytime you want. I'll take good care of yore brother jist lak he was my own. Hirum's gonna choose the baby in his share of the booty an' he'll live with us jist lak fambly." Then lowering her voice she said to me, "You jist keep sittin' on that trunk, Sugar Booger, an' if anyone complains, we'll claim it's baby clothes an' goes with him." She nodded and winked. I went all cold inside and almost lost my seat. Jerry was rocking to and fro and crying to himself. I lifted him into my lap and held him tight. In my own sorrow and dispair there weren't any words I could say to comfort him.

My heart sank. So that was how it was to be. Joseph, Jerry and I were booty just like the cargo on the boat, to be auctioned off like the rest of our property. Sam Mason stood up on the front of the boat. "All right, people, git quiet an' we'll git started. This here boat's in pretty good shape, should bring near a hunnert dollar on the market. We kin either sell it up the river or if you need the lumber for a shelter, you could have it for say ninety dollars or pesos silver or we would take gold." He grinned and I noticed a front tooth was missing.

"I'll take it out of my portion of th' share," the man who had captured Jerry said.

"Or pay th' balance if yore share don't come to ninety."

Mason grinned — an ugly leer. "Jobe an' Smittie an' Willie didn't have no family, so we will divide their shares among those of us that made it back. Paddy's widder ort to git his share for the care of herself an' little Paddy, there." He indicated a woman and tyke standing at the edge of the crowd. She didn't look very upset about Paddy not coming back. "All the food stuff will go into th' store an' we will share it with all the cooks as the need arises," Mason continued. "All the rest of th' gear will go in th' pile to

31

be divided up into nine shares, one for each man who went and Paddy's widder, an' one for th' community. I'm takin' th' girl for my first share an' givin' up my second choice to boot."

Each man and Paddy's Widow in turn chose something from the booty for his share. Hiram chose little Joseph and some other item, saying the child "weren't no bargain, jist 'nother mouth to feed."

Paddy's Widow chose Jerry. He cried and clung to me all the more. She made no move to take him away. When the first round of choosing had finished, the crowd decided their share. There was a lot of shouting back and forth, but since the crowd was heavily weighted with women, the community shares were largely trunks of clothes and kitchen hardware. The choosing started around again after Sam Mason passed on the second round and the choosing continued until there was nothing left that anyone wanted. I noticed no one wanted Pa's plow and seed. No one in this crowd looked ambitious enough to plow or plant; the items had no value to them on the island. The women began going through the trunks and kitchen gear and more than one squabble broke out over one item or another.

From the edge of the crowd a young man called out, "Sam, how much money value you put on that woman you chose?"

Mason had jumped down from the boat and was arranging the items he had chosen. He raised his head slowly and for an' instant glared at the questioner, but quickly put on a grin to hide his discomfort. Everyone stopped and it got very quiet. Sam Mason was in a spot. If he said I was too valuable, the others would demand him to return some of his booty. Setting my value too low might cost him some.

"Why, I don't know, Tom, I thought she would be worth twice what th' average share value was, so I skipped my second turn." He paused as if in thought. "I guess we should leave it up to th' boys to determine what that value is."

I could see some sly grins and winks shared in the crowd and one of the raiders rubbed his chin as if in deep thought then said, "Some of this gear is mighty worn, at second look an' not as valable as I first thought. Thet flatboat's made a few more trips down th' river than we thought, an' Will took two turns to git it . . . I'd guess one round weren't wurth moh'n twenty, twenty-five dollar, woun't you, Jeb?"

Jeb looked thoughtful. "Waaal," he spoke

slowly as if in deep thought, "I'se jist lookin' at this here stuff an' thinkin' th' same thang. Might be mor'n twenty dollar, say twenty-five to thirty uld be more lak it."

Sam squirmed. He knew he was the object of some joshing, but it could turn against him.

"Considerin' Sam was the leader of this here outin' an' should git the lion's share, how much would you say that there girl mought be wurth?" asked Tom to the men. Tom was taking the heat off of Mason by allowing the men to decide and left room for Mason to save face.

"She's moughty young, but looks sturdy enough and in good health. Seems to have right smart of Injun blood and might be hard ter tame," mused Jeb.

[Here Zenas interjected that his Grandmother Ruth, was light skinned, but with the jet-black hair and features of her mother.]

One of the other raiders spoke up, "Goin' price for a Injun ain't much these days, but she's got at least fifty percent white in 'er, I'd guess on th' open market she might take fifty, sixty-five dollars."

There was a murmur through the crowd. Sam Mason dug at the sand with his toe. "You men shore got me in a fix. I don't think thet girl's worth mor'n thirty, forty

dollars, even with some white blood in 'er."
Hoping to deflect any criticisms of his deal-
ing, he said, "I'll think it over a couple days
an' let you know somethin', Tom."

Tom stood up and turned as if to go. "I
ain't gonner take any of your cast-offs, Sam
Mason, an' I don' want any damaged goods,
I'm willin' to pay you a hundred dollars for
that gal, right now." The crowd roared with
laughter.

"Why, I woudn't take less'n a hunnert fifty
for her," Sam shot back, then caught himself. The crowd roared again.

Tom whirled around. "I got a hunnert
twenty-five gold *burnin'* my pocket," he said.

Sam was caught in a bidding war and
knew he would lose. "A hunnert fifty or
nothin'," he fairly shouted.

"Sold!" yelled Tom over the roar of the
crowd. He strode to the front and plopped
down a leather bag with a clink on the deck
of the boat. "Jeb, count out a hunnert fifty
out of them gold coins an' give 'em to Sam,
I've got me a woman! An' dont you git any
sticky fingers, I'll be watchin' you!"

Even I had to smile at the audacity of this
man in tricking Sam Mason out of his gain.
Jerry looked bewildered at all the goin's on,
but seemed to like the one called Tom. I
certainly preferred this young man who

hadn't raided and murdered my family over that cold-blooded killer Sam Mason, especially when I found out that he already had a woman living with him.

Someone tapped my shoulder and Paddy's woman stepped around beside us. She had frizzy red hair and fair skin, as did the child she was carrying and when she spoke it was with a heavy Irish accent. "Sure an' it's the child I'll be needin' for the chor-r-res aboot the place, but he needn't be spendin' all his time wi' me. If he keeps the wood chopped an' watches the child, I'll feed him two meals a day an' he can stay wi' you if it pleases 'im."

Then to Jerry she said, "Come over first thing the morr-r-row an' chop me some wood an' I'll see you git a good meal for your labors, boy. Me name be Rose an' here's Little Paddy for you to watch arter."

She had a kindly smile for him and Jerry stood up and with a little bow said, "Yes ma'am, I'll be there soon's I find the way."

"Twon't be hard to do, boy, we live just a short way from Tom Finn's," she replied with a little pat on his head and turned to speak a few words to Maudie, who held Joseph quietly sleeping in her arms.

"She said I could stay with you, Ruthie," Jerry whispered in Cherokee. "Do you really think I can?" I nodded, but my heart was full of doubts about what was in store for us. Tom Finn was a pirate and could be just as cruel a man as Sam Mason or any of the others in this bunch.

As Rose left with Little Paddy in tow, Maudie stepped over to where I still sat on the trunk. "You jist sit there until this crowd thins some, child, an' we'll get Hiram to lug that trunk home when there's not many left to see where it came from. Way things work 'round here, I'll be keeping the baby, but you an' the boy there can see him anytime you want, jist like he's still your brother. I mought need your help corralin' him an' Shawna, 'specially when this tyke gits to walkin'. I've decided to name him William after my pa," she said smiling down at the sleeping baby.

"His name is Joseph Harris," I said firmly.

"Not now that we've 'dopted him," Maudie replied just as firmly. Then cocking her head in thought, she mused, "We can call him William Joseph Cates."

Too numbed and tired from all the things that happened to these two or three days, I didn't reply. Jerry just sat on my lap and stared at nothing. He was gently rocking to and fro.

"Maudie, oh Maudie." It was Tom Finn

calling from the boat. "I'm gonna hep Will git this here hull up on the bank an' wreck it down so's he kin build onto his house. Would you mind takin' my woman home with you, an' I'll come by for her 'bout sundown?"

"Be glad to, Tom," Maudie replied. "Soon's Hi carries this truck home, we'll be on our way."

Hi looked up from inspecting the boat at the not-too-subtle hint from Maudie and shook his head. He came walking toward us wiping his muddy hands on his already muddy pants. "What is it you want, woman?" He pretended to grump. "I shore got me a handful whin I bought you, wonder if I could git a refund from that no-good river rat that sold you?" Though his voice was gruff, his eyes were merry behind his full beard. I recognized him as the one who had grabbed Jerry on the beach and Jerry must have too, for he drew back against me closer.

"You wouldn't know a good deal if it bit you on the hind sides," Maudie shot back then in a lower voice, "now grab that trunk an' git it to the house 'fore someone gits 'spicious an' raises a fuss."

Hi blinked his surprise at the trunk as I stood up. Then he quickly grabbed the handles and without hesitation strode off up the bank toward the cluster of huts.

"Come along, children," Maudie called as she fell in behind Hi. "I 'spose you haven't et for a while, neither, an' I got vittles waitin'."

They led the way toward the middle of the row of huts to one that sat under a huge chestnut tree, seeming to lean against its trunk for support. Three little barefoot girls were playing around the door. They looked to be about five, three and two years old. They stopped their play and solemnly watched our approach.

"Look what Daddy brought us from the river," Maudie called, "a little brother for you!" The girls gathered around Maudie as she bent over to show the sleeping child. I caught an involuntary sob before it came out. Jerry just stared and pulled closer to my side. For all his ten years, he seemed to be very small at the moment. Tears were running down his cheeks again. The girls cooed over Joseph, then the youngest whom I assumed was Shawna clouded up and for a moment I thought she was going to cry, but Maudie quickly rose and strode to the doorway.

"We gotta feed these children 'fore they starve plum to death," she called. At the door she nearly ran into Hi as he was coming back out to return to the boat. "Don't expect me to be feedin' you after dark, Hiram Cates, unless you hie yourself back here an' chop some wood for the stove *early* this afternoon!"

"Since when did *you* start givin' orders, woman, we got plenty to do gittin' that boat wrecked out an' I don' know when I'll be back," he shot back, but he winked at us as he passed.

"Come on in, child," she urged as we hesitated at the door, "you can hold little Will while I stir up some food for you."

The inside of the hut was dim under the canopy of trees, and as my eyes grew accustomed to the dimness, I noticed the dirt floor was well swept. In the corner was a cookstove that also served as heat for the house. The furnishings were a crazy contrast in opulence and poverty. In the middle of the room stood a magnificent oak table with planks under the feet. Around it were three wooden crates and a nail keg set on end for chairs. At the head was a fine chair with arms that obviously did not go with the table. In the corner closest to the stove was a low handmade bed obviously for the children. A corner across the room was walled off with sheets of canvas. Maudie proudly shoved back the curtain to reveal a mahogany bed with tall posts and resplendent with linen canopy. Each leg stood in a small container of water to keep ants out of the bed, as was the custom in that region. A candle in a silver stand stood on a crate near the head of the bed. "Hi got this bed from a barge up from New Orleans, ain't it beautiful? Won't be too long 'fore we have a reg'ler home here if Hi's luck holds." She smiled. "Now you rummage through that trunk an' find little Will some clean clothes while I git busy in the kitchen."

The trunk did have some baby clothes in it, along with things Ma had packed for the boys to wear. Tears fell on Samuel's linen Sunday shirt. In one corner were even two of my dresses. In the middle of the trunk wrapped in oilcloth and tied up with string was Papa's family Bible. I grabbed it and held it close for a minute then replaced it in the trunk. I called Jerry in and washed his face and put a clean shirt on him.

Maudie appeared in the room with a drawer taken from the wardrobe in the main room and lined with a quilt. "Here's a bed for the tyke. It ain't fancy, but it'll do." She gently laid Joseph in it and sat it in the middle of the bed. "I mind he'll sleep good there for a while. Poor child is worn to a

41

frazzle. Come on, Ruth, dinner's almost ready." That was the first time anyone had referred to me by name since we had left that awful bayou.

The kitchen consisted of the stove, a large stump that served as a table and the ever-present wooden crate nailed high on the wall for storage. On one side of the stump was a hollow where bread was made and the hominy was pounded. A water bucket with a gourd dipper stood on one corner. In spite of the rude furnishings, Maudie had made an appetizing meal of beans, hominy and fried salt pork. There was even a leftover biscuit from the warming oven. She filled a tin plate, fished a fork out of somewhere and sat Jerry down at the table to eat. He fell to with gusto. The smell of the pork frying recalled my hunger and I was soon eating as well. Jerry finished and asked for seconds, which soon disappeared.

"Goodness, boy, Rosey's got a real job if she's gonna feed you. That was nigh as much as any man would eat!" Maudie smiled. "The nice thing about this place is that we mostly have plenty of food, so don't you worry 'bout that!"

"Yes ma'am," Jerry mumbled, "thank you." His eyes drooped and he nodded a little.

"You're wore out, too, ain't you, boy?" Maudie's voice was soft, "Ruth, take him to the bed yonder and tuck him in, a nap'll do him good."

Little Jerry stumbled toward the bed and I helped him with his shoes and tucked him under the covers. "Lie down with me, Ruthie," he begged pulling on my arm, so I lay down and he turned to the wall, holding my arm tightly across his chest. I hadn't realized how tired I was until then and it wasn't long until we were both asleep. Sometime later, I felt a quilt being spread over me and tucked under my shoulders. The warmth spread over me and I was asleep again.

I awakened to the sound of Maudie's voice outside the door. It was dark in the room with nothing but a single candle burning in the kitchen corner. ". . . don't care what you say, Tom Finn," she was saying, "that girl is plum wore out from her trials an' she needs restin' up 'fore she does anything else."

"Yes, but I boughten . . . ," his voice was begging.

"We all know what you *boughten*," put in another female voice, "but even in this Godforsaken place we have some morals above the heathen, an' you ain't gonna bed that girl withoutin' a marriage of some kind! Now you jist git on down to that shanty of yourn an' we will take care of the details."

In my sleep-muddled mind I thought it must be Rose talking.

It must have been Hi who spoke next, "We better do what they say, Tom, 'fore we git the wrath of all th' wimmin on this island atter us!" He chuckled.

"But . . ."

"No buts, Mr. Finn," Maudie put in, "you jist git down to that shanty an' leave the girl be. You got a lot o' cleanin' an' fixin' up on that pigsty—an' it shore needs a lot more furniture fer decent livin'!"

That was the last I remembered as I drifted back into sleep. Jerry hadn't moved a hair, but slept on. Oh to sleep the blessed sleep of a child!

I awoke to the familiar sounds of someone stoking up the fire in the stove and thought for a minute that I was home with Papa adding wood to the fire before I realized where I was. The middle child who was named Roda was staring down at me and sucking her thumb. "Why ou take me bed?" she asked without removing the thumb.

"Be quiet, Roda, an' leave them alone," Hi half whispered.

I lay very still under the quilt, then got up

quickly and shook out my clothes when Hi left the house for a minute. Maudie came from the bedroom corner with Joseph nursing contentedly. She had on a clean blouse and I noticed her hands were freshly washed. "Are you awake, child?" she asked. "Goodness but you could have slept through a storm, I imagine you don't even know what day it is!"

Jerry slipped to the edge of the bed and pulled his boots on. "Rose called last night an' said to tell you she would have your breakfast ready with the last of the firewood, if'n you gits up early enough, boy. I 'magine this ain't too late for a bite. Perlina, show him where Rosie lives, will you, then git you back here on the run or you won't git no breakfast!"

The five-year-old who must be Perlina grabbed Jerry's hand. Jerry looked at me questioningly and I smiled and nodded to reassure him as Perlina pullled him through the door. "Rosey's house be iss way." Her voice faded away.

Maudie pulled her blouse down and wiped Joseph's face with a cloth, then handed him to me. "Hold Will while I fix Hi's breakfast." She turned toward the kitchen.

Joseph gooed contentedly and drifted off

to sleep. I carried him to his bed and set about helping with the household chores. I could hear Hi chopping wood in the yard as I fluffed the bedclothes and made it up. Then I brought Joseph in his bed in and set it in the middle of the bed. Roda and Shawna climbed up and sat watching him solemnly.

Soon Hi came in at Maudie's call and sat down to eat. When he finished, he stood up and wiped his hands on his pants. He looked meanfully at Maudie. "You wimmin better git busy with yore plannin' an' doin', Tom ain't gonna wait long!" With that he gave her an affectionate slap on the bottom and whirled toward the door, avoiding her swing with the wooden spoon in her hand.

"You mind your manners, Hiram Cates!" She was blushing, but there was a smile tugging the corners of her mouth.

"I'll be back afore dark," Hi called from down the path to the water.

"I swear that man has no more manners than a mule," Maudie blustered turning back to the stove. "Gather the girls up for breakfast, Ruth, I have some news to tell you atter we've et, 'an we got a lot of work to do."

Perlina came through the door and scrambled for a place at the table. "Miss

46

Rosie's comin' ober wif yittle Paddy afer breakfas," she said breathlessly. "We can pay wif him when you works."

"Thank you, Perlina," Maudie said with a smile. "Now eat up before company gits here." The girls wolfed down their oatmeal and rushed out the door to await the arrival of "Yittle Paddy".

"Now, Ruthie, let's git this kitchen cleaned up, we've got a lot to do to git ready for a wedding day."

CHAPTER 3
MAUDIE CATES'S STORY

In the shock of the events I had gone through the last three days, I had spoken little except to Jerry. Now, with Joseph in as good hands as possible under the circumstances and Jerry seemingly out of harm's way, a little rest had allowed me to think about myself. "I won't be married to any pirate, or be a slave to any man," I vowed.

Maudie looked at me somewhat sadly. "I know how you feel, child, but you ain't in genteel company here an' these men don't trifle. If you don' git along as best you can here, th' catfish in th' river will be pickin' yore bones. Believe me, Ruthie, I seen it happen more'n once!"

We wus, my husban' an' his folks, floatin' downriver with goods fer New Orleans when they cotched us'ns under a bank in the middle of the night. We never seen them, the first I knowed was when they wus a turrible thump beside me an' my husban' wus jerked away and thrown in the river. The same thang happen to his pa, an' my mother-in-law and I were left alone in the world. They trussed us up an' floated down to a island jest like this'un. It's island ninety-four, called Crow's Nest Island by the river rats an' pirates. There they sold off ever' thang they didn' keep fer theirselves. Hiram were'n on the raid, an' he bought me away from them. I fought somethin' fierce, but it weren't no use, he jist conked me on the head an' when I woken up, I wus layin' in the bottom of a canoe, all trussed up agin an' Hi was sittin' in the back pad-dlin' up the river toward this island.

"Lie still, woman, yore all trussed up an' if'n you tilt the boat, you'll sink shore," he said. "I bought you fair an' square an' yore mine now. Believe me, if'n you had staid with that bunch of cutthroats, yore life would hev been short an' hellish. I jist wants a good stout woman to cook an' clean an' maybe be a woman to me if'n she wants, an' you fit the bill better'n any I seen in a while."

He talked to me kindly an' quiet-like all that day as he paddled the boat up that big river. At noon, we pulled to the bank an' he let me out to walk aroun' some an' git a

49

bite to eat an' drink, but he kep a rope 'roun' my waist an' hobbles on my feet. After lunch, he trussed me agin in the bottom of the boat. "Twont do for you to stick yore head up, if'n any o' these river rats sees you, they jist might git a notion," he says.

That night, he pulls into another island an' up under the bushes. "We'll stay the night here," he says, "an git to home some time tomorrer." After a meal, when it was good an' dark, Hiram tied me up agin then waded out in the river an' tied the canoe to an overhangin' tree limb. When he had waded back, he got up close to my face so I could see an' said, "That boat's the on'y way off this island, an' now it's perteckted by th' snakes an' aligators 'til mornin'. We'll sleep here with the fire 'tween us an' th' water an' thet'll keep any hungry 'gater from disturbin' our sleep."

Then he untied my hands an' tied one end of th' rope 'roun' my waist an' tother 'roun' his. The foot ropes wus loosed an' with one foot tied to one of his feet, he twisted the knot to the waist rope to my back. We laid down on his bedroll, clothes on, I wouldn' even take off my shoes, but Hi laughed an' took off his boots. With me on my side, he snuggled up to my back, an' I wasn' too unhappy 'bout that atter the talk 'bout snakes an' gaters! Hi put his arm over my waist an' was soon fast asleep, but I don' think I slept a wink all night. Each time the fire burned low, I would punch him an' git him to put on another stick of wood.

Th' light was jist peekin' under th' brush when we got up. Hi fried us some salt pork and thet with hardtack an' coffee made our breakfast. "If'n you promise to behave, I'll not tie you up today," he says, then he wades out an' gits the boat an' we gits under way. They wus other boats on the river, but Hi keeps well clear of them on the east side. 'Long 'bout mid afternoon, he points out this island 'way cross the water on the west side of the river. "Thet's our home over there, we'll wait 'til near dark to git there." Further upstream, he pulls for the west bank an' we stretch our legs a little. Hi tells me 'bout th' island and th' people livin' here, mostly outlaws an' ne'er-do-wells run out of the States.

"We're a pretty rough crowd," says he, "but we takes care of our own, jest like I intends to take care of you. I have a good tight house an' you'll be warm an' dry there."

He tells me the island is known and avoided by travelers who know the river and that it is impossible to escape without a boat. The west side of the island is only 'bout a hunnert yards from the bank, but the current is so rough and swift there that no one could cross it swimmin' or floatin' a raft.

Just after sundown, when other traffic on the river had tied up for the night, we git in the canoe an' Hi pulls for the middle. We drift down the three or four miles and pull into the bank just at last light. Hi pulls the canoe up high on the shore an' takes me here to this house. "This is yore home, now an' you can tend it as you see fit. I on'y ast thet it be kept clean an' my meals ready an' good when I'm here," he tells me. "Light a fire an' I'll fetch you a tub an' water an' you kin git a bath an' clean up. Don' stick yore head out th' door while I'm gone, they'll be someone watchin' an' they might be a little rough on you."

This here stove was the first one I ever seen an' it took me some time to learn its workin's. Most o' the others have to do with a fireplace. I busied myself gittin' a fire goin' an' in a few minutes Hi came back luggin' a tub in one hand an' a big bucket of water in t'other.

He sets the bucket on the stove an' the tub nearby. "I'll go down an' git yore kit out'n th' boat an' when th' water's hot 'nough you can git cleaned up."

He was gone agin, but I daren't stick my head out the door. When he got back with my trunk, he says, "I'll be outside while you bathe. You kin sleep in the bed an' I'll sleep here on th' floor by th' stove."

He said thet to put my mind at ease, I guess. When the water was hot, he poured it into the tub, an' handed me a store-bought bar of soap still in the wrapper, the first I ever seen!

"I'll be outside while you bathe, call me when you are dressed." With that, he went out an' closed the door. I heard him talkin' to someone as I took my bath. I taken my time with the bath, rubbin' off the grime an' soakin' my sore arms an' legs where the ropes had been. With the last of the hot water, I washed my hair. Hi had laid a cloth on the chair for dryin'. He called it a Turkish towel. I had never seed one like it, but it shore did feel good when I dried with it.

A few minutes atter I was dressed, I opened the door a crack an' told Hiram I was done. There was four or five men standin' an' sittin' 'round an' as they rose to leave they hoorawed Hi with some rough talk. Hi came into the room with a smile. He took the tub out and hung it on a peg in the outside wall. When he come in, he warned me that the camp wus guarded all night and no one wus allowed outside 'til mornin'. I wus so skairt of whut 'ud happen next I wus shakin', but Hi wus almos' gentle when he tole me to git to bed an' he 'ud see me in the mornin'. I laid for a long time stiff with terror, but he stoked the fire an' blew out the candle an' I heard him lie down on the bedroll.

"Are ye tired, Maudie?" he ast.

I didn' answer for a moment, then I said, "Yes."

"Well, don' you worry none, jist go to sleep an' you'll be safe," he says an' he was soon asleep.

I tried to listen for a long time, but it prob'bly weren't too long 'fore I was asleep. I did'n know what the time wus when I woke, but Hi's bedroll wus rolled up in the corner an' he wus gone. Lookin' 'round the room, I could see that Hi wus neat fer a man, but there wus lots of things needin' done that a man jist didn' know or care to do. I set myself about doin' the housework an' had done quite a bit when Hi came back 'bout mid afternoon. They war't much food in the house, but I made do with whut I had an' there wus a tol'able meal cookin'. I had a pile of dirty clothes in the middle of the floor, an' the kitchen clean an' arranged to my likin'. They wus more furniture than now, but it got wiped out by the flood a couple year ago, an' we're jist gettin' back on our feet.

After Hi had eaten, he pushed his chair back an' looked at me. "I shore don' reckon on sleepin' on the floor in my own house fer long . . ." He paused a moment to let that soak in then said with a big grin, "So I went out and gotten me the makin's for another bed. I'll put it in here near the kitchen an' I got some canvas we can hang 'round yore bed so you can have some privacy." Then he looked me direct in the eyes an' said, "Maudie, I won' bother you none 'til someday you mayhap be willin'. 'Til then I sleeps here in the big room when I'm home an' you sleep on the big bed."

An that's the way it wus 'til I was ready to be his woman, but that's a whole 'nother story. One day I ast him why he didn' jist take me when he first brought me here, an' he said, "I always believed wimmin an' horses wus much better when they wus gentle-broke."

I guess he be right 'bout thet. He's my man, thick an' thin an' I been gentle-broke for good.

Then Maudie looked me straight in the eyes

an' said, "Now Sugar Booger, thet Tom Finn are young, hot blooded an' impatient an' he's not likely to b'lieve in gentle breakin' his woman, so we are goin' to have to figger some way to corral thet young buck. Me an' the other wimmin on the island are gonna help you ease into this married life!"

Zenas leaned back in his chair and watched the sun setting across the basin. The Organs and San Andres were casting long shadows and the basin was taking on its deep purple hue of evening. "That should be enough to keep you busy for a while, son, I got my chores to do and you got a long drive ahead. Next time we get together I'll tell you 'bout Grandma's pirate weddin'."

Mrs. Sophie stepped to the door and said, "Won't you stay for supper, Jim? It's almost ready." I thanked her for the invitation, but excused myself because of the long drive ahead of me.

CHAPTER 4
THE HOUSEWARMING

It was Wednesday of the next week before my duties allowed me to return to the Meeker place. I gathered some produce from the garden to take to them and departed in time to arrive at the Meekers' shortly after noon. Driving south on Highway 54, I could see Culp Peak and the ridge running southwest from there to the point near the Meeker house and as I turned off the pavement, I glimpsed the glint of sunlight from the tin roof of the house. The dust raised by a car could be seen from Meekers' as soon as it left the highway fifteen miles away, and I always found them awaiting my arrival, a glass of cold water on the porch stand and the couple sitting in the rocking chairs. It became our custom for me to sit on the steps and visit a while, talking of the local events and happenings, then Mrs. Meeker would excuse herself and return to the house, while Zenas gathered his thoughts and continued his story. He eased himself into the chair

57

and hooked his heels on the front rung. "This is how Grandma Ruth used to tell the story of how she got her first house!"

As Maudie was ending her story, I noticed that women were gathering from the several huts and shanties around. We stepped out into the yard and Maudie began introducing them to me as they would arrive. There certainly was a cross section of society there. Some were pleasant faced and clean and others were slovenly unhappy wretches. I learned a lot about them over the next months and years. Generally, the cleaner happier ones were from the working class of people and most were not there voluntarily, but had made up their minds to be as happy as possible under their circumstances. The more slovenly had come to these conditions as some man's wench or wife and would have been just as unhappy in a cabin or the grandest floored and shingled house. Give me three minutes in another woman's home and I will tell you her outlook on life.

"Ladies," Maudie announced, "we are fixin' to have a weddin' — as if you didn't already know that! We'll need the tables under the trees cleaned off an' dishes brought out, food an' drink prepared, and gen'ral cleanup of the place. Rosie, why don' you an' Nancy an' Louisa see to the food from the stores, an' the rest of us'll mosey over to Mr. Finn's place an' see if anythin's worth keepin' there."

Maudie led the way toward the edge of the settlement and my heart sank when I saw the hovel she headed toward. If it wasn't the worst dwelling on the island, it was well below the worst. All it looked like was a bunch of logs and boards leaned up against a pole fastened between two trees with brush piled over it to shed some of the rain. The opening — for you couldn't call it a door — looked more like a hole in a brush pile where some creature denned up.

Maudie stood with her hands on her hips surveying the mess and I just stared, getting angrier by the moment. "I swear I've seen better pigsties than this," she vowed. There were mumbles of agreement all around.

One of the women, I think it was Minerva Conner, called out, "Tom Finn, air you to home?"

"Course not," sniffed Maudie. "Won't no pig stay in that mess longer than he has to. Well, let's look inside an' see if they's iny-thin' worth savin'." She carefully lowered her head and peeked into the hut. "Nothin' much in here, 'cept junk an' dirty clothes," came her muffled voice. Then the whole wall on one side of the door pushed out and fell with a sigh. "There, that looks better with the window open," said Maudie.

The other women were laughing at the sight of her standing there over the collapsed wall in the midst of the remains of the hut. "Maudie, don't you think we should open the window on the back side an' git some ventilation in here?" asked another of the women as she gave the back of the lean-to a shove.

In a moment, all of them were pushing down walls and giggling like schoolgirls. "There," called one as they stood in the midst of the destruction, "that should git the place aired out!"

"Let's git the valu'bles outen, 'fore the roof caves in," laughed another.

Looking around, we found a few items of small value, an iron skillet with a broken handle, a Dutch oven with one leg broken off, and a pile of clothes thrown into one corner of the ruins. The bed wasn't much more than a bunch of raggedy quilts and blankets piled under a canvas tarp.

"Looks like all those clothes an' quilts is good for is a good washin'," observed one of the women. "I washed this mornin' an' the fire's still goin'. I'll go start the kettle boilin' an' we can dump it all in an' bile 'er clean."

As she started away, Maudie said, "Ruthie, pile all these clothes in the crate there an' take them to Helen's to wash. Me an' the girls will clean up here a little."

As I left with the crate full, Maudie and the other women were piling the brush under the ridge pole. Before long, the kettle was boiling and we were shaving soap into the water and piling in the clothes. I took the paddle and kept the clothes sloshing and stirring in the hot water. The water turned turbid, then pure muddy brown like the river. "This looks like a two-kettle washin'," Helen muttered.

We dipped out the clothes and dumped the water from the kettle. Several trips to the well and a few more sticks of firewood later and the clothes were happily boiling away again.

A thick wave of smoke wafted across the camp and I heard one of the men call out, "Fire!" Two men came running from the dock toward Tom Finn's. We ran after them and arrived just as Maudie was explaining as we looked at the remains of the Finn manse going up in smoke. "Wus cleanin' house for the weddin' an' it jist flamed up an' burned real sudden. Must hev bin a

61

spark from one of the chimblies. We jist got the valu'bles out in time."

One of the men looked at us and grinned. "Looks 'spicious to me, but it couldn't hev happened to a more dersarvin' place. Thet wus th' fust thang built here, an' Tom moved into it when ol' Jed left. 'S wonder it stood 'til now." He winked and started back. "Looks lak ol' Tom'll hev to build him a new honey cabin, now."

Maudie turned to me. "Well, Sugar, looks like we'll jist have to postpone yore weddin' 'til Mr. Tom can git 'nother house." She smiled. "Let's gather this stuff up an' we can store it at our house. Wonder how Rose and the others did at the store."

There wasn't much to carry and Helen and I hurried back to the wash kettle. The water wasn't so muddy as the first, so we rinsed the clothes and hung them to dry on the community line strung between trees.

At the store, the women were gathered around Rose and she was explaining what was there. "We has a bag o' rice an' a bag o' beans, the flour be weevily, but not beyond use, an' one o' the jugs o' molasses be filled wi' fine rum, ef I does say so me-self! I hid it away where no one will be findin' it."

Maudie was thoughtful. "It's gonna take

Tom a few days ter build his house, thet'll give us some time to git things arranged. Mayhap we kin git someone ter run down to New *Mad*-rid an' pick up a few items fer us. Some fish would go good with the rice an' beans. I'll bet we could git some of the men to fish for us."

There was a shout from the river and two canoes pulled under the trees and up to the bank. Out stepped several of the men including Hi, Tom Finn and the younger Sam Mason. Helen had told me that the elder Sam Mason who was the pirates' captain had been killed in '03.

"We seen th' smoke from up th' river an' thought you'uns mought need some help," one of them called. "Whut burned?"

There was a general babble from the crowd, "Tom's house caught fire . . . burned to the ground . . . saved what we could . . . don't know what started it . . ."

Finn ran a few feet up the bank to see the smoldering ruins. "Whut caused that . . . ?" He stopped and stared at me. "You burned my house so you . . ." With hands clenched into fists, he started toward me and I backed up a step or two.

"Hold on there, Tom Finn," Rose shouted stepping in front of him, "Ruth be about washin' yore filthy clothes up to Helen's

63

whin the fire started an' wern't nowhere near that brush pile you called a house."

"Th' very idee you lived thet way an' x-pected a woman t' keep house in it makes my blood boil," chimed in another lady. There was a general agreement to that by the other women and they gathered around Tom in the most threatening way. He blinked and backed up a step or two. "Well I intended to make it better . . ."

"Th' proper way t' do things, to 'make it better,' as you say, is to do it *b'fore* you gits a woman!" Minerva interrupted.

Tom was now confused and surrounded by a seeming sea of irate women. "But . . ."

"Don't you 'but' us, Tom Finn. You git busy an' build a decent house for this girl or you don't git no . . ."

"Now see here . . . ," Tom began, his anger rising again.

The other men had by this time gathered around, some sitting on the boats or logs, some standing at a safe distance, watching with barely disguised amusement.

"Hold on, Tom," called Sam Mason with a big grin, "seems like th' ladies got a point or two there, an' anyhow you don' got no home for a woman to keep. Looks to me yuh better git busy fixin' up a place t' live an' while yore at it, it should be decent 'nough to keep a woman in."

"I heered talk of a weddin' an' party in th' works," put in another man through his pipe smoke. "Thet could take some time doin'. With a little help, you could fix up the old Barlow house livable, an' th' wimmin would hev time enough to cook us up a feast." There was a chorus of assent from all to that and Tom Finn looked around him perplexed at this turn of events.

"W-e-l-l . . . ," he faltered.

"Tell you what, Tom, we men'll hep you work thet place over the next couple days an' th' wimmin kin prepare us a feast wuth 'memberin'," put in Hi.

"W-e-l-l . . ."

"Good, it's settled, then," Sam Mason sang out. He seemed especially amused at Tom's predicament, probably remembering how Tom had fleeced him out of getting me for himself.

For the first time, Maudie spoke out, "We have plenty of beans an' rice, but no meat. Someone needs to hunt us up a deer or bear on th' shore, an' some of you fishermen needs to cotch us up a mess 'o fish."

"Yes an' someone needs to go down to New Mad'rid an' see ef they has eny fresh veg'ables we coud buy," Rose put in.

"I reckon if we put in two hard days' work,

we could have the Barlow place livable," mused Hi, "but it ud take eight or nine of us doin' it."

"I'll go down to New Mad'rid tomorra an' see what they have," Sam volunteered.

"You kin let me off afore the first bend an' I'll try for a deer, we almos' allus gits one there," said a barefoot man in a buckskin shirt and breeches.

"I seen lot o' fish jumpin' at the upper end of th' island yesterday, me an' th' kids could catch a pretty good mess tomorry," another man said.

There was general agreement all around and the women began planning the meal and dividing up the chores to be done in the next two days.

"So you men'll be for fixin' up the house an' be done in two days? Thet'll gie us time to fix the feast an' prepare for the weddin' on the third day!" Rose Monahan said.

"Shore," replied Sam, "an I'll be back by noon on the second day with whatever I can find and maybe John'll have us some meat by then."

Tom Finn looked a little dazed and confused. Whatever plans he had in his mind had been blown away by the events of the morning. First he had lost his "house," then the plans he had for me had been usurped

66

by a bunch of women with the men chiming in. He looked at the faces around him, his jaw working soundlessly.

"Come on, Tom," said Hi, slapping him on the back, "let's look at thet shack an' see what we will be needin' to fix it up." He winked at the rest of the crowd and started off behind Tom who was striding away slowly. "Ruth you come with us an' give us some advice on what to do," Hi called over his shoulder.

I looked at Maudie and she and Minerva were nodding approval. "You go ahead, child," Minerva whispered, "might be a chance to learn more about that boy."

You may wonder why I put any trust in these pirates, but I had no choice. I was totally dependent on them even for my life. I therefore determined to be as helpful and little trouble as possible, to be quiet and compliant, uncomplaining. It seemed the only way Jerry and I could survive in that place. Mostly up to this time, I had kept my mouth shut and my thoughts to myself.

The Barlow place was in the middle of the camp, set back a little from the other houses on the pathway. It looked as well built as any, but it had been empty a while and had been scavenged a bit, the front door and windows were missing and the inside was bare of any kind of furnishings except for the universal kitchen stump, which was rooted to the ground and couldn't be taken. There was daylight streaming in through several holes in the roof and some places where the chinking had fallen out from between the logs that made up the walls.

Hi surveyed the house, kicking at wallboards, poking at the low eaves of the roof, and kicking through trash in the corners. "Looks like there ain't much to do, Tom, it'll take us longer to git th' goods we need than t' put it all t'gether."

I watched Tom Finn closely. He looked around gloomily, then seemed to brighten some at the things Hi was saying, getting caught up in the prospects. "I recollect some lumber and a door we could git frum thet wrecked flatboat down under th' first bluff — ef it's still there, but it'ud take us all day to git there an' back," he mused. "If we git a early start, we could make th' run there an' back by sunset. I suppose we could git th' place in shape in one day."

"I 'magine some of th' boys'ud hep us out with thet," Hi replied.

"I'll git th' tools together an' loaded an' we can start 'fore daylight." Tom was enthusiastic now. He started out the door, then turned to me. "You kin clean up th' place to suit yoreself, an' when you git that done, go to th' clay pit ahind th' houses an' git chinkin' for th' walls."

Only the second time he had spoken directly to me and he was giving me orders like a servant or hireling! My temper flashed, but I caught it in time. "I need furniture and kitchen furnishings, too. There was plenty of that on my boat if you can get it back."

Now it was his turn to get mad. "Don't go gittin' sassy on me, you'll do with whut I got!"

"Which is nothin' but two broke pots and a pile of rags," I shot back, "and they wouldn't be clean if I hadn't washed them!"

He seemed taken aback at that and hesitated a moment. "I'll see to that whin we git th' place in order." He turned on his heel and strode off down to the shingle.

Hi was looking on with a grin on his face. "You got spunk, girl, an' I guess you'll need it to git along with thet boy. You kin bet Maudie an' th' others'll back you up, may even be a little ahead 'o you in places," he chuckled. "I'll git you a tamp for th' floor an' you can borry a broom someplace 'til you kin make yore own. Won't take much t' fix this place up dry an' sound. Git th' boy t' bring you some firewood from my pile 'til

69

you hev time to git some chopped yoreself." He chuckled again. "Never a dull moment 'round here," and out the door he went.

I looked around in the gloom at the empty dirty cabin. Our place in Tennessee had been much better than this, with strong logs and tightly fitted, a loft for the boys to sleep in and a big stone fireplace for Ma's kitchen. I didn't know what they had when they started out, but Pa was industrious and worked hard to make us a place that was safe and sound. What a far cry from that this was! Thinking of Ma and Pa at home then seeing them laying on that cursed beach and Sammy gone in the wilderness probably lost forever, I was overcome by grief and I leaned against the stump and cried great sobs.

After what seemed a long time, someone touched my arm. It was Jerry. He had brought over a load of firewood and piled it by the fireplace without my hearing him. "It's gonna be okay, Ruthie," he said. "We'll git along here together." He put his arms around my waist and squeezed tightly. I held him and tried to control my grief.

"Maudie said t' tell you supper was on," he said after a moment. "I brung you a load of wood for tomorrer when you start clean-in'." He pointed proudly. "I'll bring more in th' mornin', an' Rose said I could watch th' girls an' Little Paddy while you'uns cleaned over here."

I noticed his hands were blistered some from chopping wood, but he had a happy smile and chattered about his day and the antics of Little Paddy. Rose had given him a big breakfast and left him mostly alone with the child while she saw to the doings of the community. She had gotten home in time to feed him a meal and send him to help me.

I dried my eyes and we walked back to the Cates house. Outside, I washed my face in Hi's wash basin, then went inside amidst the bustle and noise. Three hungry girls stirred around the table setting out dishes and spoons. Joseph lay on the bed kicking and gooing, as contented as I had seen him since we had gotten here. Maudie and the girls adored him and Hi was pleased to have him here. I could see that he would be well cared for, but I wondered what kind of life he would have here among a gang of river pirates. Maudie saw my reddened eyes and her face softened. "We had a long day, Sugar Booger, but we got things in hand some an' thet Tom Finn's gonna be easier t' handle atter this."

She turned to the stove and began ladling

71

out stew for the girls and pushing them toward their seats. I moved to help, but she gently pushed me to a chair. "Sit down, child," she said softly, "you've been through a lot an' I got this all in hand." She placed a steaming bowl in front of me and a large square of corn bread. "Eat an' you'll be feelin' better," she commanded.

The stew was good, potatoes, onions and venison in a thick broth. I didn't know where the meat came from or how she got it all done along with the rest of the day. Hi had already eaten and was sitting outside by the door smoking his pipe. I could see him stretched out lounging and watching the light fade. We cleaned the dishes and set them up. Maudie lit a candle then went out to sit with Hi while the girls sat on the bed and played with Joseph. Shawna grew sleepy and curled up in a corner of the bed and was soon sound asleep. When he got fussy Maudie came in to feed Joseph and put him to bed and the rest of us began preparing for bed. I made the pallet for the girls near the stove and Jerry washed up and sat removing his boots and yawning. We left Shawna where she was and Jerry was soon fast asleep too.

Hi came in and closed and bolted the door. Looking around, he stretched and headed for the bedroom. "Put out th' candle 'fore you go to bed, girl." He disappeared through the curtains. I blew out the light and quickly got into my gown and into the bed.

The next thing I knew, Hi was stoking the fire in the stove. He went out softly and I heard him going down the path to the boat. I hurriedly put on my dress and was seeing to the table when Maudie came in.

CHAPTER 5
ARNSTED WOOD'S ARM

This was our third day on the island and we were just finishing breakfast when Minerva Conner came to the door. "Arnsted's arm don't look good, Maudie, he ast if you would come look at it as soon as you kin."

"Tell him I'll be right over soon's I git my kit," Maudie replied.

"I'll see to the dishes and children," I volunteered. "You go on and see about him." I sure wasn't up to seeing that arm after three days and I'm sure Arnsted didn't want to see anything of me.

Maudie went into the bedroom and returned with a small box that clanked when she set it on the table. "Hi found this doctor's kit on one of the flatboats they caught. It has come in handy, though I don't know whut half the doodads are for," Maudie said as she put her hair up. "I'll be back as soon as I can." She hurried out the door.

I finished the dishes and got the girls dressed. Little Joseph was asleep in his bed and I picked it up and we went off to the Barlow house.

Jerry came up the path from Rose's. He had Little Paddy in tow. "Rose'll be here soon's she gits the dishes washed up," he called. "I can watch after the girls while you work." He seemed proud of his new responsibilities. I was cleaning out the trash when Rose came over with her arms loaded. "Where's Maudie?" she asked.

"She went to see Arnsted Wood. His arm is not doing any good."

"I'll go on over and see them." Rose laid down her burdens. "Maudie may need some help. That arm didn't look good at all yesterday." She hurried off and I went on with my cleaning.

It was sometime later that the two women came back. Their serious looks told me all had not gone well. Maudie told me how the arm was swollen and discolored and there were red streaks running up the arm almost to the shoulder. The blow had run down the bones almost like the meat was sliced off. The men had folded that back on the arm and wrapped it tightly and it hadn't been unwrapped or cleaned since coming to the island. Maudie cleaned it as best she

75

could and poured some rum over it to cleanse it, but she wasn't optimistic about the outcome. "Someone's gonna be takin' thet arm off or we'll be buryin' thet man soon." She shook her head.

Mama had taught me some healing plants that might help heal the arm, but on this island there would be none of them growing and it was sure I would not be allowed to go to the riverbanks or roam the woods looking for them. I wasn't ready to help that man much anyway after what had happened to my family. When I was a little older and had read the Good Book some, I understood my responsibility to love my enemies, but it wasn't to be three days after my family had been murdered.

"Faith, an' you be a cleanin' divil, Ruthie," declared Rose looking around at the room, "a mite more, an' the place be good for livin'!"

"I need to chink the logs and clean and tamp the floors yet," I replied. "Does the storage place have any sulfur? I would like to burn some to rid the bugs and spiders," I asked.

"They's all kinds of stuff up there, an' we kin go look," said Maudie. "Rose knows the stuff more better than me, why don't you two go up there an' look an' I'll run down where the floor tamp be. I think I saw one of Helen's tykes totin' it down to her place."

It took some poking around at the store, but we finally dug out a small jar of sulfur. Maudie had sprinkled down the floor and was in one corner using the floor tamp when we got back to the house. I found the clay pit and dug up a bucket of clay for the chinking. Rose and I mixed mud and chinked while Maudie tamped. Tamping was hard work and we all took turns at it. When we quit at noon to feed the children, most of the chinking was done and half of the floor was tamped. After eating, we finished the floor and chinking. Someone produced some old canvas we hung over the door and two windows. Building a fire and setting the sulfur in the middle of the room to burn, we returned to Maudie's to rest and begin supper.

"I don' 'spect those men to git in much afore sunset," Maudie said as she stirred the stew pot. "We'll feed the girls an' git them bedded down early an' I'll keep the stew hot fer Hi an' Tom."

With the children fed and bedded down, the room quiet and dark and only a candle giving light, I lay down on the bed and was soon fast asleep, leaving Maudie sitting by the door waiting for the men. I was careful to keep my dress on and covered myself with a blanket.

It was very late when the canoes pulled on to the beach. I heard the muffled voices of Hi and Tom as they came up the path. Maudie had stirred and was ladling up the food as they came through the door. I lay very still and didn't open my eyes. It must have been Tom Finn standing over me, for I heard Hiram sit down at the table and ask for a cup of water in a hushed voice.

Maudie's voice whispered from very near, "That girl has worked herself to the bone fixin' up yore house, Tom, you can sleep there tonight better'n you ever slept in that hovel of yor'n. Come on over and have a bite while it's hot afore you go to bed."

They moved off and I drifted in and out of sleep listening to the muted sounds of people eating and whispering the news of the day.

"Arnsted's arm an' it looks bad," Maudie whispered. "I think he is either going to lose it or die."

"They's a doctor at New Mad'rid, seen him myself when I wus down to there last month," Tom replied.

". . . got enough to finish th' house . . . ," from Hi.

". . . git yore self to bed, Tom, things will

be busy tomorry!" from Maudie.

Creaking chairs and low murmers, the door opening . . . Maudie calling out down the path, "Mind the sulfur burnin' in the house, Tom, set it outside an' open the doorway so's you won't choke. They's a fire in the fireplace."

The door closing and bolt falling, candle out and the soft swish of the bedroom curtains parting and closing . . . I drifted into a sound sleep.

It seemed only a moment later that there was a pounding on the door. "Hiram, Maudie, wake up, it's Tom. We need yore hep with Arnsted, he's taken for the worse!"

I jumped up and unbolted the door and Tom pushed his way in. Hiram was coming through the curtains as I lit the candle from an ember in the stove. "Whut's he like, Tom?" he asked as he pulled his gallouses over his shoulders. He sat down in his chair and started pulling on his boots.

Maudie's head poked out between the curtains. "Speak up, Tom, I'm gittin' myself dressed."

Little Shawna stirred and the two girls on the pallet sat up rubbing eyes and murmuring. "A light was on at his place whin I passed, so I stuck my head in to see how he wuz an' they wuz bathin' him with cold cloths an' his fever wuz high. He stopped groanin' atter a while an' jist went limp, thet's whin I come fer you'uns." Tom paused to catch his breath. "Is he still breathin'?" Maudie's muffled voice came.

"Yup, but he 'pears awful pale, an' th' fever won't quit," Tom replied.

Maudie came bustling through the curtains. "Jerry, run down to Rose's and git her up. You can stay there an' watch Little Paddy 'til she gits back. Lay down, girls, an' go back to sleep, Ruth will stay with you while we're gone. Let's git, Hi."

The three hurried out the door and I stood in the doorway and watched Jerry as far as I could see. I heard him banging on Rose's door, saw a light come on and the door open to let Jerry inside. I closed and bolted the door again with the latch string out.

The girls had laid back down except Perlina. Her eyes were wide and her lip quivered. "Mommie 'on't be gone yong, will she?" her voice trembled.

"No Perlina, they will come back soon as they have Mr. Wood better," I replied.

"Will he die like Mr. Jed did whin he got dat hole in he chest?"

"I don't know about Mr. Jed, Perlina, an' I don't think Mr. Wood will die right now.

They should take him to see the doctor, to make him well, but I don't know if they can until he gets better."

"Don' yike Papa bein' a pirate," she cried softly, "it be dangrus an' he mought git hurted yike Mr. Jed an' Mr. Arnsted. Mommie says we will go 'way someday an' Papa'll do sompin' safer."

It won't be something safer like taking your family down the river to a better life, I thought, the anger rising in me unexpectedly. Then my throat got a lump and I was almost crying thinking about the past loss of my family and the anxiety of this little girl for hers. Pirates don't need to have families, I thought as I retrieved Joseph from his bed. I sat in Hi's big chair and held the sleeping baby close. Perlina came and crawled onto my lap. She touched Joseph's hand and his little fingers wrapped around hers. They both drifted off and I was sitting there holding them when Maudie returned in the gray morning light. She looked tired and disheveled as she came in. "Lands, child, have you been there all this time?" she asked. Not waiting for a reply, she went on explaining the events of the night, "We finally got his fever down some an' he come round to groanin' an' mumblin' — out of his head — so the men decided to take him

81

to the doctor at New Mad'rid. We wrapped him tight an' put him in the big canoe an' three o' the men are takin' him down. Hiram an' Tom's takin' their plunder over t' the Barlow place. They wuz quite a pile of it at the beach. I'll fix 'em some breakfast, an' holler 'em up whin it's ready."

I laid little Joseph in his bed and started the salt pork frying while Maudie rolled out biscuits. It seemed strange that flour would be so plentiful here. We hardly ever saw it in the hills where I grew up. With the coffee boiling hot, the biscuits brown and the meat and beans hot, Maudie went to the door and cupping her hands hollered, "Whooo, HIRAM." She watched a moment, then turned back into the room. "They're a-comin'," she said.

Joseph was stirring and fussing, so she picked him up and began nursing him. I had a fresh bucket of water on the stand and Hiram and Tom washed up before coming in. I served them breakfast and noticed that both had dried blood on their clothes from handling Arnsted Wood. They looked tired, having had a hard day and hardly any sleep. Now, they had a hard day's work ahead of them. Neither one said a word or hardly looked up while they ate.

The food seemed to pick up their spirits

some and by the time they were through, they seemed to have regained their vigor. I poured them the last of the coffee and Hiram pushed back in his chair. "We got all we needed from that ol' wreck an' more," he said. "Soon's th' others git there, th' boys'll hang th' door an' frame th' winders in. I kin mend th' roof while they do thet an' we mought hev a tight house by sundown. Sam should git back around noon an' you gals kin git th' feast goin'."

Maudie sniffed, "A lot you know Hiram Cates, we been preparin' since the sun come up yestiddy, else they won't be no doins tomorrer!"

Tom Finn spoke directly to me in a kindly way for the first time, "Th' insides look to be in good shape, fair. We found some furnishin's in th' wreck. Ya kin look at them an' pick out whut you wants. I may git us a table an' chair or two today if'n th' tradin' goes good."

"Might come high," Hi chuckled. The men must have been giving Tom a hard time about all that was going on.

Soon they were gone and I started setting the table for the youngsters who were stirring around. Maudie sat loving Little Willie, as she called Joseph. She seemed totally attached to him even in this short time and I

83

felt better about her having the care of him.

Soon we heard the sound of hammering coming from the Barlow place and we hurried to clean up the kitchen to get over there and see the doings. Hiram was on the roof nailing down shingles, and Tom and a half dozen men were working on the doors and windows. Outside the door was a pile of material and other things from the wrecked boat. Without speaking, Tom nodded for me to sort through them.

They had found some pewter pots and pans, banged a bit, but usable. Some of the tablespoons in the pile were bent and needed straightening. There was a small wooden box that could serve as a cupboard when nailed up in the kitchen corner and a nail keg that would do for a stool. The other things I could find no use for, some of it Tom might possibly be planning to use.

I picked out the best of Tom's raggedy clothes and took them to Maudie's to press. Young Sam Mason pulled in to the beach about noon with a couple of deer and baskets of fresh fruits and vegetables which soon disappeared to various cookstoves and fireplaces for preparation. We spent the afternoon cooking and I pressed clothes for myself and Tom Finn.

It wasn't very late when the men came in

tired and dirty from their day's work. They had finished early and Maudie sent them both off to the river to bathe while she prepared supper. Both were so tired they hardly ate and Tom stumbled off to the new house to bed before even the sun went down. Hi sat by the door and smoked his pipe. Soon he came in and was off to bed early too.

We learned the next day when the big canoe got back from the doctor's that he had to take Arnsted Wood's arm off at the elbow. The men had to hold him while the doc sawed and cauterized the stump. Arnsted was unconscious and pale as death when they left him. They left the doctor with money enough to care for Arnsted's needs and some left over. We never saw him again. Sam Mason said Arnsted lived, but a one-armed pirate was no good, so he went on up to Cape Girardeau or Saint Louis. I guess Ma's hatchet made a more honest man out of him. I couldn't help thinking that he only got part of what he deserved. It was later in life that I realized that the Good Lord could forgive even Arnsted Wood and all the other pirates and that my hatred was hurting only me.

We had been watching a cloud build up over

the Organ Mountains south of San Augustin Pass and now it towered over the basin. Black rain was pouring out of the bottom and flashes of lightning lit the late afternoon sky. Suddenly a huge bolt of lightning shot out from near the top of the cloud and arched high over the basin to strike one of the peaks of the San Andres mountains twenty miles away. It was more than thirty seconds before we heard the clap of thunder rolling across the basin and bouncing off the hills around us. "Looks like it hit Black Mountain or Bear Peak," Zenas allowed, "they're both in line from where we sit an' it's hard to tell one from the other."

I folded my notepad and rose to go, calling a goodbye to Mrs. Meeker. "Better hurry, Jim, it'll be a good race to see which gets to town first, you or that cloud." Even as I looked, it seemed the cloud was already moving up the basin. "I'd pay fifty cents for another melon like the one you brought last time," Zenas called as he stepped down from the porch. "Bet we don't get a drop out of that cloud." I started the car and began my race toward town.

CHAPTER 6
A PIRATE WEDDING

"W-e-l-l-l, I guess you want to hear how Grandma married Grandpa," Zenas said as he spat the last watermelon seed into the yard. "It must have been pretty much of a nightmare for her for I only heard her speak of it a few times, and never did she talk of it while Grandpa Meeker was livin'. Here's the way she told it."

I didn't sleep well at all the night before the wedding, if you could call it a wedding. I tossed and had bad dreams and woke and cried and worried. If I had thought I could get away, I would have jumped in the river, but I had to stay for the sake of Jerry and Joseph. I was up well before any of the rest of the household, having given up the thought of rest. I stoked the fire in the stove and drew a fresh bucket of water from the community well. By the time Maudie was dressed, I had water hot on the stove and breakfast started. "My goodness, child, ef you wasn't goin' off today, I'd keep you 'round here helpin' me," she said as she came through the curtains.

Joseph was happily nursing. He seemed to be very contented and was growing stronger by the day. Jerry left for the Monahans and we got the children fed before Hi came in. He seemed rested from the last couple of days. Most of the men on the island were lazy, preferring to let their wives or someone else do the work, but Hiram Cates was not that way and neither was Maudie for that matter. Their place was always the neatest and the children the cleanest on the island, maybe due mostly to Maudie, but Hiram was a hard worker in his own right.

We spent the rest of the morning and into the afternoon cooking and preparing for the feast. About mid afternoon, the women began gathering the food to the outdoor tables. A whole herd of excited kids descended on the tables, eyes bright looking at all that food. Soon the men began drifting over and Tom Finn arrived wearing the shirt I had pressed for him and the same dirty britches he had worn the day before. I heard one of the women scold him for not wearing the clean clothes, to which he growled, "I changed shirts for this silly meetin' an' thet's fer as I'm goin'."

"First meal's ready," Rose called and the men gathered around filling their plates. As soon as they moved away to eat, the children gathered and those that couldn't serve themselves were served by the women. That being done, the women filled their plates and we sat down, some on the ground, some on blankets or quilts brought from home. There was lots of talk and visiting and I wondered how much there was to talk about closed up on this little island with no contact with the outside world. I found that the wilderness off the island was no better in those days when there were so few people in the country. In fact, there were more people to talk to on that island than any-where else I lived for years afterward.

The children kept coming back for more food and everyone ate until it was mostly gone. Feasts like that were rare on the island and everyone thoroughly enjoyed them-selves. When the men were smoking and the dishes gathered and stacked, Helen Fields reached behind a big tree and brought out a newly made broom. She came and gave it to me. "Here's the first present for yore new home." She smiled.

A grizzled old pirate they called Sary stood up and called out, "Folks, we got no preacher nor priest tuh do th' nupt'als, but we kin do lak th' Cajuns in th' swanps does an' call it a weddin' 'til th' real thing happens along." There were grins and winks among the men, most of whom had dispensed with any formality of wedding their mates.

"Whut they does," Sary continued, "is that they takes a new broom an' jumps over it three times an' thet sarves es a weddin' 'til th' priest comes around, usually in a year or two. So here's th' broom an' here's th' man an' here's th' woman, whut say ye we have our own weddin'?"

There was a shout of ayes from the men and they pushed Tom Finn out from amongst them. "I don' need no weddin' for a *boughten* woman . . . ," he growled, but the men would have none of that and they made a ring around him moving him toward the middle of the circle where I stood with the broom.

If I could have, I would have melted into the ground. It was all I could do to keep from crying I was so angry, but I determined not to show a sign of weakness nor give any of them the satisfaction of seeing my despair. Someone took the broom from me and laid it on the ground. Rough hands, some that had been used against my family not four days ago, shoved Tom Finn up beside me. "I ain't . . ."

"Oh yes you are, Tom," one of the grinning men swore.

"Now to do this proper," Sary called out, "yuh hold hands an' jump over th' broom once, turn 'round th' bristle end an' jump over agin, then ya turns 'round th' handle end an' jumps agin an' thet makes it legal."

"Take her hand, Tom," someone called, and I shuddered as he touched me for the first time. I was surprised that his hand was soft, but I learned that they were that way because he was too lazy to turn them to work like decent men do.

"Now jump!" Someone pushed him and he stumbled over the broom as I hopped over. "No, no, Tom, wrong way." The crowd was laughing at his fumbling around and they jostled him around the broom the right direction. The men kept pushing him right on around the broom and over it again. "Not th' same way agin, Tom," they laughed as I turned correctly and he started the other direction again.

To my surprise, he jumped over the broom enthusiastically and before I could regain my balance started off toward the house, pulling me down as he went. The men were now roaring with laughter and it was the women who stopped his progress long enough for me to jerk my hand free, get up and brush my clothes back into place.

"Hold on there, Tom Finn!" Maudie shouted. "We heven't even cut the cake!" Before he could regain his equilibrium, the women were pushing him back to the tables where a cake stood by a bucket with a dipper in it.

"Maudie baked you a cake an' Rose mixed us up a punch fit for the gods," Minerva had to holler in his ear to be heard over the hubub.

I noticed several women wiping tears of mirth from their eyes and the men were still enjoying their laugh over the events of the last few minutes. "Cut the first slice, Ruth, an' serve yore new husband his first meal." Maudie was nodding at me meaningfully. I cut a slice of the cake and filled the cup pushed to me. Tom fairly grabbed them from my hand and wolfed down the cake. He took a long drink from the cup, but stopped about halfway and looked closely into the cup, then he drank the remainder and reached for the dipper. Someone handed me a small cup filled and one sip told me where the jug of rum had gone.

The men must have guessed what was happening, for they pushed up and all filled their cups. Several of the women had cups as well, but on the whole they were more restrained than the men. Tom had finished his second cup and was reaching for the dipper again, when Maudie took me by the elbow and led me away from the crowd milling around the cake and punch. "Let's jist stand aside an' watch, Sugar Booger," she said with a grin.

Several of the other women nodded knowingly when they caught my eye. Everyone then joined in the festivities, the children getting the bulk of the cake and the adults working diligently on the punch. Tom Finn was in the midst of it all and I noticed that every time his cup was emptied, someone filled it up for him.

Soon there was much merriment and laughter and Tom seemed to have forgotten me. He began bragging on his manly prowess and one of the younger men challenged him to a wrestling match. Someone drew a big circle on the ground and in a trice they were going after each other. Neither could quite get the advantage and every time one of them got thrown out of the circle, the men gathered round threw him back in. It was a good hour before the two were worn out and the match just petered out. Tom's shirt was torn almost off and he was covered with mud and sand from head to foot. Someone handed him his cup — filled again — and the party went on. It seemed everyone was drunk, even some of the women, when the sun finally settled on the horizon. The bucket of punch which had mysteriously stayed filled all afternoon went dry and people began wandering away towards their homes.

Tom Finn suddenly became aware of the quietness. He looked over where I was sitting on a split log bench with Rose. "Rosie, ain' 'at my boughten woman sittin' 'ere with you'uns? S'time we got home," he slurred, stumbling over to us and almost falling over the bench.

I drew back in alarm, but Rose squeezed my arm and said, "I guess it's time, all right, Tom, let's git on to the house."

Taking one arm and motioning for me to take the other, she started off down the path with Tom stumbling along. He became very boisterous singing bawdy songs and bragging loudly about what he was going to do on his wedding night. I must have been crimson with embarrassment, but Rose was just laughing with him and leading him on his unsteady way to the house.

When we got to the door, Tom paused weaving a little, then very seriously said to

Rose, "Now Rosie, you knows th' custom o' th' auld country tha' th' groom carries th' bride o'er th' thresssh-'old' an' I'm gonna do thet now." With that, he tried to pick *Rose* up and carry her through the doorway. Rose and I both were almost overcome with mirth.

Tom Finn looked at us puzzled and turned and walked into the house. "Thisssh is *my* house an' I' gonna bed my woman right thar on thet bed," he said, weaving slightly. As he moved toward the bed, Rose tapped him smartly on the back of the head with a heavy bottle that seemingly came from nowhere. With a sigh, Tom Finn sank to the floor and lay very still.

I was aghast. "Rosie, you've kilt him," I whispered.

"Faith an' begorra, no, child," she said, "me faither ran a tavern in the auld country, an' he knew just how t' tap the rowdy ones wi'out harmin' 'em. He'll sleep all the night an' be all the better in the mornin' 'cept'n for a rum headache whin he wakes up. Jist you give him a little hair o' the hound that bit 'im an' he'll mend right well."

She set the bottle on the stump and I noticed that there was a swallow or two of the rum in the bottom.

"Kivver the boy right where he lies, child,

95

an' yuh kin sleep safe an' sound knowin' he won't be movin' none, an' he'll sleep late a'mornin', too. I doubts he'll feel worth much all day, with what he put away in him today. Anyhow, this be the weddin' gift the women thought you would like the best, girl, a good night's sleep wi' no interruptions on yore weddin' night!"

She grinned mischievously, gave me a reassuring hug and went out the door. "Jerry's sleepin' wi' Little Paddy an' me tonight, so don't you worry none," she called from down the path.

I lit a candle and found an old blanket among Tom Finn's old rags and covered him. He was sleeping soundly and snoring some, but didn't move at all. I quickly put on my gown and lay down in the bed and was soon sound asleep.

The sun was bright when I awoke with a start. Looking furtively over the edge of the bed, I saw that Tom Finn was layin' just as we had left him the night before. Quickly, I dressed before he stirred and went about the household chores, several times stepping around the prone body. It was past noon before he stirred any and it must have taken him an hour to get awake enough to sit up and take notice of his surroundings. Spying the bottle still sitting on the stump, he crawled over to it, dragging the blanket with him. Picking up the bottle, he turned and propped up against the stump with a groan, fumbling with the stopper. I reached down and taking the bottle unstopped it and handed it back to him. With one long pull he drained the contents. Wiping his mouth on the back of his hand, he leered at me. "Well, woman, how did yuh like yore weddin' night?"

I smiled. "Just fine, Tom Finn, just fine!"

Zenas concluded his grandma Ruth's story with a flourish, quoting her: " 'And that was my pirate wedding!' she would say."

Zenas sat very quietly for a few minutes, his head on his chest, while I finished up my notes. "Tom Finn wasn't very well liked by the pirates, being lazier than the rest and too mouthy even for them. He was a drunkard even at this young age, being just about twenty years old at the time. He was a bully, but could not stand up to anyone when trouble came. Grandma didn't like Tom Finn at all, they got along like dogs and cats, I suppose."
He chuckled at a sudden recollection. "She did say that he came home drunk once and tried to beat her, but she got away after a few blows." He picked up his Grandma Ruth's words again.

■ ■ ■ ■

When I had recovered my nerves a little, I went back to the house. All was quiet and when I looked in, he was passed out on the bed. I laid a blanket out on the floor under the edge of the bed and rolled him off the bed onto it. Then I rolled him up in it and tied him up tight. I cut a strong hickory stick from the woods and whipped the daylights out of him with it. He was so drunk that he didn't even wake up entirely, just lay there and groaned and hollered some.

When I had run out of strength and the anger in me quieted, I sat down there on the floor and cried. After a while, I got up and washed and threw away the switch and untied the rascal. Then I went over to Maudie's to visit a few minutes and hold Joseph. He was crawling everywhere and the girls had a time keeping him out of trouble. They all loved him so much, even Hi doted on him, that I was glad things had worked out as they did. Jerry seemed to find his place in the community, too. He spent his nights mostly with Rose and Little Paddy, but stayed with me some too, especially when Tom was gone.

I helped Maudie cook and feed the children, then about sundown I returned to the house. Tom Finn was still laying where I left him, so I left him there and went to bed. Daylight was just beginning to creep into the room when he began tossing and groaning, trying to wake up. The sun was full up and I had done most of my chores before he sat up. He was groaning and sore all over and he never could explain the welts and bruises all over his body, but he suspected I had something to do with it. I never told him, but he never came home so drunk again and always left me alone when he was drunk.

Jesse was born in October of 1807. I never knew the exact day, but I set it down as the fifteenth in Papa's Bible. He was strong from the start and Maudie and Minerva Conner said it was the easiest birth they had ever seen. In a few days I was back to nearly normal. Tom Finn had gone off on one of his stealing trips and Jesse was three weeks old before he showed up. He was proud of the child and bragged to the other pirates about him and how many more he was going to have. I made up my mind then that there would be no more that I birthed for him, and there weren't, thanks to his drunkenness and some herbs Mama had taught me about.

The pirate gang operated between the mouth of the Ohio and the mouth of the Saint Francis, but mostly above the Chickasaw Bluffs. Fort Pickering was on the fourth Chickasaw bluff where Memphis is now and they generally gave it a wide berth. They would cut across to the Natchez Trace and rob a few travelers there, but since the capture and hanging of the elder Sam Mason, they mostly liked to hit unsuspecting boats along the lower Ohio and on the Mississippi River.

Tom Finn never shared his parts of the booty with me and I was dependent on the charity of the other women and the stored goods for my and little Jesse's sustenance. I never did get used to wearing or using things stolen from others. Knowing that most of the original owners were murdered only made it worse. My constant prayer was that God would forgive me for using the stolen goods and punish severely those that had stolen them and murdered the innocent owners.

CHAPTER 7
ISLAND LIFE
1806–1809

"Grandma and Uncle Jerry lived on the island without leaving from late summer, 1806 until January of 1812. She was as much a prisoner of the river as of the men who constantly guarded the camp. The east channel of the river was the widest and main course of the river. On the west side, the channel was only about one hundred yards wide, but very swift and treacherous. It was called the Chickasaw Run and was the second most dangerous stretch of river next to the Devil's Race Ground down below the second Chickasaw Bluff. No one dared challenge the Run and the occasional hapless navigator who tried always met with disaster. Grandma said that not one boat made it through the west channel the whole time she lived on the island, though the Indians routinely shot the rapids in their smaller canoes.

"Most boats on the river traveled in groups for mutual protection, more from the river pirates who infested every part of the river than from the Indians who lived along its banks. It was the boats who traveled alone or strayed too far from the group that the thieves preyed upon. The river was too treacherous for night travel and the boats all tied up at night, either along the banks or to some island. It was then that the pirates would sneak into their midst and try to conquer the most prosperous looking boats. Mostly, these were immigrants moving from the states to new lands and not aware of the dangers on the river. Very few of the victims lived to tell of their misfortune.

"Though they were tightlipped about their activities when on the island, Grandma learned how the pirates operated from things dropped here and there by the men or their wives. They were a bloody bunch. Some were educated men driven from their homes by misdeeds or bad luck, and some were the scum of the earth who didn't belong in any society.

"Grandma Ruth kept mostly to herself, tending house and child and reading the family Bible. She mostly avoided the other women except for Maudie Cates and Rose Monahan. They were rough frontier women, but kindly to Grandma and helped make life more tolerable. Tom Finn was gone most of the time, either on forays with some of the other men or off alone on some secret mission of his own making. When he was at home, he was usually drunk and spent most of his time laying around the beach talking to the other men who happened to be there. No one knew where he was from and it was pretty certain that his real name was not Tom Finn. Most of the men did not use their given names, but some name made up or borrowed from their past. The others were too dull or depraved to care about changing names and lived with the name they were born with — names hated and despised by decent people with whom they came into contact.

"Maudie and Rose sometimes talked of leaving the island. Maudie wanted Hiram to move on and take up the life of an honest man, but Hiram was very careful to avoid the subject, knowing that their lives would be forfeit if the other pirates caught them in the act of leaving. If they ever escaped, it would have to be secret, swift and complete. They would have to move far and fast with no traces to avoid the wrath of the pirate gang. They watched the children growing with the apprehension that they would soon join this outlaw society without a chance of choosing a more civilized mode of living. Grandma Ruth told of their final escape:"

■ ■ ■ ■

One morning as I was working about the house watching Jesse play on a blanket on the floor, Jerry came running into the room. "They're gone!" he said breathlessly in Cherokee.

"Who-all went," I asked idly, thinking that he was talking about the pirates leaving on another raid.

"Maudie an' Hi an' Will an' th' girls, an' Rose took Paddy an' went with 'em," he replied wide-eyed.

"Oh, they're not gone, Jerry, they were talking about going fishing this morning and I bet they slipped off without you because you always catch the most fish," I laughed.

"No, no, no!" Jerry grabbed my arms and shook me. At thirteen he was an inch or two taller than me and the work around the island had made him strong. "They left in the night and took a long canoe Hi had hidden on the lower end of the Chickasaw Run where no one would look. They left everything but some clothes and food they had accumulated. I followed their tracks and saw where they slid the boat down the bank!"

I was still doubtful that they had left, so we went over to the Cates house. Everything was in place just as I had left it yesterday except that no one was there. It was eerie how quiet it was. Trying not to attract too much attention, we went over to Rose's and found the same thing. Jerry led me out the back door and we followed a track through the dewy grass into the edge of the woods. Jerry hurried on and I tried to keep up carrying little Jesse and shielding him from the limbs and vines that got in the way. I could hear the Run splashing and flowing before I saw the water.

Jerry stopped and waited for me to catch up. There on the bank of the river were a profusion of tracks in the sand. Lower down, there was a long skid mark left by a boat's keel running down into the water. Where they had launched was below a little shoulder of land that stuck out and shielded the water from the rushing current somewhat and I could see that by hugging close to the island a boat could avoid the main current and reach the calmer water in the lee of the island. It began to dawn on me that the two families had actually left. I sat down hard in the sand at the edge of the bank and stared at the tracks and the skid mark and the water. Some of the tracks were barefoot and plainly there were Joseph's tracks among them.

"Why would they go an' leave us?" Jerry whispered. He sat down beside me and gathered the struggling Jesse up between his knees.

"I don't know, Jerry, but they sure did and they took Joseph with them!" That realization hit me and my eyes suddenly filled with tears. I laid my head on my knees and sobbed. First the murders of Mama and Papa, then Sammie is left in the wild to some unknown fate, now little Joseph was gone. All the ones dear to me left in my world were Jerry and my baby. At this moment, it seemed that nothing worse could happen. After a minute or two, Jerry pushed Jesse onto my lap and the child's chubby arms wrapped around my neck. He couldn't understand why I was so sad.

Jerry stepped into the bushes a ways and came back with a leafy limb. "They'll have a better chance if we wipe out their tracks," he said. He slid down the bank and with his bare feet wiped out the tracks in the mud. Then wading into the water, he splashed water over it until all marks were gone. At the edge of the woods, he began sweeping the limb back and forth until all the tracks in the sand were gone. I stood holding Jesse and blinking back the tears. It was as if he was erasing the people and brother we loved from the earth. Why would they leave us without saying a word? How would we ever find them again, especially our beloved brother who had grown into such a happy-go-lucky four-year-old cherub?

"We'd better git back afore someone misses us," Jerry said as he tossed the limb into the current.

Back through Rose's back door without being seen, I washed my face and combed my hair. Jerry washed all sign of mud from his hands, legs and feet and changed his trousers. "Maybe if we kept on like nothing has happened, the others won't notice them gone for a while," Jerry said. "I'll keep pre-tendin' that ever'thin' is normal here an' you kin help cover for the Cates es long es we kin."

It was a good idea, so after talking it over a few minutes, he went out to the woodpile and began chopping wood. I stayed inside for a few more minutes, then went out, call-ing back as if talking to Rose in the house. Saying something cheerful to Jerry, I walked on up to my house. All day, I kept busy about my routine of housekeeping and watching Jesse. Once or twice I looked at the Cates place, but all was quiet.

Late in the afternoon, Minerva Conner stepped through the door. "Where are those

Cates?" she asked as she scooped up the running Jesse and hugged him tight. Jesse squirmed struggling to escape and continue his chase of the junebug crawling away.

"They were talking about a fishing trip to the upper end of the island last night and I suppose that's what they did," I replied. "Jerry was put out they didn't take him. It's getting late, I imagine they should be back soon," I added.

"If you see Maudie whin she comes in, tell her I got Roda's dress made an' I need to measure her for the hem," she said.

Minerva loved to sew and was always making something for someone. We visited a while, then she left to fix supper for her brood. I lit a candle and fed Jesse his supper, bathed him and put him to bed.

In a few minutes, Jerry came in. "Rose took all the beans an' flour with her an' I been hungry all day." He plopped down in a chair. I got busy and dished him up a big bowl of beans and broth and got some corn bread out of the wooden box I laughingly called the safe. "Wonder how long 'fore they're missed?" he asked between bites.

"Probably not much past sunrise, I would guess," I replied.

"I lit a candle in Cates' house when I come by," he said. "That should put them off a little."

We talked a while then he left to go back to Rose's so there would be someone around there, too. After I saw that he had reached the house and shut the door, I closed and barred my door. Tom Finn had been away but a little while and it wouldn't be like him to come back before a month so I left the latch cord inside and went to bed.

All was quiet until nearly midmorning when I heard voices and someone calling from the direction of the Cates' house. Looking out, I saw Minerva standing in the Cates' doorway. She was calling and waving to a couple of the men at the beach. Seeing me, she called for me to come up. I grabbed Jesse and hurried over. "They ain't been no one here since I come by last night," she called as I neared.

I tried to look surprised. "I thought I saw a light when I went to bed last night, I think they must have come home late," I said as I walked up. Looking around, it was obvious no one had been there. I went over and touched the stove. "It's cold."

"I don't see no sign of fish or fishin' poles," Minerva said. At that moment, one of the men stuck his head in and asked, "Whut's goin' on, Minerva?"

"Th' Cates went fishin' yestiddy an' ain't

come back," she said.

"Maybe they decided to stay overnight," the second man said. He yawned and turned to wander back down to the beach. "Com'on, Dan'l, they's still a couple o' pulls in thet jug, yit." The two wandered off. Jerry was chopping wood, and Minerva called to him. "Have you seen any of the Cates today?"

Jerry shook his head no, then put the ax down and walked over. "Rose didn' come home last night, an' I just thought they must hev decided to fish all night," he said as he neared. "I bet they'll come in soon, those girls'll be too hungry to stay out longer."

"I don' know, I wouldn' think they 'uld keep those kids out all night in the mosquiters an' sich." She shook her head. "You don' 'spose they had some kind of trouble, do you?"

"Not likely," Jerry said. "Hi is with 'em an' he kin take good care."

"Jus' the same, I wonder 'bout 'em," said Minerva.

"If you think we should, Jerry could go up to the point and see if everything's okay," I put in. Jerry gave me an exasperated look. "I got chores Rose left me with," he groused.

"Just the same, if they need help, we

should go see," I replied.

"Run on up there, Jerry, an' we'll feel better knowin' they're safe," Minerva urged.

Jerry pretended to hesitate. "Go on Jerry, and take your pole, might be if the fish are bitin' you could catch us a batch," I said.

"Okay, but you got to make it straight with Rose," he replied. He wasted no time getting his fishing pole and started up the trail to the point of the island.

"I'll feel better knowin' they is all okay," said Minerva. "They's too many dangers 'round here with Injuns an' outlaws an' sich."

I stifled a chuckle, thinking about a pirate's woman worrying about outlaws. We watched Jerry disappear down the path and visited a few minutes before Minerva left to see about things at her house. "Let me know when he gits back, Ruthie," she called.

I was getting the laundry ready for washing when I heard Jerry yelling from the direction of the path. Looking out I saw him running as fast as he could. He got to me out of breath and unable to speak. He was as white as a sheet and his eyes seemed to bug out of his face. I began to get alarmed. "What is it, Jerry?"

He bent over with his hands on his knees. "Dead man," he panted. He had to say it twice before I could understand.

"Dead man?" I asked. "What are you talkin' about?"

"They's a dead man in th' water on th' point," he replied as he began to catch his breath.

"Who was it, Jerry?" I almost whispered, thinking it could be Hi.

"I couldn't tell, he was facedown, but I don't think he was from th' island." He was getting calmer but shuddered at the thought of the dead man as he found him.

The inhabitants had a secret signal they were to give to the everwatching guards if something were wrong or danger was near so I gave the signal and several men converged on us as we stood in the yard.

"Whut's wrong, Ruth?" It was Minerva's husband Thadore who asked as he walked up.

"Jerry's found a dead man on the point where Hi and Maudie were fishing with the girls. Not a sign of anyone else up there."

The men at once gave the signal for everyone to gather around them, as all activity had ceased when I gave the secret signal. "You wimmin gather up th' children an' git to th' strong house with 'em," commanded Sam Mason. Motioning to three armed men, he said, "Th' rest of you men arm up an' be on guard whilst we visit th' point an' see whut's goin' on," he ordered.

Motioning to Jerry to lead the way, they quickly disappeared down the path. The rest of us began gathering children into the strong house, which was the former home of the elder Sam Mason and now young Mason's home. The men appeared one by one with their guns and assumed preassigned defensive positions around the compound. All was quiet for a long time, and it soon grew very hot and stuffy in the crowded house. Several babies began to fuss and one of the women stuck her head out of the door and asked the nearest guard if they could sit outside the house and cool a bit. After asking the men around the area, it was decided that we could come outside if we stayed close and ready to retreat at any moment. It was much cooler outside and the babies soon quit fussing and began playing around on the ground.

We sat down and held whispered conversations about the events. Pretty soon one of the men who went to the point returned and announced that there indeed was a body at the point, but that it wasn't anyone the men had seen before. He said the rest of the men were making a sweep of the area down to the compound for any sign of Rose and the Cates. It was another hour before men began to appear from various points along the north edge of the clearing. Jerry was with them, flushed and sweating from walking through the woods and brush. He looked very pleased to be included among the searching men and it occurred to me with a start that he would soon be grown enough to go on their pirating missions with them. I determined then and there it would never happen so long as I breathed.

"We didn't see hide nor hair of any of th' Cates or Rose an' her kid, though they was lots of tracks an' their fishin' gear layin' about," Sam Mason spoke up. "Let's sweep on down th' island to th' end an' make sure they're not there, *nor anybody else,*" he called.

Taking several more men who had guarded the camp, they fanned out to span the island and began moving toward the downstream end. "Fire yore gun if you finds anything," Sam called as they disappeared into the woods, Jerry included. After waiting a little over an hour with no sounds of a signal, the crowd began to relax and scatter to their respective houses to prepare supper.

Soon the men straggled back in. Jerry hurried to my house. "They didn' find a thing."

He grinned happily. "Th' ones who were by the Run never noticed th' place where they hid th' boat. I heard them speculate that some River Rats had grabbed the lot of them an' that Hi had got one of them afore they did him in, an' they must hev made off with th' wimmin an' children. They're gonna put on a double watch fer a while in case someone gits any more idees," he said with a grin.

This turn of events was a great comfort to us, since there was now no suspicion that the Cates had escaped the island and probably no search would be made for them. This would insure their safe escape and wherever they were, little Joseph would be safe from the pirates. I prayed that they would all be safe and that Hiram would finally give up his ways and seek honest means for supporting his family.

As days went by the pain of the event lessened and we gradually resumed the day-to-day routine of the camp without constant thoughts and speculations of what might have happened to our friends. Tom Finn passed through, only staying a few days and hardly paying any attention to Jesse and me. He spent less and less time on the island and even less time with us when he was there. I didn't mind that a bit, but we still remained prisoners on the island with few friends and no way of ever leaving. Occasionally I drew the attention of one of the other pirates, but I mostly was able to resist their advances by one ruse or another and they eventually left me to myself. Even young Sam Mason kept his distance, being under the watchful eye of his woman, who was a force within her own right.

Chapter 8
The Year of Waters

Zenas said that the Cates' escape occurred in the late summer of 1809. His grandmother stayed on the island two more years a virtual prisoner, unwilling to leave without taking Jerry with her and knowing how difficult it would be to escape unnoticed with a babe in arms. Nothing noteworthy happened until 1811, which began with the greatest flood in memory inundating the Ohio and Mississippi valleys. This is the narration Ruth Harris gave about those days.

Each spring the river flooded, but the spring rise in 1811 was the worst we experienced on the island. The rise began as usual, then suddenly in the middle of the day the water rapidly rose several feet covering the whole island. Jerry and I had become accustomed to preparing for the rise as the others did by placing several days' supply of food and clothing in a johnboat pulled up by the door of the house. The first I knew of the big rise was when I heard Jesse splashing and laughing by the front door. Looking out, I saw that the water was almost coming in the door. I grabbed Jesse and my pack of valuables and set them in the boat at the same time yelling "flood" as loud as I could. Tom Finn came reeling through knee deep water and Jerry was splashing from the other direction. By the time they got to the boat it was afloat and water was pouring into the door of the house. I hurriedly closed the door and scrambled into the boat just in time to catch Jesse's shirttail as he tumbled over the end, laughing all the time. He loved water and was at home in it from the very beginning.

Tom Finn fumbled over the end of the boat almost upsetting it. Jerry stood at the other end and braced against Finn's thrashing. He grabbed the rope and towed the boat to the nearest large tree and wrapped the rope around the trunk, then gingerly hopped in. It was astonishing how fast the river rose. Jerry was constantly hoisting the rope up the tree trunk and it was fortunate that the tree limbs were thirty feet or more above the ground. Several of the island inhabitants were swept away and the rest had to take to the boats and tether to the trees to be safe from the waters. The water rose until it was lapping on the roof of our house. The upstream end of the island soon gathered trees and debris enough to stifle the current to a great extent and we only had to contend with the backwater currents.

Tom Finn lay in the bottom of the boat and slept off his drunk. He woke up mid-morning of the next day sick and grumpy. All he could do was berate me for not including a jug of whiskey in the boat. I cooked a meal of beans and rice in the fire box and offered him a bowl. He quickly ate it, then almost as quickly lost it over the edge of the boat. After that, he lay and groaned and cursed us as the rocking of the boat kept him in a state of nausea. He finally quieted down after dark and slept loudly through the night. The next two days were just like the first for us until he finally convinced a couple of his buddies who had a jug to paddle over and get him. He left us with a curse and we sighed with the relief of being rid of him. He never came back to our boat and we only saw him a time or two after the waters receded.

We saw many strange things as we rode out the flood. All sorts of animals, dead and living, floated by. I saw my first buffalo in the flood. It was dead and no telling how far the carcass had come. One day we saw a roof from a barn or house floating by with a cow standing disconsolately astraddle the ridge. How in the world did she get there and how far did she float down that river? One morning we heard a dog whining and looking about we discovered a very large black-and-tan hound laying on a half-submerged door. The current had pushed him into the backwaters and it had actually floated from the south to the north which was against the main current of the river, of course. Jerry and Jesse were intrigued with the dog and called and talked to him for quite a while. The dog would listen and occasionally wag his tail, but we could tell that he was near the end of his rope. Finally, Jerry jumped into the water, swam to the door and pushed it over to our roof. The dog needed no encouragement to hop on to the roof. He shook himself and walked up to the ridge and laid down, wagging his tail at Jerry. I let out enough rope from the tree so that I could pole over to the roof and Jerry beached the boat up onto the roof. I filled a bowl with our now-daily fare of beans and rice and handed it to Jerry who set it before the dog, who eagerly ate it to the last grain of rice and licked the bowl clean. Then he wagged his tail and looked at me and burped. We laughed and Jesse tumbled over the end of the boat and climbed the roof to sit down beside the hound. They became fast friends and in the days and years to come were inseparable. Jerry named him Mississippi after the flood that brought him to us and he immediately became "Sippie" in four-year-old language.

The boys begged me to let them sleep on the roof with Sippie, but I didn't trust the soundness of the house or the river enough to allow it, so they both settled down in the moored end of the boat to sleep as close to Sippie as they could. Sometime in the night I sat up to see that Jesse was properly covered against the chill and there was Sippie wedged in between the boys with his head laying on both boys' hips. A few thumps of his tail told me everything was okay and I went back to sleep.

The waters receded so very slowly that we were beginning to worry about having enough food to outlast the flood. Jerry discovered that the backwaters around the camp were teeming with fish seeking shelter from the current and feeding off the bottom and we didn't have to worry about hunger anymore, though we did get awful tired of fish after a while. Others around the camp were in the same condition as we were and it was a worry about what we would do for food after the river fell, since anything left behind would be ruined and not usable. It was ten days before the high ground the camp was built on reappeared above the water and much of the island remained under water for weeks.

Of course, the camp was a wreck. Several of the hovels had collapsed and floated away piece by piece. The ones remaining were a mess inside and it took us weeks to clean them all up. So many were without homes that we worked as teams cleaning and sleeping two or three families to the house. When one was cleaned, we moved on to another and in that way got all the places remaining livable. Our house stood the flood well; I think if the chinking between the logs had not washed out, it would have been damaged worse. As it was, the currents had little trouble flowing through the house. In doing so, it carried away any item that could fit through the cracks. Most of our things that stayed were plastered against the wall. While we cleaned houses, the men gathered logs and flotsam from the river and fashioned houses and temporary shelters for those who had lost their houses.

All the food was ruined and we dumped it into the river. An unexpected advantage of this was that the fish gathered and fed off the food and the men and boys kept us amply supplied with fish, which was our only source for food for several weeks until the river fell enough that it was safe for the men to navigate and go to the mainland for game. The men had learned to bring me the hide when they killed a deer and I could tan it like my mother had taught me and we could sew clothes out of it. In this way, I kept the boys and myself adequately dressed without having to depend on the hand-me-downs stolen from some poor innocent traveler.

It was late summer before things finally returned to a somewhat normal life, if that is what you could call life in a pirate camp. Sippie had grown and grown. We had thought he was nearly grown when he came to us, he was so big, but he just kept getting bigger. One of the pirates thought he must have some Mastiff blood as big as he was. He loved the boys and took special care of Jesse. If I missed Jesse, I could call the dog and here they both would come, or if Jesse slipped away without Sippie, I could tell him to go get Jesse and it wouldn't be long until I would hear them come tumbling up the path. He was a good watchdog and he slept on the floor by the door.

Of course, Tom Finn hated him — well really, he feared him — and Sippie disliked Tom. If Tom came around drunk, Sippie wouldn't let him in the house, the result being that Tom rarely got in. When he came sober, Sippie would always stay between Tom and Jesse and watch Tom Finn's every move. Tom would have killed the dog if he got a chance, but Jerry and I kept them separated. Jerry was going on fifteen years and nearly as tall as Tom Finn and stronger, too. I think that had a lot to do with Tom keeping in line.

Chapter 9
The Great Shake

One September night in 1811, we were surprised by a bright light in the skies. It shone down through the thinning leaves of the trees and we all went to the beach on the north end of the island for a better view. It was a very bright star with a long luminous tail — some called it a comet. My grandfather on my mother's side had told us of another time when a Star-with-a-Tail had appeared and of the fearful things that had happened to the people as a result so it was with a sense of foreboding that I watched the skies as it appeared night after night.

There were other signs in the sky. At the end of November, just before sunrise, two huge shafts of light shot up from the eastern horizon until they were almost directly overhead, then just as swiftly they receded. I alone saw this and didn't mention it to anyone for fear of stirring up false worries, but I pondered them in my mind.

There was a big stir among the men about the first of December. They gathered in groups talking in low tones obviously making plans for some big event, probably involving piracy. Curiosity ran high among the women about what was going on and there was a lot of spying on the men. Piecing little tidbits gathered here and there, they deduced that the pirate gang was going downriver below the Saint Francis to an island and stage from there on several raids. There was confusion about which island they were going to, some said it was Stack Island and others heard it was Crow's Nest Island. It took a few days for us to find out that it was island number 94 and was called by both names. Almost all of the men were going, with only a couple to stay and guard the camp. One day Jerry came in wide-eyed and excited. "I'm goin' on th' raid!" He fairly danced with excitement. I didn't say anything, but made up my mind then and there that he would *not* be going on *any* pirate raid. Pretending interest, I asked, "When are you leaving?"

"First thing tomorrer mornin'," he replied. "I gotta git my things together." He began stuffing a bag with clothes and things he would need for the trip.

"I'll fix you a big supper tonight," I said. "No tellin' when you'll git a good meal again goin' with that bunch. I saw some poke growin' in that little clearing on the south end, run down there an' gather us a bunch an' I'll fix you a good mess of 'em with salt pork just like you like it."

As soon as he and Jesse were out of sight, I hurried up to near the north point of the Island where I had seen some Trout Lilly growing. I gathered several leaves and quickly returned to the house and began cooking supper. Soon the boys were back with a big bag of poke. I soon had it boiling on the fire. Along with that was a large venison steak and I stirred up a pudding for dessert. I ladled out two helpings of the poke and quickly stirred the finely chopped Trout Lilly leaves into the remainder. It was late when I finally called supper and both boys were starved. I gave Jerry the largest cut of steak and a large bowl of the Trout Lilly–laced poke. He was so excited about the trip that he hardly stopped talking long enough to eat, but he did finish, then he cleaned up the leftovers from Jesse's plate.

Not long after that, we went to bed in anticipation of the planned before-dawn departure of the men. Jesse fell right into the blessed sleep of a child, lying on his back with his arms thrown back, never to move until morning. Jerry talked on and on in the darkness until he finally dropped off to sleep. I listened for a long time, but there was no sound from him save his gentle breathing. I began to worry that my "medicine" wouldn't work. I drifted off to sleep and it was almost time to get up when I heard Jerry groaning. He rose and I heard the door open and close. In a few minutes he returned only to leave hurriedly again and I heard him throwing up outside the door. He returned to his bed and was groaning softly until it was time to get up. I dressed in the dark then lit a candle and began stirring up the fire. "Better git up, Jerry, I'll have a bite for you to eat before you leave," I spoke softly.

He stood for a minute and then rushed for the door. In a few minutes he came back looking as white as a sheet. His skin felt pasty when I checked him for fever, and he was bent over with stomach cramps.

"What's wrong with you, Jerry, you are white as a sheet!" I pretended worry.

"I'm real sick, Ruthie," he groaned and sat down carefully on the edge of his bed.

He only protested a little when I said he wasn't going to leave that sick and I brewed him some sassafras tea. While he was cautiously sipping that, I stepped out into the darkness and told Thel Fields who happened to be passing that Jerry was very sick and would not be able to go with them. It only took Thel one glance to see that the boy was really sick and he nodded and quickly left. In a few minutes, we heard the boats slipping down the beach into the water. With a small splash or two, they were gone and the island sank once more into the predawn quietness.

Jerry was sick most of the day and I fed him venison broths. By evening, the effects of his "illness" were almost all gone and he began to feel much better. He went to bed with the sun and slept soundly all night. I was relieved, but most relieved that he didn't go on the raid with those low-down pirates. After we had talked quite a bit and he had time to think about it, I think Jerry was glad he didn't go also. The lure of escaping the island and its boring routine was great and he had seen a chance to do that, but had not thought about what he was escaping into with those marauders. He was safe from becoming one of them for now, but what about the next time he had a chance to go with them? I worried about it.

Because Jerry didn't go, they took one of the men appointed to guard the camp and when Jerry was up and about, Dan Sowell, the single guard left behind, gave Jerry a musket and pistol and made him the night guard. This was a new responsibility and kept him busy patrolling at night. He cleaned his guns and slept most of the day and prowled around the camp all night.

The rest of us began thinking and planning for the Christmas coming up. It was one of the few days in the year that offered some relief from the monotony of everyday life on the island.

The comet was still making its nightly appearance and I had never gotten over the foreboding it gave me whenever I saw it. The fifteenth of December was an oppressive day on the river. There seemed to be a mist hanging in the air and the sun shone only weakly even though there were no clouds. Even the animals and birds seemed restless and more active than ever. The myriads of birds migrating south would rise from their roosts in the trees crying loudly, then settle down again only to rise in another panic. This went on all day. Sippie was restless, lying down near my feet or next to Jesse, only to leap up almost in a terror and rush for the door of the cabin. I must have let him out a dozen times only to hear him scratching at the door a few minutes later. Just before dark, I fed Jerry and he resumed his nightly rounds of the camp. Jesse and I went to bed and Sippie seemed to settle down and lay on his bed by the door.

It was well after midnight when I was awakened by Sippie's frantic whining and pulling at the bedclothes. Jesse awoke and started toward the door, I supposed to let the dog out. I was setting my feet on the floor when Jesse gave a little cry and I saw that Sippie had pushed him out of the door. I rushed after them and as I got to the door, there pealed the loudest clap of thunder I have ever heard. It was a long and hollow and vibrating sound. Almost immediately I was thrown down as if some mighty hand had pulled the ground out from under my feet. Screaming, I grabbed Jesse and hugged him tightly. Sippie cried and pushed against us trying to bury himself under our bodies. Desperately, I crawled away from the house to more open ground.

The birds rose in solid masses screaming and calling in panic, while trees swayed and broke and fell all around us. It seemed the ground rose several feet, then fell again and I could hear great waves beating against the island shores. The river seethed like something boiling and there was the sound of a mighty wind in the wildly swaying trees, though not a breath of air was stirring. It seemed hard to breathe. People were screaming. Another sound came to our ears, it was the roar of the vertical banks along the river falling into the water. I thought of the many boats that would have tied up under those bluffs and was sickened by the thought of those tons and tons of soil and trees falling on them.

The ground rose and fell again and I became sick and threw up. After every roar of a bank falling, huge waves beat against the island, washing up several feet on the banks. I could hear the sounds of timbers cracking in the houses around us. Our own cabin swayed drunkenly and the door fell off. Dust boiled out as the roof collapsed, but the walls stood even though they were tilted badly out of plumb.

I could hear cries and sobs all around me and someone at the edge of the camp was calling frantically for help. I became aware that my own voice was among the other cries and I was calling for Jerry. "I'm coming," he called and I soon saw his form lurching and crawling over the heaving ground. His rifle was slung on his back and his clothes were torn and soiled. A trickle of blood ran down his temple and cheek from a split in his scalp at the hairline. Sippie whimpered and crawled across the ground to him. "How did you git out here?" he asked in wonder, but didn't wait for an answer. "I'll git some covers from the house." And before I could stop him, he was crawling through the doorway. In a moment he reappeared with an armload of quilts and bedclothes. I wrapped ourselves in them and only then realized how chilled I was.

We lay huddled together until dawn. It was impossible to stand long for the shakes came time and time again, sometimes regularly and other times at ragged intervals. Some were small and some were quite violent. Sippie could somehow anticipate when one was coming and we learned to watch him and brace ourselves for the jolts.

Others began to congregate around us and some went around to rescue those trapped in their houses. They found Minerva Conner who was the one calling for help, her legs pinned under a log. She was nursing her infant child and waiting for her rescuers. When they pried the log up enough to release her, some grabbed her under the arms and dragged her out from under the log. Minerva screamed and fainted and they saw that her left leg was broken below the knee. Quickly, they grabbed sticks for splints and set the leg, binding it tightly in the splints. When Minerva came around again, she was encased in blankets and splints and one of the older girls was holding the infant.

In the daylight, the river was frothing in its agonies and foam covered the surface. It looked like a boiling, poisonous cauldron and we were loathe to even get near it. The shocks were still coming and we could see great waves rolling across the surface some after the shakes and always after some bank had fallen into the river. It grew eerily quiet, the birds having left for safer lands and the only sounds we heard were falling trees and an occasional snapping timber or limb. Entire trees floated in the current as if in the spring floods and there were boats fully loaded without a person on them, their fate unknown. The Chickasaw Run was choked with trees and the stream seemed wider. Foaming water rushed over the trees and beat against banks and trunks.

As we began to take account of all who were present on the island, someone asked, "Where is Dan Sowell?" We hadn't missed him until that moment.

"He was headed to the beach to check on the boats when the shakes started," said Jerry. "I'll git down there an' see whut he's doin'."

Between shakes, Jerry made his way to the beach. He was gone a long time and I began to get concerned when I saw him returning. He had to walk slowly to keep from being thrown to the ground and it took quite a while for him to walk the hundred yards or so from the beach. "Did you find him?" someone called and Jerry nodded, but I could tell by his face that something was not right. Sitting down heavily beside me, he took some moments to catch his breath.

"Well, whut's he doin' down there while we're sittin' here tryin' to hold on to a shaking world?" asked Helen Fields.

"He ain't doin' nothin'," Jerry replied. "He's dead. Looks like he was leavin' in one of th' boats an' a tree fell on him. Th' boat was smashed out in th' water an' he wus pinned under th' water."

There was a silence for a moment, then a babble of talk. "You say he wus leavin'?" someone asked.

"Uh-huh, an' thet ain't th' wurst of et," Jerry gritted. "They ain't a boat left on th' island. By his tracks, I could tell he pushed them off to drift away, he done it a-purpose," Jerry spat.

So we were left stranded on a shifting island in the middle of a raging river, a couple dozen women and as many children, without any means of saving ourselves save our own wits. Our only hope of rescue seemed to be with the men who had left earlier on the raid. If they learned of our circumstances, they would surely try to get back to our aid.

We lived outside from that time on, fearing the dilapidated houses would fall in on us if we returned to them. Indeed, several of them did in the following days and jolts. Jerry and some of the older boys recovered canvas sheets that we strung up and made tents for shelter. It was fortunate that the weather was mild during that time or we would have suffered much more than we did.

Gradually, the severity of the shakes lessened, though there still were several a day. The river calmed down and resumed its steady flow, and the traffic gradually picked up, though not as heavily due to the rivers north of us being frozen for the winter. We looked daily in vain for the men to return. Some thought we should flag passing boats, but most were fearful of the consequences if it became known that we were the families of pirates. In the end, we waited and hoped for the return of the men. Christmas came and passed almost unnoticed and as the days passed it became apparent that no rescue was coming from the men on Crow's Nest Island.

It looked more and more like we would have to seek rescue on our own, which meant we would have to flag down boats to rescue us. This was not a very reliable way to get help, since one of the ways pirates operated was to lure boats to the "rescue" of someone on shore or island, then ambush the unsuspecting boat. Experienced boatmen would not fall for such a ruse.

I spent much of my time reading Papa's Bible and at times several would gather around and I would read aloud. We sang hymns that we could remember and prayed.

The children were much affected by the happenings, being terrified and screaming when the harder jolts hit. Most clung to mothers and the older children. We didn't have to worry about them wandering far. Sleep for all of us was fitful and it wasn't unusual to find one napping any time of the day. All of us showed the signs of anxiety, eating little, listless, temperamental and impatient with others. Almost any time of day or night the sounds of crying could be heard, from either child or adult. Those were some of the darkest days of my life, save for the time after the murders on Humpy Bayou.

The days dragged by at a faltering pace, then on the morning I calculated as January 22, 1812, *[Actually, it was January 23. — J.D.]* a second great shaking occurred just at sunrise. I had just added wood to the fire and stirred the ashes when the familiar rumbling struck and I was just able to reach the sleeping boys before quakes as violent as the first hit. Again, the trees trembled and shook and the sound of wind where there was no wind was heard. This time, there were few birds to scream, since they must have sought quieter lands to spend their migratory time in. The shakes were just as hard as the first episode, only the ground continuously quivered between jolts. All day long, they came, some as hard as the first and the ground rumbled constantly. At first, the well went dry, then it collapsed in on itself.

In the daylight, we could see the effect the shakes had on the river and land around us. Huge fountains would suddenly rise from the depths of the river and shoot water and mud and other debris sometimes as high as thirty to forty feet into the air. Bubbles of air rose from the bottom and burst on the surface with loud booms, such as we had heard in the darkness of the first big shake. In places, sucks would occur where the river would whirl about some fissure in the riverbed and suck water and anything that was borne on it into the vortex, to disappear forever. The water was so laden with mud and sand that a third of a bucket of water would settle in the bottom as sand and muck.

Trees called sawyers were released from the bottom of the river and bobbed to the top, to be gathered against other trees called planters that were secured upright to the bottom and unmoved by the current and shakes, great jams were so constructed. As we watched, a huge piece of land, maybe forty acres across the river suddenly sank into the water, causing a huge wall of water to well up and rush across the surface, then almost as quickly it reversed and rushed over the now-sunken land until only the tops of the trees were visible above the water. The whole channel of the river constantly changed, writhing back and forth like a huge snake.

All of these events inspired such awe and terror that I found myself crying and sobbing aloud with my face and the front of my dress soaked in tears. Some fainted and few could look on the scene long before averting their eyes and burying their faces in their arms. And still, the ground shook and quaked.

Gradually, the shaking subsided and we could again move about with relative ease. Jerry pushed through the brush and fallen trees to see how the Chickasaw Run was doing. In a few minutes he rushed back. "It's gone!" he hollered.

"What's gone, Jerry?" I asked.

"Th' Run's gone, th' island's pushed up against the far bank!"

"What on earth are you talkin' about, Jerry, the island can't move that much!" I replied.

"Come see for yourself!" he said defensively, so several of us pushed our way through the brush to the edge of the island. There where the Run used to be was a wall of soil about three feet higher than the island surface and pushed up tight against the island. There was a line where the sand of the island met the black soil of the other bank and it was plain to see, though just as unbelievable that the two banks of the Chickasaw Run had joined and the Run was no more. To tell which had moved was impossible, but as we watched, the two masses of land moved and shook in unison, indicating that at least for now, they were joined together.

Helen grabbed my arm. "We can git off!"

she whispered. Then louder, she hollered, "We kin git off. Let's run!" She began to climb the bank.

"Wait!" I cried. "We have to tell the others and get our things together!" By now, she had scrambled to the top of the bank and stood looking back until another shake tumbled her back on to the island.

"Yo're right, Ruthie, we need to git ever'one over as quick as we kin."

CHAPTER 10
ESCAPE TO NEW MADRID
JANUARY 1812

As we ran back to the camp, my mind was rushing a hundred miles an hour. We had to gather as much food and clothing as possible. We had to get everyone off the island. We had to get Minerva and the little ones through the brush and over the bank.

"Jerry," I called, "git the boys and start cuttin' us a path through that brush. Send a couple with shovels to the bank to knock down a path so we can get our things up it. Be sure to make it wide enough. Now move!"

Helen was calling the women to pack up and giving orders for them to hurry. I grabbed two of the tent poles and made a travois out of them and the canvas, then I piled all our foodstuffs and clothes on it. Frantically, I showed the other women how to make the travois Indian fashion and store all their belongings on it.

We could hear the boys chopping brush

and pulling it out of the way and they had a decent path started by the time we were ready to leave. The travois would not get through until the path was cleared all the way, so we pushed through the brush with the children and put them up on the bank. Some of the older girls herded and carried them back a long way from the bank and most of the adults helped clear the path. It seemed forever before it was clear enough, but we got a reasonable path made. The big logs couldn't be moved or cut up, so we had to pull the travois over them. It was hard work, but we finally got all of them through and up the ramp the boys had dug. All that was left was to get Minerva over.

"Look at the ramp, Ruth," Jerry whispered.

I looked and saw a small band of black soil sticking up above the level of the ramp. One of the two pieces of land had moved vertically. Either the island was sinking or the bank was rising. Either way, we had to get off the island and back away from the river to higher ground. Someone had dumped out a travois and several of us ran and dragged it back to where Minerva sat on a log across the path. She had hobbled as far as she could on her own before giving out in exhaustion. Laying her in the travois, four of us grabbed a corner and we struggled down the path and over the logs. Others rushed to help and it took four of us to lift Minerva above our shoulders and four or five others on top to pull her up the vertical bank.

It was nearing dark and we still had much to do, but we stood still for a moment and looked at that cursed island. Most of us had lived there for years without ever leaving and a large part of our lives were left there. How one could have mixed feelings about such a place, I don't know, but I guess it was the leaving of the familiar and striking out in a huge world we didn't know that caused us all to look back. Another jolt suddenly struck and one of the boys tumbled over the bank. As he scrambled back up, he called, "So long, prison island."

"Goodbye, Hell's island," someone said.

"Goodbye, home," another chimed.

"Good riddance, stinkin' hole!" a louder voice called from further back on the bank. "We're free!"

"Let's git!" And we all turned our backs and hurried to the children.

We decided that we should get as far from the river as possible, so gathering all things up, we pushed through the brush. Soon the forest grew denser and the underbrush faded out. We found ourselves in a familiar virgin forest where the trees grew to fantastic sizes and the forest floor was as clean as a park. Except for detouring around the fallen timber, walking was much easier and we made good time traveling. It was now near pitch dark and the ground began to descend, so we determined to stop and make a camp until daylight.

Stumbling around, we gathered enough dead wood for a fire. Someone had thought to bring a bucket of coals and we soon had a fire going. As the blaze grew, we gathered around its light and began making camp. Some of us erected tents, while others of us spread our canvases on the ground and made beds on them. By sharing covers and canvases, we made a huge pallet on the uphill side of the fire and soon all the children were piled in it and gradually the squirming turned to sleeping and quiet settled over the camp.

Sippie found Jesse and wormed his way under the covers next to him. In a moment his head popped out of the cover beside Jesse's and with a sigh of contentment, he lay down. I knew I would not have to worry about Jesse for the night.

The boys were still gathering firewood and we women gathered around the fire storing things and making the camp more secure.

"Well, where do we go from here?" Minerva asked. She was propped up against a tree trunk, her leg sticking out awkwardly in front of her. Her face was pale, but there was an air of relief about her that the rest of us shared.

I felt almost giddy. "We have to find help before long while our food holds out," I said.

"New Mad'rid is somewheres south of here along the river, if anythin's left o' it," said Helen.

"Even if nothin's left of it, there ought to be some people left," put in another.

"First, we've got to find water aroun' here and fix a meal or these kids'll starve," said another.

"We need to be whur the men kin find us," one of the women said.

I thought, "They'll play whaley finding me!" Tom Finn was a bad dream in my past and if I never saw him again, it would be soon enough.

"We should wait 'til daylight an' find water, then we can git our bearings and maybe head for New Mad'rid," I suggested.

"That looks like the best plan," said Minerva. "I for one am wore out." I took a canvas sheet and spread it near her. With my help, she was soon on it and covered

146

warmly with a blanket. Giving the children another look to see that they were all snug and covered, we all lay down for a night's rest.

The boys kept the fire going brightly all night and most of us slept soundly. I drifted off wondering what the future would bring. Surely, it would be a place where the ground didn't shake and there were no pirates. I hated the big river that had brought so much pain and had held me prisoner so long. If I never saw it again, I would be happy. Jerry and Jesse and I could find a place where we could live secure and safe. Maybe we could go back and look for Samuel.

Morning broke bright and clear, but it was cold. The children huddled around the fire or wrapped up in their blankets on the beds. Several of us started out in various directions looking for water. One of the younger boys found a spring near the base of the ridge we were camped on and not far from the camp. The water was turbid, but after it sat a while, we could dip some clear water off the top. It wasn't long before we had rice and beans boiling merrily and the children began to stir around.

While we ate, we discussed what route to take to get to New Madrid. The boys had explored the bottoms west of us and said that they were wet and boggy, so we decided to stay on the ridge as long as possible. It looked like it paralleled the river, so we could probably get to the village with little trouble.

Finishing our meal and packing took time and it was midmorning before we got going. We took turns, two at a time, pulling Minerva on her travois. It was hard going and no one could last long pulling her. The other travois were tiresome, too, and the children who were walking didn't move so fast. We had lots of rest stops and didn't get very far. In the early afternoon, we stopped and cooked a meal. After resting a while, we moved on until evening when we found a good spot to camp for the night and slept. This pattern of travel was repeated for three days, until we reached New Madrid midday on the fourth day.

Before the shakes, New Madrid sat on a high bank of the Mississippi at the head of a great oxbow bend of the river, the upstream side actually flowing north before continuing its southward flow. It afforded the town a clear view of the river several miles upstream and downstream. It was the afternoon of the twenty-seventh of January when we entered the town — what was left of it — cold, tired, dirty and hungry. Most of the houses were severely damaged, not a chimney was standing and several roofs had collapsed into the homes. Few of the inhabitants were living inside, but had erected tents and shelters safely away from the structures standing akimbo and leaning ominously.

The townspeople met us with indifference and it was very apparent that they were in the same condition as we were and could offer us no assistance. In consequence, we moved north of town and set up camp separate from them. The older boys began to explore the area and bring in firewood, which was plentiful because of the quakes. The ground continued to shake and it seemed that the movements of the ground were more often and more pronounced than those up by the island. We wondered if we had chosen the wrong direction to travel but it was a much longer distance to any other settlement on the west side of the river. None of us had any desire to be near that river.

We turned in early that night though our rest was fitful because of the shakes. Minerva was exhausted and looked pale and shrunken. She ate little then drifted off, to sleep for nearly twenty-four hours. It was after daylight before the camp began stirring much. We fixed a big breakfast and fed the starving little ones.

Jerry and some of the other boys were up and gone heaven knows where before any of the rest of us had stirred and it was mid afternoon before we saw anything of them. All four of the boys were carrying sacks bulging with provisions and Jerry had a twenty-five-pound sack of flour on each shoulder. They triumphantly set their sacks down in the middle of camp and began unloading their contents of food — cured hams, potatoes, dried fruit, bacon and a lot of other things.

"Where in the world did you get this stuff, Jerry?" I was afraid they had stolen it somewhere.

"We found a faltboat stranded 'way up on the banks of a creek over west of here. It must have been washed up there by the shake. No one had been near it and it's loaded with goods," he explained. "We can get three times this stuff off'n it when we need it!"

"Well, we need it for sure," put in Helen. "The kids won't hardly eat beans an' rice, an' I'm gittin' awful tired of them myself!" She began arranging the provisions under

150

one of the tents. One of the women opened a bag of flour and began mixing up a pan of biscuits while another had a skillet of bacon frying and was slicing big slabs of ham and throwin' them into the hot grease. The aroma drew people like flies and we ate as the food was cooked, not waiting for the meal to be served whole.

Last to be ready were the biscuits. Someone opened a jug of molasses and we ate until the last biscuit was gone. Looking around at the children, I began to laugh. Jesse had molasses and bread crumbs from the tip of his nose to his chin and he was picking sticky crumbs off his chest and eating them. None of the others, including some of the older ones, looked any better.

We found a big cast-iron kettle at one of the abandoned houses and the boys carried it into camp, set it over one of the fires and filled it with water. We put up canvas walls around the fire and when the water was good and warm herded the children through the tent, washing and scrubbing them to the tune of their protests. Dirty clothes were piled in a corner and whatever we could find clean replaced them. Some of the smaller children were put to bed without anything on because there was nothing clean they could wear. Soon quiet settled over the camp as full tummies and clean bodies made heavy eyelids. I filled a pan with warm water and took it to where Minerva lay. With Helen's help we three bathed her except for the broken leg which remained bound. We looked at each other and almost in unison said, "Now it's our turn!"

The fire was stoked, the kettle was refilled and when the water was hot, we women all bathed with little thought of modesty. One by one we slipped off to our beds and a sounder sleep was never seen in that camp.

The boys had kept a discreet distance from us and when the morning came they were the only dirty ones in camp. While some of us cooked breakfast, one of the mothers stoked the fire under the kettle and had it refilled. When it was warm, she grabbed her son by the ear and led him to the bathroom. "Now you git in there an' wash an' whin I think yore clean enough, ya kin hev breakfast — an the same does fer the rest of you'ns!" she said, hands on hips and looking around at the half dozen remaining dirties.

There was some halfhearted groaning but no loud protests. I caught Jerry's eye and with a nod and motion of the spoon in my hand, seconded the command. He suppressed a grin and headed for the kettle.

Breakfast over, it wasn't long until the bathroom was turned into a washroom, and the boiling kettle filled with shaved soap and dirty clothes. By noon the bushes all around were covered with drying clothes. We suspended washing for the day since clothes were slow drying that time of year. It was three days before all clothes and beds were clean and dry and the place began to look like a decent camp. Some of the townspeople were amazed at our proficiency in setting up a camp and we didn't tell them how we got so much experience, having determined not to reveal who we were and where we had come from.

While we washed and some of the boys carried water for us some of the others returned to the stranded flatboat and brought in more provisions until we were well stocked. They secured the boat and piled brush around it so it would be hidden. This wasn't done out of selfishness but necessity since the townspeople were hesitant to share their supplies with us — at any price.

Game was unusually scarce, having left the area for firmer grounds. It took Jerry and the boys several days of hunting to bring in one deer. After that, their hunting was haphazard. We were used to seeing and hearing birds of all kinds by the thousands migrating south for the winter or north for the summer but with the first shakes, they rose with an awful din of screaming and squawking and totally disappeared. The eerie silence they left b'hind was most disturbing.

If I hadn't seen it for myself I would imagine that I was in another world, but this was Louisiana and this was the Mississippi River and the vision and feelings was of a hell on earth. Everywhere there were great fissures opened in the ground; they opened and closed with the constant to and fro and up and down movement of the earth, like the waves on a lake. There were large and small craters in the ground where geysers had spewed forth black woods and dust and sand with an awful roaring and whistling. Some of the craters built up six or seven feet high. There were sounds too. The earth groaned and rumbled sometimes sounding like thunder deep under the ground that vibrated on our feet. It was almost like the land was in great pain and that sound still comes to me after all these years. The air was heavy and stank of sulfur and decay. Sometimes it was hard to just breathe. It seemed at times that the light of the sun grew dimmer without the presence of clouds or dust. Thinking back on it I wonder if it wasn't my eyesight that grew dimmer from the anxiety and fear I felt. Often we would be overcome and many times I sat holding Jesse and Sippie close, covered with a blanket as if we could close out the happenings around us.

The children were most affected by the shaking, they clung to us and panicked whenever they lost sight of their mother or the one caring for them. The motions of the earth caused much dizziness and it wasn't unusual to see someone throwing up after a strong shake. We learned to watch the animals for they knew when a strong shake was coming and when they stood still or braced themselves by spreading their feet wide or crouching, we called out to everyone near and braced for a shake. Part of the town nearest the river began sinking and b'fore it was over, ended up under the river — not because the river ate away the bluff — it just sank. Trees could be heard falling any time of the day or night. There were great tangles of them where a fissure had opened or the ground had risen into a ridge, tossing them off like weeds behind a plow.

Jerry was struck with a great restlessness and we hardly saw him. He would come in about sunset, sometimes famished, always tired and dirty, and would fall exhausted on his bed and be instantly asleep. Then he would be gone before daylight. I learned to leave him something to eat where he could find it when he arose. I don't know if it was because of the shaking earth or because he had been cooped up on that island so many years that made him so restless. Sometimes he would sit a few minutes and tell us what he had seen and done. Jesse was wide-eyes and ears to hear him and I was afraid he would try to follow Jerry but the shakes kept him close to me.

One day Jerry came in early, quiet and pale. I could tell something unusual had happened but didn't pry. I got him a heaping plate and he picked at the food absentmindedly. Sippie seemed to perceive his mood and lay with his head on his feet but Jesse was excited to see him and sat beside him asking a hundred questions. Jerry laid down his plate and grabbed Jesse in a bear hug and held him a long time. Tears were trickling down his cheek.

"Ruthie, I saw a terrible thing today," he said as I sat down beside him. "We was over south of here a ways and found a Injun village all abandoned. I was looking through the huts when I found a little girl pinned under a roof beam an' dead. She was about Jesse's age an' they left her where she lay. After that we was more careful looking 'round an' they was five more Injuns layin' dead where they fell. It looked like the rest panicked and run and never come back."

We were quiet for a moment then I said, "I can imagine how you felt, Jerry, but how do you think those Indians felt when the earth started shaking? They must have been terrified most to death. No telling what they thought was happening. Even here in this town I hear that several men panicked and left the country with no thought of their families left behind. There's no telling what people will do in an emergency. That's why you need to think about things and train your mind what to do in those times. Remember what Ma and Pa did when those pirates showed up? They didn't panic and run because they had resolved beforehand to protect the family regardless of what happened and they stood and fought. Four pirates died and Arnsted Wood lost his arm subduing them. I heard some of the pirates talking later about that fight. They said it was the most costly raid they had made and they didn't look hard for Sammie and would not abuse us b'cause we were from fighting stock. Even after they were dead, Papa and Mama protected us by their resolve."

Jerry pondered on what I had said a moment then I asked, "What do you suppose we should do about those bodies?"

"They should be buried proper, I guess, but they was in a awful condition. I couldn't touch them."

"Maybe we could get some help and go see what can be done," I said.

"Johnny an' Clell was with me an' they'll help us an' mebbe some o' th' others." He seemed to brighten a little.

"Well finish your supper and see if they will and maybe some of us can go and help too," I said, rising.

"Me too, me too!" chirped Jesse.

"We'll see, Jesse. It's not going to be a good trip for little ones," I said.

"Me big 'nough," he said, standing as straight as he could.

The older boys said they would go back to the Indian camp, and Helen volunteered to go with us. Minerva was mending well, even moving around on crutches a little and I made arrangements to leave Jesse with her but when it came time to go, I couldn't part with him knowing how chaotic things were and how we had lost Sammie and little Joseph so he trotted happily along with us.

Sippie coursed ahead of the boys who carried borrowed shovels, with Jesse working to keep up and Helen and I following behind.

The village sat under the trees at the edge of the woods looking out on a large prairie. Most of the mud and stick houses had fallen in and the area gave evidence of a hasty departure. The floors of the Indian huts were dug down a foot or so and the excavated dirt used to build up a dike around the hole to keep out the rain.

The smell of death and corruption was strong. Sippie's head first went up, sniffing and whining, then went to the ground, following the scent. After looking in a couple of houses, he found the one with the child in it and bayed. The little girl must have been killed in the first big shake and the advanced state of decay made it impossible to move the body. Two of the others, a man and a woman in separate houses, had apparently died in their sleep and were still rolled up in blankets. A huge tree had fallen over one of the huts and looking into the debris two bodies could be seen, but there was no way to move them. In one of the two huts that were comparatively undamaged, a very old woman sat huddled in her blanket against the center pole. She didn't look injured in any way and may have died of fright or old age, being too feeble to run away. It was a testament to the desertion of the area by the animals that the bodies had been undisturbed by wolves or other scavengers.

We sat down on one of the fallen trees and the boys looked to Helen and I for advice. "We can't move the child to a grave, so we will have to bury her where she lays," I said.

"But we *could* move the sleeping ones in their blankets to where she is," put in Clell Conner, Minerva's son.

"Where I was raised, the ground was too rocky to dig graves," Helen said, "so we laid people out near the top o' the ground and built rock coffins 'round 'em."

"We ain't got no rocks here, but there are sure a lot of logs layin' 'round, we could use them for the coffin," one of the boys said.

"First, let's clear away all the stuff from this hut an' make room, then we'll move the others over here and build a grave over them," Helen suggested.

The call for action appealed to the boys and they set to clearing the rubble from the collapsed hut. They chattered constantly while working, making plans on how to build the grave and what materials they would use. Last to be moved was the log resting on the body and it took all of us lifting and prying with poles to move it. We laid it out as one of the sides of the crypt, then the boys rolled three other logs in place to form the other three sides, all on the top edge of the sunken floor space.

Jesse had been very quiet the whole time, clinging close to my skirt and I was surprised when he tugged and handed me a blanket he had found from somewhere. "Cover the little girl, Ma, so her won't be cold," he said gravely. I folded the blanket and covered the child with it. That helped to lift our gloom a little and the boys hurried off to bring in the other bodies.

By grasping the blankets they were wrapped in, they could carry and drag the bodies easily without handling them. The old woman came first. She was very light because of her advanced age and starved condition. They gently laid her by the little girl and placed the other two bodies on either side leaving the child and granny in the middle. Gathering the smaller poles used for the walls of the huts, they laid them across the logs for a roof. A second layer laid at right angles to the first was added and on top of that we added thatch from the roofs; then the boys shoveled dirt over the whole grave, making a pleasing appearing mound for their resting place. On a thought, the boys piled more thatch over the hut where the other two bodies lay and shoveled dirt over that but they had grown tired and the result was not as nice as the first grave.

Foraging through the ruins we found several spears and bows and the boys stuck them up at the head of the grave. They hung other items they found on poles stuck up around the grave and when they were satisfied they sat down and surveyed their work.

"I think that makes a good grave," said Johnny Fields.

"Shore does," agreed Clell.

"Leastwise they got a burial an' th' animals won't trouble 'em," Jerry said rubbing dirt from his hands. "Ruthie, are we s'posed to say somethin' for a funeral?"

I started to speak when Helen said, "We could say the Twenty-third Psalm together." I was very surprised for Helen always seemed of the roughest sort and I never thought of her as having any sort of religion. She started off, "The Lord is my Shepherd, I shall not . . ." And the rest of us that could joined in.

When we finished, all were quiet for a moment, then little Jesse spoke up, "An' t'ank you, Yord, for this food we are about to receive, a-a-a-*men*!" Giving an emphatic nod on the end.

We laughed, realizing we had worked all morning and into the afternoon without eating. I brought out a bag of biscuit and ham sandwiches and we sat on a log and ate. Helen's jug of water was welcome and I fished out a cookie for each of us to top off our meal. I got one bite of mine before Jesse commandeered the rest. The sun was sinking and we hurried back to camp before dark.

Thinking back on the whole affair, I was touched by the thoughtfulness and responsibility of the boys in the matter. I'm sure Jerry was touched by the similarity of the little girl and Jesse, but something beyond that struck a chord in the hearts and minds of all the boys. That all people deserved the dignity of a proper burial, whatever that may be in different societies and under different conditions, was somehow naturally ingrained in their minds. They showed a natural maturity beyond their years and most likely beyond that of their fathers in the same situation. I was proud of all of them, as was Helen, who made it a point to mention it to the others in camp.

The people of New Madrid were quite diverse in their origins. At any time, one could hear Spanish, English, French or German spoken, many with a word or two of native tongues thrown in. Not far from our camp was a camp of mostly French people who were from a community called Little Prairie south of New Madrid. They were destitute, even in worse shape than we had been. We helped them all we could and as we got acquainted, they told us the stories of their experiences. Mr. George Roddell was an American living with his family at Little Prairie, and owning a mill there. When the shocks began the family abandoned the house for open ground. On the tenth shock, a thirty-yard-wide swath of the east bank of the bayou where he was standing sank for as far up and down the bayou as he could see. At the same time, the swamp on the west bank was pushed up and became dry land. Both the mill and the house fell with the ground and the mill turned over. The family fled in panic but was stopped by a large crack in the ground. The eleventh shock hit and all the ground was broken up. Great quantities of water blew with great force from the ground, roaring and whistling, spurting sometimes as high as fifteen feet and carrying with it all forms of debris and sand, falling back as a black shower on the land. The ground was shaking so hard that it was hard to stand, with a constant rumble coming from deep in the earth. The trees were crashing into each other, being blown out of the ground, or splitting and falling. At the same time the land seemed to be falling and the water rose until it was waist deep on a man. Mr. Roddell attempted to lead his family out of the water but was hampered by falling into crevasses and craters hidden beneath the water. The geysers continued to spurt around them some as high as ninety feet, spitting mud, water, rock coal and sand.

Mrs. Roddell said they would have frozen to death in the water, except that it was warm, probably from coming from deep in the ground where the earth was hot. They waded more than eight miles before finding dry ground. The whole town of Little Prairie was thrown down and sank beneath the water and all the people fled to Francois Lesieru's place. There they heard that the country north of there was not affected, hence the whole community except for an old Negro too feeble to go walked the thirty miles to New Madrid only to find that it too was destroyed, though not as completely as Little Prairie.

They were too exhausted to go further and decided to remain until help could arrive from the river traffic. So here they were, destitute with only the clothes on their back and little else. They were a miserable lot and would have fared much worse save for the flatboats found abandoned along the river and washed up on the shores. In time the cargoes from these boats gave them enough to get by on.

We never knew what happened to the crews of those boats except to speculate that they had been washed away by the violent agitations of the river. Many of the foundered boats had their cargoes soaked as if a mighty wave had washed over the boat. Very few bodies were mentioned of in our area but there may have been many found downstream from us. It became plain that more were lost on the river than on the land.

Chapter 11
The Fourkillers

As time passed, I became more and more concerned that Tom Finn and the rest of the pirates would show up and I was determined we would *not* be present when they arrived. Jerry and I kept our ears open and our eyes peeled for some sign of a way to escape. He began to hang around the river and learned a lot from the travelers who stopped by. One day he came back in a high state of excitement. He had a small barrel hoop and stick and after showing Jesse how to roll it he left it with him and two or three other boys to master. When he came into the tent he motioned me to come close and whispered, "I got some news about the pirates today!"

I caught my breath. "What was it, Jerry?"

"I was fishing off th' bank when a boat came up the river and docked, so I wandered down to see if there was any news from downriver. A man named Sarpy was th' captain and he was on his way to Saint Louis from Natchez. He was telling about th' damage from the shakes downstream. The night they first hit, he had tied up to an island for th' night only to cast off and move when he discovered some menacing-lookin' men there. It was awful dark an' they didn't move far an' tied up on a low bank. They took th' precaution of not makin' any lights or fires so as to be hidden. Th' shakes hit an' they were barely able to hold on to th' land, there was so much agitation. One of his men jumped ashore in a panic an' they never saw him agin. Sarpy said the ground moaned and groaned — just like here — an th' waves was fierce like to swamp th' boat . . ."

"What about the pirates?" I interrupted.

"I'm gittin' to that." Jerry was enjoying the tale and suspense. "Well, guess whut they saw th' next morning when th' air cleared?"

"I — don't — know!" I said in frustration.

Jerry leaned closer and whispered, "Th' island was gone! Guess what it's name was!"

"Crow's Nest?"

"Yeah, and all th' pirates went with it! Leastways nobody's seen 'em since!"

I sat back and pondered that for a minute. Gone! They could some or all be dead or

168

they could have escaped and floated away down the river, nobody could be sure. Tom Finn could be among the living or the dead, we didn't know.

"Jerry, we have to keep this to ourselves and hope the others don't hear about it," I said. He nodded. "Maybe this will give us more time to plan our escape."

I nodded. "I hope they are all gone to hell and sizzlin'! It couldn't happen to a more deserving bunch, but we don't know where they are for sure. We need to get out of here as fast as we can but how and where can we go? Saint Louis or Cape Girardeau aren't far enough and we sure can't go downriver. We have to plan something they wouldn't expect."

"Let's wait a day or two an' see what shows up," Jerry said. "I've got an' idea or two that might pan out."

"What are you thinking about?" I asked but he stayed mum, so I nodded and went back to my chores. In a few minutes, Jerry left and I watched him disappear into the woods.

A few days later, Jerry saw a boat tie up to the bank. A man and his wife and small child hopped off and the crew unloaded their baggage and quickly shoved off downstream. Jerry heard the man introduce himself as Lonza Fourkiller. He had been to North Carolina to visit kin and was returning to the Western Cherokee country. He inquired where he might buy some horses but the bystanders didn't know of any available nearby. Jerry had stepped up and said, "Come with me and I can give you lodging for the night." Then in Cherokee he said, "I know of some horses that are available, but they are unknown to these men."

The man made arrangements for their baggage to be delivered and as they walked toward our camp Jerry explained that our mother was a Fourkiller.

"I remember the family well," Lonza said. "Sarah is the daughter of my father's uncle, but we were not well acquainted."

I was sitting watching Jesse play when I saw them hurrying up from the river. Jerry was leading a little boy about three years old by the hand and the man and woman, who was obviously with child, followed.

"Ruthie, this here is th' Fourkillers, an' they need a place t' stay for th' night," he said as they walked up.

"Welcome to our home," I greeted them in Cherokee, "what is ours is yours."

The man smiled. "I am Lonza, this is Lydia and our son Riley." Lonza was short for a man, but he had the barrel chest and

170

large muscled arms and legs of a man used to strenuous activity. His wife Lydia was very small and looked tired. She sat on my stool with a sigh and smiled and said, "I get very tired these days traveling. The motion of the water has kept me upset for days. It's good to sit on something that isn't moving!"

I smiled because even then, the ground was in almost constant motion, like waves on a lake. "Here, it isn't the water that has waves. I don't see how this can go on for long without another big shake."

I began to fix supper while Lydia rested and we visited. I was surprised a few minutes later when I looked up and Jerry and Lonza had disappeared. Their baggage was delivered and we spent a few minutes stowing it in a safe place. Jesse was busy playing with Riley and Sippie and only pointed toward the woods when I asked where the men had gone.

Supper was ready and we were just sitting down to eat from the plates in our laps — that being our only "table" — when they came up from the opposite direction than what Jesse had pointed out. I dipped food from the pots into the tin plates we had found and they sat cross-legged on the ground and ate. We conversed in Cherokee, which was easier for Lydia to understand. Jerry and I told them of our experience being stolen and marooned on the pirate island, the flood and the quake.

Lonza was most interested in the shaking grounds and what had happened since they had begun. He said the church bells had rung and the springs turned muddy in North Carolina with the first shake. The animals were alarmed and there were loud booming noises. Turning to Jerry he said, "I think seven horses would be adequate. Riley would ride with his mother and two packhorses could carry all our gear. The five you have are in good shape, we only need two more."

I stared at Jerry. "Where did you get horses?"

"They were strays left by th' Injuns and some settlers. I didn't steal them, if that's what you're getting at."

"I won't have you becoming a common thief, Jerry Harris!" I was mad at the thought that he might have taken what belonged to another.

"Honest, Ruthie, they were left by th' Injuns, and some settler over that way left his horses penned up. They would have starved if I hadn't found them and I've been taking care of them ever since. Anyone leaving their horses t' starve in a pen don't deserve t' have them an' I'll tell that man to his face!"

"Just the same I won't have you bending the rules or taking what's rightfully someone else's!" I replied.

Lonza had been listening. "I agree with you, Miss Ruth, and in this case from all I can see, Jerry has done the right thing by the penned horses, and the Indian ponies were left to run wild so the previous owners would have no claim on them. I will ask around tomorrow and see if I can purchase two more horses for our trip."

"What trip? Where are *we* going?" I asked.

"West!" Jerry said with a grin "Those pirates would never think of looking for us there — if there's any of them still living."

"Some of our people have settled around the Little Red River. We are hoping to return there before Lydia's time comes. It would be a great help if you go with us," said Lonza.

"Oh, please come with us, you will be very welcome," Lydia added, smiling.

"How can we travel on this shaking land?" I asked. "The animals won't go when the shakes hit and we might never get any-where."

"The ground wasn't shaking at Paducah,

so I think this shaking is over a small area," replied Lonaza. "Even if it isn't small, we will have to learn to live with it wherever we are. Wouldn't you be safer where the pirates can't find you?"

I thought this over. Going west into the wilderness would most likely rid ourselves of the threat of the pirates returning. I knew that it appealed to Jerry. He had often talked of moving west, partly out of curiosity and partly because that was Papa's dream. The Fourkillers knew the way and it would be a safer trip for all with our numbers. The thought crossed my mind that there might be danger in trusting strangers we barely knew, but Lonza was distant kin and I believed they were honest and sincere. The more I thought about it, the more the doubts faded away. "All right," I said, "we will go west with you, but we will need to go quietly and not let anyone know our plans."

"It should be easy so long as no one finds Jerry's horses. I will purchase two or three more if I can. That would only serve to move the three of us and no one would suspect that you were going along," Lonza said.

"We'll need to stockpile food and pack things secretly for the trip," said Jerry. "I'll get things from the boat and hide them where the horses are. We can leave most of this stuff here, like we had just gone off for a bit and no one will suspect what we are doing until it's too late."

Lydia had been quietly listening. "We could leave early like we were on our journey and you could sneak away in the night and meet us someplace."

It all sounded good and we sat up a little late making plans. Lonza was to begin looking for horses to buy and Jerry would begin to collect provisions for the trip at the farmstead. The three Fourkillers would leave with a show the day before our set departure and wait for us at the corral. Jerry would "escort" them out of camp, go to the corral and help pack for the trip. He would return late in the evening before dark with the news that they were well on their way. All would seem normal and we would go to bed as usual only to rise after the camp was quiet and leave. It took careful planning for us to pick the things we had to have from the few things we would leave behind to throw off any suspicions for a while.

Finding horses proved harder than we thought and it was several days before Lonza with Jerry's help found some that could be bought. It turned out that they could only get one decent horse, but they bought two mules that would do, one fit only for packing, the other one would do to ride if need be. They cost more than they would normally have but Jerry came up with Tom Finn's stash of silver to make up the difference. We kept the animals hobbled and Jesse and Riley had a grand time helping Jerry stake them out and care for them. I was anxious about the little ones being around strange animals but Jerry and Sippie kept a close watch and the horses and mules soon got used to having them around. The boys were ever gathering grasses and feeding them. Jerry taught them how to approach the animals safely and was ever present when the boys were around them.

Meanwhile, the Fourkillers made preparations to depart. Lydia and I packed their things so they would ride on the mules, and Lonza fashioned packsaddles for them. All were busy for a few days. I packed our things quietly and stowed them with the Fourkillers' baggage. One of the last things I wrapped and that most carefully was Papa's Bible. I would keep it with me; it was too valuable to trust to strange mules.

CHAPTER 12
THE HARD SHAKE
FEBRUARY 7, 1812

All was set to depart. We had decided that the Fourkillers would leave on the morning of February eighth and that we would depart that night and meet them at the corral. Depending on how things went, we planned to be on our way immediately. The ground continued to wave gently and there was much stumbling about because one might take a step only to find that the ground had subsided more than expected or one might stub a toe on a rising wave. The young ones made a game of jumping from crest to crest or running down the valleys until they rose again and they tumbled to the ground. Adults and animals were not so happy with the conditions.

Toward evening about twenty boats tied up at the beach and Jerry was happily visiting with the boatmen until supper. We retired early on the night of the sixth, conscious of an increase of the frequency of the waves and the increased agitation of the animals. Sippie whined and crept close to Jesse and the horses were very restless. It was with much trouble that I finally drifted off to sleep.

I awoke suddenly from a deep sleep with Sippie howling in my ear and desperately trying to claw his way under the cover between Jesse and me. The horse and mules were moaning — an awful sound I had never heard from horses before. Jerry and Lonza rushed to them and tried to calm them while holding to their halters. They made no move to run away, but stood heads down with legs spread as if bracing themselves. Then we heard it, a dull rumbling from far away and under the ground that grew and came nearer at a high speed, much like the rumble of a train as it approaches.

The trees began to weave and sway and they sounded as if they were in a windstorm, limbs breaking and trunks crashing down, but there was no wind. Now as the rumble seemed to near, there were crashes of thunder under the ground that thumped our bodies as we lay huddled together. Loud explosions rang in our ears and there were hissings and whistling sounds followed by the sounds of rushing water crashing down. We were pelted with gravel and sand mixed with warm water. I looked out from under the quilt in time to see Jerry, Lonza and the animals flung violently to the ground as it was jerked from under their feet. The ground moved several feet and we were flung by it like leaves flipped from a blanket. A large fissure split the ground several feet from where we lay and a cloud of dust and sand was thrown up.

Water that was gushing up in many directions flowed into and quickly filled the fissure. Another shock and the fissure slammed closed sending water and sand spewing high into the air. The ground rolled and waved and boiled violently so that we couldn't have stood if we had wanted to and thunder and cracks and booms loud as cannon pounded us from beneath. The very ground vibrated and the gravels rattled against each other while the sand hissed ominously. We could hear the riverbanks falling into the river with great roars and the sounds of the huge waves they produced fading as they crossed the waters, then growing louder as they reflected from the far bank and sped back, only to be met by the giant wave from another collapsing bank and sending great waves high into the air roaring like a great storm.

There was a flash of lightning and the sky

began to glow red. Lightning flashed continually and the air was filled with the stench of sulfur that made us gag and retch. The glow grew brighter and brighter until we could see plainly the things around us. I could see Jerry struggling to hold down the head of the horse so he couldn't stand. The mules lay as if frozen in place, not struggling at all and Lonza lay between them, and an arm around each neck. The children were huddled to us and sobbing and crying loudly. I heard someone screaming and looked at Lydia, but her mouth was clamped shut, her face pale and eyes wide and bulging. Slowly the screaming subsided and as if coming from a fog, I realized that it was my voice I was hearing, though at first I had thought the sound was coming from far away.

Looking around I could see no one standing, though I knew many people surrounded us. Not one tent was standing and looking through the haze toward town, I could not see one house, only piles of logs and rubble where they had once stood. I could hear the boatmen shouting, "Cast off, cast off!" The vision was unreal, geysers of sand, water, rotten wood and coal shot up in every direction. Some were small and some very large, shooting as high as the tallest trees and throwing their contents great distances all the while hissing or whistling and roaring.

In between the geysers were fissures or rifts in the ground, some emitting gasses and water but most just yawning holes from a few inches wide to several feet wide. Some would open and close as waves passed over the ground and some were suddenly formed as the crest of a wave split and broke open. We became terrified that a rift would open and swallow us then close over us crushing our lives in a deep tomb. Water sloshed and ran over the ground. What part of us wasn't soaked by the geysers was wet by the water flowing back and forth. It filled the fissures and saturated the ground so that the very soil seemed turned to liquid and sloshed about with the movement of the land.

Gradually the violence of the shakes subsided, though there were still some hard jolts and the ground kept moving between them. The glow of the sky remained, though I think that by this time it was subsiding somewhat. There were still flashes of lightning and in their light I could see glimpses of the river and the boats that had cast off. They were rapidly moving with the rushing current. Then Jerry was there grasping my arm so tightly it hurt. "It's goin' backwards!" he shouted.

"What's going backwards?" I asked.

"Th' river!"

"That can't be," I replied. "See the boats going downstream?"

"Ruth, that's th' *left* channel, it should be flowin' toward us, not away!"

"But the boats are moving away from us, so it must be the downstream channel," I still insisted.

"Stand up, Ruth, and look again," said Lonza. He stood, feet spread wide braced against the movements and leaning on a pole he had picked up. Cautiously, I stood, fell, rose again and bracing myself against Jerry, I looked at the river. I didn't need to wait for a flash of lightning to see that the downstream channel was to the right and the boats were fast disappearing "up" the left channel. Still, it took me a moment to realize that the mighty Mississippi was indeed flowing backward! One boat remained tied to the bank where New Madrid had once stood.

"Where's th' water goin'?" Jerry wondered out loud.

"Maybe there's a big hole up there and all the water's going into it," Lonza speculated.

"D'yuh think maybe the ground's sinking?"

"Maybe so," Lonza replied. "I think we

should get away from the river as soon as we can and find higher ground." Another hard jolt hit and he stumbled a couple of steps trying to keep his feet before sitting down unceremoniously with a splash. Thinking about it now, it was amusing, but no one thought it funny at the time.

"I don't think we'll get those animals to move for a while," Jerry said, looking at the still-prone mules and the horse struggling to maintain his footing.

"Possibly so," Lonza eyed the animals.

"Just the same with you, if I have to walk, I'm getting out of here as soon as I can!" I vowed.

"I will go with you," Lydia spoke for the first time. Her lips were pressed in a straight line and her face was pale in the flashes of lightning. She had not risen, but remained seated in the receding water with Riley pressed close to her bosom.

"We have a lot of packing to do, now that we can move without raising suspicions," Lonza said. "Let's take stock and see if we would need to repack your things before we go. By the time we get that done, the shakes may be quieter and the mules will want to move."

I thought for a minute. We had packed the bare essentials for the trip, but now what clothes we had left behind could go, along with the canvas tent and some of the other camp gear that would make the trip easier. Walking, stumbling and crawling, I got to the fallen tent and began sorting things for packing or leaving behind. Lonza and Jerry pulled the canvas and poles out of the way and began making a travois and loading it. It was impossible to leave the frightened boys and Lydia sat with them and Sippie, watching and making suggestions.

The dawn was coming and we could see things more plainly. "Look, the river has turned around!" exclaimed Jerry. We turned and beheld the river returning to its old flow. We watched the river rushing down a rapid of falls about a mile upstream from where we stood, and as we watched, the torrent grew and roared as it tore over the falls, tearing at the banks and filling the riverbed below. It was an awesome thing and we watched in fascination the oncoming flood. I began to wonder if the banks could hold the water, but they did and we were in no danger from it where we stood on the ridge.

"Look, here comes a boat!" Jerry shouted.

We held our breath as we watched two flatboats tied together shoot the falls. Thankfully, they kept the boats lined with the current and came through with nothing more than a good soaking.

In a few minutes, the boats tied up to the beach and we walked down to see the men. Two or three of them were laying on the bank, exhausted from their efforts, and the Captain, Mr. Mathias Speed, was talking to some of the men from town. "We were tied up to the west bank opposite island number nine when the Hard Shake hit. Quick as possible, we cast off and submitted ourselves to the whims o' the river. We worked all night trying to keep upright, with waves sometimes washing knee deep across the decks. The river gradually calmed down and we were approachin' number ten at dawn.

" 'Glory be, Captain,' Joshua said to me, 'we been four hours comin' four miles! I swear the river must hev run back'ards!' And indeed it must have, for there was a current all night, I could feel it with the tiller, but couldn't tell which direction we were goin' in the dark. I don't know how long it flowed backwards or how far we went upstream."

"Look!" someone called. "Another boat's comin' down the falls!"

We all turned to watch in fascinated horror as another flatboat shot the rapids, whirling and dipping crazily. We were relieved to see that no one was on the boat. It shot down the falls and dipped far down into the backwater at the bottom. Gradually, it floated into calmer waters, got caught in an eddy and floated back upstream toward the falls. Turning crossways in the current, it went into the foot of the falls and dipped so low under the water its deck disappeared. Suddenly, it bobbed clear and floated placidly on the current, gradually sinking until with a sigh from the crowd it disappeared under the river.

"Thank God no one was aboard her!" someone said.

"Must have jumped when they saw the falls," commented another.

"I'm sure we wouldn't have made it in a single boat," Mr. Speed said, "having the two tied together gave us quite a bit more stability than one boat would have had. That and having a good crew that stuck with it," he added, indicating the exhausted men on the bank. "That falls must be twelve, fifteen feet high and at least three quarters of a mile long."

As we climbed back toward the tent, we became aware of a new sound, a far away roaring of waters.

"Listen!" called Jerry. "Where's that comin' from?"

"Sounds like there's another falls some-where downstream," said one of the men.

"I'll bet ol' Mathias stays tied up 'til he knows whut thet is!" said his companion.

And that's just what Ol' Mathias did! Some of the bolder men took a canoe and floated downstream to the falls. They came back late in the afternoon and said the falls was as high as the first one and eight miles downstream. Imagine hearing the river roar from that distance!

Zenas leaned forward in his chair. "I've heard others talk about the Mississip running back'ards in those days, heard everything from a few hours to a few days, heard that it made a lake in Tennessee that ol' Davy Crockett named Reelfoot after an Injun that lived in the area. Grandma's story that the river ran backward only about four hours seems more accurate than days. Even then, there was a lot more water than necessary to fill that lake 'lessen it's mighty big and deep — an' what about the water coming down from Saint Louie? It had t' go sommers. All in all, there musta been a big flood all up and down that valley. It's a wonder anyone lived through it!"

CHAPTER 13
EARTHQUAKE CHRISTIANS

We don't know exactly when this event oc-curred chronologically, but it seemed to Zenas and I to fit here the best. There is the possibil-ity it could have occurred before the Hard Shake, but not likely. — J.D.
  Ruth told the story just like this.

We were working as fast as conditions would let us when I looked up and was startled to see a crowd of people standing silently watching us. It seemed that all of the survivors of the island were there along with the Little Prairie people, and there were quite a few townspeople in the crowd. We looked at each other for a few seconds. Then Mr. Roddell stepped forward and removing his crumpled hat and bowing a little said, "Ma'am, some of the women from your group say you have a Bible. Could we read from it a bit?"

"Of course you can," I replied. Wiping my

hands on my skirt, I carefully unwrapped Papa's Bible. It was too precious for me to trust to a stranger's hands so I said, "If you will all gather around the trunk and sit, I will read you some passages that come to my mind at this time."

By the time I had seated myself on the trunk and leafed through the Bible for the scripture I wanted to read, everyone was seated as near as possible. The only sound they made was an occasional whimper or word from the little children. Someone brought a lantern and held it swaying by my shoulder. Looking over them, I was struck by their rapt attention to me and it was a little scary. They weren't still, for they moved and bobbed on the waves running through the ground and for a moment I felt I was floating above a sea of bobbing heads. It gave me a start and I diverted my eyes back to the scripture.

[Here, Zenas stopped the narration and said, "Grandma always took up her pa's Bible and read the scriptures she read back then as she told this story and we always listened carefully to what she read. I am taking up that same Bible and will read those verses just as she did and has them marked off in the Book."]

I thumbed to the back of the Book, looking for the comforting words at the end of

Revelations. I turned to Chapter 21 and began reading.

And I saw a new heaven and a new earth; for the first heaven and the first earth were passed away; and there was no more sea. And I John saw the holy city, New Jerusalem, coming down from God out of heaven, prepared as a bride adorned for her husband. And I heard a great voice out of heaven saying, "Behold, the tabernacle of God is with men, and he will dwell with them, and they shall be his people, and God himself shall be with them, and be their God. And God shall wipe away all tears from their eyes; and there shall be no more death, neither sorrow, nor crying, neither shall there be any more pain; for the former things are passed away."

And he that sat upon the throne said, Behold, I make all things new. And he said unto me, Write: for these words are true and faithful. And he said unto me, It is done. I am the Alpha and the Omega, the beginning and the end. I will give unto him that is athirst of the fountain of the water of life freely. He that overcometh shall inherit all things; and I will be his God, and he shall be my son. But the fearful and the unbelieving, and the abominable, and the murderers, and the whoremongers, and sorcerers, and idolaters, and all liars, shall have their part in the lake which burneth with fire and brimstone; which is the second death.

Sometimes I would pause and think about what I had read and the comfort it gave me. Still the crowd sat and didn't make a sound. I tried not to think of the bobbing heads and turned back to the Gospel of John, chapter 14 and read portions through verse 17 of chapter 15:

Let not your heart be troubled; ye believe in God, believe also in me. In my Father's house are many mansions: if it were not so, I would have told you. I go to prepare a place for you. And if I go and prepare a place for you, I will come again, and receive you unto myself: that where I am, there ye may be also. And whither I go ye know and the way ye know. Thomas saith unto him, Lord, we know not whither thou goest; and how can we know the way? Jesus saith unto him, I am the way, the truth, and the life: No man cometh unto the Father, but by me. If ye had known me, ye should have known my father also: and henceforth ye know him, and have seen him. If ye shall ask anything in my name, I will do it. If ye love me, keep my commandments. And I will pray the Father and he shall give you another Comforter, that he may abide with you forever: Even the Spirit of truth: whom the world cannot receive, because it seeth him not, neither knoweth him: but ye know him: for he dwelleth with you, and shall be in you. I do not leave you comfortless: I will come to you. These things have I spoken unto you, being yet present with you. But the Comforter, which is the Holy Ghost, whom the Father will send in my name, he shall teach you all things, and bring all things to your remembrance, whatsoever I have said unto you. Peace I leave with you, my peace I give unto you: not as the world giveth, give I unto you. Let not your heart be troubled, neither let it be afraid. This is my commandment, That ye love one another, as I have loved you. Greater love hath no man than this, that a man lay down his life for his friends. Ye are my friends, if ye do whatsoever I command you. These things I command you that ye love one another.

There was a long pause and I thought we had finished but no one moved. Then someone in the crowd said, "Read more, Ruthie!"

We sat for nearly an hour and I was growing hoarse from so much reading, so I turned to Psalms 23:

The Lord is my shepherd: I shall not want. He maketh me to lie down in green pastures: He leadeth me beside the still waters. He restoreth my soul: He leadeth me in the paths of righteousness for his name's sake. Yea, though I walk through the valley of the shadow of death, I will fear no evil: for thou art with me: thy rod and thy staff they comfort me. Thou preparest a table before me in the presence of mine enemies: thou annnointest my head with oil: my cup runneth over. Surely goodness and mercy shall follow me all the days of my life: and I will dwell in the house of the Lord forever.

Someone called, "Read 24, Ruth."

The earth is the Lord's, and the fullness thereof: the world, and they that dwell therein. For he hath founded it upon the seas, and established it upon the floods. Who shall ascend into the hill of the Lord? or who shall stand in His holy place? He that hath clean hands, and a pure heart: who hath not lifted up his soul unto vanity, nor sworn deceitfully. He shall receive the blessing from the Lord, and righteousness from the God of his salvation. This the generation of them that seek him, that seek thy face, O Jacob. Selah. Lift up your head, O ye gates; and be ye lifted up ye everlasting doors: and the King of glory shall come in. Who is this King of glory? The Lord of hosts, He is the King of glory. Selah.

By the time I had finished the psalm, my voice was barely above a whisper, so I closed the book and looked helplessly at the people. A man in the back stood up and said, "I think we should pray." The men that had them removed their hats and I noticed some of the women covered their heads. "Our Father," he prayed, "we thank thee that thou hast preserved us and brought us thus far. And now like the children in the wilderness, we beg of thee manna for our provision. Lead us safely from this wilderness as thou led the Children of Israel out of the deserts into the Promised Land. Lord, if it be thy will, stop the earth from shaking and give us rest. We repent of our sins" — this to a chorus of amens and groans — "and lean on thee for our safety and preservation." He paused for a long moment and I thought he was through, but he hadn't said the amen, then in a choked voice, he said, "Lord we beg thee not to lay our sins on our innocent children, but protect them and preserve them. If we must, as we deserve, pay for our past sins, let each man and woman bear their own punishment, but spare the children." There was another long pause, then, "Amen."

There was a chorus of "amens" from the crowd and someone began singing "Rock of Ages" and we all joined in. As it died away on the last verse, someone else began singing the "Old 100th."

Praise God from whom all blessings flow,
Praise Him all creatures here below,
Praise Him above ye heavenly host,
Praise Father, Son and Holy Ghost,
A-men.

As if in answer to our prayers, the shakes subsided and we could stand in fair comfort. The crowd began to disperse quietly and I sat with head bowed, overcome by the events of the moment and saddened by the thought that out of three communities brought together by catastrophe, there could be found only one Bible. Lydia's arm came around my shoulders and she softly kissed my cheek. "Thank you, Ruth" was all she said.

"Yes, thank you, Ruth," Lonza agreed. "Now, let's get packing and see if these mules will lead us out of this 'wilderness' to a promised land — or at least one that doesn't shake and move!"

CHAPTER 14
A NIGHT WITH THE ANIMALS

We were finally packed, but the animals were in no mood to move. While we waited on them to become calmer, Jerry and Lonza checked out the condition of the trails through the woods. Lonza came back with a serious look on his face. "The woods are sure torn up. It will take us longer than we expected to get out to the corral. Jerry has gone to check on the horses and will try to bring one back to help us out if he can."

We had given up on moving that day and supper was almost over when Jerry appeared leading one of the Indian horses. "They was all okay except that a tree had fallen across th' corral fence. Th' horses couldn't git out — an I don't think they would have if they could," he added.

We went to bed early and slept fitfully, the waves in the ground gradually growing stronger. There was another hard jolt in the early morning hours, but it passed and we

197

slept until dawn. It seemed that all the bad shakes occurred in the night for some reason and that was the worst time for us. The dawn was dreary and it felt colder. We could still hear the roar of the downstream falls, though it may have been some fainter. The upstream falls had quietened considerably as the current ate away at the soft sands and soil.

The animals were calmer and Jerry led one of the mules around to see how he would cooperate and move. It seemed to be willing to move about so we ate a hasty breakfast and were loaded up and moving out as the sun peeked weakly over the river. Everyone walked since the going was so slow and we were unsure of the animals' reactions to the occasional shakes. The Indian pony pulled the travois and seemed accustomed to the task. After the hard shake there was a general exodus from the area. People were moving north and some were packing to follow. We waited until there were others between us and those in our camp. When no one was on the trail, we started out that way also. When out of sight of camp and other eyes, we quickly turned west then southwest toward the corral. Lonza went back to the trail and covered our tracks so no one would notice we turned off. When the boys grew tired, Jerry put them on the horse he was leading. Later, Lydia took turns riding with them.

The going was slow with many detours around fissures and sinks full of water. It seemed that the many small ponds were pushed up and drained, while the high ground had sunk and filled with water. There were places where the ground had sunk so far that only the tops of the trees were above water. Some of the sinks covered many acres. You could tell where the ponds had been by the amount of black and rotten matter left behind.

A few of the fissures were dry, some being shallow and some several feet deep. In places, there were tall trees split in two, one half standing on one side of a fissure and the other on the other side several feet away. It was a strange sight and we took note when we saw them. Piles and runs of white sand indicated the presence of blows and geysers. The movement of the ground subsided more and no new fissures appeared to us. It was late evening when we got to the farm place and corral. The horses there were glad to see us and called as we approached.

We made camp next to the corral and soon had supper on the fire. Jerry and

Lonza saw to the horses with Jesse and Riley busily helping and chattering all the while. It was exciting to them to be moving after all the inactivity of the island and New Madrid. Lydia looked tired, but she was happy to be moving toward her home. At supper, Riley complained of his legs hurting. When Lydia pulled up his shirt, his legs were red and chaffed where he had sat on the horse. "I can tell right now, young man, that you will have to wear trousers if you are going to ride a horse!" she said.

Jesse's legs were chaffed even through his trousers and I rubbed fat on both of the boys while Lydia stitched up a pair of Jesse's pants to fit Riley. He was proud of his first pair of pants and strutted around the camp until Lydia made him take them off for the night — not without protest.

The men put up a shelter for Lydia and I and the boys to sleep under and soon after dark we all turned in. The horses moved as close to us as possible and Sippie was soon squeezed between the two boys and sleeping soundly. The gray of morning was just beginning to show when I awoke suddenly. Something unfamiliar had disturbed my sleep. I lay still a few minutes listening, but there was no sound, yet something was not right. Slowly, I turned on my stomach and raised my head.

What I saw was the most startling thing I have ever seen. I thought I must be dreaming and it took me several minutes to realize that what I was seeing in the fog and gloom was real. In the garden and yard of the fallen house and all around the corral were dozens of all kinds of animals, foxes, coons, bears, wolves, deer, panthers, wildcats and buffalo, all side by side. I could hear the horses breathing close behind me. The deer were panting as though in some distress. They were all turned toward our camp and none seemed to be afraid of our presence. It seemed that they took comfort in us being there.

There was none of the natural enmity one species held for the other, rather they seemed to take some kind of comfort from being near us in these strange movings of the earth. Jesse stirred next to me and I heard him catch his breath. "Wow, is this Noah's Ark?" he whispered. Riley looked up and in turning kicked his mother, who turned to see what we were looking at. I glimpsed Jerry and Lonza lying motionless and watching. As it grew lighter, the animals began moving off into the forest and prairie, still showing no aggressiveness toward each other, though many were prey to the others in normal times. By the time we had risen and stoked the fire, all were gone except for a couple of scavenging raccoons and the buffalo who slowly grazed across the little prairie. The horses seemed glad we were moving around.

"They started coming in as soon as we went to bed," Jerry said, "and I watched them all night. Every time I looked, there would be more of them and they packed closer and closer to each other as more of them came."

"Once or twice when I woke up, there would be a coon or possum lying against my legs, and the deer were almost stepping on me," Lonza said. "I would have gotten up if I hadn't been afraid of starting some kind of stampede."

How strange that night was! It was almost like the scripture told of the lion lying down by the lamb and a little child leading them. But for the other witnesses there, I would have long ago decided it was a dream. Even now I sometimes think it must have been. I will never forget that morning.

The boys were full of excitement about the animals and chattered on and on, asking a thousand questions. We hurried around and cooked breakfast while the men repacked and loaded the animals. They

divided the packs and the things on the travois between the two mules and one of the
farm horses that looked like he would
submit to a pack.

"We should get to the Pemiscot River
today and if we are lucky, maybe Little
River," Lonza said. "I will saddle two of the
new horses for you ladies to ride, but I think
it would be best if you led them until they
are used to travel and we know something
of their nature." He saddled the farm mare
and one of the Indian ponies with side-
saddles brought from New Madrid. "Lydia,
I think the pony would be best for you and
Ruth can ride the mare. Jerry, you lead. We
need to go as near west as possible and
hopefully hit the Pemiscot a little after
noon. From there, we will determine if we
can reach the Little River before dark."

The ground still moved and waved and
there were still shocks and jolts from below.
We were well warned when a jolt was coming because the animals would stop dead
still with legs spread and head lowered and
wait. Sometimes they would groan and we
knew that the jolt would be harder than
usual. If we were riding we would hold on
tight and if we were walking we would get
to the end of the reins and sit down if possible. The trees would sound as if the wind

was blowing and we could hear limbs cracking and falling but less and less of the trees fell. More than once we were thrown down if we hadn't had time to sit and I was worried for Lydia, but she was always seated or braced in some way and she didn't fall once.

The stress on mind and body was especially hard on the children at first but they soon learned to respond to the signals of the animals and prepare. It became a game with them, calling "Jolt!" to each other and seeing who could sit down the quickest. Yet, they shook and rocked to and fro and sometimes cried. Someone would always go to them and hug them for reassurance and after a few moments they were better and ready to go.

CHAPTER 15
RIVER OF SAND

The forest was very congested with fallen trees and limbs, not at all like the open mature forest it had been and with the new ponds and swamps we spent much time detouring around the obstacles. Late in the afternoon Lonza called a halt to our march and we made camp while the men picketed the animals and scouted ahead for an open route. Lydia and I and the boys were in bed by sundown. My last vision was of Jerry and Lonza sitting by the fire talking and my first vision in the morning was of the stoked-up fire and the sound of the horses being brought into camp.

Breakfast was quickly eaten and we began our trek as we had the day before, with Jerry leading his horse, the boys chubbing along after him, chattering like two squirrels in a walnut tree. Lydia followed then me. Lonza brought up the rear, leading his horse and the spare pony. Jerry was a good guide but the going was as rough as the day before, with many detours around ponds and fallen trees. The boys soon tired and climbed up on Jerry's horse. "Seems like there's less fissures an' geysers. Ain't th' sand they threw up pretty an' white?" he called.

It was amazing how white the sand was. Lydia picked some of it up and it was so fine the breeze blew it when she sifted it through her fingers. Near noon we came upon a pond of several acres that was filled with a mound of the sand. The ground around it was littered with fish thrown out of the pond. The horses rested and grazed around the edges of the clearing while the boys and Sippie romped in the sand. We ate a light lunch of leftovers and the boys lay down on a pallet with Sippie happily between. All three slept and we rested for about two hours while the horses fed.

We had to waken the boys when it was time to go but they were soon romping through the sand and we were under way before they noticed and ran to catch up.

"I judge the Pemiscot to be about two hours west of here, Jerry," Lonza called from the rear.

"Maybe th' going will be easier and we can make it in four hours!" Jerry called back.

Indeed, it seemed that the travel got better by degrees as we went on. There were almost no fissures and fewer of the trees had fallen, though there were still the round blowholes occasionally. Even so, the travel was slow and it was over three hours and near sunset before we reached the edge of the flats of the river which still lay hidden in the trees.

Jerry stopped by a spring flowing between the roots of a huge elm. "This might be a good place to camp for the night," he said, looking quizzically at Lonza who nodded in agreement. The boys and Jerry began gathering firewood and building a fire while Lonza unloaded and picketed the horses. As soon as the fire was going Jerry hurried and helped Lonza rub down the animals and lead them to the water and grass below the spring. The boys were tired and hungry and still chafed from riding. It wasn't long after they had eaten and been rubbed with fat that they were sleeping soundly on the pallet. Sippie lay quietly at their feet, watching us as we rested a few minutes before retiring.

"When we get to the river, Jerry, we will want to cross over right away while it is shallow and follow it down about two hours to a trail that cuts west to the ford on the Little

River. I don't know what shape the trail will be in but we should stick with it as much as possible so we can hit the river at the ford. Otherwise we'll hit the canebrakes and have a hard time moving," Lonza said.

Jerry nodded. He was proud that Lonza trusted him to lead and worked hard at finding the best route. Soon we were all turning in. Sippie wormed his way between the boys and with a contented sigh lay his head on his paws and slept.

I awoke in the gray of dawn with water slowly dripping on our canvas shelter. It must have sprinkled some in the night and the rain was dripping down through the leaves. It was colder here than in the Mississippi bottoms and we shivered as we stoked the fire for breakfast. The horses snorted and stomped and seemed to be anxious to move in the chill air and it wasn't long after eating that we were under way.

Jerry led us across the flats toward the river, ever detouring around the obstacles and bearing to the right as much as possible so as to cross the stream where it was smaller. A canebrake blocked our access to the water and we had to walk upstream quite a distance before the cane was thin enough to push through. It was still so thick that I could only see the back of Jerry's horse but I knew he had reached the river by the shouts of joy and laughter of the boys. Jerry stopped so suddenly that I almost ran into the horse. "Move over, Jerry, so we can get through!" I called. Jerry led the horse out of the way and I stepped out of the cane.

At the sight of the river, I stopped dead still and only a sound from behind me brought me to my senses enough to move and let Lydia and Lonza through. They too stood and stared. The boys and Sippie were romping in a river of the whitest sand we had ever seen. It mounded almost head high in the middle of the old bed. Water trickled along the side of the sands, trying to force its way back into the bed and we later discovered the same was occurring on the other side. There was debris and dead fish pushed high up on the canebrake, indicating the violence with which the water was thrown from the river by the sand.

"Well I'll be switched," muttered Lonza.

"Riley, Jesse, get yourselves down from there right now," Lydia called. The boys ran and rolled down the slope and Sippie romped down in a cloud of sand. They paid no mind to the water wading through as though it were a day in summer.

"What do we do now?" Jerry asked.

"We'll have to find a way across, and that may not be easy," Lonza opined. "Let's move upstream and see if the sand peters out somewhere. That sand may be quickie with the water running through it and maybe under it. We'll have to be careful where we cross."

Lonza led the way now. The going was easier for a while, then the cane grew right down to the riverbank and we had to leave the river and detour around it. We must have gone three miles to gain two up the river. At last Lonza stopped in a clearing behind the canebrake. "There's no use us all traipsing up this river to find a crossing. We can make camp here and rest the horses and Jerry and I will look for a likely crossing."

There was no argument from Lydia and I so we unpacked and hobbled the horses and made lunch for the boys who were soon napping on their pallet. Meanwhile, the men had left and were exploring the stream. The sun was well down and the boys were romping when they returned, tired and dirty.

"We found a crossing and I think we should cross today," Lonza said as he led up the horses. "It looks like rain and I want to cross that river before it rises."

We hurriedly loaded and were soon moving up the river to the crossing. The river may not have been as wide here, but the sand looked to be piled just as high. The water was somewhat less and that was a good sign. Jerry led his horse out on the sand and he sank pretty deep into it, but he struggled through and made the other side. He came back and took my horse over the same track, but the loose sand offered no better traction. Lydia and I struggled across while the boys and Sippie lightfooted it over rolling and laughing.

"Jerry, I don't think these mules and the horse will make it loaded," Lonza called. "I'll unload them and you come get one of the mules and take him across with the end of the rope. We can pull the packs over the top of the sand easier than they could carry them."

The mules seemed to struggle less than the horses did in crossing. Jerry put the rope around a stout looking sapling and looped it over his saddle horn. When the first pack was tied on, he led the horse along the bank of the river, pulling the load straight across. The pack kept bogging down on the uphill pull and Lonza had to keep lifting it out of the sand, but when it reached the top it came downhill easily. Jerry stopped before it got to the water and lifted it over to dry ground.

We heard Lonza chopping with the ax and Jerry coiled the rope and struggled to the top of the sand where he slung the rope to Lonza. "Take this log and lay it across the top of the sand, Jerry, and lay the rope in the notch. It should keep the rope from digging into the sand and the packs from bogging down some."

The log helped a lot and the second trip was not as hard as the first. Lonza cut another log and they laid it a few feet from the first one on the other side of the crest and the rest of the packs hardly bogged down at all. In the meantime Lydia and I had decided to find a likely spot for a camp since it was growing dark and we would not travel any further this night. The threat of rain prompted us to look for high ground away from the river. Riley and Jesse gathered firewood and by the time the men were through crossing, supper was cooked and the boys had eaten.

"We got everything over," Jerry said as he came into the firelight and plopped down. They had used the three saddle horses to pull the loads over and now they were hobbled and quietly grazing along the riverbank. Both men were too tired to eat much and were soon rolled up in their blankets asleep. They had forgotten to put up the canvas shelter, but we were able to spread it and make a decent shelter before the fire. Snuggling in on either side of the boys and Sippie, we talked a few minutes before drifting off to sleep.

"We didn't make much headway today, did we?" It was more of a statement than a question.

"No, we didn't," Lydia replied. "At this pace, it will be next summer before we reach home — if we don't wear out before!"

"I don't care where we are so long as we are away from that river and the ground doesn't shake!"

"Do you think Tom Finn will come looking for you — if he's still alive, that is?"

"I hope not. I don't think so. He's so lazy and he can always buy another woman so long as there are pirates on the river," I replied.

"Did he care for little Jesse?"

"A little at first. It was more of a 'Look what I done' type of boast to the other pirates. As Jesse grew he had less and less use for him — and for me. He cared more for his jug and silver."

"I'm glad Jerry found his silver before you escaped."

"He had known where it was for some time and he would occasionally take some out and hide it for us, so we actually had two stashes to dig up when we left. That would be the only thing Tom Finn would come after, but if the island finished sinking he may think we and the money were all lost."

A drop or two of rain splatted on the canvas and the fire hissed. I got up and put a pile of live coals in the Dutch oven and covered it, then added wood to the fire and banked it as much as I could, hoping the rain wouldn't drown it completely out. When I came back, Lydia was asleep and I lay down thinking about the last month's events. As I drifted off to sleep, I thought how it was so good to be free again and I vowed that never again would I submit to captivity.

I awoke to the steady patter of rain and Jerry was rigging another canvas side to the shelter to make room for himself. He pushed me over some and muttered, "Raining" before he was sound asleep again.

Morning was gray and dark. The rain had slowed to a heavy mist and haze lay over the river bottom. We could hear the flow of the water and were glad we had taken the trouble to find higher ground. The horses stood under the trees for shelter and the packs hanging in the trees dripped. The fire was dead but the coals in the oven were still alive and we soon had a fire going with the dry wood from under the shelter. The boys sat up sleepily and then plopped back down with groans when they saw the rain. Sippie lay at their feet with his head between his paws and looked gloomily at the world.

"I think the rain will lift soon," Lonza offered. "Let's sit tight for a while and maybe the travel won't be too unpleasant when we move."

He would have ignored the weather if it had only been him and Jerry, but his suggestion was out of consideration for the women and boys he had along with him. We didn't protest and after breakfast sat down under the shelter and busied ourselves with little things we had neglected on our journey. Lonza rummaged through the packs until he found a long strip of canvas about a yard wide. He sat down and began sewing. "Jesse, what do you suppose I'm making?" he asked.

Jesse was busy playing with Sippie and glanced at the work. "Don't know."

"Don't know, sir," I corrected.

"Don't know, sir."

"What do you think it is, Riley?"

"Are you making me britches?" The ones he had were kind of baggy and he had been asking for pants that "fit me like Jerry's" but there had been no time for sewing.

"No, not britches, but something you and Jesse can use," Lonza replied.

Jesse stood up and bumped his head against a shelter pole. "Ouch! Is it a saddle blanket?" he asked rubbing his head.

"No, but you are getting warm."

"What is it, Mamma?" Riley asked.

"I don't know, Riley, what do you think it looks like?"

"It looks like a long sack with a hole in the middle," said Jesse. "Are we gonna put something in it?"

"Two somethings," Lonza said pulling heavy thread through the canvas with his needle.

"What?!" the boys chimed.

"Critters."

"What kind of critters? Will they bite?" Riley asked.

"Wel-l-l, I've known one of them to bite, but I don't know about the other one," Lonza studied his work critically.

"Hmmm," said Lydia with a smile, "only two critters and one of them bites, what could they be?"

"I don't want any if they bite," said Riley.

216

"I don't think he has bitten anyone for a while," said Lonza. "He may be grown past that by now."

"I've been bitten by one of those, and I guess that means they both have bitten in the past," I said.

"Do we have to have them if they bite, Mamma?" Jesse asked.

"We couldn't do without them, for sure," Lydia laughed. "I don't think either one of them bites anymore. They should have grown too old for that by now."

Lonza stood and walked over to the horses, Riley and Jesse padding along behind asking a hundred questions. He caught up one of the Indian ponies and led him back to camp. Laying the canvas over the horse's back with the pockets he had sewn on each side, he caught up the girth ends and tied them.

"Are we gonna get the critters, now, Pa?"

"We sure are, and I've got one now," Lonza said, scooping Riley up in his arms.

"I not a critter, Papa," Riley protested. "Momma, tell him I don't bite!"

"No, but you have before," Lydia laughed. "I have the scar to prove it!"

The pony stood patiently while Lonza stood Riley in the sack. "Now you won't get your legs chafed when you ride."

He lifted Jesse into the sack on the other side of the horse's back. "You're so tall, Jesse, I think I will have to cut some holes for you to put your feet through and you can ride sitting down. Riley, you can either stand or sit in the sack."

"I want holes just like Jesse," he said.

"Let's see how this works out and we might cut leg holes later," Lonza said. He led the horse around camp with the boys dangling from each side. They were pleased and the horse seemed to take his new chore well.

"I think that will do fine, but someone will have to lead the horse to keep these two from taking off on their own," he said.

About midmorning, the mist stopped and the clouds lifted, though the day remained dreary. We broke camp and were soon lined out traveling down the right bank of the river of sand.

The boys were thrilled with their new saddlebags and happily chattered as they rode. That poor pony had more patience than Job and I'm sure he was a little deaf too! He plodded along while the boys wriggled around, alternately standing and sitting, swinging their legs by the horse's belly. Eventually, they became accustomed to the ride and with our admonishments took consideration of the horse and stopped making sudden movements.

To our surprise, the river was filled with the white sand the entire length we traveled it, which must have been a good ten miles. It was full of sand as far downstream as we could see when we left it on the trail to the Little River ford, though the water from the rains was beginning to wash its ways back into the riverbed. We now followed a well-used trail, which must have been established for some time by the local inhabitants of the region. Travel was getting easier and easier as we left the Mississippi valley behind us. The ground was hardly moving and the land didn't show as much damage as we had experienced in New Madrid.

The Little River was a small stream; the ford was wide and shallow, barely reaching to the horses' bellies and we crossed quickly with no trouble. Sippie must have swum less than twenty feet before striking bottom and romping out of the water. The only place we climbed upward in this country was out of the riverbeds. The ground seemed flat and boggy with many streams and much standing water. The forest was heavy with cypress in the low places and a great variety of hardwoods in the better drained places. At times, the brush was heavy and in other places, the forest was open with no under-growth. Gradually, the land became drier, though if it rose any, it was not discernible.

The trail turned southwest and after a mile or two, we came into a large field overgrown with brush and saplings. As we neared the center of the field we came into what had once been a village. Nothing was left of the houses except mounds of rotted logs, mud and thatch. Dried cornstalks marked places where the grain had been stored or spilled. Pottery, whole and broken, was scattered about. We came into what had been a central plaza and Jerry stopped to let the horses rest. "What is this place, Lonza?" he asked.

"Many, many moons ago, this land was occupied by many villages such as this. The people lived in houses the year round and raised many varieties of food, corn and other grains, squash, melons. Each village was independent and there were no enemies so they lived in peace and security. It was this way all down the Mississippi and up the Arkansas.

"One day word came from the south that strange men had come into the land from the east. They were light skinned, rode on the backs of strange animals and spoke a strange language. Though they were ragged and starved, some of them wore hard shiny shells while others had hardly anything to cover their bodies. Their weapons were long knives and lances and a long stick that spat fire and made a loud noise with clouds of smoke. When the people heard it, they fell down flat and some died.

"At first the people were afraid of them, but their chief professed friendship and the village welcomed them. They stayed many days and gradually gained strength from the abundant food they were fed. One day their chief indicated by signs that they wanted to visit other villages to the south and the village headmen were glad to take them to the nearest village since their stay had been overlong and burdensome on the people. In this way, the strangers passed through the land, visiting village after village, but a strange thing began to happen. The people of the villages they visited began to get sick and die.

"It was determined by the elders and seers that the strangers had cursed the land and poisoned the people. Soon word spread and they were no longer welcome in the villages. The people went out against them and drove them away. Still the curse spread and those that did not become ill and die fled to the highlands west and north of here. Even then, the curse sometimes followed them and many, many died.

"The strangers crossed the Arkansas and somewhere south of the river their chief died. They buried him in the Mississippi so the natives would not know and find his body. From there, they passed over the great river and back to the land they had come from. But the curse remained and soon the land became empty because the people either died or fled. No longer do they plant and harvest, but they long ago joined other tribes and are a people no more and so remain. Even to this day, the land is empty of all peoples in spite of the fertility and abundance of foods and animals. That is the legend of the people of the Low Lands, passed from generation to generation by our fathers.

"Of course, we now know that the strangers were Europeans from Florida, the land of the Seminole and that they wore metal armor and had swords, lances and guns of iron. We also know that the 'curses' were white man diseases that the red man had no defense against. White man diseases have killed more red men than all the swords and guns that can be found; we must always guard against them," Lonza concluded.

Even the boys were listening closely to

Lonza's story. Looking around me at the hundred or more mounds, I shuddered to think that these were once the homes of hundreds of people who either died or ran. Ran and yet still died. And how many hundreds of other villages from here to the Arkansas valley suffered the same fate? Even if the two races who mixed their blood in my veins had ever lived in peace and harmony, the same horrible results would have occurred. They would most likely occur again with the white man's measles, mumps, whooping cough, chicken pox and smallpox ever present. I shuddered.

Without another word, Jerry hoisted the boys into their packs and led the way silently down the trail going west from the plaza. We camped on a hummock well hidden from the trail that night.

Chapter 16
The Trail to Flee's Settlement

It was late afternoon when we came to the wide and muddy Saint Francis River. Lonza led us through the bushes downstream a couple of hundred yards to a small clearing on the bank. Removing his boots, he waded around almost to his waist feeling the bottom with his feet.

"The canoe isn't here, it must be on the other side. I'll have to go over and find it," he said as he tied his boots across his saddle. "I want to cross the river tonight if we can, so you wait here and I will go see if I can find that canoe and bring it back."

He disappeared into the bushes and soon we heard him splashing into the river. When he came into sight, the horse was swimming and he swam most of the way across. They scrambled up the bank and disappeared from view.

While we waited, Jerry unloaded the packs and rubbed down the animals with straw from the tall grass. We didn't see Lonza again until he came into view paddling a canoe. "Jerry, bring two packs and put them in the boat. Then help Ruth and Jesse in and I will take them over," he called.

As we pulled away for the far side, Sippie danced on the bank, barking and whining. Finally, he waded out and swam for the canoe. He didn't catch up until we were on the far bank, then he shook and ran around Jesse, making it plain to all where his allegiance dwelt. Jesse was thrilled that he had followed and the two ran and frolicked up the bank. I held the canoe while Lonza unloaded and carried the packs up the bank. On the next trip he brought over Lydia and Riley with more packs. It took two more trips to get all the gear and tack over.

Lonza was just pulling out from the bank to help bring the animals over when Jerry appeared at the ford riding bareback on one of the farm horses and pushing the rest of the animals into the water. They struck for our side and swam steadily until they stood on the bank dripping and blowing. "Good work, Jerry," Lonza said, "I couldn't have done it better myself!"

Jerry grinned and looked at me. They didn't know that he had never even seen that done before, much less done it himself. To me it was an indication of his growing maturity, though probably an ordinary chore for boys who had not been kept captive like Jerry had. I was proud of him. Lonza returned the canoe to its hiding place while we made camp for the night.

Breakfast over, Jerry and Lonza began loading the packs on the animals. "We won't go far before we come to Crowley's Ridge. The travel will be more pleasant for us, but more work for the horses," he said as he helped Lydia into the saddle.

The boys and Sippie romped ahead down the trail and Lonza led the way with Jerry behind driving the pack animals. The trail grew broader and before long we began to climb a long slope. We came out on top of a low rounded hill and beheld a low ridge of hills above us that stretched north and south as far as we could see. The soil was a fine yellowish loamy — sandy type — quite different from the black gumbo of the bottoms. It looked as if it had been piled up in the middle of the river bottom, for on the west side was the same black gumbo flats. There was no great difference in the forest on the hills, except that there may have been more oak and hickory than in the bottoms.

The ground still shook here, but not as

violently as near the rivers to the east. There didn't seem to be as much damage to the land and not many trees were fallen due to the shaking. The trail turned southwest along the length of the ridge and we followed up and down the gentle hills. In the valleys were little streams that, save for the stirring of the shakes, were clear. It was nice to see them and I looked forward to camping near one.

At the nooning, Lonza said, "This is the fifth day on the trail and the animals need a good rest. This evening we will find a good camp and take a day of rest. We need to find a place where the animals can get plenty of grazing and we can do a little hunting."

Jerry nodded. "I'm getting hungry for fresh meat. I've been seeing lots of deer sign along and we could use the hide for new moccasins."

"It will give us time to wash the clothes we've worn since leaving New Madrid and there are a couple of urchins needing cleaning too." I eyed the boys who were reveling at not having a bath every three or four days.

Jesse grinned at me, and Riley said, "Me not dirty!"

"Oh yes you are, young man," Lydia laughed, "and we're going to scrub off at least one layer of dirt as soon as we can!"

Riley frowned and reached for another cold biscuit.

We were soon on the move again, the boys riding in their saddlebags. It wasn't long before the swaying of the horse had them both nodding and they sank to the bottoms of the bags and slept.

Gradually, the ridge widened until we were surrounded by the gently rolling hills and could no longer see the bottomlands. Here it would be hard to imagine that this was just a narrow strip of hills in the middle of delta bottoms and not the foothills of our Tennessee Mountains or some other mountain range.

As Jerry led, Lonza would occasionally leave the trail to check out a valley or stream for our camping place. He didn't find anything that pleased him until very late in the afternoon when he came trotting up behind us and called for a stop. He waved for us to follow and turned and retraced our tracks for a ways down the trail where he stopped and waited for us to catch up. "I found a place." He grinned. "Follow me close, the brush is heavy for a ways."

Lydia had remarked on the brush as we had passed through it the first time and we surmised that it must be the result of an old burn that had cleared out the trees and allowed the brush to grow. Lonza pushed his way through, weaving and dodging the thickest with the rest of us struggling behind. I wondered how the boys were doing being scraped by the limbs, but I didn't hear any complaints.

The brush opened up and we were out in a large meadow high with dried grass for the animals. Lonza continued down the slope and we soon came to a clear stream with a wide pool filling the banks. The forest grew right down to the bank on the opposite side of the stream, which must have stopped the old fire from burning any farther. There was a wide flat on our side just right for a camp.

"How does this look to you?" Lonza grinned.

"Oh, it's perfect!" called Lydia. "Why don't we build a cabin and stay a while?"

"Because you would soon be homesick to see your people and our home in the hills before we finished building," Lonza answered as he lifted the squirming Riley out of his pack. Jesse had already freed himself and was heading for the creek. I turned to help Jerry with a pack when I heard a yelp and a splash. Riley was trotting toward the creek as fast as his chubby legs would go and Lonza was right behind. Just as Riley got to the bank — where Jesse had popped up out of the water spluttering — he tripped and went headlong into the water too! Lonza was only a step or two behind and he stopped at the edge of the bank and laughed at the two tykes struggling and sputtering in the shallows. "Bring the soap, ladies, the lads are anxious to get cleaned up!" he called.

As calmly as if she were getting ready to wash dishes, Lydia was already digging through the packs for the soap and cloths.

"I'll get them some clothes, Lydia," I called as she hurried to the creek.

Lonza had sat down and taken off his boots and taking the bar of soap, he waded into the water and grabbed one of the boys by the collar. "Whooo, this water is co-o-l-ld, Jesse," he said as he stripped the struggling boy and began scrubbing him down. Almost as quickly as you could say it, he dipped the boy through the water, sending a trail of soapsuds with the current and in the same motion, handing him into the waiting towel held by Lydia.

Meantime, Riley had scrambled out of the water and headed up the hill, Jerry in hot pursuit. "Me clean, Jerry, me clean!" he yelled.

"Not yet, but you soon will be!" Jerry said,

scooping him up and whirling back to Lonza. I handed Lydia the dry clothes for Jesse and turned to help Jerry strip the clothes from Riley — just in time to see Jerry trip over Sippie and the three of them fall over the bank!

Lonza ducked as a huge splash soaked him from head to foot. Both boys came up with a whoop and I could swear Sippie yelped under water. I laughed until I was too weak to stand.

Lonza grabbed the struggling Riley. "Here, Jerry, grab his pants legs and pull."

Off came the pants, moccasins and shirt and before he could yell again, Riley was being vigorously scrubbed. Another scoop through the water and he was wrapped in my cloth and arms getting rubbed dry.

Lydia had sat down with Jesse in her lap and was laughing so hard tears were running down her face. I looked at Jesse still wrapped in the towel. His lips were blue and he was shivering. "We need a fire quick!" I called.

"Don't look, Ruthie, we're in the tub!" Jerry called back.

Lydia covered her eyes and laughed harder. "Oh my!" she exclaimed as she sat Jesse down and tried to rise. "Ruth, it's up to us if a fire gets built."

Averting my eyes from the bathers, I hurried up the hill looking for a good site. To my surprise, I found an old campfire on a bench above high water with some firewood stacked nearby. I piled sticks on the ashes and swept around for leaves and dried grass. Lydia came over the bench edge with flint and steel and we soon had a little blaze going. The fire was catching good when the men appeared in clean clothes and leading the packhorses. Jesse and Riley huddled wrapped in blankets and shivering, though they now had warmed considerably after their dunking.

"I never saw a more clumsy bunch of men," I tried to say with a serious face, but failed.

"I never saw two boys more anxious to get a bath," laughed Lydia. We both broke into peals of laughter while the boys grinned.

"I guess they wanted to get it over with quickly." Lonza laughed. "Uncle always said humor was pandemonium remembered in moments of tranquility."

"Well, we've had the pandemonium, but I'm still looking for the tranquility!" Lydia laughed. "You should have waited for hot water like Ruth and I."

Lonza was laughing too. "Once you're

wet, you might as well get clean and get it over with."

Jerry called from where he was unloading the horses, "Has anyone seen that cussed dog?"

"You leave that poor dog alone, Jerry Harris," I called, "he deserves a bath as much as you do!" I looked at Sippie shivering between the two boys and wagging his tail and started laughing again.

It didn't take long to have supper on the fire and by the time the men came back from staking out the horses we were ready to eat. Riley and Jesse had warmed and were exploring around the camp. They finished supper with droopy eyes and were asleep in their blankets before we had cleaned up the dishes.

Lonza had been quietly smoking his pipe and I knew that he had something on his mind. "I'm not too surprised you found a fireplace here," he said. "There are a few Quapaws still living on Crowley's Ridge and we should keep an eye out for them. I don't think there would be any danger from them, but you can't be too careful — or watchful. We will need to keep track of the horses and boys at all times as long as we are on the ridge and probably from now on until we get home. In two or three days, we will hit the foothills and there are more people there — red and white. Some of them are pretty rough and we will have to be on guard for any mischief they might want to pull. Jerry and I will get up early in the morning and see if we can find us a deer or two. If we are lucky, we will have venison steaks for breakfast. Get the boys to gather a lot of wood, we will smoke jerky for our trip across the bottoms. Once we start out again, we will probably have only one more day on the ridge."

"Lydia, why is it that we are the only two without a bath around here?" I asked.

"Probably because we aren't clumsy." She giggled.

"Jerry, take these kettles down and get us water," I said, "we are going to have a warm bath before bedtime!" I stoked the fire with another stick or two. Jerry brought the two kettles and nestled them down in the coals, banking them up around the pots. Lydia and I gathered up clean clothes and towels and when the water was steaming, we each took one and headed into the dark by the stream.

"Watch that last step by the creek," Jerry called lazily, "it's a doozy!"

We undressed and standing on our dirty

clothes sponged and soaped ourselves. It was too chilly to enjoy bathing too much, but it felt good to wash off the grime of the last weeks. Dipping the cold water from the creek, we washed our hair then rinsed with the warm water. We were both shivering by the time we were dressed and it felt good to get near the fire again.

The men had set up the shelter and laid out the pallet. The boys were already in it and a soft thumping from under the covers told me Sippie was already in bed too. The fire was banked and the packs were laid around it to prevent it from being seen too far away.

Lying by Jesse, hearing his soft breathing and looking into the most starry sky, I thanked the Lord for preserving us thus far. To some, this might be a rough life, but after island life, it was like heaven to us. Looking back I think the hilarity we shared over the silliness of boys falling into the creek was as much about relief from our bondage and being out of the danger of the shakes as anything. Freedom! There's nothing like it, no matter how hard it is!

I awoke to a frosty morning with just a hint of light in the eastern sky. One of the men was stoking up the fire. The horses were snorting and I knew they were being moved to water and better grazing. With a couple of whispered comments, the men moved off on their hunt and I lay and watched the stars blink out one by one. The boys stirred and Sippie wormed his way out of the covers whining to follow the hunters.

"Where you go, Sippie?" Jesse called sleepily and the dog returned wagging all over and laid his head across Jesse's chest. Riley pushed against his mother to make room and Lydia rose with a laugh. "I guess I had best just get up seeing I've been kicked out of the covers!"

We left the boys and dog rolling and laughing on the pallet and hurried to get the day's work done. It was good to know we wouldn't be traveling today, but there was much to do and not a lot of time to do it in. After we had made the biscuits and set the water boiling for rice, we gathered the dirty clothes and piled them by the creek. While I scrubbed, Lydia supervised the boys in gathering wood. She showed them how to dig a long trench and arrange the wood in it so it would make hot coals over which the meat could be hung. The boys kept to their job hauling wood and tending the fire and I was surprised at their tenacity.

"Well, they are playing with fire . . . ," Lydia said, and that did explain a lot. She spied the men returning with two carcasses on the horse and hurried off to put the rice in the water and set the biscuits cooking.

I was surprised when I looked up to see that Lonza was wearing buckskin and carrying a bow and quiver. That explained why we hadn't heard shots — a sound that carried far and that other ears might hear.

The men hung both carcasses on the limbs of a burned out snag of a tree and quickly began to skin them. They gave Lydia a hindquarter from the smaller deer and the aroma of roasting venison soon filled my nose and made me put the washing aside for better things. What a feast that was! Biscuits drowned in brown gravy, molasses, a thick slab of roast over rice and strong black coffee. We ate until all was gone except for a portion of the roast we set aside for later.

"Jerry, have you ever jerked meat?" Lonza asked.

"No, but I remember watching Ma and Pa do it back home."

"Well, we've got a lot to do, so sharpen your knife and let's bet busy."

"I want another roast for the trip," Lydia called from where she was feeding Sippie scraps and the gravy scrapings.

I returned to the washing leaving the boys

in Lydia's care. Soon, they came bouncing along on the back of one of the horses with Jerry and splashed across the creek.

"We goin' to cut yimbs for the vinson, Ma," Jesse called. His voice was jerky in rhythm with the jogging horse's steps.

The day was filled with many chores and passed quickly. Lydia and I worked hard on the deerskins getting them ready to make into moccasins and clothes. By late afternoon, all the things we could think of to do were done and we had an early meal. Afterward we walked down the creek a ways. As we entered the woods on the edge of the burn, we could hear water running and splashing over some obstacle. A little further on, we came to a beaver dam.

"So that's what made our pool," Jerry whispered.

We backed away from the bank and hid in the trees. Before long, a head popped up and after looking around a moment, the beaver swam toward the far bank. Three more heads popped up and swam after the first. On the bank they began romping and playing on a slide they had made into the water. We watched them for some time. The boys could hardly sit still. One of the adults may have seen some movement, for he slapped his tail on the water and instantly the other beavers dove in and disappeared. A moment later a large gray head poked through the bushes and out stepped a wolf sniffing the ground and looking around. It was more than Sippie could stand and he gave a ferocious growl. We stepped out with Jerry holding Sippie's collar. The wolf, not alarmed at our presence, watched us for a moment then disappeared back into the bushes.

"Big dog!" Riley said.

"Bad dog, Riley," said Lonza. "Don't play with him."

Our presence revealed, we returned to camp and soon turned in. I was jolted from sleep by Sippie's low growl. He was crouched between the boys and staring intently toward the fire trench. Sitting up and grasping Sippie's collar, I watched intently for several moments before I saw movement. Gradually, I perceived a large form crouching at the edge of the fire pit. It seemed to be eating something on the ground and I realized that it was licking the juices that had dripped from the meat as it smoked. Thank Goodness it had been stored high in the tree for the night. I only hoped the form was not a tree climbing cougar. The coals in the pit were stirred by something falling in them and I saw two yellow eyes glowing behind a long snout. A thump of something hitting the wolf sent him scampering into the dark. Then the silhouette of Jerry emerged into the faint light from the coals and tossed several sticks into the fire. After a moment he turned back into the dark and I heard him sit down against the packs. The men had not mentioned that they were on watch in the night and it dawned on me that they had probably been doing so for some time, most likely since we had started. Sippie carefully backed up between the boys and lay down facing the fire. With that, I lay back and slept soundly knowing there were two on watch for us.

Morning broke dark and cloudy. When I went for water there was ice rimming the pool. The air had a chill dampness and we wasted little time packing and getting under way. The animals were greatly refreshed and seemed eager to be underway. Lonza led us through the woods at an angle that soon intersected the trail and we took up a good pace. The trail was broad and travel was easy.

The shakes and trembles had mostly died out and there was very little evidence of damage. We were grateful they were diminishing, meaning that we were leaving the quaking area. That night we camped on the western slope of Crowley's Ridge just before the trail dipped back into the flatlands.

"It's about thirty miles to the Black Rock crossing on the Black River, and the Cache River to cross between," Lonza said at supper. "We will do good to get past the Cache tomorrow and I suspect it will take another day to get to the far side of the Black. We'll be out of the bottoms then and the travel will be easier again." By this, he meant we would be in hills and not slogging through thick gumbo mud and water.

"I'll be glad to get back to hilly country," I said, "flatland is not for me!"

"If we stayed there long, we would have to grow webs between our toes." Lydia smiled.

"Tomorrow will be long, so turn in early," Lonza said, knocking the ashes from his pipe.

We cleaned up supper and turned in with the boys. They wiggled and squirmed before finding sleep and Lydia and I talked.

"Ruth, have you thought about what you want to be called when we get back to people?"

"I plan to drop the Finn name and go by my maiden name," I replied.

"Won't that raise questions when they hear that Jerry is your brother and has the same name?" she asked.

"I have thought about that. Do you think it would be a problem?"

"I think it may raise some questions that you might not want to answer. Is there another name you might go by?"

"I guess I might use Mamma's maiden name and go by Fourkiller. What do you think?"

"That would be the next best thing if you don't use Finn or Harris."

"If I never hear the name Finn again, it would be soon enough for me! And Jesse won't have it, either. From now on, I will be 'the widow Fourkiller and son Jesse' to all comers. I don't suppose it would stretch things too much to say that my husband had died in the shakes."

"That seems to be the thing that most likely happened," Lydia replied.

Whether Tom Finn was dead or not, to me he died when the shakes hit and we escaped the island. No matter what his disposition was, he was dead to me. I only hoped he stayed that way! I struggled with the thought that the pirates might all be dead. My moral standards resisted rejoicing in their demise, yet I knew the world would be better off without them preying on innocent people.

"Sometimes my anger wells up and I fervently hope they all got their just desserts, then I'm ashamed that I would rejoice in the death of another," I said.

"I know, but with them gone, a lot of good innocent people may live out their lives peacefully."

Yes, I thought, that's true. The boys had finally settled into sleep and Sippie's tail thumped occasionally signaling that all was well. Lydia sighed and I knew she was asleep too. Stars flitted through the broken clouds and the rising moon lined them with silver.

Almost the next moment, it seemed, it was morning and I heard Jesse bringing up the mules. The fire was stoked up and the big black coffeepot boiling away when I got there. It didn't take long to get some steaks frying and the beans from last night warmed. Two sleepy heads appeared and just as quickly ducked under the cover as Sippie pounced. The three tumbled out and rolled toward where Lydia was ladling out beans on plates. Lonza cut their steaks into bites and they sat down on the packs to eat. They certainly were enjoying this travel and we were grateful for that. It was a joy to see them having so much fun.

The air was cold and damp and the clouds

seemed to skirt just above the treetops. As we got on the trail, it began to rain lightly and soon became steady. We had wrapped the boys in blankets before stuffing them into the packs and Jerry covered them with a piece of tarp. All we could see were the lumps of two heads above the horse's back. The prattle told us they were still comfortable. The rest of us covered ourselves as best we could and rode on. The trail ran due west straight as an arrow except for the creek crossings and we only stopped for a few minutes at noon because of the rain. Lonza seemed concerned about the crossing at the Cache.

Mid afternoon found us on the banks of the turbid river. High on the bank was a log raft and the men set about tightening the ropes that held it together. When it was pushed down to the edge of the water, they loaded some of the packs and Lonza and Jerry poled Lydia and Riley across while Jesse and I held the horses — well, I held the horses while Jesse supervised. One more trip with the raft got all people and gear over then Jerry drove the animals across. They only swam a little way in midstream. Soon they were standing on the bank blowing and shaking off the water. Jerry quickly dried and donned the dry clothes I had for him. As soon as the packs were loaded we moved on.

Camp that night was soggy and uncomfortable. The fire sputtered and smoked and never did get going good. We put up the shelter and all crowded under it. The animals stood under the trees and dozed. I thought the night would never end. Jerry finally got up and disappeared into the darkness. I heard him stirring the fire, then all was quiet for a while.

We started our seventh day of travel earlier than usual and munched on jerky as we rode. The boys were quiet and soon I saw that they were asleep under their tarp. In the early light, we noticed the trees were covered with ice. Fortunately, the ground was still warm enough that it didn't freeze and the footing remained good except for the mud. By midmorning the sun burned the clouds away and the ice was fast disappearing. Our spirits rose with the sunshine and the boys came out from under the tarp and clambered to get out of the packs, but it was too muddy and slippery.

We had the good luck of finding a ferry at Black Rock. It was a small boat and we got the packs and people over in two trips. The animals had a long swim and Jerry bought hay for them.

This was the first people we had encountered since leaving New Madrid. The ferryman was a white man who had married a Delaware woman. They had a log cabin and small farm with a lean-to barn and a few head of cattle. They were quite glad to see us and we took our noon rest by the cabin and spent a pleasant time sharing news with them. They were most curious about what we knew about the shakes and we told them what we had experienced. I could see some doubt in their eyes when we told about the geysers and islands sinking. Overall I don't believe they gave our story too much credibility. It was a fantastic experience and I don't blame anyone for doubting us if they hadn't seen it for themselves.

"How is the trail to Flee's?" Lonza asked the man who was called Zack Hartwick.

"Waal . . . I thinks it's purty good," he drawled. "Ain't been . . . nobody come this-a-way since October . . . but several hev been through goin' west. Ain't none o' them . . . come back an' complained none," he spoke between pulls on his pipe. "Weather's gonna . . . be yore worst problem from here on . . . been lucky so far . . . no snow and the temp-a-chure's been warmer . . . 'an usual."

"I expect it will change soon," Lonza surmised.

"Aaup, . . . yore right there, son."

"How's the game 'round here?" Jerry asked.

"Game's good." He nodded. After a long pause, he added, "I 'spects ya kin . . . git plenty, but the big stuff may be . . . a little scarce. Osage huntin' party come through this fall . . . Whut they didn't kill, they scairt off . . . Cricks is full o' beaver an' they makes good eatin' . . . Ye should find some turkeys an' the bears may come . . . out'n ther dens some if'n it stays warm a few days . . . 'Course, ye mought go in his den atter 'im . . . if'n ya gits too hungry."

"We won't be fishing any bears out of their dens this trip," Lonza said, looking directly at Jerry. "Don't want to be caught on the trail in winter with a clawed up hunter."

"Aaup, yer right ther," Zack allowed, "s'bad 'nough bein' on the trail 'thout nursin' someone stove up."

Alice Hartwick was a pleasant woman with a ready smile. She was some younger than Zack, neatly dressed and there were two small children toddling around the cabin. She spoke English well and was very happy to have women to talk to.

"I have family living up the White River,"

she told us. "My father is Chief William Anderson and my sister, Mekinges, lives with him. They live in the bottoms between the James fork and the Beaver Rivers."

"We have heard of Chief Anderson and Mekinges, as well," said Lydia. "Everyone speaks highly of them."

Alice beamed. "It's good to hear that they are respected. I hope to go there next fall when the crops are in. Perhaps we will meet along the way."

"Our cabin is on Middle Fork of the Red River. It would be out of the way for you not being on Fallen Ash Trail, but you would be welcome," Lydia said.

[Here Zenas interjected that he was using the modern names of the streams because they would be identifiable.]

"I been hearin' 'bout the villages ther . . . an' at the junction o' South Fork an' Archer's Creek . . . They any good trail up to Bear Creek Spring?" Zack asked.

"Yes, there are good trails between the three villages and there is a good trail from South Fork down to the villages on the Arkansas River as well," Lonza answered.

"Been thinking 'bout goin' that-a-way . . . an' tradin' some at the villages," Zack spoke through a cloud of smoke.

"You would be welcome if you come,"

Lonza repeated Lydia's invitation. "Now, I think it's time to be on the move."

Horses and mules were caught up and loaded and soon we were taking our leave of the Hartwicks. "Three days to Flee's," Lonza sang out from behind us as we took the trail. "The sooner, the better," Lydia said softly to me. I knew she was getting tired and needed rest. Hopefully, we could get a few days at Flee's Settlement for her to rest up before moving on to their home. Almost immediately we entered hilly country, then after a few miles we descended into the Black River valley again. The trail stayed on the bottoms close to the hills and near sunset we arrived at the Strawberry River. There was a campground there, and Jerry looked inquiringly at Lonza. "Let's cross over now and we'll camp at the campground on the other side, Jerry," he called.

We waited while Jerry carefully crossed the ford. The clear water only reached the horse's belly, so he came back and placing the boys on the back of their horse and tying up the saddlebags, he crossed over. Lydia urged her horse close behind and was soon across, the rest of our caravan following. The campsite was up the trail a ways and we were soon cooking over a nice fire. Immediately after supper, I made Lydia

249

retire to the pallet over her protests, but I noticed that before I was finished cleaning up and getting the boys ready for bed, she was sleeping soundly.

The Strawberry River marked a transition in the land. It was the first clear stream we had encountered because we were close to where it flowed out of the hills. From then on the streams were smaller and for the most part clear. They abounded in fish and game was much more plentiful there. The type of vegetation was changing and though much of it was similar to our Tennessee hills, there were many new plants and bushes I had not seen before. We began to see groves of pine trees along the hillsides, but their needles were shorter and the cones smaller than the ones in the east. Lonza called them short-leaf pines. They seemed to grow as large as our long-leafed variety; many would have taken two people holding hands to reach around them.

There were more and more signs of human activities as we traveled, once even passing through a group of abandoned huts Lonza said was an old Osage camp. I noticed that the men kept the horses hobbled at night and were more cautious about letting them stray far. Before retiring, they were tied close to camp. Because of their caution, I slept lightly and awoke several times during the night, but we were not bothered by any unwelcome visitors of the two-legged variety.

For two days, we traveled southwestward, then on the morning of the third day, the trail turned northwest and we entered the valley of the White River. The trail stayed close to the hills and we only occasionally got glimpses of the river bottoms and the river. Near what they called the Dennison Bottoms, we left the river altogether and followed up a small stream that ran behind a hill they called Eagle Mountain. There on a flat were scattered a dozen or so log cabins. We had gotten to Flee's Settlement February 18, 1812.

[I suppose that by now the reader has noted that sometimes the conversation of the partici-pants in this story have spoken near perfect English and other times the language has been heavily colloquial and rough. This is because neither Zenas nor I know the "slang" of the Indian languages. Therefore, the "slang" language is when some rustic form of English is spoken and the more proper English is when some Indian or other language is being spoken. — J.D.]

As we rode into sight of the settlement, I could see mothers calling their children in from play. In those days, the sudden appearance of strangers was cause for concern and it paid to be cautious. Several of the men sauntered to their doors and one or two sat by their steps smoking. You could be sure that their rifles were within reach.

"Howdy, Jake, how's fishin'?" Lonza called to the nearest settler as we rode by.

"Why, it's purty good, Lonza," Jake replied. "We been lookin' fer yuh nigh on to a week. The shakes hold yuh up?"

"I reckon it did some, they were much worse where we were than here," Lonza replied. "Come by Rice's cabin tonight and we'll tell you all about it."

Lonza continued to hail people as we passed by each cabin and the children were let out of the houses to continue their play.

We had passed by most of the cabins before Lonza pulled up at a dilapidated cabin with the door hanging on one leather hinge. "This is Henry Rice's cabin. He said we could use it if he was still gone on his trip south to the Arkansas River. Looks like it needs some repair."

The men began unpacking the horses, and Lydia and I approached the house tentatively. I pulled the door back a little and the last hinge gave way, the door slamming down on the ground.

"So much for that." Lydia giggled. There were circles under her eyes and I could tell she was very tired.

Stepping over the threshold log, I peered into the gloomy room. There were no windows and it was dark and dank. A fireplace stood at one end and must have been the only source of light in the house.

"Jerry, can you rustle us up some firewood?" I called.

"Shore, Ruthie," came the muffled reply, "soon's I git this pack set down."

We stepped back outside in the light and watched the unpacking proceedings. It was cold and blustery and the air felt damp. "Feels like rain — or snow!" Lonza said in passing. "What does the house look like?"

"Too dark to tell until we get some light," Lydia replied.

"We have candles in one of these packs, Ruth, I think it's that one," he said pointing to one in the pile. I untied the rope and opened the sack.

"No, that's not the one," Lydia said. "Let's look in this one." She struggled with the knot, then gave up in frustration. "I wish I had a knife!"

"Let me try my hand," I said. It took some struggle, but I got the pack open and found the box of candles just as Jerry rode up dragging a dead treetop and swinging a bucket in one hand.

"I borryed a bucket o' fire from the neighbors. We'll have a fire goin' in no time," he said as he swung down and hurried into the cabin. We broke off limbs and piled them on the pile of coals in the fireplace. Soon a fire was going.

"Chimney seems t' be drawin' good, guess there's no 'coons nestin' up there," he said as he peered up the chimney.

There was a chattering, and dirt and soot from the mud-and-stick chimney showered down in his face. He pulled back sputtering and rubbing his eyes.

"Guess I wus wrong," he muttered.

We could hear scratching and scrambling, and dirt continued to fall on the fire. There was a cry from one of the boys outside and Jesse hollered through the door, "Git the gun, Jerry, they's a coon on the roof!"

Sippie started baying and when I looked he was bouncing around and barking at the racoon who sat on the peak of the thatched roof and fussed back at him. A shot rang out from behind us and the coon tumbled over backwards and disappeared. Sippie charged around the house and we could hear his fierce growls as he attacked the ra-coon.

We turned to see where the shot had come from and beheld a barefoot man in buckskin walking through the powder smoke. He was short and stocky with a full beard of ash-blond hair. "In the name of one wife an' four hungry kids, I claims thet coon fer my table," he called.

Lonza laughed, "Well if there's anything left when Sippie gets through with him, he's yours, Jobe Pike."

Sippie trotted around the cabin with his head held high and the coon in his mouth. Proudly, he laid the carcass at my feet and barked.

"Looks like most of him is left." Lonza laughed and shook hands with Mr. Pike. "This is Mrs. Ruth Fourkiller and her brother Jerry Harris. Jerry, shake hands with Jobe Pike from Alabama."

They shook hands and Jobe Pike looked up at Jerry. "Looks like yore gonna be a long drink of water whin you gits yer growth," he drawled.

"Thank you, Mr. Pike, I'm pleased to meet you," Jerry replied a little embarrassed.

The boys were dancing around the coon and poking him with sticks. "Bang!" Riley yelled, pointing his stick like a gun at the coon.

"Boys! Let Mr. Pike's supper alone," I

scolded, but Jobe didn't seem to mind.

" 'S' okay, Miz Fourkiller, I'd jest 'soon hev thet coon twice dead afore I skins him anyway." I couldn't see if he was smiling behind that beard, but his eyes twinkled. To Riley, he said, "How'd yuh like a warm cap made out'n thet there coon's skin, young man?" Riley's head appeared from behind his mother's skirt, his eyes big, and he nodded.

"Did the groun' shake whur you wus, Lonza?"

"I'll say it did. Come over after supper and I'll tell you all about it."

"Mought do thet if'n I gits 'roun soon 'nough." Jobe Pike picked up the coon over Sippie's protests and nodding to Lydia and me, took his leave. I heard him call, "Emmy git me my skinner, I got supper here!" as he neared the first cabin.

"The fire is going good, ladies, will supper be long?" It was early, but we could tell that Lonza was eager to talk to the settlement men and it would be good to get an early start to sleep. "Jerry can store the packs inside while I repair the door and we can eat a little early if you like."

We took the hint and hurried back to the cabin. Inside, I lit a candle from the fire and turning, surveyed the room.

"Look, Lydia, a table and chairs!" I exclaimed, then laughed at myself for thinking how nice a rough-hewn table and rickety chairs looked to me.

Lydia laughed, too, "Now if we only had a chandelier and wine in fine glasses, we would have our castle complete!"

"I'd settle for a plank floor instead of dirt, if you don't mind," I replied.

"Let's hang velvet curtains over that big window, the sunlight hurts my eyes."

"You call in the maids to do that, and I'll go to the kitchen and get the cooks busy on supper." I laughed.

Jesse brought in the food packs and placed them gingerly on the table, testing its ability to hold the load. It held with a creak or two. Nodding, he returned to his chores. In no time, I had a pot boiling for the rice and a big serving of the jerked venison frying in the skillet. The boys were drawn in from their explorations by the aroma before dinner was on the table. We fed the men and boys, then when they were finished and were sitting outside, Lydia and I sat down and ate.

"Do you suppose that corner bed would be more comfortable than sleeping on the floor?" she asked.

"It might if it didn't already have occupants," I answered, thinking of all the vermin that might be waiting there.

Lydia laughed, "I suppose it might be safer to wait for new padding at that."

Jerry stuck his head in the door. "Lonza said not to use the bed before we change the ticking." He gathered up the old straw and took it out the door. I tested the rawhide ropes that made up the framework of the bed and they seemed strong.

"We could spread the buffalo robe over them and make a pallet for the boys," I said. "They are light enough that they would be comfortable on it, but I doubt we would."

"That's a good idea," she said, "I would sleep sounder without two little feet running up and down my back all night."

"Me too!"

We laughed and soon had a bed made for the boys. Nearby, we made our pallet in front of the fireplace. We left the men to their own devices for their sleeping accommodations. I could hear strange voices outside and knew the men of the village had gathered to hear Lonza tell the news from the East and going to the door, I called the boys in for bed. They protested, but we were firm and they were washed and sent to bed with promises of a more thorough bathing on the morrow. Two or three giggles and comments and all was quiet.

The murmur of voices outside told us that the men were settled in for a long talk and it wasn't long before Lydia and I were bedded down and asleep.

Sometime later I heard the rattle of sleet on the thatch and the door opening. Jesse laid an armload of wood by the fire and adding some sticks stoked the fire up a little. By its light, the men laid out their rolls and after a couple of whispered comments were asleep. The bed creaked as Sippie bounded up on it and making three circles bedded down at the boys' feet. I watched the firelight playing on the underside of the thatched roof and listened to the sleet. Gradually, it faded away and I knew it had turned to snow. A draft came under the door and the fire flared a moment, then slowly began to die. "How fortunate for us to have this cabin to sleep in on a raw night with sleet and snow, Lord," I thought. "It wasn't fortune, but Providence," I thankfully replied to myself as sleep came again.

It seemed only a moment later that the door opened and a subdued light fell across the floor as a blast of fresh air swept across us and up the chimney. I heard Lonza laugh. "Ladies, it's time to get up, you've slept through half the morning!"

"And how about you," Lydia retorted, sitting up and rubbing her eyes.

Jesse sat up and looked around, then plopped back down. "Boys, you should see this snow!" Lonza called from behind the door. Three heads bolted up and eight bare feet scrambled out of the bed and to the door. The snow had piled against the threshold log until it was level with the top. Expecting to walk on top of the snow, Riley stepped out and his foot sank to the ground sending him facedown in the snow and ice.

"Yeooow!" he cried, as he sat up, his face full of snow except for two wide eyes under his long lashes holding up a ridge of flakes. Sippie bounced through the door and yipping and burying his nose under the snow ran around and around, slinging snow everywhere.

We laughed and Lonza reached down and lifted Riley back on the log, brushing snow out of his face and hair. Jesse helped by brushing snow from his clothes.

"It's co-o-o-ld!" Riley shivered and dashed back to the bed, Sippie close behind, for the fire was yet to be stoked.

Jesse stood in the open door and stared at the first substantial snow he had seen in his young life. "Listen, Ma, you can hear it falling," he called.

I stepped to the door and enclosed him in the blanket I had wrapped in. It *was* snowing so hard you could hear it falling. The rest of the world was hushed and no one was in sight. Only the smokes wreathing from the half-hidden cabins spoke of others present in this white world. Another gust of frigid air hit us and we stepped back as Lonza closed the door.

"Looks like it's set in for the day, we got here just in time," he said.

Jerry was building up the fire and Lydia was sitting nearby combing out her long black hair.

"I'm hungry," Jesse called from the bed where he had retreated with Riley and Sippie.

"We'll have breakfast in a trice," I replied and threw on my long robe. While the food was cooking, the boys dressed themselves and danced around the room, exploring every nook and cranny.

After we had eaten, I sent Jerry for water while Lonza saw to the animals. They had gathered in the shelter of a heavy growth of cedar behind the house and were as comfortable as possible. I put the water on the fire and waited for it to warm. Lydia had stripped Riley and he was standing in a kettle of warm water being scrubbed down to the tune of his protests.

"Be quiet, Riley, or I'll roll you in the snow!" Lonza said. He sat on the door sill smoking his pipe and watching the proceedings with amusement. "Well, ladies, I stretched my reputation for telling the truth last night."

"How is that?" Lydia asked, scrubbing on a rusty neck. "Be still!"

"I told the men what happened at New Mad'rid and they couldn't believe all that I said." He chuckled, "Blamed if I had a hard time believing it myself and I saw it happen! I imagine you will have a lot of questions to answer from the women of the camp."

"Well, I'll tell them the truth, believe it or not!" Lydia declared.

"Good girl; but don't tell them any more than they ask for, it's such a fantastic story it *is* hard to believe. Who would believe that islands moved and land sank and the Mississippi ran backwards without seeing it for themselves?"

"I still have a hard time believing it and that we are free from those pirates. Sometimes I wake up and wonder if Tom Finn will come back to the island today, then I realize where I am and that with the Lord's blessing, I may never have to look on his being again," I said.

"Oh, I hope so, too, Ruth." Lydia was toweling Riley off and wrestling with him on the bed as he giggled and tried to escape.

I threw the bathwater out and started another kettle warming for Jesse's bath. "I took a bath at the creek, Ma," he protested.

"Yes, and it smells like you need another one today, young man," I replied. He too was stripped, scrubbed, dried and dressed.

Lydia had been digging through the packs and came up with a sack of oats. "I've been saving this for a convenient time and this looks like the right time to have some oatmeal. If we get it on the fire soon, it should be done by suppertime."

Oatmeal was almost everybody's favorite, but it took so long to cook, it was impractical to cook it on the trail. I retrieved a box of dried apples and had a pie baking in one of the Dutch ovens. The aroma filled the cabin and made us all hungry again. Supper would be a real treat.

It snowed heavily all day and about sundown, the skies began to clear. "We're in for a couple of cold nights now," Lonza predicted.

With almost a foot of snow on the level and the cold settling in, it didn't look like we would be moving any time soon. I was glad. We needed a break in the traveling and the rest would do man and beast good. The hard part would be finding feed for the livestock.

Zenas said, "Grandma and Uncle Jerry never talked much about the shakes, 'cause the happenings was too fantastic for common folks t' believe. Ever onct in a while they would mention something about it or tell us 'bout it if we urged them. I remember an old man Uncle Jerry called Clell Conner coming through the country onct that wus a kid with Uncle Jerry on the island. He spent a couple o' nights with us and he and Uncle Jerry stayed up 'way into the nights talkin' 'bout them times. I listened and it was a fantastic tale they told. I 'spect it all meant more to me after hearing a stranger confirm all the things Grandma and Uncle Jerry had described."

CHAPTER 17
UNCLE JERRY'S STORY
FEBRUARY 1812

"I think this is the place to start tellin' some o' Uncle Jerry's version o' this tale," Zenas said as he sat deep in his chair and sipped hot coffee. "Course, some of it overlaps Grandma's story at the first, but he had some good adventures on the rest o' the trip up White River and I'm tired o' all that woman talk."

After the noonin' on February 18, Lonza took the lead an' I rode drag b'hind the packhorses. We wus headin' northwest up the White River bottoms over close to the breaks. I could see the river ever once in a while, but we mostly had trees both sides o' the trail t' block any long views. They weren't much game sign here, this close to the settlement, they had all been hunted out. I wus shore glad we had thet deer t' see us through the visit t' town.

Late in the afternoon, the trail led away from the bottoms and up a draw in the hills.

We came out on a flat an' there was the settlement.

Cabins set helter-skelter each side o' the trail. Lonza knew most of the men an' spoke t' 'em as we passed. They 'ould relax some as they recognized him and I got the distinct feelin' ever' one of 'em wus within reachin' distance o' ther rifle. It wus a trait I got used to in the wilderness.

We were near through the village when Lonza pulled up in front of a run-down cabin. "Here's Rice's cabin," he called, an' we all stood down. Them two scamps an' the dog was ever'where at onct an' into ever'thing. They shore was glad t' git their feet on the ground. We got the packs off'n the animals an' they found a good place t' roll. Grazin' was scarce in town, but they found some nourishment here and there.

It looked like rain so I hied myself off to the woods an' drug up a good sized deadfall top fer fuel. On the way back, I stopped by the nearest cabin an' asked the missus for a bucket o' coals for our fire. She scooped up a generous portion an' I hurried it back to Ruthie. After we got the 'coon out'n the chimney (which Jobe Pike shot off'n the roof), the fire caught good and things settled down some. While dinner wus cookin' I stored the packs in a corner o' the cabin an'

Lonza put new hinges on the door that had fallen down. It wus the same ol' fare o' venison steaks with gravy an' rice, but it shore tasted good.

While the wimmin cleaned up an' got the boys t' bed, Lonza an' I sat outside in the dusk an' he smoked his pipe. I hadn't taken up the custom yit, so I jest sat an' watched the mules nose through the bed ticking I had thrown on the ground.

"Hope those mules don't get lousy, nosing through that straw." Lonza chuckled.

"Hope *I* didn' git lousy throwin' it out!" I replied.

A shaft of light appeared from Jobe Pike's open door and Jobe headed our way. I heard him call, "Evenin', Jake, evenin' Huz," an' two more shadows took form of men comin' up the trail. As they approached, Lonza called, "Evenin', men, pull up a chair and set."

"Humph," said the one I recognized as Jake, "looks like we'll have to sit on our fist an' lean back on our thumbs afore we git a chair."

"Jerry Harris, I want you to meet Jake Moss and Huzkiah Hall." Lonza and I had stood when the men had walked up.

Jake Moss's hand was hard and calloused and he had a firm grip I suspicioned was not his best. His arms were large and there were long rows of scars down his right forearm. "Pleased to meet you, Jerry," he said.

Huzkiah Hall was tall and slim. He wore buckskin from head to foot. He was an extremely quiet man — most of the others called him Silent Huz or just Silent — but his handshake was warm and frendly. "Jest call me 'Huz,' it's easier." He grinned.

Jobe dragged my fire log over in front of our seat and the three of them sat and began building smokes in their pipes. All was quiet for a while. I retrieved a burning stick from the fireplace and the men passed it around.

Jake got his clay goin' first. "Well, Lonza . . . how's things in the East?" between puffs.

"Doing right well, I suppose, rain's been good and crops about average. Madison's still President, and lots of people are talking about moving west."

Huz nodded.

"I heered they may be war with ol' England agin," Jobe put in.

Lonza nodded. "Looks that-a-way, all right. People are getting awful tired of this impressment of our sailors. It's getting so a man going to sea doesn't know when — if ever — he'll get back."

"Redcoats is stirrin' up Injuns agin us north o' here," Huz observed.

"They's itchin' fer it . . . all right," Jake agreed.

"Air we still livin' in Missouri Territory . . . or hev they named us somethin' else?" Jobe asked.

Lonza chuckled, "Still Missouri, Jobe, and they were talking about Louisiana becoming a state this year."

"I've lived in two territories 'thout movin' a inch from this place, an' I'll bet you a bob-tailed nag I'll sit right here an' hev another new address 'fore them politicians is through 'ith us!" he growled.

[Zenas paused at this point to pass on Jerry's confirmation of the correctness of Jobe's prediction. "Shore enough, he was right," Uncle Jerry would always laugh. "By 1819, they wus callin' them in Arkansas Territory, an' Flee's Settlement wus goin' by another name. Last I heerd, they had named it after some politician named Bates. I'm not even sure it covers the same ground now."]

"Here comes Drew," Jake observed. Another man walked up. He was as tall as me and I noticed that he didn't make a sound as he walked. He jist seemed like a shadder movin' 'cross the ground an' I was surprised

269

Jake even seen him, much less knew who he wus.

"Howdy, Lonza," he spoke softly an' stuck out his hand.

"Howdy, Drew, I'd like you to meet Jerry Harris. Jerry, this is Drewery Moss, late from Kentucky."

"Glad ta meet yuh, Jerry." He shook my hand with the same firm grip as the others.

"How's the family?" Lonza asked.

"They's all fine. Ma's carryin' another one, due sometime in the spring," he replied. I discovered later that the Moss cabin was fair overflowin' with children. They wus nine or ten of 'em an' it seemed like one was always on the way. "Oh, Ma sent some milk over for the tykes, said they likely hadn't had some for a time."

He handed me a bucket and I took it in the house. Lydia poured it in a crock with a lid an' sent the washed bucket back with many thanks. Drew took the bucket, turned it upside down an' sat on it.

" 'S'purty bad whin you has t' bring yore own seat whin you visits yore neighbor, ain't it, Drew?" Jobe Pike chuckled.

"Ol' Rice wern't much fer fine furniture, an' I didn't see any on the pack train comin' through this evenin'," Drew drawled with a grin.

I heard one of the boys call "jolt" an' th' ground shuddered, the cabin door opened and all five occupants stood in the doorway. We all braced for more, but after a few moments and nothing else happened, we relaxed.

"Yuh say it's worser over on the river, Lonza?" Jobe asked.

"Much worse," Lonza replied. There was a pause while he pulled on his pipe. "We were in North Carolina when the first shake hit. A lot of things shook off the walls and out of the shelves and broke. Some people said they heard thunder and I heard all the church bells ring. The ground shook for quite a while and the wells turned muddy. At New Mad'rid, they said the shakes were so hard you couldn't stand. Timber fell everywhere and large areas sank into the ground until you could only see the tops of the trees above the water."

"Sounds bad enough," someone observed.

"Yuh say the ground sank?" Jake asked.

"Yes and there were great geysers of water and black coal pouring out of the ground. A place called Little Prairie was knocked flat and the people had to wade water for eight or more miles to get out of the flood."

"Must hev near froze to death," Huz observed.

271

"No, the water was warm," Lonza replied.

" 'S'at so?"

"They speculate the water came from deep in the ground where it was hot, or from near some volcano."

"Volcaner, huh, whur wus it?"

"There wasn't one on the surface, that we saw," Lonaza replied. "That happened on the first shake in December. There was a lot of damage in New Madrid and they were all living outside the houses when we arrived in January. The hardest shake came on February seventh just as we were getting ready to leave. All the houses collapsed and it was a long time before we could stand without being thrown down."

"How many wus kilt?" Drew asked.

"We could only count five or six in the settlements that we knew of. One woman died of fright and a nigger drowned in a fissure that opened up. One boy went into the woods looking for livestock and never came back."

"I found six Injuns killed in a village near New Mad'rid," I added.

"It seems the Indians suffered the most harm," Lonza said.

"They wus mighty scairt around here, too," said Jake. "All left the country headed west. Don't know why they went that direction 'stead o' any other."

"They knew the damage was worser east o' here," Huz said. "Got the messages by their secret ways. I talked to one of the Osages on his way with his family. He said the shakes didn't hit the upper White River an' that's where they were goin'. He was some scairt — said it was a bad day whin the best place was the Bad West. They thinks the east is good," he added.

All the men seemed impressed by this long speech by Silent. In fact, it wus the longest talk he made all night.

"You come down the rivers after the first shake, Lonza?" Drew asked.

"Yes, I got to New Madrid in January just before the Hard Shake. Jesse and his sister, Ruth Fourkiller, were prisoners of pirates on an island in the Mississippi when the first shake hit and they escaped to New Madrid. We met them there and were staying with them."

"Prisoners, huh? I heered of sich whin we passed through Saint Louie," Jobe said. "How long wus you kept, Jerry?"

"They kept us almost six years. I was given to th' widow of one o' th' men Ma an' Pa kilt in th' attack. She wus good t' me, bein' she had been stole and bought herself. We all got off th' island while th' pirates wus gone on a raid and th' river shifted its bed." I didn't tell them that the land shifted, for I could tell they was havin' t' swallow our story twice t' b'lieve it.

"They wus buyin' an' sellin' *white* folks?"

"About half o' th' wimmin on th' island wus bought or stole by th' pirates," I replied.

"Someone ought ta hang the whole bunch!" Jake spat.

"They may all be dead," I replied. "We heered th' island they wus stayin' on sank with th' first shake that moved the river."

"Good 'nough for 'em," said Drew. Huz nodded and drew on his pipe. The glow from the bowl lit his eyes and high forehead.

"Tell yuh the truth, men, yore story's plum fantastical," Jobe observed. "I know the ground kin shake, but those geysers spurtin' hot water an' groun' splittin' is shore sompin' else."

"We-e-l-l, the groun' did swaller a bunch of them Israelites in the wilderness," Huz drawled.

"I never knowed Lonza t' tell tall tales, meself," said Drew.

"Thet's right, I reckon, but yuh gotta admit them wus fantastical events, he's talkin' 'bout," replied Jobe.

"Well, you can bet it's all *true*!" I said hotly.

"Sometimes I had trouble believing what I was *seeing* myself," Lonza said mildly. "I don't blame you for not taking it all in."

"Time will tell," Jake added.

"Feels like rain," Drew said, looking up.

"Gonna snow," Silent Huz said matter of factly.

A drop of cold water hit my cheek. I brushed at it and it felt icy. Another drop hit and bounced off my shoulder. We could hear the sleet hitting the dried leaves and limbs of the trees and getting heavier and heavier. We stood up.

"Guess it's time t' go 'fore the sleet freezes my toes," said barefoot Jobe.

We said our good nights, the four men hurrying off to their homes. Lonza sighed and turned to the door. "Well, Jerry, story-time is over, let's get to bed, I'm tired."

We went in and I fastened the door tight t' hold out the weather.

It was still snowing hard when we got up late the next morning. I guess everyone was so tired we all overslept. The snow wus level with the door sill an' Riley tried to walk on it. All he got wus a face full of snow. After breakfast, the wimmin started bathing the boys. I knew they'd be on me next for the same thing an' I wasn't ready for a bath, so

I put on my boots, grabbed my gun an' sneaked out the door while they wus busy.

The only signs of life in the settlement wus smoke from the chimneys. As I walked toward the trail, I spied a set of animal tracks, though it was hard to tell jist whut made them in the soft snow. Thinkin' it might be one of the Indian ponies gone astray, I follered them west out o' the settlement. The tracks wandered here an' there across an' old cornfield an' I could tell where the animal had pulled on some of the old cornstalks an' browsed on 'em. Lookin' down the trail, I could see whur he had come back to it, so I follered him on into the woods. The snow was comin' down hard, but here in the woods the trees shielded me some from it. I could hear its soft swish as it fell. It was coverin' the tracks fast, so I knew they must be pretty fresh an' the crittur warn't far ahead. I couldn't see too far because of the snow covered brush, but onct or twice I heard a soft snort. Turnin' a corner in the trail, I got a glimpse of a horse's hind end goin' aroun' another turn. It warn't one of ourn, but I thought it might be one of the settlers' an' I hurried to ketch up.

Th' trail started up a rise an' it slowed the pony some so that I thought I could catch up afore he got to the top. Lowerin' my head agin the snow, I hurried up the hill with the horse not more than a hundred yards ahead. I had cut the gap in half whin I looked up an' the pony had stopped an' was pullin' on some bushes by the trail.

I stopped dead still myself, starin' at the blanket that wus draped over the pony an' there wus someone layin' under it! I called an' the pony looked up, but there was no movement from the rider. I thought of my rifle an' pulled it out'n the buckskin case an' checked to see that it was in firin' order then called agin an' the pony turned as if to go on up the hill. He was some ganted and stumbled when he moved. I called, "Whoa" an' he stopped and looked back at me over his shoulder. Still no movement from who-ever wus under thet blanket. I could see the toe of a moccasin stickin' out, but thet wus all. The Pony turned agin as if to go on, but stumbled an' almost went to his knees. By this time I wus hurryin' toward him an' he got some skittish, so I stopped an' started talkin' to him soft an' easy. He stood still an' listened, but was still nervous.

I realized thet bein' a Injun pony, he might understand Cherokee better than English, so I switched languages. It worked, his ears pricked forward an' he turned to look me straight on, liftin' his head an' sniffin' the air. "Come on, boy," I called, holdin' out my hand, "come on." He took a couple steps toward me an' I stood still. Ears cupped toward me, he stopped an' sniffed the air agin. I wus speakin' the right language, but I didn't smell familiar like the Injuns he knew. "Come on," I urged, then started talkin' t' 'im soft an' friendly. He came three or four steps closer, paused, then came on all the way to my hand. He sniffed it, then snorted and drew back some, so I talked to him more — never takin' my eyes off'n the blanket — an he looked me over. Pretendin' to graze on the snow, he moved one step closer and sniffed the bottom o' my buckskin pants. This seemed t' satisfy him an' he stood still lookin' at me. I slowly reached up an' grasped the rein, all the time talkin' to him soft an' easy.

There wus still no movement from the blanket an' I didn't know if there wus anyone alive under there or if whoever wusn't gonna rise up suddenly an' ax me in the head. Somethin' wus stingin' my eyes an' I realized that it wus sweat, my insides felt all shaky an' I near ran away. Then I looked into the horse's eyes an' saw how near to collapsin' he wus an' knew I had to help him almost as much as whoever was on his back. I couldn't work with one hand an' after *some* thinkin' 'bout it, I leaned my rifle against a tree an' made sure my knife wus handy. Talkin' an' rubbin' the horse's neck, I slowly worked my way down to his shoulder. Liftin' the blanket, I saw the back of a head covered with long black hair. I wus so skairt I watched for movement for several seconds. They wus none. I spoke softly in Cherokee. Still no movement.

Carefully, I lifted the blanket more an' saw a long stain o' blood runnin' from the body down the horse's side. There was also a furrow burned along the horse's shoulder that must have been made by a bullit. It looked like he had lost a lot of blood from it as his foreleg was covered in dried blood down to where the snow had washed it away.

Th' bare shoulder I saw wus white as death an' I had almost decided thet the horse wus carryin' a corpse when I saw the fingers move in a pettin' motion on the horse's side. Just by instinct an' relief, I grabbed the hand an' it feebly gripped mine.

"Good work, Jerry, yuh caught up to him afore I could head 'im off."

I jumped as if I had been shot. There on the other side o' the horse stood Huzkiah Hall. He wus within touchin' distance o' me an' I didn't even see or hear him walk up, I wus so concentratin' on the horse an' its load. I wus shore put out with myself for bein' so poor a scout thet I let someone slip up on me like thet.

Huz must have noticed, 'cause he said, "You was concentratin' on the right things, Jerry, don't let my slippin' up on yuh bother. I seen the horse halfway through the settlement when I come out this mornin' an' I took the back trail to head him off. You were faster comin' up ahind an' caught up. Now, let's see what we got here," he said as he lifted the blanket off.

It wus a Injun naket to the waist. They wus a hole in the back o' his left shoulder that must have gone clean through from the track o' the blood down the horse's side, an' a furrow runnin' along his right ribs that had bled some, but not as much as the shoulder.

I spoke to him in Cherokee, but there wus no response. Silent spoke in another language I come to recognize as Osage an' the man responded by noddin' his head slightly. Huz wus lookin' him in the face on his side o' the horse. After some questions from Huz an' some whispered replies from the man, Huz took the blanket an' ripped a long strip from the edge an' handed it t' me. "Thet wound in the shoulder'll start bleedin' agin whin we move him, Jerry, an' it don't look like he has too much t' spare right now. We're gonna have t' lift him up an' off the horse an' whin we do, you slap this rag on thet wound as fast as you kin."

I took the rag an' folded it on one end. I intended t' slip it between the man an' the horse, but the wound had stuck to the horse's hair. "Wait, Huz, he's stuck to the horse!"

"We gotta git him off this horse; it couldn't carry him to the settlement." Huz came around t' my side and scoopin' up some clean snow, he packed the back wound with it. The man shivered, then laid still while Huz felt around between him an' the horse. "We might could soak 'em with snow 'til it comes loose. Thet's 'bout the only thing I knows t' do. Tell you what, Jerry, you git back to the cabins an' git another horse t' carry this man whiles I try t' soak him loose. Yuh could git some more blankets an' some-thin' hot for him t' drink while yore about it. Some of the others will help you."

This last he had to call, for I was already on a trot t' town. The snow was still fallin' an' it was hard to make any time, but I did the best I could. It was farther than I had thought. I had been concentratin' so much on catchin' the horse, I didn't pay any attention t' how far I had come. I burst in on the cabin all out of breath.

"Where have you been, Jerry?" Ruth asked, lookin' up from her sewin'.

"Me an' Huz found a man all shot up an' near dead up th' trail, can you git me somethin' hot for him t' drink, an' I need some blankets. I'm gonna git a horse," I called, runnin' out, Sippie rompin' after me. Lonza was comin' up from the breaks with a big load of forage on one o' the mules whin I found the animals.

"Huz has a man all shot up on th' trail, I need a horse for him t' ride," I called.

Lonza dropped the reins an' slipped the knot on his load, lettin' it fall off on both sides. "Here, take this mule," he called. "He has a broad back and an easy gait." I grabbed the reins an' pulled the mule up to the cabin, Lonza close b'hind. Just as I reached the door, it flew open an' Ruthie almost ran into me with her arms loaded with blankets an' a buffalo robe. Jesse was right b'hind with a jug of steamin' coffee.

"We need to fix up the bed if the man is to have a place to rest." She looked at Lonza.

"Can you and Huz get along without me, Jerry?" At my nod, he said, "Good, I'll get the bed ready."

I threw the covers across the mule an' grabbed the jug of coffee an' was gone. The mule seemed to sense the need t' hurry an' in the end I had trouble keepin' up with him. Huz wus still workin' to separate the man from the horse. I tied the mule to a limb an' hurried around to the man with the coffee. Huz said somethin' an' the man nodded slightly. He raised his head to take a swaller or two. It wus awful hot an' he winced a little. I scooped a little snow an' put it in the pot. It cooled it some, but wus still plenty warm. He took another drink, more this time.

"Ahh, he's loose." Huz gritted his teeth at the sight of the wound. We set him up on the horse an' Huz bein' taller held him up while I wrapped the strip of blanket around him to cover front an' back wound. I gave him another longer drink of the coffee an' looked him over for the first time. He must not have been much older than me, though it was hard t' tell in his condition. He never opened his eyes an' it looked like one was swollen shut. There wus a large lump an' bruise on the left side o' his head an' I noticed rope burns on his wrists an' ankle. His right foot was bare.

"Looks like he had a tangle with someone an' come out second," Huz whispered.

"Let's git him up on thet mule an' back t' the settlement." He led the mule closer an' spread the robe over his back, fur up.

I carefully lifted his leg an' swung it over the horse's back an' afore I could git around t' help, Huz had picked the man up like a little kid an' set him on the mule. The injun laid down on the mule's back with a small groan, the first I had heard from him.

"Reckon he'll ride like thet," Huz said. "Bet it's a whole lot softer thin thet bony horse's back!"

I covered the man with the rest o' the blankets an' Huz led the mule down the trail. I grabbed my gun an' the horse's rein an' follered. It's a good thing Huz went slow, 'cause that horse could barely walk. I talked to him a lot an' he seemed to understand things wus gonna git better. Roundin' a bend, we met Lonza an' Jobe hurryin' up the trail. I noticed they both carried their rifles.

"Who yuh got there, Huz?" Jobe asked in a low voice. He never looked at us, but wus constantly scannin' the woods. Lonza came up on the other side, doin' the same an' lookin' up our back trail. I wondered at this an' later learned thet renegade Injuns an' white men baited traps an' ambushes this way, knowin' decent men would natcherly help someone in trouble. It wus an' old, old trick an' I could have fallen into a trap.

"Young Osage buck, been worked over somethin' fierce," Huz replied. "I don't think he wus follered, he wandered through the settlement early an' Jerry cotched up to 'im afore I got 'round the back trail."

"Come through the settlement? I'll git Drew an' we'll back track 'im a ways jist t' be certain they ain't no skunks follerin'."

"I'll ketch up to yuh in a minit, soon's we git this man settled," Huz replied.

Th' sky had lightened some by the time we got back t' Rice's cabin an' the snow wus just spittin' a little now an' then. A breeze had come up an' snow wus blowin' off'n the trees some. The wimmin saw us comin' an' were standin' in the door waitin' fer us. They wus a couple of other wimmin there from the other cabins that I didn't know. Huz gently lifted the man off the mule like he was nothin', carried him into the house an' laid him on the bed. He quickly stepped back as the wimmin crowded in an' with whispers an' murmurs began to doctor on the man.

"Looks like we got him in good hands," Huzkiah said to me, "let's see to thet horse." He strode out the door, me close behind. The horse stood jist whur I left him, his head hangin' down low. I spoke t' him as I walked up an' he only lifted his head a little.

"Take him down in the cedars, Jerry, an' I'll send some corn fer 'im." Huz hurried off.

It took some coaxin' t' git him started movin' agin, but he perked up some under the cedars where the snow wusn't so heavy. I brought him whut wus left o' the fodder Lonza had gathered an' the horses hadn't eaten an' he eagerly ate on it. Takin' some grass, I began rubbin' him down, not that it would do any good, the shape he wus in, but it would comfort him some.

"Pa sent some corn t' feed him." I looked up an' there stood a boy 'bout ten years old holdin' a bucket with a couple o' quarts o' corn. Without waitin' fer me t' take it, he stuck the bucket under the pony's nose an' the horse eagerly went to the bottom an' wus munchin' away.

"Thet ought t' perk 'im right up," I said, but the boy had already disappeared up the trail home. While the horse munched the corn, I fetched him a bucket o' water. He eagerly drank, but I didn't let him have much, thinkin' the corn an' too much water might not be good. He went back to the corn bucket an' licked it clean, then givin' a satisfied snort, he resumed his meal on the fodder. I tied him to a tree with a long rope an' left him contentedly munchin' away.

Th' wimmin had unwrapped the bandage me an' Huz had put on an' were washin' an' packin' the wounds with herbs an' such. They wus workin' on the bullit burn on his side an' washin' him some. One of the wimmin wus cookin' some broth over the fire an' I noticed the woodpile wus growin' low, so I went out an' chopped more firewood. The cleanin' an' fussin' over the patient wus over whin I went back in with an armload of wood an' the cook wus spoonin' the broth into the man as fast as he could take it.

"Jerry, did you see any prickly pear cactus under the cedars?" Lydia asked. At my nod, she said, "Good, go get me two large pads, please."

I dug around under the cedars an' found the pesky cactus. The pads wus small, but I got the biggest of them and brought them back to Lydia. She peeled the skin an' spines off them and liftin' the bandages placed them over the wounds. "There, that should do." She sat back and covered the man to his chin with the blankets.

Th' sun wus goin' down an' it wasn't 'til Jesse an' Riley loudly mentioned it that I realized that I wus hungry as a mama wolf.

Lonza came trampin' in from scoutin' the back trail an' with exclamations of surprise at the late hour, the wimmin hurried off to their cabins t' begin supper an' Ruthie an' Lydia bustled around to fix our meal. The wounded patient lay quietly asleep.

Over supper, Lonza told us about their trip trailin' the horse. "That horse came down the river and circled up to the settlement. We followed his trail up the hollow past Blue Spring and out on top of the hills. He stayed on top of the ridge and the tracks came down from the north. We followed quite a ways and there were no other tracks, so he wasn't followed as well as we could tell in the snow. There's a cave away up there they call the Blowing Cave and Drew thinks that's where the horse came from. Tomorrow, some of the men are goin' to go up there and see. The rest of us will stay here on watch. We don't know who this man is, he may be good or bad. Right now, he's too weak to do us harm, but we will need to keep an eye out until we know more about him."

"Why would an Osage be ridin' a Cherokee horse?" I asked durin' supper.

"Why I don't know," Lonza replied, "I didn't know the horse was Cherokee."

"He knew what I was sayin' t' him whin I

288

talked Cherokee, but not whin I spoke English."

"Mayhap we'll know in a day or two, right now, we need to get some sleep. It may be a long day tomorrow." Stokin' his pipe, he headed for the door.

It wus cold when we stepped out and I could see stars peekin' around the clouds.

"It's clearin' off, gonna get pretty cold tonight," Lonza observed. "Better get in some extra wood." We chopped on the treetop and hauled in a few armloads of firewood.

"Jerry, that sick man got our bed," Jesse said as I stacked the last armload. He an' Riley had been mighty proud that they got the bed an' the rest of us slept on the floor.

"Well, I guess you'll have to sleep with th' men on th' floor." I tried to keep from smilin'. "We will have to guard th' women tonight, so you kin help me watch."

"Okay," he said reluctantly. "Where we gonna bed down?"

"You pick a spot between th' door an' th' women's bed an' I'll git our bedroll."

It took some thought an' we had to move the bed twice b'fore he was satisfied, but he climbed under the covers an' jabbered a while before he drifted off to sleep. Riley opted to sleep beside his mother. Onct or twice in the night I woke to find one or the other of the women checkin' on their patient. Toward daylight, I fed the fire some wood and it was burnin' brightly when we got up before dawn. We were finishin' breakfast whin there wus a knock on the door and Huz called out. Jesse ran to open the door.

"Thought I would check on the patient afore we heads out," he said as he stepped in. Goin' over to the bed, he said a few words in Osage and the man opened his eyes for the first time I had noticed.

They had a short conversation, then Huz turned to us. "Says he and his family was stayin' at Blowing Cave when some men pushed in an' joined them. There were two Cherokees an' four French trappers. They beat him an' tied him up an' made his wife an' mother serve them. He slipped his ropes an' was gittin' away when they saw him an' shot at him. He doesn't know how long ago that was, but it was afore the snow began."

Lonza nodded. "We don't need those people roamin' the country, do we?"

"Nope, we don't," Silent said firmly. "I think we need to pay a visit t' Blowing Cave an' see whut's goin' on."

CHAPTER 18
BLOWING CAVE
FEBRUARY 20, 1812

"How many are goin' with you, Huz?" Lonza asked.

"Right now, jist Drew or Jake, whichever thinks he kin go, I 'magine it'll be Jake, but yuh never know with them two."

Lonza smiled. "Looks like we'll be here a few more days until the weather moderates and our patient is better. I wouldn't like to be caught on the trail by that Blowing Cave bunch."

"Nope, wouldn't be no good."

I wus listenin' close an' I guess they noticed my interest. "We could use 'nother man or two, but we need most to stay an' guard the settlement," Huz mused.

"I will stay here with the women and patient," Lonza said, "but Jerry would be free to go if you could use him."

Ruthie started at that an' I saw her start to speak, then she closed her mouth an' turned away to fuss with Jesse an' Sippie.

"Might be good fer him an' us, three's a lot better'n two agin six."

"What do you say, Jerry, it could get rough, do you think you could hold up your end?" Lonza asked. I looked at Ruthie, but her back wus turned.

"Shore he could," put in Huz. "Kin yuh shoot, Jerry?"

"I've practiced a lot on th' island," I replied.

"He's a good man around the camp and on the trail, Huz. I think he would work out well for you and the experience would do him good."

Huz nodded. "Git yore gear together, Jerry, we'll travel light, jist a blanket an' 'nough food for three, four days. Any longer'n that an' we'll hev t' shoot somethin'." He turned toward the door. "Take a goodly amount o' powder an' lead, we may need it," he called over his shoulder. "We'll be back in a few minutes." Lonza stepped out with him an' I could hear the hum o' their voices.

I wus already diggin' through my things gittin' ready. Ruthie sighed, "I'll get you some food, Jerry." In a few minutes she brought me a bundle an' I tied it up in my blanket roll.

"This will be the first time we have been

apart in a long time, Jerry, you be careful and do us proud." She kissed my cheek an' I got a lump in my throat.

"Can me go, Jerry?" Jesse wus tuggin' my sleeve.

"Not this time, Jesse, yuh have t' take care o' the wimmin." I gave him a bear hug an' he ran off with Riley and Sippie.

My rifle wus by the door an' I wus puttin' the last touches on my pack whin I heerd the voices o' the men returnin'. I rushed out the door an' almost ran into the side of one of the Injun ponies. He wus saddled an' Lonza wus holdin' the reins an' talkin' to Jobe Pike.

"Goin' on the scout, air ye, boy?" Jobe called. "Mought be a mite rough in places, but ol' Silent'll take good care o' yuh! You jist keep low an' watch him an' yuh'll come out fine. Take this here cap I made fer the tyke, it'll fit an' keep yer ears warm." He handed me a coonskin cap with the tail draggin' b'hind.

I bristled a little at Jobe talkin' down to me like that, but didn't say nothin'. Jobe wus a talker an' a lot of whut he said wus just noise.

"This pony should be good, Jerry, he's the best of the three." Lonza handed me the reins. "Take this pistol; you could need it."

It wus his own an' I opened my mouth t' say no, but he pushed it into my hand. "I've got my other one in the cabin and my rifle. I doubt I'll need it. We'll stay here a week if we don't hear from you sooner, then we will probably have to leave, weather permittin'. I will leave our destination with Jobe and you can follow when it's safe to do so. Be careful and learn all you can from Huz. I know you will do good." He shook my hand and held the horse while I mounted. Huz had ridden up an' it wus Drew follerin' b'hind on a little dun-colored mule.

"We shouldn't be gone mor'n three, four days. Huz's wife is Osage an' kin talk to the Injun, should yuh need." Drew had taken over the talkin' duties now he wus with us.

Silent Huz turned his hoss an' led the way. We headed northeast along a maze of sluggish creeks an' canebrakes, Drew bringin' up the rear. They wus just a shadow of a trail on the high ground, then Huz turned sharply right down the hill an' across the creek. Another sharp turn left down the bank an' we wus soon crossin' another stream comin' in from the north. "This's Pheiffer Creek," Drew said quietly. "We'll hit Poke Bayou an' travel up it quite a ways."

Nothin' stirred. The snow wasn't so deep in the woods, but the limbs wus heavy with it an' we got showered purty often. It wus colder 'an blue blazes, but the sun wus bright an' I wus glad we rode mostly in the shade o' the trees, or we would of gone blind. Poke Bayou wus nice an' large an' Huz turned up the stream. The trail meandered a lot, goin' around the canebrakes an' such, but stayed generally with the bayou. Once in a while, it would take up over a hill an' cut off a bend. The stream got smaller an' clearer as we climbed an' whin the sun wus overhead, we came upon a cave with a big sprin' gushin' out of it. On a little flat, Huz stopped an' we let the horses brouse on the grasses stickin' up out o' the snow while we ate lunch.

Not far above the spring, we crossed the bayou an' cut across the hill back down to where a creek flowed in from the left. Huz stopped an' we moved up to hear whut he had t' say, "Ef we come in frum the north, we kin see whut's goin' on at the cave frum the bluff. They wouldn't be watchin' fer visitors from up there an' we mought jist s'prise 'em."

"Sounds good." Drew nodded. "We kin camp on the divide an' be in place afore daylight."

Huz nodded an' without another word turned up the creek. It wus rough goin' without much of a trail an' we slowed considerable. The sun was sinkin' fast whin we come to a spring that's now called Tate's Spring flowin' into the creek. We rested a minute an' the horses watered before goin' on up towards the divide. Jist es dark wus fallin', we come to a little bluff whur the creek fell over it an' there we dry camped with no fire. Huz clumb the bluff an' disappeared over the top o' the divide. I found a pile of leaves in the lee of the rock an' burrowed in for the night.

After a while, Huz returned without a sound bein' made — near spooked me. "I smelled smoke on top, must hev come frum the cave," he whispered. The leaves rustled some whur he burrowed in, then all wus quiet, 'cept for an occasoinal sound frum the animals. I slept light an' whin I heard the leaves stirrin', crawled out into the night. A sliver of moon an' the stars wus the only thing that tole me which way wus up. Otherwise, all wus es black es ink.

Drew whispered in my ear, "Wrap yore gun in yore blanket an' follow Huz. We'll git ourselves fixed on the bluff an' wait fer light."

I didn't know how t' foller someone I couldn't see, but whin he climbed the rocks, I could see his shadow agin the stars, an' by stayin' low, I could skylight him as he moved up the hill. We moved across the divide an' down into another gully. Goin' downhill, I couldn't see or hear Huz at all, so I jist follered the gully. After a while, the trees opened up some an' I could see Huz silhouetted agin the stars. We come out on a flat an' Silent stooped to his knees. I follered an' in a few feet came to the edge of the rock that rimmed the blackest hole in the ground I ever seen.

Drew crawled up beside Silent. "Cave's over there to the left," Huz whispered, but I had trouble findin' anythin' beyond my nose in the dark. A little ember lit up below an' I knew where the camp wus. After a few minutes, Huz backed away from the edge an' we follered.

"The breeze is blowin' down the valley an' ef we stay here long the blamed Injuns'll smell us. We'll work our way 'round the bluff to the right 'til we're opposite the fire an' wait fer light." He turned an' wus off with me strugglin' to keep up an' not fall off the rock. When we were movin' through the cedars growin' in the thin soil on the shelf, I felt a little safer. Silent disappeared an' I stopped dead still. I felt Drew near an' he whispered, "He's checkin' the bluff t' see where we are." After a moment Silent whispered from ahead, "Not quite far 'nough." And we continued creepin' through the cedars.

Another hundred yards an' Silent turned back left an' I follered. Whin he got on his knees, I did too an' we crawled to the edge of the bluff. "Missed it a little, but this is good 'nough," he whispered, then backed away. In the trees, he whispered, "Cut some limbs off'n the back sides of these cedars fer a bed an' screen t' hide ahind."

We cut limbs without a sound an' when I had an armload, I carried it to the bluff. Makin' myself a bed on the rock, I unsheathed my rifle an' laid it down on the bed, then covered the barrel with another limb. It was still black as the insides of a cow an' I covered myself with my blanket an' dozed some.

When I opened my eyes agin, it seemed the black wasn't so thick an' I saw some embers from the fire across the valley. Lookin' up to my right, I could see that the stars wus dimmin' in the east an' there wus a hint of gray along the ridge. It wus almost daylight afore anyone stirred in the camp. An Injun rose from behind some rocks to the right o' the cave an, wrapped in his blanket, wandered down to the fire. He added wood an' squatted an' watched the fire catch. Presently, another Injun appeared out o' the mouth of the cave an' squatted before the fire. We could hear an ocassional comment from one or t'other, but couldn't make out the words. After a few minutes, one of them called gruffly to someone in the cave, "Get out here and cook!" The stockinged head of a man appeared draggin' a woman. He roughly shoved her toward the fire an' said in Cherokee, "Cook!" Regainin' her balance, the woman busied herself with cookin' a meal.

Another man left the cave an' close b'hind, an' older woman was pushed an' stumbled out holdin' a baby in her arms. Two more men lazily sauntered out an' sat by the fire. I gripped my rifle an' b'fore I could move, Silent signaled "no" with his eyes.

"Hold on, Jerry, we may be here all day b'fore doin' anythin'," Drew whispered.

Silent's nod was barely perceptible.

I settled myself down for a long watch. Pa an' Grandpa Fourkiller had taught me to still-hunt an' I thought I knew how t' stay still a long time, but Drew an' Huz took me to a new level in thet d'partment. How they could lie still that long wus beyond me. Next t' them, I felt like a worm in hot ashes, but they never complained. It warmed as the sun rose an' a south wind came up, shakin' snow from the trees an' meltin' it into puddles an' runs. B'fore long, the water wus drippin' off the bluffs in a reg'lar torrent.

Life in the camp wus rather slow an' lazy save for the men abusin' the women an' givin' them all kinds of chores. I don't think Silent or Drew took their eyes off the camp an' its surroundin's all day, an' I tried t' learn as much as I could about it. Two or three times we munched jerky, but it wus shore hard watchin' the women cookin' steaks for supper. I durn near drooled. Drew punched me in the ribs an' grinned 'thout takin' his eyes off'n the camp.

The gloom of sunset came early in the valley an' the camp began t' settle down for the night. One o' the Frenchies moved off down the canyon an' disappeared b'hind the same rocks the Injun had used the night b'fore. One by one, the others disappeared into the cave. When all had been quiet for a while, Silent started crawdaddin' back from the bluff an' we follered. He led us through the cedars back to where the hillside come down to it an' sat down on a log there.

"They must hev a purty good shelter inside the cave t' sleep there with the wind blowin' through," he observed.

"I remember all those boulders layin'

around in there, an' I bet yuh could git out'n the wind purty easy with a little work," Drew said.

"Be a good place t' fort up."

"Less'n we figures out how t' kill all six with three shots, we're gonna hev t' dig the remainin' ones out'n thet cave."

"Less'n we kin git 'tween them an' the cave somehow." Silent scratched his chin.

"Did you see how much wus left o' thet carcass they been eatin' off'n?"

"Looks like they have jist enough fer breakfast," I put in.

"Betcha someone goes huntin' tomorry," Drew said.

"They won't climb th' bluffs fer thet, I'll bet," I replied.

"Nope," Huz said, "th best huntin'll be over on Punkin Creek, down the hill."

[The lower end of what was once called Pumpkin Creek was later named East Lafferty Creek after an early settler. — J.D.]

"So . . . if they go huntin' tomorrow, they'd be one or two less we 'ould hev to fight left at th' cave, wouldn't they?" I asked.

"More like one er two out huntin' we could take care of in a permanent way," Drew corrected.

"Which way d'yuh suppose they 'ould hunt the creek?" Silent asked.

301

"We-l-l-l, I'd head *up* the creek m'self," Drew reckoned.

"I'd guess so, too. Squeezin' 'tween the hills b'low, they wouldn't have much open space whur the deer 'ould be."

"Still . . ." Drew thought a moment. "They *could* go that-a-way . . ."

"Let's go back an' see to the horses an' we can make our plans there," Silent said as he stood up.

I hurried t' git in as close ahind 'im as I could. I shore didn't want t' be left wanderin' 'round thet mountain in the dark by myself! It felt good t' be movin' agin after that day an' we made good time goin' the two miles or so back t' where the horses wus. They had eaten out the circles where they were tethered and were glad t' see us. We watered them an' tied them up lower down on the branch where they could reach the water, since we might not git back fer a couple o' days the next time out.

Munchin' on our meals, Drew an' Huz discussed how t' best go about conquerin' the gang at the cave. "Ef no more than two or three go huntin', we could either take the cave or the hunters an' lessen our odds a lot," Drew said b'tween chews of jerky.

"Two go huntin', we take 'em, three go, we got a choice t' make, four go huntin', we takes the cave."

"Shore be nice t' greet the hunters frum *inside* the cave when they come back with thet fat doe fer my supper." Drew chuckled.

"We still don't know whether they'll go up or down the creek t' hunt. What say you an' Jerry take the hill on the upper side o' the canyon an' I'll git me to the lower side. We got 'em either way they go an' the other side kin catch up?"

"Sounds good. We need t' git a good ways from the canyon so's they won't be hearin' any shots at the cave."

"We need meat too, we'll let them do the huntin' fer us, then take 'em." Silent said this with a straight face.

Drew slapped his leg an' chuckled, "Yuh wants t' wait 'til they cooks it, too?"

"I likes my steaks jist so an' they 'ould git it wrong if they did it, no, I'll cook my own." He only hinted at a grin.

We waited around for a couple o' hours, then headed up t' the divide. The quarter moon wus jist risin' an' we wanted t' hurry past the cave so we couldn't be silhouetted agin it in case someone was watchin'. Reachin' the shelf o' the bluff, Silent split off t' the left an' Drew led the way along the right side o' the canyon. We stayed well back in the trees, but still, whin we got nearer the cave, Drew slowed 'way down. After some huntin', we found where we had cut off the cedar limbs. Makin' our way to the bluff, we moved our beds back from the edge so's the dyin' limbs wouldn't give us away. On down at the mouth of the canyon, we hid ourselves among some big blocks o' rocks an' curled up in the leaves fer some shut-eye.

Drew stirred an' I wus instantly awake. I lay very still for a few seconds and got my bearings. We were in a narrow alley between two huge slabs o' rock about four feet thick thet had broken apart. The leaves piled inside were nice to burrow into, but any movement made 'em rattle, so we 'ould hev t' git into position afore anyone neared. Motionin' fer me t' stay still, Drew moved out o' the alley an' came back in a few minutes with an armload o' cedar limbs. "Take these an' pile 'em up on the back side o' the rocks an' I'll pile some on the front side. You watch out fer the back door up the hill, an' I'll watch the valley."

I arranged my limbs so no one could see us from up the hill an' Drew had his arranged with a peek hole through the limbs. "I think I kin see whur Silent is," he whispered. "See thet oak log layin' on the hillside? It's the best spot."

The sun wus toppin' the hill afore anyone showed up. "Here they come," Drew whispered. "There's one, an' two an' . . . thet's all. Jist two, now which a way will they turn?" I dared not move, my eyes searchin' the hillside b'hind us, but there was no movement there.

"He weren't ahind the log, I see him up the hill a ways." Then I heard Drew curse. "Thet's not him, they's two on the hillside over there an' they're above the log, git over here!" he hissed.

I turned quickly and the leaves rattled like a squirrel goin' through them. At first, I couldn't see anythin', but then there was a movement and I saw a pair of legs step by an openin' in the trees. A second pair appeared close b'hind an' I knew we wus in trouble.

"They're gonna see Huz any minit," Drew hissed. "Put yore sights on the hind man an' I'll shoot at the front un. *Don't* shoot till I count three!"

I couldn't see anythin' movin', so set my sights a little ahead of where the two had last been. The two men b'low passed out of sight under the rocks an' I worried where they wus, but thet didn't matter so long as Huz wus in trouble. Every once in a while, we got a glimpse of them movin' along the bench, but they wus movin' away from us an' soon were out of range.

I glanced at Drew. Sweat wus runnin' down his cheek. "Whur's Huz, whur's Huz," he muttered over an' over. Try as I might and look as I might, I couldn't see anythin' on thet hillside thet moved or looked like someone was hidin' there. Even the Injuns wus gone. Nothin' stirred. Drew never moved his eyes off'n the hillside. "Yuh see them other two, Jerry?"

"I ain't seen hide nor hair since they disappeared under th' edge o' th' rock." I turned an' scanned the valley. A movement 'way up Punkin Creek caught my eye an' I got a glimpse o' one o' the men goin' up the creek. "They're still goin' up the creek," I replied in a whisper.

"Whur's Huz?" he asked agin.

"I don't know, yuh suppose he's okay? We ain't heard a thing, could be he's follerin' those two scoundrels."

"I ain't seen a *thing* move thet tells me whur he is," he said, more to himself than to me.

"He *has t'* be follerin' them other two, hadn't we orter be follerin' our two?" I asked. "They're gittin' 'way up th' creek an' we might lose them."

Drew weren't long in makin' up his mind. "Yore right, Jerry, let's move!"

Leavin' our plunder b'hind, we scrambled over the rock an' headed up the creek. Drew stayed away from the trail an' we hurried as fast as we could without makin' noise, jumpin' from rock to rock an' avoidin' the dead leaves whur possible. Next t' him, I sounded like a horse plowin' through the brush. I sure learned a lot from him about trailin' quiet on that trip.

Presently, he slowed considerable, then stopped an' squatted down. "They're up there 'bout a couple hundred yards, sittin' under thet big sycamore." He nodded toward the creek. Trouble wus there wus a dozen big sycamores whur he wus pointin' an' it took me a few minits t' see them sittin' with their backs t' the tree, one side an' 'tother, an' almost invisible.

"Still huntin'," Drew whispered, "we gotta git closer." Lookin' around, he picked up a small limb with the leaves still on it, an' tied it on to the top o' his head so's it hung in front o' his face. He could hardly see, but it made good cover. "Git rid o' thet coonskin hat, er you'll git yore punkin head shot off by one o' them coon-hungry Injuns." He grinned. I stuck the hat in my belt an' found a bunch o' leaves t' tie on.

Drew backed away an' moved in a wide circle 'long the hillside in a crouch. He dropped t' his knees an' crawled a few feet to the top o' the knoll. Fer a long time, he watched the men under the tree, then so slowly I didn't notice at first, he began crawlin' toward them. Whin his heels disappeared, I slowly poked my head over the top. I could see one o' the men sittin' under the tree an' after a few seconds made out the knee o' the other one on the far side. Drew had slid down 'til he was layin' aside a big log thet had fallen down the hill. He slithered alongside of it 'til he was up in the limbs o' the old top. He wus 'bout a hunnert yards from the men an' he laid an' watched.

Lookin' at the layout, I thought about whut I could do t' help. I remembered us passin' over a wash a ways back an' lookin' for it now, I saw thet it ran mostly toward the stand o' sycamores an' I could git closer to them by crawlin' down it. The only drawback would be that Drew 'ould be on the opposite side o' the tree an' we couldn't see each other. Crawlin' back, I rolled into the ditch an' began inchin' my way down it. I dared not look up an' my back tingled with the thought thet one of them Injuns might be standin' over me an' laughin' at my crawlin' along. I'd be helpless in this position.

The ditch got wider an' shallower as it crossed the bottom an' I finally had t' stop or run out o' cover. Carefully, I peeked over the edge. There wus a tree b'tween me an' the Injuns an' I couldn't see either o' them. Crawlin' back'ards several feet, I took a peek and could see the man nearest t' Drew. I crawled back'ards a few more feet so's I could git a bead on the man sittin' on the opposite side, the one Drew couldn't see frum whur he lay. Proppin' myself up ahind some grass an' leaves, I watched the men. Nobody moved, it must hev been fer hours. I got drowsy an' almost dozed off. The snow had gone, but the bottom o' thet ditch wus wet an' it grad'ally soaked through my clothes and on through my skin to my bones, it seemed like. I lay there 'til I wanted to scream an' charge those two scoundrels sittin' so dry an' comfortable under thet sycamore. Still, no one moved.

The sun had passed overhead an' wus jist startin' down the afternoon side whin I heard a soft snort on the hillside opposite side o' the creek. I dared not move. Strainin' my eyes as far t' the left as I could, I still couldn't see nothin', nor any movement. By lowerin' my head b'low the edge o' the ditch, I could turn an' look up the hillside. It took me a while t' see them, but movement showed me whur a mouse-colored doe browsed on the floor o' the woods. Another snort from up the hill told me the buck wus on watch. Soon, two more does an' a couple o' yearlin's came into view through the brush. They wus all pointin' to'ard the creek, probably plannin' on a drink. Now, I had t' strain my eyes to the right t' see the Injuns. No one moved.

Slowly, ever so slowly, I unsheathed my rifle. I checked the flint. Ever'thin' looked good an' dry. I couldn't risk the noise o' cockin' it 'til it wus time t' shoot. My mouth wus so dry I couldn't spit.

The deer moved nearer. Now I could see the buck higher on the hillside. He wus a fine lookin' one, 'bout six or eight points an' nervous. One o' the deer reached the water an' after lookin' around lowered her head t' drink. There wus a sudden crack of a rifle an' one o' the does up the hill a ways leaped straight up an' landed in a heap. The drinkin' deer panicked an' 'stead o' turnin' an' runnin' up the hill, leaped across the creek an' ran across the bottom fer the hill an' right b'tween me an' the Injuns. I ducked as the other man shot at the runnin' deer. Crack, the deer wus so close I heard the whump o' the ball hittin', then her thrashin' around. Whin I looked, she wus layin' not mor'n twenty-five feet from me, her head pointin' back towards the creek.

"We got two of them, Pierre!" I heard one of the men call in Cherokee.

I wus in a sweat, trapped in the bottom o' thet ditch, fixin' t' be shot like a stuck pig! It seemed I couldn't think fer a moment. The bulky rifle wouldn't do no good with me layin' in this ditch. Even if I s'prised one man by jumpin' up an' aimin', he would still git the first shot off, an' if he missed, the other would surely not. I rolled over on my back an' Lonza's pistol in my pocket thumped me in the chest. The pistol! I could use it faster than the rifle, but it wus less accurate . . . *but not at close range,* say— twenty-five or thirty-five feet! I would have t' wait until they were that close an' still only git one shot off. Well, at least I would git one afore the other got his shot off. I pulled out the coonskin an' dried the gun good. The charge wus good an' I chanced cockin' it afore they got too near. As I turned over, t' git ready, I heard one of the men exclaim, "Somethin's movin' in that ditch!"

In an instant, I grabbed the hat an' waved

the tail in the air, jist showin' a little o' the fur like it wus a coon's back, movin' towards the creek an' disappearin'.

"Just a coon in the ditch, get him too, we could use the pelt." The second voice sounded further away. Maybe I got lucky an' only one wus comin' t' the deer near me. I held my breath. I could hear steps now, an' whin I looked, I could see the top of the Injun's head comin' straight at me, lookin' down the ditch fer the coon. He hadn't seen me yet an' still he came closer an' closer. Twenty feet, fifteen feet his rifle held ready. I couldn't wait any longer. As quickly as I could, I sat up, my back against the bank aimin' square at his chest with both hands. He stopped with a grunt of surprise, his rifle comin' to bear when I shot. The ball hit him hard an' he fell backward an' wus still. I scrambled for my rifle, lookin' desperately for the other man but he wasn't in sight. Crack! Smoke billowed from Drew's gun in the treetop. I didn't see where he wus aimin', but in an instant, a shot wus fired at him from b'hind a tree by the creek. Still, I couldn't see anythin'.

They were both reloadin'. I eased my rifle over the bank an' aimed for the tree. If anythin' showed, I wus firin'. His rifle muzzle came in sight an' I could see him takin' his ramrod out'n it. In a second, the muzzle appeared around the opposite side o' the tree aimin' for Drew. Takin' careful aim, I squeezed off a shot at the rifle barrel close to the trunk of the tree, hopin' t' spoil his aim at Drew. It must have worked, 'cause the barrel lowered for an instant, then came back up just as Drew fired.

Like an idiot, I sat there watchin' 'stead o' reloadin'. The man fired agin at Drew, then appeared from b'hind the tree with a yell runnin' straight at me! You can bet I started reloadin' — *and* quick! By the time he had covered half o' the hundred yards atween us, I could tell he wus gonna win the race.

Standin' up, I clubbed my rifle an' waited on him. I never saw a man run so fast. There were ten yards left between us an' he was bringin' his clubbed rifle up when a shot from behind an' above dropped him. His speed carried him a few steps then he fell an' slid a little on the grass. I only took three steps t' reach him, but it wern't necessary to do nothin', he wus dead.

Drew wus trottin' down from the hill an' I looked to where the shot had come from an' saw Silent. I was all of a sudden awful shaky an' jist sat down right there 'tween those two corpses, not twenty feet apart.

"You okay, Jerry?" Drew asked.

I nodded. If I had needed to speak, I would have thrown up. I sat an' finished reloadin' with shaky hands.

Drew stooped an' turned over the nearest man. He was a Frenchman with a neat hole in his breast near the heart. "Nice shot, Huz," Drew said when Silent walked up.

Silent grinned. "Thought I wus ahind the log, didn't yuh?"

"At the canyon? Yup, s'where I'd a been," Drew replied.

"Too easy." Huz wus grinnin' from ear t' ear. "I wus settin' up the hill under a bresh pile."

"Whur's the other two Geezers?" Drew asked.

"Why, they's both under thet bresh pile, now." Huz wus still grinnin'. "Didn't hev time t' git no deer, though."

"Which reminds me." Drew whirled on me. "Why didn't yuh wait 'til they had gutted the deer afore you started shootin', Jerry? Now, we got all thet work fer ourselves!"

I looked up at him sharp, but I knew he wus joshin' whin I seed his grin.

"Usin' thet hat fer a decoy wus purty smart, Jerry," Silent said. To Drew, he explained, "He swung thet coonskin up an'

314

wiggled his tail like it wus goin' down the ditch. Twas the first time I knowed some o' you two wus around — thought I wus gonna hev t' take care o' the whole crew by myself."

"Well, I shore didn't know whur he had disappeared off to," Drew replied. "Shore wus a gutsy thing hidin' out in thet ditch!"

"Right smart, gittin' 'em in a crossfire," Huz said. "Sounded like a reg'lar war there for a minit."

"Let's git these deer dressed an' head back t' finish our job," Drew said. He got out his knife an' started workin' on the nearest one.

Silent looked down at me. "You sure you're okay, Jerry, no holes or blood anywhere?"

"Nope," I replied.

He looked at me closely. I guess I must of looked pretty peaked at the time. "Good, go up the hill there a ways," he said, pointin' across the creek, "an sit ahind somethin' whur you can see both of us an' all around. Don't let anyone slip up on us while we're cleanin' those carcasses." I started toward the creek, my legs feelin' awful shaky. Wadin' across with Huz, I stopped a minute an' scooped me up a drink or two an' washed my face. The water wus cold an' I felt better.

CHAPTER 19
THE RESCUE

I found a big rock t' sit under an' watched the whole valley while I reloaded the pistol. Drew an' Silent made short work o' the deer, jist field dressin' them. When they was ready, they motioned me down an' I carried Huz's rifle while he shouldered the deer 'cross the creek.

When we got to where Drew wus, he shouldered his deer an' led the way into the woods. He stopped in a sheltered place among some big rocks an' dropped the deer, looked up an' said, "Rest a spell, Huz, an' let's talk this over a little, I been thinkin'."

Huz laid the deer down an' looked at Drew. "Whut's on yer mind, Drew?"

"Hev yuh thought how we wus gonna git those other two out'n thet cave?"

"Nooo, I ain't."

"Ef they holes up in there, it may take an' army t' git at 'em. We need t' lure 'em away somehow. I been thinkin', whut ef they think we wus a couple o' these here fellers an' we could somehow got atween them an' the cave? We could do thet ef we put on the clothes these here is wearin' an' carried the carcasses up the trail while they wus down to the fire."

"I ain't int'rested in wearin' no dead man's clothes with holes an' blood on 'em!" I blurted out. Both men looked at me surprised then chuckled.

"Well if you hev a better idee, let's hear it," Drew replied.

"I'll think on it," I said, half mad.

Silent rubbed his chin. "D'yuh s'pose they have a sentinel sleepin' outside, now thet there's only two of 'em?"

"Dunnow . . . ef it wus, we might could sneak up on him an' then wait fer t'other t' come out," Drew replied.

"Ef we'uns could git atween him an' the cave, we could grab him as he went back, then we 'ould have t' lure t'other one out somehow."

"We need t' do it in the dark so's they couldn't see us."

"What if you two got atween him an' th' cave an' I came along th' path an' scared him into goin' fer th' cave?" I interjected.

Drew nodded. "Sounds good, we could

trip him up on the path an' dispose of him quiet-like."

"How we gonna git t'other un?"

"Dunnow, mebbe we could lure him out some ways."

"Ef we gits the first one, one o' us could wrap in his blanket an' sit by the fire. T'other one'd come down t' sit by him whin he wakes up," I suggested.

"Hev t' be someone who looks Injun an' 'bout the same size." Huz wus grinnin' at me.

"They's both Frenchmen," I shot back.

"Thet sounds good, but whut ef they both sleeps in the cave?" Drew asked with eyes narrowed. "We 'ould hev t' catch 'em both at the fire an' git atween them an' the cave."

"Got t' worry 'bout whur the wimmins is, too."

"Yuh think they 'ould hep us?"

"Doubt it, they won't know us frum Adam."

"If they's both in th' cave, we could lay a deer out by th' fire an' whin they seen it, they 'ould come down, bein' hungry an' all," I offered.

"Yeah, an' one o' us could be cookin' a steak an' thet 'ould lure 'em even more!" Drew brightened up.

"Yore alus wantin' a decoy, Drew, how

'bout you bein' it?" Huz wus chucklin'.

"Gimme thet pistol an' my sticker an' I *will,*" he shot back.

"So-o-o, we got two plans," I put in. "One if the guard sleeps outside an' one if they both sleeps in the cave?"

"Sounds 'bout right, let's go see whut the 'rangements is at the cave. We may hev t' come up with 'nother one," Drew answered.

Silent nodded an' without another word, shouldered his deer, picked up his rifle an' led off down the trail. Drew grunted an' followed. I covered the rear an' kept my rifle ready. It took most of an hour t' git back to the canyon. Huz left the trail an' climbed up to the rocks Drew an' I had hidden ahind. Lookin' at Drew's deer, he said, "Let's stash your'n sommers an' we'll use this smaller un fer our bait."

I clumb a white oak an' pulled the carcass up atter me. Layin' it across a couple o' limbs near the trunk, I tied a couple o' the legs to the limbs with leather strings. Whin I got down, Drew asked me, "Think you could climb the bluff an' spy on the camp frum there?"

I nodded an' started off. Drew grabbed my arm an' said, "We'll check out the trail to the cave an' meet back here in the crack whur we slept last night."

I nodded agin an' left. I started up the hill to the bench that led to the bluff. It wasn't long 'til I was shakin' an' tired. Not havin' anythin' to eat 'cept jerky for a couple o' days left me weaker'n a kitten. I slowed down an' whin I gets t' the top, I sat down fer a few minits. The sun wus gittin' low an' I hurried along the shelf o' rock well back out o' sight from the valley. It wasn't hard t' find the place where we cut the cedar limbs an' grabbin' a few that were still pretty green, I crawled out to the bluff.

At first I couldn't see anyone, the camp looked deserted, even the fire wus burnin' low. The slightest movement told me thet Silent an' Drew wus hidin' in the rocks by the trail, very near t' where the guard's hidin' place wus. I heard muffled voices comin' frum the cave an' the younger woman appeared with one o' the Frenchies close b'hind. They went toward the fire, the man givin' the woman a shove or two along the way. I could feel my pulse racin' in my temples an' my heart thumped so loud I thought it could be heard. "If you let that fire get this low again, I'll beat you 'til you can't stand," he growled through clenched teeth. I inched my rifle out a little.

The woman began gatherin' sticks and stokin' the fire up, while the man sat watchin' an' cursin' her. I began t' tremble an' the valley took on a reddish glow 'round the edges o' my vision. "Tell her I'll beat the old woman again if she doesn't get a move on." It wus the second man standin' in the mouth o' the cave.

Both of 'em were in my sight an' the captives were not in the way. Drew an' Silent couldn't see the man in the cave, but they could git atween the man at the fire an' the cave if they caught on t' whut I was about t' do. Slowly, I brought my rifle up an' aimed at the man in the mouth o' the cave. I held my breath a moment to make sure o' my aim. I couldn't afford t' miss. Then I slowly squeezed the trigger. The crack o' the gun bounced off the walls o' thet canyon an' roared like a cannon. Through the smoke, I saw the man throw up his arms an' fall backwards.

The man at the fire leaped up, lookin' first at whur I lay, then turnin' to look at the cave. It seemed that instantly the woman wus in motion an' with a scream o' rage swung a large stick o' wood with both hands at the remainin' bandit. He turned to her just in time to take the first blow full in the face, stumblin' back'ards an' fallin' as a second blow took him in the ribs. Instantly, she was astride his body an' usin' the stick like a tamp to beat the man's head agin an' agin.

I had seen frum the corner o' my eye that Huz an' Drew were on the move the instant I fired, but by the time they got to the fire, the fight wus over — or almost . . . the woman looked up as they approached an' with another scream, advanced toward them, the bloody stick raised t' strike.

I stood up an' called in Cherokee, "We're friends! We're friends! You are safe now and your husband is safe with us!"

Drew an' Huz hed been backin' away an' Huz set the butt o' his gun on the ground an' leaned on the barrel. Drew turned an' hurried to the cave. He stooped over the other bandit where he had fallen out o' sight, then advanced into the cave.

I called agin, loud as I could, "We are friends, you are safe." In a moment, the older woman came out clutchin' the baby in her arms. She hurried to where the younger woman had collapsed in a heap near the fire.

"Think ya kin come on down, now, Jerry, tell the wimmin I goin' t' git the deer an' not t' kill me whin I come back!" I could see his grin, then he turned an' went back down the trail.

I called to the women, "We have meat for

you. Your husband is safe at Flee's Settlement and all the bandits are dead. My friends cannot speak Cherokee, but you can talk to the Silent One in Osage. I will be down there in a moment."

Pretendin' I needed t' sit down to reload, I brought out my powder horn and reloaded. Truth wus, I couldn't hev stood another minit, my legs wus shakin' so. I took my time an' when the shakin' had slowed, I rose an' began my trip down the canyon. It took me half an hour or more t' git to the cave, an' I didn't hurry. The smell of roastin' meat met me down the canyon an' I felt so weak that I didn't know if I could make it to the camp.

I came out at the mouth o' the cave an' stood there a minit catchin' my breath. Lookin' toward the cave, I could see the feet of the man I had shot where he had fell b'hind the rocks. Down the hill, the women were preparin' a meal, while Huz an' Drew who wus bouncin' the baby on his knee watched. I remember walkin' down to the fire as carefully as I could, the strain o' the last few hours descendin' on my shoulders like a weight. I didn't think Silent or Drew knew I wus there until I sat down on a boulder b'hind them. Without even lookin' around, Huz said, "Battles shore wear yuh out, don't they, Jerry?"

The older woman brought me a cup of scaldin' hot coffee an' smiled a toothless smile. "Welcome to our camp, my son," she said in broken Cherokee.

"Thank you, Mother," I replied in the traditional greetin' of our people.

"My name is Zilkah and my son's wife is Morning Starr. My son is called White Wolf and we call the boy Little Chief," she said with a smile.

Morning Starr came to us and spoke to me, "You said he was at Flee's, is he well?"

"He was shot in two places and had lost a lot of blood, but th' women were takin' good care of him when we left. He told us about you bein' captive here, but didn't say what his name was."

She smiled and said, "We owe you our lives, it is something we can never repay. I must hurry to my husband. Can we leave soon?"

Speakin' to Drew and Silent, I said, "She wants to git to her husband as fast as possible."

"Tell her that we will leave as soon in the mornin' as they are ready. Wonder where their horses are?"

I relayed his reply to Morning Starr, "Do you have any horses?"

Huz spoke to the mother in Osage.

"Yes, the horses are penned up in a canyon down by the creek. I can get them tonight."

"There will be no need for them tonight, we can do that in the morning," I replied lookin' longingly at the steaks roastin' over the fire.

"Oh, you must be starved, I forgot about cooking. I'll have you a meal in no time." She hurried back to the fire.

"Jerry, the next time we go into war, you are goin' to *have* t' tell us whut plan three is afore yuh starts it." Drew still hadn't turned t' look at me, but his shoulders were shakin' with mirth.

"I just couldn't help myself, Drew, that sorry scoundrel pushin' the woman 'round like that made me fightin' mad."

"I should say it did!" Silent wus laughin' too. "I tole Drew t' git ready fer action whin I saw that rifle muzzle pokin' out'n the cedar. Shore glad yuh got the one in the cave . . ."

"An didn't miss 'im," Drew put in.

"We could of taken care o' the other one, but someone beat us to it." Huz chuckled out loud and Drew laughed so heartily the women looked up. Huz said somethin' in Osage an' they both smiled and resumed cookin'.

"By the way," I said, "where is th' other one?"

"Beat up so bad in the head we couldn't of eat lookin' at him, so we drug him off the hill," Drew replied.

The women approached with three steamin' hot steaks an' more coffee an' we set ourselves to the serious job o' eatin'. I finished my steak just as another was plopped on my plate. It wus gone in short order an' I had to refuse delivery of a third one Zilkah offered me, but the hot coffee wus welcome.

Drew leaned back an' rubbed his belly contentedly. "Best I've et in days, you fellers er gonna hev t' feed me better ef yuh 'spect me t' be goin' on many more wars with yuh," he said.

Huz grunted, "Nex time I goes with you, I'll hev t' git cotton for my tired ears."

Drew just grinned. "We need t' be seein' 'bout our horses, they'll hev et ever'thin' down to the dirt by now."

Silent nodded. "Be dark in a minit. One o' us could go back an' git 'em an' we could meet up on the ridge in the mornin'."

"We could take the trail down spring crick frum there," Drew added. "Whut's yore pleasure, Huz, wanna git the horses?"

"I could, I guess, with the wimmin here t'

wake yuh up in the mornin', we wouldn't be takin' the chance that you 'ould sleep through the day whiles we waited on the ridge fer yuh."

"Huh! Yuh'd think I wus the onlyest one t' sleep while the sun shines, but I seen you sleep 'til noon more'n onct!"

Huz chuckled and without another word, picked up his rifle an' blanket an' started down the trail.

"Well, boy." Drew sighed. "Thet feed set my mind t' nappin'. Think I'll check out the sleepin' 'comodations an' git some shut-eye. Yuh kin hev the first watch an' git me up whin the big dipper handle is stickin' straight up." He wandered up the hill to the cave.

The women had finished their meal an' were preparin' for the breakfast an' the deer fer travel tomorrow while the boy played around the fire an' chased minnows in the stream. He didn't seem to notice how cold the water wus. I sat on a rock by the fire an' watched.

"How did my husband get to the settlement?" Morning Starr asked.

I wus tellin' her how he wus layin' on the horse's back under a blanket an' how Silent an' me caught the horse an' discovered him. Our conversation wus slowed considerable while Morning Starr interpeted to her mother-in-law. "He was in pretty bad shape when we left, but the women were takin' good care of him and he was safe and warm." I didn't want t' be too incouragin' an' give them false hopes. Morning Starr was relayin' this to Zilkah whin Drew come bustin' out'n the cave kickin' a pile of blankets. With a grunt of disgust, he kicked them to one side. "Lousy," he spat.

Morning made a face. "Filthy Frenchmen." She shuddered in disgust.

Zilkah said somethin' an' spat on the ground. It wasn't hard t' figger their feelin's 'bout the outlaws. Although the Osages were more casual about their cleanliness, the Cherokee took care to keep theirselves clean, bathin' often an' wearin' clean clothes. Ma took a bath in the creek ever' day in the summer an' well into the fall days. She always made us clean up ever' day, an' the thought of vermin sent her into a tizzy.

"Tell our friend he may sleep near our beds where the lice don't come," Morning Starr said.

Drew nodded whin I told him an' bowed to the wimmin. "Thank you, but I would not disturb your sleepin', though I will find a place nearby out'n the wind."

The wimmin smiled an' nodded whin I relayed his message. Drew turned an' reentered the cave.

I found a good spot near the mouth o' the cave where I could watch the whole area an' made me a nest agin the rock wall. It must hev been too comfortable 'cause I had a whale of a time keepin' from noddin' off. Each time I looked at thet dipper handle, it seemed it hadn't moved a hair. My eyelids felt like they had lead weights on them an' I caught myself noddin' off a couple o' times. I knew I had t' git up an' move aroun' to keep from sleepin' on the job, but just couldn't git myself up fer it.

I jerked awake from a sound sleep. Little Chief wus snugglin' against my side an' we were both covered with another blanket.

"Rest, Jerry, I will watch for you," Morning Starr's voice came low from the other side of Little Chief. There was a little tug on the blanket an' I knew she wus sittin' close t' Little Chief, keepin' him warm on that side. The boy gave a sigh an' laid his head on my arm under the cover an' that's the last I knew of my watch.

Suddenly there came a long high-pitched sing-song cry from down in the valley. I found myself standin' in the early dawn, rifle in hand searchin' for the unseen source of that cry.

"It is only Zilkah singin' her Dawn Chant," Morning Starr whispered. "All is well."

My heart wus thumpin' so loud I could feel each beat an' I wus a little shaky frum wakin' thet sudden, so I sat back down, careful not t' sit on the boy who had laid over my spot whin I jumped up. Zilkah's song continued on an' on. We sat there listenin' to that sad, eerie, bittersweet song. At last it trailed off into silence an' we sat as in a spell rememberin' those hauntin' notes. It was the first of many times I have heard the Dawn Chant an' I have never forgotten it. Even now though far away from the Osage, I can hear it in the mornin' light. I miss it an' I dread it. I cain't describe it.

" 'Bout time I took over the watch, ain't it Jerry?" Drew wus standin' by the mouth o' the cave grinnin' at me.

"Might be if you was to take the day shift. I reckon Morning Starr took the bulk of the night shift."

The lump under the blanket that wus Little Chief stirred and a small hand grasped the edge o' the blanket an' jerked it down, showin' his tousled head an' mischievious dark eyes. He grinned at his ma an' said,

"Me hungry, Mother."

"We will eat soon, my Little Chief," she replied and moved toward the fire where Zilkah was already stirrin' around and cookin'.

Drew came down an' sat on a boulder nearby.

"What should we do about all these bodies layin' 'round?" I asked.

"Twas up t' me, I'd be tempted t' let them lay where they are an' rot, but it'd spoil the use o' the cave for ever'body, I s'pose we need t' haul them off sommers."

"Maybe we could take them down th' valley an' put them under th' brush pile with Silent's two," I replied.

"An' while we're about it, I suppose you're gonna want t' have a proper buryin' for those two on Punkin Creek." Drew grinned.

"Shouldn't leave things undone, an' ever'body deserves buryin' — well most ever'body."

"I s'pose yore right, Jerry. B'sides ef some o' those scamps' friends finds them layin' out like thet, they mought take exception t' it an' seek revenge on someone. The settlement air too close t' ignore an' Lord knows we got 'nough troubles without invitin' more!"

"We could git th' horses an' carry them away while th' wimmin pack up. Morning Starr, how far away are th' horses?" I called.

She looked up from the fire. "They are two washes over, down the creek," she replied, then with a smile, "You could have them here before we eat if you hurry."

"How many are there?"

"They had three after White Wolf took one."

I relayed this to Drew, and he said, "Tell 'er we'll skin on down there an' git 'em afore breakfast, an' ask her where the halters is."

"They hung them high in a cherry tree on the trail down the hill there," Morning replied to my question.

Drew an' I hurried off t' retrieve the harness an' the horses.

Goin' down the creek, Drew pointed out the trail up the first wash. "Thet's the trail to the ridge whur Huz'll meet us." The second wash was really a small valley that we westerners would call a box canyon. There was a brush fence across the mouth an' we could see three Injun ponies grazin' by the little branch thet trickled down. It took us some time t' catch them since we were strangers an' they wus not used t' white men's smell. "No use t' try ridin' . . .

these critters lessen you . . . wants t' break one o' them," Drew said as he struggled t' calm the horse he wus holdin'.

I finally got the horse I had caught calmed enough t' lead, an' then the third horse nickered an' walked right up to Drew an' his horse! "I'll be switched," he said. "Why didn't we cotch him up first?"

"Dunno, but git that halter on him quick 'fore he changes his mind!" I called.

I could open the gap just enough t' let one horse at a time through, then tied my horse to a tree an' helped Drew git the other two through. "I suppose we should close the gap, Jerry, an' let the grass grow fer the next ones t' use."

Except for horse orneriness, the trip back to the cave was uneventful an' we stepped up our pace when we got a whiff o' what was cookin'. Little Chief was already eatin' from a bowl of stew. He looked up an' grinned mischievously at us as we approached. By the time the horses were tied up, there were two steamin' bowls of the finest venison stew waitin' on us. Even after the steaks the night before, I was still hungry an' it didn't take me long t' git around thet stew an' another bowl, too.

Drew sighed an' wiped his mouth on his sleeve. "Thet wus deelushous." He grinned at the wimmin. Zilkah offered him a third bowl, but he declined. "Tell the wimmin we got some chores t' do while they pack an' we'll be back soon's we're done."

Morning Starr nodded an' Drew picked the tamest horse an' led the way down the bank to where one of the men wus layin'. I almost retched when I saw his bashed-in face. It would've been hard t' imagine a face was ever there. It took us some time t' git the body over the pony's back an' even then he didn't like it at all. The second body up by the cave wasn't much easier, but we got him loaded. It didn't take us near as long t' find the old dead treetop where Silent had hidden, but it was hard gittin' the horse to it, the hill was so steep. We laid out the two next to their partners an' piled more brush on them.

"Won't keep the critters out, but it'll make it hard fer them t' drag one off." Drew rubbed his hands on a clump of grass. Turnin' down the hill, he called back, "Better hurry, Jerry, the parson's already waitin' at the cemetery."

The other two bodies were layin' where we had left them. They were untouched but there were wolf tracks around them. "Damned scavengin' wolves," Drew muttered. A half dozen buzzards hung in the trees an' flapped their wings at us as if scoldin' us fer disturbin' their feast.

The gulley I had crawled down was pretty deep further up the hill, so we dragged the bodies up there an' rolled them off the bank an' caved as much of it off on them as we could.

"Parson, thet wus a right nice ser'mony said over these two scalawags, even if they didn't desarve it," Drew said as he shook the imaginary parson's imaginary hand. "Now me an' Jerry hev t' be gittin' on, thur's a lot t' do t'day an' we're gittin' a late start!" he called over his shoulder as he grabbed the lead and started down the hill in long strides.

To our surpise, we met the wimmin at the foot of the cave canyon. They had packs on both ponies, and Little Chief was perched atop one of them holdin' on to a rope an' grinnin'. They had even retrieved the second deer from the tree an' packed it on.

"Good work, let's go!" Drew called, not breakin' stride an' movin' on down the trail.

"Gooderkessgo!" Little Chief echoed, his heels beatin' agin the pack. The wimmin laughed as they fell in b'hind Drew. I pulled drag. We were soon puffin' up the draw an' Drew was 'way ahead 'til he looked back an' seen the wimmin strugglin' t' keep up.

"Sorry, ladies," he called as they neared. "We'll rest a minit here an' let you ketch yore breath." Morning Starr nodded an' relayed the message t' Zilkah whin I told her.

After a few minits, Drew started off at a slower pace an' they kept up the rest o' the way up. Huz was sittin' next to a small fire nursin' a cup o' coffee whin we got out on top o' the ridge. "Wipe yore feet at the door an' come on in, the coffee's hot," he said as we walked up. It didn't take us long t' empty the pot an' Morning Starr dug around in one of the packs for a snack for Little Chief. She plopped him atop his pack an' started stowin' the coffeepot an' cups.

"Guess she's anxious t' git." Huz grinned. "Best we move along er git left." He said somethin' to Zilkah and she spread a blanket over his saddle and climbed on. I gave Morning Starr my horse an' she was soon astraddle. It wus the practical way t' ride a horse, but the first time I had seen a woman ride that-a-way. Even Lydia had rode sidesaddle.

"Better mount up, Drew," Huz called, "it's gonna take some herdin', t' keep them wimmin frum stampedin' an' killin' them horses!" He led the way down the ridge in long strides an' I wus left on drag agin.

Our trail follered the ridge fer several miles until the ground sloped off gently to the creek. We follered the creek a ways, then crossed it an' cut over the hill straight to'ards Flee's. Toppin' the hill, we could see Eagle Mountain above Flee's three or four miles away. Zilkah began chatterin' somethin' an' Huz called to Drew, "Better take these wimmin on afore we hev a runnaway. Ef them two go roarin' into the settlement alone, they might think they wus bein' attacked by a herd o' crazed squaws!"

Drew nodded an' broke into a canter, the wimmin followin', leavin' Little Chief squallin' an' beatin' the packs with his heels.

"It's okay, Little Chief," I called. "We'll have t' git th' packhorses in."

Huz fished in his pocket an' handed him a chunk o' jerky and he quietened down. "Thet yowlin' prob'ly skairt the game fer miles around," he fussed. "Hev t' go five miles, now, jist t' find sign."

The rest of the trip in was uneventful an' we pulled in to the settlement just as the last light of day faded. All seemed quiet. Lights shone dimly from the cabins an' I saw a pipe glow as someone drew on it by Rice's door. Silent gave a wave an' without a word moved on toward his cabin. Little Chief an' I pulled up to the door as Lonza rose to meet us. Takin' the sleepy boy down, I carried him to the door an' his grandmother took him there.

Lonza wus already loosenin' the packs an' layin' them by the door. We took the deer an' hung him up from the ridge pole. "Cold enough to freeze it solid by mornin'," Lonza muttered. "How was your trip, Jerry?"

"It wus good," I replied. "How's White Wolf?"

"He is gainin', but very slowly," Lonza said an' I gathered that he wasn't doin' all that well by his reply. "Mayhap he will show more improvement with his family here."

We led the horses into the cedars with the other horses an' there wus a lot o' snortin' goin' on when we left.

"Tell me what happened, Jerry," Lonza asked, so I told him what we did while we were gone. When I had finished, Lonza took a couple of pulls on his pipe an' nodded. "You did well, sounds like. Aren't you glad you had the pistol with you?"

"Shore am, an' I'll be buyin' one th' first chance I git!"

"They're good in a tight spot or close quarters, but give me a rifle for accuracy any day," Lonza replied. "I suppose we will be leavin' here in a day or two, weather permittin', and make the last leg home. Have you and Ruth talked about what you are goin' to do?"

"No, I guess we just assumed to see you through to your home, then decide somethin'. Prob'ly build a cabin an' do a little farmin' an' huntin'."

"You'll be welcome to stay with us until spring and you can get settled on your own. Lydia could use the help, with the new baby comin' and keepin' the house together."

"Thank you, Lonza, we'll be glad to help, but we shore don't want t' be in the way."

The cabin door opened a crack an' Ruthie stuck her head out. "Jerry, are you there? I have some supper ready for you, wash up and come on in."

"By gosh, I forgot all about you might be hungry," Lonza exclaimed.

She just reminded me how hungry I was, not gittin' the chance t' eat much on the trail. They had fixed a washstand by the door an' I washed my face an' hands in icy cold water an' rubbed dry on the cloth hangin' there. It seemed awful hot an' stuffy in the little cabin after the last few days in the open an' I wus shure t' sleep outside t'night with all that crowd in there.

Jesse an' Riley both came runnin' to me, jabberin' an' tuggin' at my sleeve 'til I had t' git down an' wrestle both of them on the floor. Little Chief sat on the end of his father's bed an' watched solemnly. Morning Starr an' Zilkah were sittin' by the bed with White Wolf, both lookin' relieved but concerned at the same time. As I stepped over t' speak t' White Wolf, Morning Starr said somethin' softly to him, and he opened his eyes. He was still very pale an' weak, but his eyes were bright an' alert. Lookin' straight into my eyes he said somethin' in Osage. "He says thank you for savin' his life and bringin' his family to him. He owes you much," Morning Starr interpreted.

That was very embarrassin' to me an' my face felt awful hot. "Tell him Drew an' Huzkiah did th' most an' I wus just along to help."

Morning Starr explained to White Wolf, then said to me rather firmly, "I know the part you played and it was *not* small. Things could have been much different if you had not done what you did. Your bravery saved our lives and we will never forget that!" Zilkah was sayin' somethin' I couldn't understand an' shakin' my arm emphatically.

Ruth was by my side with a steamin' bowl of stew an' a big cup of coffee. She leaned against me gently and said, "Here's some supper, Jerry, I'm so glad you are back." Her eyes were bright an' a little misty. I

340

grinned an' hugged her tight, food an' all. Sittin' cross-legged on the floor with two boys hoverin' over or climbin' on my back, I tried t' eat without spillin' anythin'. The bowl wus only half empty when Ruthie ladled it full agin. I wasn't unhappy about that, I can say! As I finished, she handed me the end o' a loaf of hot bread an' a big spoon of butter. She laughed at my surprise, "Yes, that's real butter an' there's plenty of it, thanks to Mrs. Moss and her cow!"

Little Chief bumped into my shoulder. "Bite," he said while Riley an' Jesse clamored for a bite too. I laughed an' we all four sat an' ate bread an' butter 'til it wus all gone. The three boys wandered off to a corner by the fire an' were soon playin' a game.

Lydia was sittin' by the fire sewin' on somethin' for the baby and smiled. "We're so glad you are back, Jerry — and safe!" she added. She looked much more rested than when I last saw her, even though I knew she had been busy helpin' nurse their patient.

Things began to quieten down and Ruth laid the pallet out for Jesse an' Riley. Little Chief had already curled up on the bed in the crook of White Wolf's knees an' was sound asleep. Zilkah brought in a pack from outside an' began makin' a pallet for her and Morning Starr. I was pickin' up my blanket an' openin' the door when Zilkah called somethin' to me. Hurryin' over, she gently pushed me out the door an' led me to the lee side o' the cabin where she had laid out a buffalo robe an' blanket. Pokin' my chest, she said with a strange accent, "Your bed," in Cherokee.

I nodded, sayin', "Thank you, Mother," and she hurried off.

Sittin' on the edge of the robe, I pulled off my moccasins an' stockings. Just before I swung into the bed, I sniffed my shirt an' decided I couldn't sleep with it another night. I stripped it off, covered up an' slipped off my pants. Rolled up in the blanket, I folded the robe over an' pulled it over my head. My hand brushed the coonskin cap. Had I been wearin' it all this time? I'll have t' give it t' Jesse tomorrow, I thought . . . an' drifted off into the best sleep I'd had in days.

Along about daylight I heard a whisper of sound, but when I poked my head out, all was quiet an' I drifted back t' sleep. The next thing I knew was when the cabin door was thrown open an' a clutter of giggles an' shushes pattered around the corner. I lay very still until three boys pounced on me yellin' an' screamin' an' bouncin'. Pretend-

342

in' to be startled, I retaliated and we wrestled around a few minutes. "Time t' git up, Jerry, breakfast is ready," Jesse yelled.

"All right, you rascals, I'm gonna throw all three of you in the creek!" That sent them yellin' for the house an' I rolled over an' reached for my pants an' shirt — which were nowhere in sight! Diggin' through the covers was fruitless an' I was about t' wrap myself in a blanket an' go in when I heard the door again an' Ruthie came around the corner carryin' a stack o' clean clothes an' laughin'. "Zilkah took your things to wash and forgot to bring you any clean clothes. We were wonderin' where you were when she remembered. Hurry up if you want anything, those boys are eatin' us out of the house."

I tried to look put out, but couldn't help grinnin'. "Wonder what they would have done if I had come in there in my birthday suit?"

"You know you wouldn't dare!"

I laughed an' got dressed under the covers after she left. It was goin' t' be a good day, I could tell. Pickin' up my bed an' the cap, I headed to breakfast.

[This is a good time to remind the reader of the differences between the ways children were raised in the two cultures. The early

nineteenth-century Anglo child was instructed and expected to be "seen and not heard." They grew up under strict rules of behavior — and severe punishment for noncompliance, called disobedience by the adult population. Under this system, the child remained a child well into his teenage years, not being considered adult until late teens or early twenties.

By contrast, Native children (and Anglo children of the frontier) were raised in an atmosphere of loving permissiveness where they were allowed the freedom to do what they pleased — up to a certain point. They were allowed to explore their world under the watchful eyes of all adults around them. In this way, for instance, they learned by experience that fire burned and was something to avoid. They interacted freely with the adults in their world and in general all adults nurtured them lovingly. Their discipline was gentle but firm and transition from children to adults began early. They became meaningful contributors to their society much younger than the Anglo child of the eastern States.

In today's world, the child is raised much as the Native child of old and we sometimes fail to recognize the stark differences between the two past cultures. — J.D.]

CHAPTER 20
DENNISON BOTTOMS
FEBRUARY 1812

It seemed like between the weather an' waitin' for White Wolf t' heal enough t' travel, we would never get back on the trail. Lonza and Morning Starr convinced White Wolf that he could not work the trappin' season and they decided to sell out their supplies, much to the pleasure of the settlers.

Wolf did purty good in the sale. There wern't much barganin' t' do, the settlement wus in such need t' buy the goods they mostly paid his prices. By late afternoon, he had some silver, a pile of purty decent furs, a horse an' a mule an' all the supplies were gone. Morning Starr an' Zilkah were busy sortin' an' storin' the goods an' Wolf sat by the door an' rested.

At supper, Lonza said, "It looks like the weather will moderate for a few days. Do you think we can be packed and on the trail by day after tomorrow?" There was silence for a moment while that soaked in, then the women looked at each other an' slowly began t' shake their heads "no" while White Wolf an' I nodded "yes" an' the boys danced 'round the table.

Lydia spoke up for the women. "There's just too much to do to get done in one day, Lonza, even though we have kept the gear mostly ready to move, we couldn't get everything done and the cabin cleaned by then. If we had two days, we could be ready to move on the third day."

Lonza frowned. "You're sure we couldn't possibly get ready in one day's work?"

"No," said Lydia, fortified with three female shakin' heads.

"We can try, Lonza," Ruth spoke up, "but there is just so much we can get done in that time. In addition, Morning Starr and Zilkah have a lot of things from the sale to pack."

Reluctantly, Lonza agreed. "But," he said, "we are workin' against time and the spring rains. If we don't get on the trail now, we will probably find ourselves livin' here until May." He was lookin' meaningfully at Lydia, who shook her head.

"We'll be ready the morning of the third day, rain or shine," she vowed.

"Very well, let's get a good night's rest

and an' early start in the morning!"

Mornin' began earlier than usual with all bustle and hurry that lasted until after dark. My first chore was to build a fire under the washtub an' haul water. After that, I wus ever'one's errand boy until after noon whin I sneaked off to see to the horses — an git a little peace and quiet.

They weren't in the cedar thicket, but their trail was plain an' I follered it down into the Dennison Bottoms where White Wolf had taken them to graze. He was sittin' under a cedar tree hidden by the branches an' still as death. The wavin' of a branch agin the wind told me where he wus. Somethin' wus up an' I pretended not to notice his location, but concentrated on the horses while lookin' around for whatever wus botherin' Wolf.

Nothin' stirred other than the horses contentedly grazin'. Walkin' in among them, I checked their hobbles, then hazed them over toward the trail so that they were between Wolf an' the settlement. That way if anythin' happened, he could drive them up the trail quickly. Then actin' casual-like, I moseyed back up the trail toward the cabins. When I was out of sight o' the bottoms, I ducked off to the left an' circled back through the brush to the edge of the clearin'. I tied some branches around my head like Huz an' Drew had showed me an' crawled under a cedar that had limbs draggin' the ground. Now, Wolf was hid on one side o' the trail an' I wus on t'other with the horses in b'tween.

Bellied down under that itchy cedar tree where I could see the whole bottoms an' startin' close an' slowly workin' out in circles from there, I searched the whole bottoms for somethin' that was not normal that would be botherin' White Wolf. I couldn't see anythin' out o' the ordinary. Thinkin' that maybe he was watchin' somethin' down by the river, I scanned the tree line there, memorizin' jist whur ever'thin' was. Still nothin' looked out of place. The other side o' the river was quiet an' I was in a quandry as to whut Wolf was watchin', so I started surveyin' the ground over agin.

Nothin' out of place close in, nothin' out a little further. Then on my third sweep, somethin' gave me pause, but I couldn't put my finger on whut it wus. Studyin' the trees that straggled out on the bottoms from the woods, I could have sworn that somethin' had changed. I couldn't see a thing but scattered bushes an' a few cedars here an' there, still I could swear there wus somethin' wrong with the view.

Somethin' Jake said about beelinin' made me think, so I set me up two sight line sticks, linin' them up on two o' the trees standin' out from the woods. By concentratin' on the area in b'tween, I set the lay o' the land in my mind, then continued my scan o' the rest of the bottoms. Nothin' was out of place there, so I went back to watchin' the area b'tween the sticks — an somethin' had changed! Whut was it? My eye had caught the change, but my head couldn't figger out jist whut it wus. I knowed nothin' wus wrong with the area on the left side of the view — leastwise, I didn't *think* so. I drove another stick by linin' on one o' the cedars at the edge of the woods dividin' the whole area in two. Agin, I studied the area either side of the new stick 'til it was fixed in mind, then I deliberately looked away an' studied the whole bottoms agin. Slowly, I scanned back to the sight line — an almost jumped. Somethin' had changed! The scene wus different, different, different, but whut was it?

With only one stick for a sight, the movement of my head might cause the sight to be changed, so I set up another stick linin' up the two sticks with the cedar tree. Agin I looked away an' it wus the hardest thing t' keep frum peekin' back along thet line, but I held away for a few minutes. When I looked back, sure 'nough, somethin' had changed.

Suddenly, I jumped. I knowed what had happened: *one o' those cedar trees hed moved!* No! I said to myself, trees cain't walk, I must be crazy, so I set another line of sight to another cedar tree. This time, I jist laid my head on my arm an' closed my eyes. My head wus near spinnin'. If trees cain't walk, then someone must be movin' it. They must be atter the horses.

After a minit or two, I looked up an' shore 'nough one of the little cedars b'tween my two sightline trees hed moved, so now I set my sights on it, then I lined up another set o' sights, my *rifle* sights.

So that was whut White Wolf wus watchin'! I chuckled. No tellin' how long this had been goin' on — th' tree watchin' the horses an' the Wolf watchin' the tree. Well, it was the Wolf's game, so I'll jist watch an' back him up if need be. Then the thought struck me, what if there are *two* or even more trees with feet? Quickly, I scanned the bottoms agin, but nothin' seemed to have changed. Still, I set me up some other sight lines dividin' the area before me into segments so's

I could detect any other movement.

We must hev set there an hour or more, me an' White Wolf watchin' the tree an' the tree tryin' t' git closer to the horses. It must hev been frustratin' for the tree, 'cause the horses kept grazin' up the hill toward the trail an' away from the tree, so thet he wasn't gainin' much ground on 'em.

A movement to my right caught my eye an' I looked to see someone comin' out o' the woods by the river. He had a deer slung over his shoulders an' was headin' for the point where the trail to the settlement entered the woods. His head was bent down an' I wasn't familiar with his walk, so I thought it must have been Ben Witt or Obed Martin. I could tell that he would come within twenty or thirty yards of the walkin' tree an' I wondered what Wolf was gonna do. I couldn't see any movement from Wolf, an' Obed, as it turned out to be, kept on comin', his head down an' not lookin' much left or right.

I sighted the cedar tree an' waited as Obed came closer and closer: fifty yards, forty yards, thirty yards. Slowly, a cranked bow emerged from the tree with the arrer aimed at Obed. I started squeezin' down on the trigger an' was almost to the point of firin' when the crack o' White Wolf's rifle made me jump. Within an instant of time, White Wolf shot, my shot went wild, an' the arrer was loosed from the tree. The horses bolted up the trail for the settlement.

Through the smoke, I could see Obed slam into the ground an' the tree began to slowly topple over. Two bare legs appeared at its base and as the tree fell, it was like a body came slidin' out the bottom of it. I was up an' runnin', my gun in one hand an' my knife in the other. Obed lay still an' I saw the shaft of the arrer stickin' out of the deer's carcass still wrapped around his shoulders. One look at the tree man told me he was down an' out an' no threat, so I continued to Obed.

Carefully, I pulled back the deer carcass until I could see that the arrow hadn't stuck into Obed, then I pulled it off'n him. There was a split in his head just above an' behind his right ear an' when I moved the deer it began tricklin' blood. I rolled him over on his back an' he gave a sigh that made me feel a whole lot better.

"He not dead?" The question in broken Cherokee came from White Wolf as he leaned over my shoulder.

"No, White Wolf, but it was a close call," I replied. He looked at the deer an' feelin' the carcass where the point was, grunted. I put my hand on the spot an' felt the arrer head pressin' agin the hide. It hadn't come through, but must have had enough power t' hit Obed hard enough t' knock him down. Obed gave another groan an' we knew he was okay.

I went to the tree an' looked at the man layin' there. Save for the breechclout, he was naked as the day he was borned, but he was a whole lot dirtier an' smellier too. His hair was one solid mat an' lousy. An' ugly welt had plowed away the hair down the side of his head an' it trickled a little blood. He was breathin' an' it looked like he would be okay except for a bad headache.

A call came from up the trail an' I looked up t' see Huzkiah stridin' down the hill, his rifle unsheathed. "What's goin' on, Jerry? I heard shots an' those horses came stamped-in' through as fast as the hobbles'd let 'em. Thought I better come see if you needed a hand in somethin'."

White Wolf began talkin' to Huz in Osage an' I could only catch a word or two. They conversed as Huz leaned over to look at the man from the tree. "Why that's a durned Digger from the flats!" he exclaimed, with a big grin on his face.

"Digger, what's that?" I asked as Huz an' White Wolf talked.

"I guess you might say a Digger's a Injun gone wild, Jerry. They live mostly in the flatlands an' swamps whur most self-respectin' Injuns *or* white men wouldn't be found. They makes their livin' diggin' roots an' 'possums out'n the mud an' are mostly too lazy t' do much more'n git by. Lookin' at the tree an' the horses, I would guess he was atter a horse, not t' ride in the bottom bresh, but t' eat." He laughed. "Bein' tame, they're easier t' catch than deer or elk."

Another groan from Obed made us look up an' he was sittin' up an' rubbin' his head. Wincin', he pulled his hand away an' looked at the blood on his fingers. "Whut happen, did someone shoot me?" he asked lookin' at us curiously.

"Not hardly, but they did git yore deer," I replied, pointin' to the shaft stickin' out o' the carcass. "It nearly got t' you, too."

"Is that a Digger? Did he shoot me?"

"It wus either him or this here tree that flung the arrer," Huz replied. "We wus jist tryin' t' determine thet." Huz said somethin' to Wolf an' they both chuckled.

"White Wolf shot the tree an' hit the Digger hidin' in this tree an' spoiled his aim, or you would have the arrer in you an' he would have been skitterin' off t' the swamps with yore deer," I said. "Are you feelin' okay?"

"As well as possible, wakin' up an' seein' my friends an' neighbors doctorin' on a murderin' Digger whilst I lay dyin'!" he shot back as he gingerly mopped his head with a rag.

"We knowed you uz okay seein' you wus jist hit in the head," Huz replied. "This here Digger looks to be okay, too, 'cept he's mighty ganted. A good bait o' venison would perk him up plenty, I 'magine. What say we cut him off a front haunch o' that deer an' leave it fer him? I don't think we 'ould be too welcome draggin' his stinkin' body in to the settlement an' he'd jist bolt an' run if he found hisself there."

"*Then* he'd be right back tryin' t' steal horse meat th' next night," I put in.

Obed muttered somethin' under his breath, then said, "Okay, but don't do much damage t' the hide, I needs it most es much es the meat."

Quickly, Huz cut off a front quarter of the deer while White Wolf and I helped Obed up an' started him toward the cabins. Huz was chatterin' Osage t' Wolf, tellin' him whut we wus sayin', an' he wus noddin' an' grinnin' as he worked. I took the rifles while he pulled Obed's arm across his shoulders an' helped him take a few steps up the hill.

I heard an unfamiliar grunt behind and turned to see that Huz had plopped the quarter on the Digger's chest. He said a few words in a language I couldn't recognize, then shouldered the deer carcass an' follered us. "Told him we ate Diggers up here, but liked deer better, but if he wus still hangin' 'round tomorrer, we might just bile him alive in a big pot. Won't see his lazy rear end 'round here fer a good while, I bet."

White Wolf must hev understood the other language, for he was already laughin' afore Huz explained hisself to us. After a ways, Obed said he felt better an' could make it on his own, so Wolf turned loose an' let him walk.

"Betchyu'll be chewin' willer bark fer a couple o' days 'ith thet knot on the side o' yore head," Huz said.

"How'd I git thet, enyway?" Obed asked.

"We figger Wolf's shot spoilt the Digger's aim an' the deer carcass took most o' the force o' the arrer, but it hit yore head a purty good blow anyway," I said. I didn't mention my shot goin' wild.

Layin' the carcass down, Huz grasped the arrer shaft an' pushed it agin the skin feelin' the point. "Don't make a lot o' sense, seein' the deer hide ain't broke an' there don't feel like the arrer has a pint on it," he mused.

"Don't poke thet arrer through the hide, I needs it es whole es I kin git it," Obed worried.

"Don't feel no point on thet arrer. S'posin' he wus shootin' a stunner?"

White Wolf was lookin' at the entry wound an' said somethin' to Huz. It wus frustratin' not understandin' Wolf an' I determined t' learn more Osage.

"Well, it *does* look like a clean cut, don't it?" Huz said. "Somethin' must hev dulled the point goin' through the deer." With a gentle pull, he removed the arrer from the deer and held it up fer us t' see.

"Dern if it ain't a metal point," Obed exclaimed.

Huz turned it around and around, lookin' at it. "Must hev hit a bone er somethin' t' roll the point back like thet. Whin it hit yore head, it wus dull es a hammer."

"Wish I had looked at thet bow he had, it must hev been somethin' powerful t' go through that carcass an' still sting Obed like that," I mused.

"Ye shore got thet right, Jerry, ef thet arrer hed kept its p'int, I'd be wearin' it now."

"Ye'd hev two places t' hang yore hat." Huz grinned.

"Go on wi' yuh, Huz Hall, someday we'll hev a contest an' find out jist which one o' us has the hardest head!"

Huz chuckled, hoisted the deer on his shoulder an' led the way up the hill to Obed's cabin. We hung the deer high in a tree out of reach o' the dogs an' wolves while Obed sharpened his skinner. Standin' on an upturned log, he began dressin' the deer. He separated the heart, liver an' kidneys an' laid them aside. The dogs circled like vultures whinin' an' growlin' at each other an' Obed tossed them pieces of the offal t' fight an' growl over. "Wouldn't hev t' climb t' the sky t' skin ef it weren't fer the dern dogs," he grumbled, "always hungry! Here's the liver, Wolf, ye needs it t' restore yore blood worser 'an I do. Jerry, would ya take this here kidney to Calidonia on yer way home? She loves t' make kidney pie an' I don't care a durn fer it."

Huz started away toward home an' Obed called after him, "Huz, d'yuh need a steak er two fer supper?"

"No thankee, I got plenty fer now, Obed."

"Never seen thet man 'thout meat, though oncet er twice I couldda swore it were skunk," Obed said quietly.

"I ain't never et skunk in my life, Obed, an' yuh knows it!" Huz never broke stride.

"Got ears like a wolf, too." Obed grinned.

Huz called somethin' to Wolf and he laughed out loud.

"Now don't you go slanderin' me in 'nother language, Huz, be man e-nough t' say it outright!" Obed called, but Huz just kept on walkin'.

We could see Lonza tendin' the horses an' we said our goodbyes an' hurried t' help. Wolf took the liver on to the cabin while I dropped off the kidneys to Mrs. Witt. She wus pleased t' git it.

"Hev ye ever had kidney pie, Jerry?"

"No ma-am, I ain't."

"Well come by after supper an' I have a big helpin' fer ye."

"Yes mum." But I wasn't too sure 'bout that!

We tethered the horses close to the cabin that night near where I slept an' I tied Sippie on a long rope next to me. I heard him up sniffin' several times, but the horses wus quiet an' he never growled. When I woke, he was snuggled up on my robe. Later, Huz came by an' said he had tracked the Digger leavin' the country fer the lowlands.

The wimmin wus right about the time it 'ould take t' git ready for the road, but by sundown, all was done an' we looked forward to an early start.

CHAPTER 21
FALLEN ASH TRAIL
FEBRUARY, MARCH, 1812

It's uncertain when the trail up the White River was named. Indeed it had several names over its lifetime, Fallen Ash probably being the earliest we know about. It was used by the Osages for their hunting forays into the Ozark Mountains, though probably it existed long before they moved into the region. Later, it was known as the Fallen Ash Military Road and ran from the Mississippi River north of the mouth of the Saint Francis northwest through Flee's Settlement, Carrollton, Fayetteville and Cane Hill to Fort Smith. A portion of the trail was one of the several Trails of Tears of the Cherokee in later years. I am here using the name Zenas used in retelling the story told by his Uncle Jerry. — J.D.

For days and days, Lonza and White Wolf discussed the best ways and routes t' get to their destinations — Lonza to his home on Little Red River, an' Wolf to his home on

the White River — he called it Ni-U-Skah
— at Swan Creek. Lonza would go directly
to Little Red from Flee's. But, for consideration of Lydia's condition, he was reluctantly inclined t' take the Fallen Ash Trail
northwest a ways to Syllamo's, an easier
trail into the Little Red River country. It
was longer but would be easier on Lydia.
White Wolf would use the Fallen Ash all the
way to Swan Creek. For hours at a time,
they sat drawin' maps in the dirt an' dis-
cussin' the country b'tween the White an'
Little Reds, talkin' mostly by sign language.
Ever' once in a while they would hit a stump
an' call Morning Starr out t' interpret. All
of us worked on learnin' t'other language
an' we could mostly git along purty well.

The men of the settlement often sat in on
these discussions, addin' their knowledge to
the map an' learnin' from the others. Obed
Martin's chance remark one day that a
certain Cherokee clan had moved up the
Flee's Settlement trail to Beech Creek
caused Lonza to give up all hope of takin'
the direct trail to Little Red. It seems his
wife's family had a dispute with this clan
an' a feud was brewin' b'tween 'em.

So it wus that in the last week o' February 1812, we rose well b'fore daylight an'
loaded up an' by the time the sun was an

hour high were on our way up the Fallen Ash Trail. Lonza an' White Wolf led with the rest of us strung out b'hind, me bringin' up the rear right b'hind Riley an' Jesse in their panniers.

Little Chief was ridin' with Morning Starr an' fussed so much that when we stopped t' tighten the packs after an hour on the trail, she plopped him on the back of the mule b'tween Riley an' Jesse. Three happier, chatterin' boys an' a more patient mule couldn't hev been found in a hunnert miles. From that time on until we parted company, that's how the boys traveled, each one takin' turns astraddle the mule.

The trail crossed over the hills, cuttin' off a big bend in the river an' comin' back to the river at Pumpkin Creek 'bout twelve t' fourteen miles from Flee's. We nooned there an' from then on, the trail follered the bottoms, the hills steep an' comin' right down to the river most o' the way. Another ten miles brought us to the bottoms o' Rocky Bayou where we stopped for the night, not wantin' t' press the livestock too much 'til they were trail hardened.

Wolf an' I staked the horses on the grass and Lonza kindled a fire while Sippie an' the boys romped up the creek banks. I looked up in time t' see Little Chief push

Riley into the water. He was laughin' at Riley's splutterin' 'til Jesse pushed him over the bank. With the two o' them splashin' an' hollerin' in the cold water, Jesse hesitated a minnit then jumped in himself. I hollered at Sippie just b'fore he leaped in amongst them, savin' him from a dousin'. Three boys came sputterin' an' splashin' out o' the water, laughin', squealin', shivverin' an' turnin' blue about the gills. Sippie met them at the bank, bouncin' an' yappin'.

Straight to the fire they ran only t' be intercepted by two mothers an' a granny. In a trice they were stripped an' wrapped in blankets, sittin' on a log like three roostin' birds while four tongues wagged furiously at them. It took the men longer than usual to do their chores an' git enough control o' their laughin' to look serious when we got back to the fire.

"You boys had your baths already?" Lonza asked, then had to turn his back t' hide his grin.

"He pushed me," came in two language unison from Riley an' Little Chief, fingers pointin' to the respective guilty parties.

"Yes, an' then *he* jumped in on his own!" Ruthie said shakin' a spoon at Jesse.

Three sheepish boys looked at us with

heavy eyes an' they soon had steamin' plates o' beans an' meat, while Ruth an' Morning Starr quickly made their pallet. Little Chief nodded off b'fore finishin', an' his plate clattered to the ground. Zilkah caught him an' gently laid him in the bed, to be follered soon after by two more sleepyheads, Sippie contentedly layin' at their feet.

Soon, we were all sittin' around the fire eatin'. Seein' the steam risin' from the dryin' clothes, Ruthie began to laugh, "No one there to push him in, so he had to jump!" She began to laugh uncontrollably, and we joined in.

After a few minnits, Lydia said, "Did you see how blue they turned? Riley was shivverin' so much, I almost dropped him!"

"Yes, and they were so cold their little thingies had almost disappeared," Morning Starr said wipin' tears, then burstin' into another round of laughter.

"That poor mule's ears were pretty loose when I staked him out," Wolf said an' Morning Starr translated.

"It's shore we won't be surprisin' anyone on th' trail with those three along," I said.

"D'yuh suppose we should give that poor mule a rest tomorrow?"

"Probably not," deadpanned Wolf. "He's mostly deaf by now." He looked tired an' still hadn't gotten his color back.

Soon, the wimmin was ready for bed an' Lonza an' Wolf were havin' their smoke. I grabbed my roll an' moved up the hill a short ways out of the light an' made my nest agin a big walnut tree, where I could see the whole camp an' picketed horses. Layin' my rifle across my knees, I settled back for the first watch. I was noddin' an' near sleepin' when Wolf raised up an' moved out into the dark for his turn at watchin'. Bein' comfortable where I was, I nestled down an' soon was asleep.

A low long growl from Sippie brought me back awake. Without movin', I looked over the camp. There was only a small glow from the fire an' I could barely make out the forms of the sleepin' camp. Lonza's bedroll was missin' an' I figgered by that it must be his watch, sometime after two. White Wolf musta stayed at his watch post too.

Sippie's growl became steady an' more intense an' I strained t' see what was botherin' him. Somethin' blacker than the night moved near the fire an' as I watched, it crept closer. The horses began t' stir. The fire flared up for a second — long enough t' reflect in the glow of two yeller eyes of a gray wolf. By his voice, I knew Sippie was ready t' pounce, so I spoke to him soft,

"Hold, Sippie." The pitch o' his growl lowered, but if somethin' didn't happen soon, there was gonna be a big fuss an' the whole camp would be roused. I could barely make out Ruthie as she raised up an' leaned toward Sippie. I shore was hopin' she had ahold of his collar. There was a thump of somethin' heavy hittin' the wolf an' with a yelp he wus gone. A moment later, Lonza approached the fire an' picked up a heavy stick he had thrown an' put it on the fire. After lookin' around a moment, he disappeared into the dark an' I drifted off t' sleep.

On the trail early next mornin', we only traveled about fifteen miles an' camped early in a great bend in the river where it turned north toward the Osage country. This was Syllamo's crossin', the place where we would part with White Wolf an' his family. Our path lay across the river an' up the creek that was named Syllamo Creek after the Creek Indian who lived there.

It was a quiet camp except for the antics of the boys who were not aware of the partin' o' the ways about t' happen. Livin' together an' goin' through the experiences we had had together made us very close an' it was with a bit of sadness that we anticipated our partin'. Instead of rushin' through the camp chores, we sat for some time visitin'. White Wolf an' Lonza were drawin' their map agin an' showin' each other where they could be found.

About midway between the Osage country on the White an' the Cherokee settlements on the Little Red, Wolf drew another river he called the Buffalo an' indicated that he spent time almost every fall huntin' there. He made it a special point t' invite me to visit them anywhere an' I determined then that I would do just that sometime. It was slap-up dark afore anyone thought about cookin' an' the boys were allowed t' stay up late playin'.

I wondered about Wolf and his family makin' it safely by themselves, but he said that there were several camps along the trail north an' that they would be welcome in them for the nights. Mornin' came early, an' it seemed that everythin' took a little longer to get done, but we were soon packed an' saddled an' ready t' go. There were lots of hugs an' tears among the wimmin. Zilkah an' Morning Starr even hugged me an' thanked me agin for rescuin' them as if I had a lot to do with it. They made me promise t' visit them afore long.

Soon they were mounted an' Wolf plopped the protestin' Little Chief in front of his mother. They moved off up the trail to the tune of his wails until a sharp word from White Wolf shut him up.

"I do believe that boy would go with us and never miss his ma and pa," Lydia said.

"You're right and these two might just go with *them* and not look back," Ruthie said, lookin' at two sad-faced boys watchin' their playmate disappear among the trees. It was a sad partin' for them, but happily it was the beginnin' of a lifelong friendship among the three youngsters.

"We're not gettin' any closer to home standin' here," Lonza said, "let's get across the river and head home!"

Crossin' the river wasn't hard, though Lonza an' I made several trips gettin' ever'one an' the horses across safely. The boys were soon caught up in the action and seemed to forget their playmate's absence for a while. We crossed on the south side of Syllamo's Creek an' the trail opened up for us along the creek bank. No one was at Syllamo's cabin, Lonza surmisin' that he had gone south to his kin for the winter.

Not far from the river an incredibly clear stream flowed into the creek from the north. When I asked Lonza about it, he said, "Part of that creek flows out of the side of the mountain north of here. There is a hole in the ground there that leads into the bowels of the earth. Some say it has no bottom. Others say it is the hole where man emerged from the underworld. An old legend says that a brave man lowered himself into the hole and was never heard from again."

I visited the spring an' saw the hole later on. That spring gushes out of the side of a bluff an' falls down to the floor of the valley. John Blanchard homesteaded an' built a grist mill at the spring after the war.

But for the time bein', we moved on up the creek. The trail climbed gently, never leavin' sight or sound of the creek. About noon, we came to a creek flowin' in from the south an' the trail turned up it. This was Lick Fork an' it was a steep climb in places. Late in the afternoon, the creek had become a trickle. There was a good campin' ground here an' we settled into it. Lookin' up stream, I could see where the creek dripped down a bluff in a box-like canyon. The trail turned to the left an' wound up the side out of the valley.

A steep climb next mornin' brought us out on the mostly flat top of the mountain. After about seven miles on top, the trail made a sharp turn toward the west an' descended into the upper Turkey Creek valley. I noticed Lonza was ridin' with his rifle across his lap an' it made me more cautious, but we didn't see any signs of life other than the wild kind.

When we stopped t' water at the creek, Lonza called me aside an' explained, "This creek is part of the Beech Creek drainage and my feudin' enemies might be around trappin' or huntin'. Keep a sharp eye and be ready for trouble until we get out of the bottoms." All was quiet an' I was glad when we started out agin.

Climbin' out of the valley, we traveled southwesterly along a ridge through hardwood an' piney woods. Late in the afternoon, the ridge narrowed to a hogback an' Lonza pointed down the bluff to the north an' said, "There's the Middle Fork of the Little Red River." Through the trees, I could see a broad river snakin' along a narrow valley, all heavy with timber. A little further along, we came to the end of the ridge an' looked down a steep mountainside at a village tucked in a big bend in the river.

"We're home and none too soon!" Lydia exclaimed as we sat lookin' at the scenery. Lonza turned an' led the way down the steep trail to the valley.

The village was mostly log cabins of all sorts with a few tipis scattered here an' there. As we passed through, people would hail us from each cabin an' a dozen kids ran along side callin'. Lonza stopped a time or two t' speak to one or another, but Lydia pressed on, anxious to get to her home. I kept the horses on the move, difficult as it was with the urchins runnin' underfoot. Right down to the river she led us an' without hesitation waded into the ford an' on across, the rest of us follerin' with Lonza trottin' up b'hind us.

"Looks like Lydia's horse has smelled th' barn an' won't stop 'til he gits there," I said as he rode up.

"That's amazin', considerin' he's never been here before," Lonza said dryly, "I think I know who was smellin' the *house* in this train."

By the time we got the horses hazed into the ford, Lydia was climbin' out the other side an' up the bank, Ruth an' the boys close b'hind. They disappeared over the top of the bank an' it seemed all the hurry was out of the packhorses. Lonza pressed on and I hazed the horses up the bank. We came out at the end of a long narrow cornfield, now fallow, an' the trail wound around the far edge of it into a cedar grove.

There at the edge of the trees was a cabin of hewed logs, set tightly together. A wreath of smoke rose from the rock chimbly an' the cabin door stood open. I could hear excited voices inside as I rode up. Surmisin' that this was the Fourkiller cabin, I began unloadin' the packs an' turnin' the horses an' mules into a corral where a log trough full of water waited them. Someone had spread hay around an' it didn't take long for the animals t' make theirselves to home.

Sippie came yappin' out of the house fol- lered by the boys. Lonza's voice called after them, "You boys stay out of the water trough — and stay close."

I stacked the packs by the cabin an' not knowin' what else t' do, stuck my head in the door. To my surprise, the cabin had a wooden floor, the first I had seen since Ten- nessee. The room was large with the fire- place takin' up most of one end wall. There were candles lit everywhere an' a tall older man in buckskin stood by the fire talkin' to Lonza. Lydia an' Ruthie were talkin' to a lady sittin' in an armchair rocker. A large pot steamed from a hook over the fire an' the room smelled of good food an' hot bread.

"Come on in, Jerry, and meet Lydia's parents," Lonza called. I stepped over to the fire — it sure felt good t' be warmin' — an met Lydia's father. "Isaac Fishinghawk, this is Jerry Harris who is Ruth's brother."

Fishinghawk held out his hand an' his grip was warm an' friendly. "Welcome to our valley, Harris." His black eyes held a friendly twinkle. He bore himself with dignity, always reserved and deliberate in his speech an' actions, callin' me Harris as I was expected t' address him formally as Fishinghawk or informally as Wash, which was a sort of nickname his people had given him.

"We are grateful you have come and Fourkiller tells me you were a great help on the trail."

"Thank you, Father, but our debt is to Fourkiller for allowing us to accompany him to this place."

"I'm told you have been through much and I should like to hear about it all in due time. Perhaps you will visit us and tell of your experiences."

"I will like that," I replied, realizin' that this was not the Fishinghawk cabin, but must be the home of Lonza an' Lydia.

Ruth caught my eye and I excused myself to go meet Lydia's mother. "Jerry Harris, this is my mother, Laughing Brook," Lydia introduced her. I bowed in way of greetin'. "I am pleased to meet you, Mother." Her face was pleasant an' you could tell that she had been a very handsome woman in her youth, much like Lydia was then. Her hair was still black an' shiny an' hung to her waist in braids when she stood, givin' her the appearance of a younger woman.

"It is good to meet you, Harris, welcome to our homes." She smiled and nodded. I could tell by their reserve and dignity that they must be citizens of import in the community and that Lydia was very proud of them. "We knew of your coming and have prepared the house and a meal for you."

I wondered how they could have known when we were arrivin', an' learned later that Laughing Brook was one who could foretell events. She had sensed our arrival an' spent the day preparin' for it.

A thumpin' at the door anounced the tumblin' arrival of two boys an' a dog all tryin' t' git through the doorway at the same time. Laughing Brook smiled. "Those boys are hungry, Lydia, get them a bowl of stew and feed them," she said.

Lydia turned to the fire, then suddenly sat in a chair by the table with a little laugh. "I think we have arrived just in time, husband," she said.

"Oh," Ruth caught her breath an' then hurried to the fire to dish out bowls of stew for the two boys. "Riley, Jesse, wash those hands and faces and come to the table," she ordered. Fishing a large bone an' some fat meat out, she led Sippie to the door.

Lydia rose cautiously and helped serve food to all of us. We sat down to the table an' all was quiet for a few minutes while we had our first meal of steamin' hot stew, bread an' coffee at the Fourkiller cabin.

Supper over, the wimmin busied themselves cleanin' up an' gittin' the boys bedded down in a trundle pulled out from under the bed in the other room of the cabin. Lydia seemed a little pale and sat down often to rest, Ruth an' Laughing Brook exchangin' glances an' carryin' on the work. The men stepped out to light their pipes an' I follered. "Looks like it may be a long night, Jerry, we should stay out of the way. Do you mind sleepin' out another night?" Lonza asked.

I was glad for the opportunity. Bein' used to the outside, I wasn't lookin' forward t' a night in the cabin. It afforded me an opportunity t' establish myself as sleepin' outside an' later I would make a shelter by the chimbly like at Flee's. Lots of nights after that, the boys and Sippie joined me, but they slept inside when the weather got too bad. It was comfortin' knowin' that Sippie was with the boys constantly an' might keep them out of any big dangers, though they got plenty of scrapes an' bangs as it was.

The men smoked in silence an' when Fishinghawk finished, he rose an' said, "I will see you in the morning, I'm sure Laughing Brook will remain here for the night. Perhaps by sunrise we will have happy news." He turned and disappeared into the night.

I rummaged through the packs and found my bedroll while Lonza spoke to the wimmin in the house. By the time he got back, I had both our rolls laid out by the chimbly an' it wasn't long until I was asleep. Several times durin' the night, I heard Lonza rise an' go to the door. In a few minnits he would be back, until sometime early in the mornin' he didn't return an' I surmised that Lydia had given birth. After that I slept soundly until I heard steps an' Fishinghawk passed by just b'fore dawn. I dressed an' rose an' not knowin' what else t' do, fiddled around the corral an' horses, breakin' the ice on the trough an' forkin' up more hay for them.

After a while, Ruthie came around the corner an' called, "Come on in, Jerry, the boys have somethin' to show you."

The boys met me at the door. "It's a baby; Mama has a baby." Riley's eyes were wide

376

an' Jesse shrugged and rolled his eyes. "I don't know how he got here, Jerry!" They raced to the bed an' Laughing Brook shushed them as they peeked over the high side. Lydia lay propped up with a bundle in her arms. I was embarrassed but she motioned me to come in. Openin' the blanket, an' revealin' a sleepin' baby, she said, "It's a boy, Jerry. We have named him Jerry Ruth Fourkiller."

I could only grin.

CHAPTER 22
A HOME AT LAST
1812–1813

*Zenas spent several years in the Little Red
River Country with his family in addition to living on the Osage River further north. From
here on, he draws not only from his
grandmother's and uncle's stories but from
his own memories and it is sometimes hard to
distinguish between the two. For instance, he
names geographical locations by their modern
names instead of using the names given by
the Indians. In writing his story, I have re-
frained from trying to make the distinction and
here relate it just as I have received it.*

Zenas's uncle Jerry is still narrating for now.

The next few days were busy for all of us,
especially Ruth, keepin' house an' helpin'
Lydia with the new baby. Parents and
grandparents were as proud as peacocks.
On the second day of the baby's life, Fishinghawk pronounced, "He shall be called
Rising Sun, because he came to us from the

east." And so the boy was called until he became a man, then he took the name given by his parents and they called him Jerry.

Lonza showed me a place nearby where a cabin had been abandoned. It was near a spring that flowed into Weaver's Creek. The cabin was fallen an' rotten, but the corral fence was in good repair, having been kept up by Lonza an' Fishinghawk.

"You can clear off the cabin and build a new one for Ruth and you, if you wish," Fishinghawk said. And so it was that I became for a time, a cabin builder. There was an abundance of flat rocks in the area an' I got the idea they would make a good floor, so riggin' up a sled of sorts, I broke the mules t' pull an' hauled in an' put in place a passle of flat rocks. When I got them squared up like I wanted, they measured thirty feet on a side. This was big for a cabin, but I left it that size.

Lonza loaned me his tools an' I cut logs an' skidded them to the cabin. I shaved the bark off an' did some shapin' up of the logs, but I didn't take the time t' square them up like Lonza's. He did prevail on me t' shave off the bottoms of the base logs so they would fit snug agin the stones to better keep out varmints. It took us a whole day t' lay out an' square up the base logs.

A thirty-by-thirty cabin proved t' be too much, so we cut it down to thirty-by-twenty with a ten-foot gallery across the front. This was very satisfactory to everyone an' was the first one like it in the valley. Summertimes after that were spent mostly in the shade of the gallery. In later years after we had it, we would move the cookin' stove out there t' save heatin' up the house. Ten feet from the end of the house opposite the chimbly, I notched in a partition wall for a bedroom. This also braced up the long walls o' the house, makin' it stronger.

Lonza showed me how t' make mortar by burnin' limestone an' mixin' the lime with soil an' water. It set up real hard an' proved better than chinkin' with clay. We had t' skid the limestone quite a ways from the outcroppin', but it paid off t' do it that-a-way. We'd lay a foundation o' white oak wood, then a layer of lime stones then another layer of wood until we had several tiers stacked up, then we set fire to it an' let it burn down. There was a lot of crackin' an' poppin' an' the boys learned t' keep their distance from the pile t' avoid flyin' chips of hot rock.

Th' chimbly was made of rounded river rocks an' lime mortar. I set a large flat rock for the hearth. It was so big that it took both mules an' four men t' git it in place, but it fit well an' I was pleased with it. Two long narrow slabs o' rock supported the mantle stone that bridged the fireplace. We built the chimbly up to the top where I calculated the ridge t' come, I laid two long narrow rocks in to match the pitches on both sides an' overlap the roof so there wouldn't be any leaks runnin' down the rocks inside. It never leaked an' thirty years later when Ruthie's boys rebuilt the roof with sawn lumber, they kept the stones t' seal the new roof.

We laid in a strong log for a joist across the top o' the walls about ten feet from the fireplace. I put a high pitch on the roof over the enclosed portion an' fitted a lower pitched roof for the gallery. Peeled poles flattened on the top side an' fitted to a ridge pole made the roof framin'. The first roof was thatch, but in later years when sawn lumber became available, I put in lath an' white oak shake shingles.

For posts t' hold up the gallery roof, I cut four cedar poles an' left the limbs stickin' out six to eight inches near the top. They were mighty handy for hangin' things on. A door an' window on the gallery, a window on the back side for the big room an' one in the endwall of the bedroom made provision for natural light. I framed the windows an' Ruth made oiled linen cloths to cover them. Heavy board shutters on the inside offered security when needed.

It took all summer buildin' an' I wasn't able t' work on it solid, havin' t' help plow an' plant corn an' a vegetable garden. When the redhorse shoaled, we spent a week catchin' them an' cleanin' an' dryin' fish on racks over a fire. There must have been millions of fish an' the river was aboil with them. The people used short nets, for longer ones would trap too many fish t' haul in.

Midsummer when the crops were laid by, Ruthie began gradually movin' into the cabin, roof or no roof. She was eager t' have her own house an' didn't want t' impose on the Fourkillers any longer. It was comfortable enough that way, the only inconvenience bein' the occasional thundershower.

When I finished the roof, I made a two-piece door with leather hinges an' hickory bolts notched into the logs for security. By September the cabin was finished an' was the talk of the villagers. Not a few of them thought it was too fancy, but after livin' in the hovels we had for so long, I thought Ruth deserved somethin' nice. It never occurred t' me that I might not live there long an' that I was puttin' so much work into the cabin for nothin', but that didn't prove out for Ruth an' she spent over fifty years livin' in that cabin. 'Course in later years they expanded the house an' covered the logs with siding, but she insisted on keepin' the flagstone floor just like it was.

Life in the village was typical of any Cherokee village. These were the "wild" Cherokee who didn't like the encroachment of the white man an' moved away from them t' maintain their own way of life. They lived mostly in one place, where they raised crops of corn an' squashes an' other vegetables. In the fall, they left the village for areas where game was more plentiful to lay in provender t' last the winter. Some families would winter in the hills where they hunted an' trapped, but they always returned to the village in time to plant.

That spring an' summer passed quickly with the cabin buildin' an' farmin', but we still found time t' git acquainted with the people of the village. There were several boys close to my age an' we would git together occasionally, playin' ball or huntin' an' swimmin'. I had t' prove myself several times an' more than once I got a good whippin', but on the whole, I give as much as I took. Most of the boys had their own ponies. They were small an' close set with great tail an' mane, generally piebald an' in later years were called Cherokee Ponies, a breed unto themselves. The boys loved to race an' bet on the races. I didn't join in because my horses were from the east an' larger an' slower, even the Indian ponies I had picked up at New Madrid.

After the water warmed in the spring, we bathed every day, as was the Cherokee custom. I would join the boys for an evenin' swim ever' day 'bout sunset. Sometimes we would sneak up the river an' spy on the girls bathin' — an' there was sure some good-lookin' ones. The family used Weaver's Creek until it got too low, then went to the Middle Fork.

After telling these stories from his Uncle Jerry, Zenas scooted his chair back into the shade of the porch and started in on some memories of his own.

I stayed with Grandma Ruth on the Middle Fork off and on for several years in my youth and I wish I could recollect all the things she and the people there taught me. It would be very valuable now in settin' the record straight about the Indian and their ways of life. The way they are portrayed now in print and picture is shallow and distorted from the way they really were back then before the white man's ways influenced their culture too much and turned them into the peoples they are today. Mostly, the Indians of today is but a shadow of what their forefathers were. The movement of civilization westward squeezed them from territory to territory, displacing every tribe, causing wars among themselves as well as with the advancing white man. I suppose the Navajo and the 'Paches are among the more fortunate, since they have been able to keep at least a portion of their ancient lands, but even their societies have absorbed the white man's ways — not that it's all bad, mind you, both cultures have benefited greatly from the mixing.

Grandma Ruth was a rather small woman, advanced in age when I knew her. I always was in awe of her, mainly because she seemed so old and she knew so much about living in the wilderness. She was what you would call spry, always two steps ahead of the rest of us and her mind was good. She knew the seasons and the flow and order of things so that when the provender of the hills and woods were ready she was prepared to harvest and preserve them. I never knew her to be caught by surprise by the movement of time and the changes of the seasons.

Folks today think that the Indian had little fare or variety in their diet, but that isn't so. The variety of herbs and plants they used would surprise you. Grandma could wander off into the woods or fields and come back with her apron full of one thing or another and cook up a dish you would swear came from heaven. She was a wonderful cook, among the best I ever knew — never went hungry when she could gather from mother nature. Sadly, most of that knowledge is lost and today we would starve where she would prosper.

There was always something good cooking over the fire or on the stove and I remember how good the house smelled when I would come in half starved. We had our sit-down meals, but I was always welcome to eat when I was hungry and no visitor entered the house without being offered something to eat as a matter of custom and good manners. It was very seldom turned down, and more eagerly accepted at Grandma's than at other homes I knew of.

I always depended on her weather prophesies, she was seldom wrong, even when she moved in strange countries — and she didn't depend on her rheumatism to talk to her, either. *[Zenas chuckled.]*

She made all the clothes for the family,

first out of animal skins, then later out of flax and cotton she grew, harvested and wove herself. I still have a bearskin robe she made me and it's as soft and pliable as the day she tanned it. We moved her spinning wheel when she came to live with us, but by then there was seldom need for it. Her life was filled with hard work and devotion to her family and friends. They didn't know it then and really didn't think about it, but the Fourkillers and Fishinghawks were to be lifelong friends and as close as kin to us all. I didn't know Isaac Fishinghawk, but his stature and renown lived long after he passed on and many are the times I have sat by the fire and heard Grandma or Aunt Lydia speak of him and the things he did. I vaguely remember Laughing Brook as a very old woman sitting by the fireplace and rocking gently as she told whoever was listening of the old days. She was well advanced in age when she passed away and they laid her beside Isaac not far from the cabin where they spent their last years.

Uncle Jerry and my pa both say Grandma was the prettiest woman they knew. Her hair was abundant and jet black until the day she died. You would think that she was all Cherokee until you looked into her eyes and they were the most startling blue.

She insisted on cleanliness in all of us and most especially in herself. She was shocked and dismayed at how casual the white people were about staying clean, especially the women. I observed that the Indian woman was generally cleaner than the white woman of that time, especially the pioneer woman.

Grandma was always saying that the high mortality rate of white infants and children was due to poor hygiene long before the doctors "discovered" it. She gained a reputation in the country of being able to heal sicknesses, especially in children. It was common for the pioneers to bring sickly infants and babes to her for healing and the people trusted her to take the child in to live with her for a time.

Good food, frequent baths and herbs as needed worked wonders and invariably at the end of a week or a month, she would return the healthy child to the happy mother, with instructions on how to properly care for it, mainly to keep the child clean and not allow any handling of it or its things with dirty hands. Those that followed her instructions were happy, those that didn't more often than not came to grief.

Sundays at Grandma's were devoted to Bible reading and rest. Gradually, neighbors began to come to hear the scripture read and she would read it without comment, saying that the Word spoke for itself and to each person as they needed it in their lives. She was among the leaders in encouraging a church to be built when a circuit preacher first came into the country and she was always there when he came to preach.

Uncle Lonza an' Aunt Lydia lived within shoutin' distance of Grandpa Sam and Grandma and their home was as much mine as Grandma's. Many times we all ate together at one or the other of the cabins. Summertimes, we would build a brush arbor between the houses or by the spring an' come mealtime, we would all meet, carryin' pots and dishes of food. Those meals were always long and pleasant and much of the business of the day was carried on and set under that shade. Grandma an' Aunt Lydia would sit there or on the gallery in the hot summer afternoons an' sew or shell peas or whatever had to be done. Rarely, you would catch them with idle hands, just rockin' an' talkin', but it did happen. Other neighbors and friends of the ladies would come to visit until the sun began sinking behind Cedar Hill an' the cool of the evenin' called them away to their chores.

Uncle Lonza was a Tennessee Cherokee, raised on a farm an' educated in a school. When he was a young man, the itch to see what was over the hill hit him an' he traveled to the Little Red River country with some of the Western Cherokees. He found that he very much liked their way of life instead of the more sedentary life of the east. Too, he could see trouble brewing between the Tennessee Indians and the white men filtering into the country.

It was here on the Middle Fork that he met and married Little Fawn, daughter of Fishinghawk. Although Uncle Lonza loved the seminomadic life of hunting and fishing, he missed the varieties of foods and vegetables he had in the east. So it was that he sold his tipi and built Aunt Lydia a cabin on Weaver's Creek. He cleared the bottoms nearby for a garden and cornfield and went back to Tennessee for the seed and implements he needed.

His friends derided him for being a Squaw Man when they found him plowing and planting and I heard there was more than one fight over the matter. Uncle Lonza was larger and stronger than the others so it was more often than not that he had more than one combatant at a time. His dominance as a fighter won him the admiration of the community and when times of trouble came to the village, they always looked to Fishinghawk and him for leadership.

I hunted with him a few times and he was the best hunter and stalker I ever knew. If there was meat in the country, he found it. He was expert with bow or gun and I never saw him miss. One of the things he taught me was to never shoot unless the shot was sure. A few times tracking down a wounded animal at his insistence an' I got the message.

After Isaac Fishinghawk died, Lonza became the unofficial leader of the community. The Indians that were left looked to him as their leader and the whites called him the Judge of Middle Fork. People sought his advice on matters and he would usually give it, but never in an imperative or dogmatic manner. He believed all men should make up their own minds about matters and gave them that option.

Middle Fork was rough country and life and the people were necessarily tough to cope with it, but occasionally people who were too rough or lawless filtered into the country. It wouldn't be long before their nature was known and the community would deal with them accordingly. Soon, you might see their backsides disappearing over one o' the hills or the worst of them that showed an intention to stay might just disappear and never be seen again. No one talked about them, not even in whispers. There was no formal law besides the law of the community and every man took it as his duty to see that life was as harmonious as possible. Eventually, that attitude of community responsibility died away with the coming of so-called "law and order" and the country got more lawless. It was like Kerry Newcomb said somewhere, "Bullies grow bold when brave men die."

Pa an' Uncle Riley were inseparable from the time they met at four or five years of age until as young men their paths diverged. Still, they were lifelong friends, as close as brothers. Along the way, I'll tell you some of the scrapes these two got into. Grandma said, "They grew up wild," but their wildness was always curbed and channeled for good by the strong adults around them. From Isaac to Uncle Jerry, they all saw that the boys were not destructive, but no one would say their antics were not always disruptive to the tranquility of the households.

Lonza, Aunt Lydia and Grandma saw to it that they were educated, learning reading, writing and arithmetic along with Uncle Jerry. Their textbook was the only book they had for a long time, the Bible, and all three were instilled with its morals and ethics from a young age. I still remember sitting on Grandma Ruth's lap and reading scripture until I was tired or stumped. Then, she would read to me, sometimes until I drifted off to sleep and awoke with the dawn in my own bed.

If I had to describe Uncle Jerry, I would say he was average sized for the day, not much over five foot six or seven, and he called himself heavy when he weighed 150 pounds. Wiry, quick to action and strong, he would burn almost black in the summer and year round later on the plains. He had little beard and wore his black hair shoulder length, tied back in summer and around his ears in winter. His dark eyes were deep-set and keen as the best. He became a crack shot with the rifle, but mostly disdained the pistols as only good for man-killing. He would grin and say he was in real trouble if he let a man he had to kill get close enough for a pistol. Mostly he avoided killing men and I only know of two he got after the time at Flee's Settlement. Never did I hear him talk of it, believing as was prevalent for the thought of the day that you did what you had to do and never talked about it to anyone. Those that did were beset by trouble and usually short lived.

I'll always remember a conversation we had one day sitting on the banks of the Arkansas fishing for bream and catfish. I can relate it almost word for word even today. He said, "Zenas, I came to a crossroads as a young man, whether to become as they say a Reservation Indian or to choose the white man's way. I studied it for a long time — over a year or two — and I saw that the old Indian ways were not constructive in the new atmosphere of white culture — that the cultures could not coexist because of very basic differences in morality and economy. Therefore I chose the white man's path even though it meant a long struggle against the prejudices of being a 'half-breed.' I learned to live and compete and excel within the white man's society using my Indian heritage to its best advantage and I have been successful in that endeavor. This does not mean that I am not Indian nor does it mean that I am ashamed of my Indian blood, on the contrary, I am proud of my bloodlines, both red and white.

"There are those who choose to cling to the old ways, however outmoded and unworkable they are in today's world. They take pride in the fact that they are a 'sovereign nation' within these United States. Yet, their 'sovereignty' is dependent on the fickle mercies of government largesse; their sovereignty is a hollow shell. They find themselves unproductive and in poverty, trapped in a system that enslaves them to a life of dependence on others for their everyday existence. They idolize the old subsistence living of the vagabond Indian, but it was a constant struggle for the basic elements of life. No matter how romanticized it is, it was hard then and in this tamed land impossible now."

In his time, he was a mountain man, Santa Fe Trail trader, meat hunter, army scout, wagon train guide, and finally horse trainer and trader of some renown. My pa ran with him for several years and they were always close.

Having told me quite a few of his own stories, Zenas now said, "Grandma Ruth's life on Middle Fork might be some interest to you, so I'll tell you some of her stories, just as she told 'em to me."

When we got to the Fourkillers' cabin from Flee's, we were hoping for some rest, but that was not to be, for the very next morning, Lydia gave birth to another son. He was a healthy baby, but Lydia was worn out from the labors of the trip carrying the child. I could not leave her like that after all they had done for us, and Laughing Brook was more than happy to have me to help with the household. The next few days were very busy settling into the cabin, washing up the trailworn clothes, watching two rambunctious boys and caring for mother and infant. The infant care was taken over mostly by Laughing Brook during the day and I helped by night. He seemed always hungry and Lydia was hard put to keep up with him for a while until rest and good food improved her own constitution. Jerry found himself a place to sleep outside by the chimney and he and Lonza kept the outside work up, which consisted mostly of chopping and carrying wood, herding the horses, hunting and watching those boys and Sippie, who was busy establishing his territory and dominance over the neighboring dogs who would challenge him.

The days went by quickly, and gradually Lydia regained her strength and was taking over more and more of the daily chores. I began to feel that we had taken enough of their hospitality and needed to move on. But where? There were no accommodations in the village, nor had we the ability to pay for them if there were. It was about then that Jerry took matters into his own hands and began building us a cabin nearby. He had grand plans and proceeded to lay a rock floor and cut logs for the walls, learning as he went and as Isaac and Lonza instructed and helped him. I don't think anyone ever worked harder than he did that summer. Many times he was busy from before sunup until after dark. He would drag himself in, eat a huge meal and sleep only to do it all over again the next day.

The walls were up and Jerry was working on the roof when I decided that it was time to move in. I know my impatience caused him some trouble, but it turned out better for him in the long run. We stretched our old trail canvas over part of the room by the chimney for a shelter and I started making house and home. It was a relief for us all. I was there to help Jerry when he needed it and he had a more convenient place to stay and sleep. Jesse and I slept in the bedroom under the stars and if he didn't give out before I went to bed, we would lie and watch the skies. It was our game to see who saw a falling star first.

It was early fall before all was finished and I made Jerry rest a few days before trying anything else. But he was the restless sort and too soon he was out and about hunting and gathering the fall fruits. The hills were full of walnuts, hickories, chinquapins, beechnuts, pawpaws, muscadines, persimmon and other foods that mature in the days of fall and we all had great fun gathering in these crops. Contrary to the custom of Indian men to avoid such work, Jerry helped greatly in the harvest. He and Fishinghawk and Lonza harvested hay and corn fodder from the bottoms for the livestock.

With the last six silver pesos Jerry had, he bought a milch cow in the village. It greatly helped in feeding three hungry boys and we all enjoyed the butter and cream she gave us. She became quite tame and the boys loved her. They were always picking some delicacy for her to eat and there was great consternation when the milk began to taste like walnut leaves. After that, they had strict instructions to show their harvestings to some adult before feeding Bossie.

CHAPTER 23
A TALE OF SILVER

"Uncle Jerry told me some stories of what happened when hard cash was introduced into the community economy," Zenas said as he settled back in his chair.

The introduction of hard cash into the local economy had a sudden and profound effect. Even though they might not possess any of the coins, all produce suddenly became valued in silver. A raw hide might be worth half a peso, but tanned, it might be worth two pesos. Thus the buyer had to provide two of the coins or something worth two pesos in trade. It was a rare occasion in the commerce of the day that the purchase actually resulted in the exchange of coins for product, and the value of the coins was greatly inflated. The possessor of a coin could demand premium products for the exchange.

Gray Wolf, who originally owned the cow,

amassed (for Middle Fork Village) a small fortune by judiciously trading pesos for goods he desired. He bought a bow made of horn backed by sinew, made — some said — by the Nez Percé far to the northwest, with his first peso. The bow owner put more value in the silver coin than the bow's value came to be. Next, Gray Wolf traded for a fine buffalo robe, but the robe was not worth a whole peso. When the robe owner saw that he could possess a coin, he threw in a fine tanned deerskin.

Gray Wolf decided that the deerskin would make a nice shirt, so he took it to the best seamstress in the village and asked her to make him a shirt with beads and quillwork. The wise woman dickered with him for a coin by agreeing to make the shirt with special decorations and throw in a pair of leggin's too. Gray Wolf hesitated, then shook his head. The seamstress threw in a pair of finely made white moccasins with stitching and beads to match the shirt. Gray Wolf agreed. He was astonished at the beauty of his new suit and wore it proudly every occasion he could. One Sabbath afternoon after wearing his finery to Ruth's scripture reading (he went more to show off his new suit than to hear the Word), he looked around at the bachelor's tipi he shared with four other young men and decided that he needed a new abode to reflect his elevated status in the village. He drifted off to sleep that night thinking about the new tipi and early the next morning began looking for one that suited his taste.

John Nakedhead had finally bowed to his wife's desire for a cabin instead of the tipi they lived in and was busily constructing one before the cold weather came. He had an industrious wife whose housekeeping was above reproach and her tipi reflected it. When Gray Wolf approached John about purchasing it, he was glad, for here was a chance to get help with his cabin construction and maybe even a coin also. Their negotiations were long and laborious in themselves, but in the end, Gray Wolf agreed to help erect the cabin walls and pay one coin for the tipi. But only if he would get the tipi when the *walls* were complete and not when the *cabin* was complete.

This was no small annoyance to John's wife, but he was satisfied with the arrangement, and she was happier when she saw how much faster the walls went up. She chinked the logs as fast as they were in place and by the time the last log went up, the cabin was livable save for the roof.

Gray Wolf disposed of his fourth peso and

happily moved into the tipi as it was. "Now I have a home befitting my status and two coins remaining," he thought, but still there seemed to be something incomplete about it all. It dawned on him the following morning when he awoke to a cold tipi with no fire to welcome him. "This tipi is incomplete without a woman," he thought. All the time he struggled to get the fire going and cast around for a morsel to eat, the thought kept recurring. At last he sat down and said aloud, "I need a woman."

It wasn't hard for him to know *which* maiden was equal to his new status; that was determined long before his newfound affluence — and was then impossible to attain because he was only a poor bachelor unable to support a wife as her station demanded. Buffalo Running would have to listen to him now that he had this wealth. He could trade for Sunflower's hand now. Therefore, at noon, the next day, Gray Wolf, dressed in his finest, tied his best pony in front of the Buffalo Running tipi. The pony stayed there until mid afternoon, mostly to make it appear that Buffalo Running was not overanxious to address the proposed marriage of his daughter, though he had to restrain his daughter from taking the pony in. Finally, with a great show of indifference, he stepped out of his tipi, stretched hugely and "noticed" the pony standing there. He sauntered over to the pony and made great show of examining the horse, calling his son over to lead the horse around while he watched with a critical eye. Finally with a wave of his hand, he sent boy and horse to his corral. Gray Wolf watched the event from his hiding place and was delighted. Now it was his turn to show restraint and he quietly slipped away to the bachelor tipi (for there was no food in his), where he and his friends discussed the coming negotiations far into the night.

It was midmorning before Gray Wolf appeared to "see" if the gift horse had been accepted. He appeared pleased and called upon the household, whereupon his mother-in-law-to-be welcomed him.

I won't bore you with the details of the negotiations that followed, but there was final agreement on the number of horses required for the father's blessings. Then to Gray Wolf's apparent dismay, the wily fox demanded one peso, silver, to seal the deal.

Gray Wolf's face fell. "I cannot part with the last of my silver (he really had two coins left), for that is to be used for the things my wife needs to establish her home," he said.

"Ah, but I will give her many things from

my tipi for that," the prospective father-in-law replied, which was nothing more than customary.

Gray Wolf thought a moment. "Perhaps if I kept two of the horses, I could part with my last peso." He pretended to have only one coin, but Buffalo Running knew better.

Buffalo's eyebrows raised. "Do you mean that it would take *two* of your horses to equal one peso?"

Gray Wolf saw the trap. "No, no, I just meant that I would need something to make up for the loss of my coin."

"I might reduce the number of horses if I chose the one to return to you."

There followed a long discussion in which it was finally determined that the dowry price would be reduced one horse of *Gray Wolf's* choosing in exchange for the silver coin.

Buffalo Running lit the pipe and they smoked. The deal was set, the wedding proceeded as was customary with the people and the happy couple moved into their new home.

In the early dawn of the next morning, Gray Wolf awoke, sat up and stretched to the light and warmth of a cheerfully burning fire. He was delighted until he saw his bride in a corner softly weeping.

"What is wrong, Sunflower?" he half whispered.

"There is no meat," she said, trembling.

"No meat? But your father said . . ."

"He said my dowry did not include meat."

"I promised that Sunflower would have the things necessary for a household, but I did not promise to feed you," Buffalo Running said firmly to the angry Gray Wolf who had showed up at his door. "You will have to provide meat for yourself . . . *or* I would sell you a deer my son killed yesterday . . . for a peso!"

For a moment it looked like the end of a peaceful family relationship, but Gray Wolf smiled and said, "I would rather *give* my silver away than have it stolen by you!" and he turned on his finely dressed heel and strode away. He was surprised to smell food cooking when he re-entered his tipi.

Sunflower looked up happily as he entered. "Someone slipped a quarter of deer meat under the edge of the tent and I found it after you left. We will eat soon, my husband."

Gray Wolf pondered that for a few moments; who could have left such a fine present? It wasn't until later that he discovered that his new brother-in-law had overheard his father laughing about tricking

Gray Wolf and had removed the best quarter from his kill and taken it to his beloved sister. Tranquility again settled on Gray Wolf's soul and he sat long, dreaming of a proper revenge on his father-in-law and what he would do with that last coin.

Speaks Softly was the best seamstress in a village known for its fine seamstresses. Though she was a widow, she lived well by sewing fine things for her neighbors and others who lived as far away as the Village at the Forks. With the peso she got from Gray Wolf, she looked to purchase a horse, but there were none in the village that she cared for. One afternoon while visiting her sister, she overheard her brother-in-law talking about an old broken-down mare who had been bred by his fine stud without the knowledge of the mare's owner, Standing Bear. "Old Bear doesn't know what he has in that old mare," he laughed.

"If the mare is strong enough to foal," his companion replied.

"You are right," the brother-in-law agreed.

Now, Speaks Softly knew that old mare, Dancer, of Standing Bear's and remembered when she was the finest horse in the valley. Standing Bear rode her on all of the special occasions and she was his favorite for many years until she finally became too old. Many of her offspring dotted the herds around the village and they were all fine animals, though she was now deemed too old to breed. So it was that early the next morning, Speaks Softly visited the corral of Standing Bear.

"Good morning, Speaks Softly," Standing Bear called from his doorway. "How are you this day?"

"I am fine, Standing Bear, except that I would like to have a horse and I can't find one to my liking. I thought you might have one or could advise me on the purchase of one."

"What kind of horse are you looking for?" he asked, his trading blood stirred.

"I would like a gentle horse I could ride and trust with my children."

Old Bear rubbed his chin in thought. "Have you looked at that buckskin over in the corner? She is ten winters and gentle."

"She seems to have too much spirit for my boys at their age. I would like one more gentle."

"Do you see the black horse with the white stocking?" indicating a six-year-old gelding he had gotten from a white hunter passing through the country. Indians seldom bothered to geld their colts and a gelded horse was not very popular with them. Standing Bear had taken him in on trade because he had made a very good deal and did not need him to make a profit. In other words, the horse did not cost him anything, but being a white man's horse, he was trained to the white man customs, including mounting on the left side, opposite from the Indian custom and therefore, Standing Bear could find no one eager to buy him.

"I would rather have a pony, they would not be so high for my boys to fall from," Speaks Softly laughed. And so it went through the whole herd, not one being found suitable for the widow to buy.

"You see why I am frustrated? It seems I can't find the horse that is just right for me," Speaks Softly mourned. "I would give a good deerskin suit for a horse to my liking."

"Would it be as fine as the one you made for Gray Wolf?"

"No, it could not, because he paid me with the silver coin," she replied.

"So the silver coin would be for a special horse?"

"Yes," she replied, then paused. "I like the buckskin, but she is too much for the boys, they need something more gentle . . . like Dancer!" she said brightening. "I could make you a suit with moccasins to match for both horses."

"I could not trade the old mare . . ."

"But I will take special care of her and the only ones to ride her — and gently — would be my boys. She would be a good starter for them and it may be that they could ride the buckskin when they are older."

"No, I cannot let her go . . ."

Speaks Softly seemed to warm more and more to the idea. "But she would still be in the village and you could see her all you wanted to and I would see that the boys would treat her with the respect she deserves."

"No, I could not part with her."

Did she detect a halt in his voice, some reluctance to end the negotiations? "Oh my, oh my," she said shaking her head. "I wish there were a way, that would be so good for us . . . ," she trailed off in thought. Then, in a softer more earnest voice, she entreated with trembling lip, "Standing Bear" — she wrung her hands — "Standing Bear, *I will give you my silver coin for both horses!*"

Standing Bear was not sympathetic, he smelled a deal after all. "I would . . . take the silver and a suit for the horses . . ."

"No, I could not do that, the mare could die any day and she's too old to be worth the full price of a horse. I'll give you the coin for the two."

"No-o-o . . . maybe for the coin and a shirt . . ."

"I'll give you the coin and a pair of beaded moccasins for the two."

"Well . . ."

"There will be a special place for the mare. What better way to end her days than to teach young boys how to be men and warriors?" Then after a moment of silence, she said, "Bring the horses to my cabin after noon and I will have the coin for you and I will make the moccasins."

The trade would be made in public so all would witness that it was agreeable for both parties.

"Well . . ." Standing Bear still feigned reluctance, but Speaks Softly saw a glimmer in his eye that gave her hope for a deal. She turned to leave. "If you come at noon, I will have a roast of deer meat for you." She walked up the path until she was out of sight, then with faster pace hurried to her cabin. Calling the boys for more firewood, she began roasting a deer haunch on a spit. She set one of the boys to turning the spit and sent the older one out to the old horse shed in the corral to clean it up and put down fresh hay and shuck out corn for the expected horses.

Such a meal she hadn't prepared in ages, there was the roast and prairie hen broth with her special spices and strong black coffee. A loaf of bread borrowed from her neighbor warmed by the fire and a dish of butter cooled in springwater.

The sun climbed to its zenith and Standing Bear had not come. She began to wonder if he had changed his mind. She had almost given up when an hour later, Standing Bear appeared riding the buckskin and leading Dancer. Quickly, Speaks Softly prepared the meal. Almost too late, she remembered that Standing Bear took his meals the old way, sitting on the ground. It took only a moment to arrange a buffalo robe before the fire with the kettles sitting on the hearth within easy reach.

When no one came to the door, she looked out to see Standing Bear in the corral watching the horses contentedly munching corn as he talked earnestly with the boys. "Good afternoon, Standing Bear," she called. "Won't you come in and eat?"

Standing Bear and the boys turned to the house, the old warrior still talking. The boys' eyes lighted up when they saw the robe spread before the fire. This was their favorite way to eat. They hung back, for Standing

Bear would eat alone as was the custom, but he motioned them to sit and eat with him which was a large compliment to the boys. Speaks Softly served quietly while Standing Bear talked long to the wide-eyed boys about the proper care for the horses.

The meal finished, Speaks Softly knelt on the robe and set a pair of beautifully beaded moccasins before Standing Bear. If anything, Standing Bear noticed, they were better than Gray Wolf's. From a small leather pouch, she took the polished peso and laid it atop the pouch by the moccasins.

"Speaks Softly, I could not put any value on Dancer that would induce me to sell her other than as we have agreed today. If you and the boys promise to give her the best of care and never mistreat her, I will let you have her." There was a chorus of "we wills" from three voices. "Very well, boys, she is yours until the first time I hear of her being mistreated, then I will reclaim the horse without any compensation for her."

"Yes, Uncle," the elder replied, while the younger slipped out the door to behold his new possession.

And the boys *did* take good care of Dancer, making her the pet of the family, even to the point that they often slipped out of the house on summer nights and slept in the shed with her. On her part, Dancer loved the boys and followed them everywhere when they were not on her back. Speaks Softly watched carefully and made sure Dancer was well fed and not worked too hard. When the time neared that she should deliver, she was sent out of the village to the corral of a man adept at treating horses and delivering foals. Surprisingly, Dancer had no trouble giving birth and the foal was a beautiful colt, well formed and marked.

When Standing Bear saw the foal, there was a great hue and cry and he would have taken the mare and colt back, but Speaks Softly stopped him by showing him the tally stick of the days she had possessed the horse. It had 285 notches on it.

"The mare was bred forty-five days *before* I bought her and we have taken special care of her, even sending her to the Horse Healer when it was time for her to foal. You cannot say that we have mistreated her, and the colt is ours because you sold it."

Still, Standing Bear complained, but all agreed that the colt rightfully belonged to Speaks Softly. The name she gave her colt, roughly translated from Cherokee, was Dancer's Folly.

Now, at that time, little attention was paid

to the breeding of horses by the tribe, but being a widow with limited means, Speaks Softly paid close attention to her two mares and when the buckskin came into season, she saw that she was bred by her brother-in-law's stud and that was the beginning of a line of great horses that took on the name of Cherokee Ponies. Speaks Softly became known for the fine horses she produced and people came from afar to buy them. She became wealthy and was the recipient of many marriage proposals, all of which she rejected.

Dancer produced one more foal that was the image of her mother two years after the colt was born. When it became clear that her time was near, Speaks Softly returned the great horse to Standing Bear. He took Dancer far up the river to a beautiful meadow beside a bubbling spring and there they stayed until he found her lying in the tall grass. Her passing was mourned by all who knew her.

Jerry retrieved one of the coins for some work he did in the village and kept it as a good-luck charm. It was to have an important part in his future.

"I could tell a dozen more tales about the silver coins, about the foolish man who would

own them all, but found that he had nothing but five pesos and no way to gain the sixth, then lost them all buying back his tipi and horses. But they would grow tiresome, so I will tell you of other things."

CHAPTER 24
THE FIRST LONG HUNT

The Long Hunts were in the early spring before the shedding of the winter coats when the pelts were at their best and where the larder was replenished after the long winter. In the fall, hunts were made to make up any shortfall the summer harvest might have. This is Jerry's story of the first and one of the last the clan ever went on.

About the last of September, the village began packin' up an' movin' out for the fall hunt. Some of them would be gone all winter, livin' in isolated camps where the game was plentiful. Come spring, they would be back for the plantin' an' growin' season. They scattered over the hills in all directions lookin' for the best huntin', the wimmin who went along gatherin' hickory nuts, walnuts, chinquapins, beechnuts an' white oak acorns when they weren't curin' the meat the hunters brought in.

Lonza, Fishinghawk an' I left the wimmin to home an' headed west into the hills. There wasn't much sign o' game for a ways around the village, but above the valley of Archer's Fork, signs of deer an' elk began showin' up. We even ran across the tracks of some buffalo — woods buffalo — Fishinghawk called them. They were so scarce they were not hunted much an' we passed up trackin' them down though I wanted to see some, having never been around them b'fore. We set up camp under the bluff on the west side o' Red Hill near the spring. From there, we could hunt the hills east or drop down into the bottoms along Hartsug Creek an' on down into Archer's Valley. There was plenty of grazin' for the three horses an' two mules.

At night we could sometimes see the campfire of someone campin' on t'other side of Hartsug Wash. Much of this territory was hunted by the people from the village at the junction of Archer's an' South Forks of the Little Red. It was much bigger than our village, havin' more bottom lands t' till an' was scattered up an' down the valley for some distance. There was a lot of trafficin' atween the two villages, people havin' kin in both places an' all. The boys in our village said there were a lot more pretty girls along South Fork an' visited there often — that is, often when they didn't git run off by the boys livin' there. We had some pretty good set-tos with them a time or two, resultin' in a lot o' bruises an' black eyes, but not real damage done.

The Archer's Valley was sure purty, with flats an' bluffs an' big timber too. In the rocks, we got a couple o' fat bears an' one mountain lion. One mornin' when I was stalkin' a herd o' deer, on the flats, I ran into a South Fork man stalkin' the same herd. Without sayin' a word, we worked together him on one side an' me on the other side, both downwind. I had my rifle an' he had bow an' arrow, so I let him git comfortable with his shot. He looked at me an' I nodded for him t' shoot an' when he did, I let go on a fine-lookin' doe on my side o' the herd.

His deer went down in its tracks an' he was up an' shot at another as it ran, makin' a good hit. The deer ran another hundred yards or so an' fell. My deer leaped a big log afore it fell an' it wasn't quite dead when I went to bleed it out. I was sittin' on the log reloadin' when he came up. "That's a nice doe you got there," he said. "Guess that's the end of huntin' *that* herd for the day. They'll run a long way to get away from the noise of your gun." Most of the Indians hunted with bow an' arrer 'cause they were quieter an' didn't frighten the game too much. I've heard men brag that they have killed three, four deer in one day from the same bunch usin' bows. They sure are a lot quieter an' faster t' "reload," but I wasn't skilled enough to be confident tryin' it.

He stood up on the log an' waved. I saw two wimmin rise up out o' the grass an' hurry our way. The wimmin paid us no mind an' set right t' work on the two arrer shot deer. We kindled a small fire an' the man sat on the log smokin' his pipe while I field dressed my deer. "My name is Jerry Harris, son of Sarah Fourkiller from Tennessee. I am living on Middle Fork with Wash Fishinghawk," I said by way of introduction.

The man nodded. "I am Isaac Tenkiller and that is Running Quail my wife and Bluebird my daughter."

I was glad to hear that Bluebird was his daughter an' not his second wife, 'cause she was really good lookin' an' about my age. By the time I was done with my deer, they were finished too an' came over to the fire. Bluebird gave me a sidewise glance an' my knees felt shaky. I got busy cuttin' out four steaks from my deer an' spittin' them on green sticks for cookin'. We settled down to cook an' eat, Running Quail cookin' Tenkiller's steak for him. "Where are you camped, Harris?" Isaac asked.

"We're under the bluff up on Red Hill, not far from the spring," I replied. "It's just Lonza Fourkiller, Fishinghawk an' me; the women stayed home this time."

He nodded. "I like to hunt that way some, too, but Quail loves to camp and she is a great help. We have to bring Bluebird along to keep her safe from all of the young bucks hanging around." He smiled at his daughter an' she blushed, but said nothing.

The steaks were good an' washed down well with creek water. It turned out that the Tenkillers were camped up on a bench west of Hartsug Creek an' it was their fire we could sometimes see from our camp. With our meal over, we loaded up for the trip up Hartsug to our camps. The two wimmin divided one of the carcasses b'tween them an' Tenkiller an' I shouldered the other two deer. Most men made their wimmin carry the loads, but some like Tenkiller helped out.

We had a good five miles t' walk, it bein' three miles up Hartsug to where my trail went up the mountain, an' the Tenkillers had t' go near as far afore their trail angled up the mountain to their camp. Tenkiller led the way with the wimmin in the middle an' me bringin' up the rear. It seemed I spent most of my life bitin' dust at the back o' some parade, but I didn't mind this time, for the view wus *some* enticin'. Ever' once in a while, Bluebird would throw me a glance an' smile. That was enough t' keep me goin' in spite of the load I wus carryin'.

Durin' one o' the rest stops, Running Quail asked if I knew a certain family livin' in the Middle Fork village. I had heard of them, but had not become acquainted with them much with all my summer's work. "They are my family and I haven't seen them for some time, do you think they are doing well?" she asked.

"I think so," I replied. "Seems like one of the boys got kicked by a pony last summer, but he got over it pretty fast." Kicks an' bruises were pretty common where boys an' ponies mixed.

"I haven't seen them since last fall, maybe we can get over there this winter for a visit."

"I'm sure you would be welcome to visit us when you come." I tried not to be too eager. Bluebird smiled, but said nothing. She seemed very shy.

It was gettin' late when we reached the place where the Tenkillers branched off t' the left an' up the mountain. I still had a ways t' go an' didn't relish climbin' that hill in the dark with a carcass on my back.

"I saw elk tracks on the ridge above the creek," Isaac Tenkiller said, nodding his head upstream. "There were fifteen or twenty in the herd best I could tell. Would you and your friends like to join me in a hunt? It's better if several go together to hunt elk."

"I'm sure we would and I will ask them tonight. When would you like to go?" I replied.

"The day after tomorrow would be good. We can meet where your trail comes down to the creek and go from there."

"I will be there before dawn. Lonza was saying that he needed an elk hide or two and I am sure Fishinghawk will not want to miss the hunt."

"Good. We will be there early. Running Quail has been anxious to have an elk hide also." Bluebird smiled and gave me one of her glances, then tried to hide her blush. I got that shaky spell again.

Without another word, Tenkiller shouldered his deer an' started up the trail. The two wimmin picked up their bundles an' followed.

"Goodbye until the day after tomorrow,"

Running Quail called.

"Goodbye, Jerryharris." It was the first time Bluebird spoke directly to me.

I picked up my load an' hurried off up the creek. It was full dark when I got to camp. Lonza an' Fishinghawk were already there an' eatin'. They had each gotten a deer an' it was plain what we would be doin' all the next day. The day dragged by slowly in spite of all the work renderin' tallow an' cuttin' jerky strips. We ate roasted ribs and worked steadily all day. Lonza and Fishinghawk were both ready to hunt elk an' we finally turned in early that night. Even so, I didn't wake up until I heard Lonza stokin' up the fire. It didn't take long t' git ready, a few bites of roast, an' a handful of meat for the day an' we were on our way.

Three shadows emerged from the trees at the creek; a few whispered greetings an' we were on our way, Tenkiller leading an' Bluebird walkin' beside me. Once or twice she stumbled an' grabbed my arm t' keep from fallin'. She held on for a moment an' squeezed my arm a little afore lettin' go. I wus sure hopin' she would stumble agin.

Th' creek began t' peter out an' the way got steeper. Isaac stopped where a steep hollow came in from the left. "The elk should be moving out on the ridge to feed soon. If some of us went up the hollow here, they might be able to get behind them and drive them around toward the head of the creek. The rest of us could be waiting for them there."

"I'll go up th' hollow," I volunteered. I hated t' still-hunt an' this way I could keep on the move an' still be useful.

"Good," said Isaac, "we can get ourselves set on either side of the ridge and hopefully you can drive them between us. Wait here until the sun is nearly up then work your way slowly up the hollow. If they haven't bedded in this one, maybe they did in the next hollow north and you can still be behind them."

"Follow them slowly, Harris, and try not to scare them into running," Fishinghawk advised. "Push them too hard and they will scatter."

I nodded. "Lonza, do you want to take my rifle and maybe get two shots at them?"

"It's a good idea, but you should keep it in case something goes wrong and you might have the only shot at them," he replied.

"If you're lucky and get behind the herd, take your time. It wouldn't hurt if you didn't get to us until after midmorning," Isaac advised.

I shuddered inside. Who would enjoy sitting on a stand in the cold half a day just for the chance at gettin' a kill? "Okay, when the stars start to fade, I will start up th' hollow."

They started up the trail an' I sat down on a rock. When Bluebird passed, she stepped on my foot. Guess she was aggravated I volunteered t' do the scoutin'. I couldn't have lived through a stand with her that close by, anyway. My biggest worry was goin' t' sleep waitin', so I made sure not to git too comfortable anywhere. The stars were beginnin' t' fade, but I still waited a little to give them plenty time to git set. When I could see individual trees up the hollow, I started out.

The first part of the hollow was steep an' I slung my rifle on my back an' went up mostly on hands an' feet. When it got more level, I stopped to catch my breath an' look around. A buck snorted somewhere to my left an' up the hill an' I started. They were there an' I was ahind them. Good luck so far. Slowly, I began makin' my way up the hill, strayin' somewhat to the left an' takin' advantage of what cover I could find.

The wind was dead calm which helped keep my scent away from them, but it was extra hard keepin' quiet, since noises carried a long way in the stillness. Presently, my eye caught a movement an' there stood a big cow. She was grazin' quietly an' showed no alarm. The more I looked, the more cows I saw. The bull elk gave another snort somewhere up ahead, but the cows showed no alarm. As I watched, they began movin' an' grazin' up the hill toward the ridge. I moved as quiet as possible through the undergrowth around to the left to the edge of a large clearing across the ridgetop.

The cows was grazin' into the clearing an' from where I sat, I could git b'hind 'em easy. Then the bull snorted agin, only this time it was from the left of me in the trees beyond the clearing! They were goin' the opposite direction from the hunters! To git b'tween the cows an' the bull would scatter them like quail an' no one would git a shot at them. I had t' git ahead of that bull somehow an' change his direction of travel. Lookin' around to my left, I could see a knob of a hill between me an' the bull. If I could git around that knob an' head off the bull, maybe they would change directions.

After about a hundred yards of quiet travel, I slung my rifle on my back an' began runnin' around that knob. Around on the southwest side of the hill, I stopped to catch my breath. I couldn't see any elk to my left which gave me hope I had headed the bull. Just then, I heard a snort to my right an' I knew I had gotten ahead of him. Creepin' slowly out from b'hind the knob, I worked my way west then back north, keepin' my eye out for the bull. He saw or sensed me afore I saw him an' snorted a warnin' to the cows. I could hear him movin' back the way he had come so I sat still for a minute or two.

Sittin' there waitin' to git a little distance atween me an' the elk, I realized the wind had come up, but I couldn't tell which direction it was blowin'. It could have a real effect on my efforts t' herd the elk an' I worried about it. Then just as quietly as it came, it stopped and the air was calm agin.

The bull was in the middle of the herd now, head high an' sniffin' the air. His nose pointed almost straight up an' his rack was layin' along his back. He shore made a purty sight, but it was the cows we wus interested in for meat an' hide. I moved toward them a little bit an' shook the bushes some. He saw instantly an' turned t' face me, snortin' an' shakin' his horns. The cows stopped their grazin' an' looked my way. I shook the bushes agin an' they turned an' trotted up the ridge, the bull pushin' them an' snortin'. I sat still an' presently some o' the cows began grazin' agin, ignorin' the bull's fussin'. Soon he grazed a few bites too an' it was time for me to show agin. I moved closer to the herd, not makin' much trouble t' hide myself, but not showin' much either since I didn't want to spook them too much.

In this way we moved up the ridge. In the exposed places, the wind hit us quartin' from the southwest. I had t' keep off on the east side of the herd so they wouldn't git my scent too much, an' this made them veer more to the left away from the head of Hartsug hollow. Somehow I had t' steer them right toward the hunters. I could see the elk crossin' a draw up ahead an' thought if it ran the right direction, I might be able t' git on the west side o' them 'thout spookin' 'em too much. Sure 'nough, the draw drained off to the west an' I crept into it.

By bending low, I could stay out of sight an' hopefully that bull wouldn't git too much of a snoot full o' my scent whin I passed upwind. Part of the way I crawled an' I heard the bull snort once, but I was afraid t' look from where I was. When I finally climbed out an' looked, the herd was movin' more toward Hartsug.

Presently, the ridge flattened out to a wide meadow on the mountaintop. I had considerable trouble figgerin' out whur those hunters was hid not seein' hide nor hair of them an' the herd was spreadin' out over the flat. I couldn't keep them bunched an' movin' without spookin' them, so I stopped an' studied the lay of the land.

Best I could tell, the hunters would be off near the head of Hartsug draw an' possibly on the opposite side o' the ridge where it was somewhat narrower than the big flat. As I watched, the cows that had wandered off to the north on the flat suddenly jerked their heads up lookin' to the north at the edge of the woods. Then they moved away, bunchin' up with the cows grazin' down the middle. I didn't know what spooked 'em, but it shore worked t' my advantage.

Now I could move them more towards where I thought the men might be. After they were movin' toward the right draw, I eased up an' let 'em graze. Herdin' had made them wary an' they spooked easy. Now, if they would jest relax an' graze, maybe the men would git good shots.

I found me a good low spot behind a bank an' laid down, my gun aimed at the herd. I wus through herdin' 'til I knew where those hunters wus an' they shore wasn't showin'. The wind seemed awful damp.

A little noise came frum b'hind me an' I caught sight of a patch o' buckskin movin' through the bushes. As I watched, the patch became a skirt an' Bluebird appeared. She shore could move quiet for a girl an' without a sound she eased up close b'side me — awful close. She must have been chilled, cause she was shiverin' an' pushed right up t' whur she wus touchin' my side head t' foot. It shore was warmin' to me, but I put my arm across her shoulders an' pulled her closer anyway — t' git her warm, yuh see.

Her smile made me weak as water inside. "Father and Mother are over there to the left under that forked walnut. Fishinghawk is straight ahead laying in the end of the Hartsug hollow, and Lonza went up a branch and should be a little to the right and ahead of us. Father sent me around to help bunch them up. We have the herd nearly surrounded and no one is directly upwind of them until they pass Lonza and catch his scent," she whispered, her lips brushin' my ear. I shivered an' she wiggled closer, if that wus possible.

We had the herd in a crossfire with the crown of the ridge above us an' if everyone stayed low, there wouldn't be any danger of gittin' hit. It wus awful hard keepin' my mind on the business at hand an' talkin' t' Bluebird. We got well acquainted an' I even took a chance an' kissed her cheek. She giggled almost out loud an' quickly caught herself.

Suddenly, the bull raised his head an' snorted loudly, pointin' t' where Lonza must be hidin'. There was a disturbance off t' my left by the forked walnut an' I knew Tenkiller had loosed an' arrow. The crack of a rifle an' billow of smoke showed me where Fishinghawk was. Even before he fired, the herd was on the move. Now they milled for a moment, then stampeded back along the ridge toward the flat — an' us. Lonza fired an' a cow tumbled head over heels. The herd was bunched an' headed straight for us, that big bull bellerin' an' slaverin' in the lead.

I stood up an' hollered an' he veered off, givin' me just enough time t' snap a shot at a yearlin' calf runnin' b'hind him. I could only git a breast shot, but it went home an' the calf stumbled a few feet an' fell. The herd thundered by not twenty feet from us. Bluebird had stayed laying on the ground, now she reached up an' untied my moccasin. When I stooped t' tie it, she touched my hand, then was gone, returning the way she came.

Heads were poppin' up around the ridge. The Tenkillers were already workin' over their kill. I reloaded then walked over to my kill an' slit its throat. It was a young bull, but maybe it was young an' tender enough t' eat without tastin' strong.

Suddenly I thought of Bluebird's tracks bein' on top of the retreatin' herd's an' of the ground where we had met. I didn't know what Isaac or Runnin' Quail would say about her bein' there so I jumped down the bank an' scuffed up the ground t' hide her sign. Lonza called an' motioned for me to come up, then he started walkin' toward where the Tenkillers were workin', an' Fishinghawk was there.

"It's for sure we aren't going to pick these carcasses up and haul them to camp," Fishinghawk was sayin' as I walked up.

"No, you are surely right about that," Tenkiller agreed. "Looks like we will both have to move camp."

"It will be a dry camp if we stay close to the meat," Lonza observed, lookin' around.

"It should only take three or four days to finish butchering these cows and curing the meat, then we can move back to the better camps," Isaac observed. "We have our meat sealed up in a cave and I think we probably will have enough with this elk to go home soon." He looked at Runnin' Quail an' she nodded agreement. Just then, Bluebird emerged from the woods and without a word began helping her mother. Runnin' Quail said somethin' to her I couldn't hear an' she glanced my way an' blushed.

Lonza turned to me. "Jerry, do you think you could get to camp and bring it back here by yourself?"

Of course I nodded, not wantin' to embarrass myself, but knowin' what a job that would be.

"You could cache the meat high in a tree and it would probably be safe. We will go back that way and pick it up on our way home," he added.

"Before you go, let's drag your kill and Fishinghawk's kill over close to mine so we can protect them better. We'll start butchering and may have most of that work done by the time you get back. Be sure to bring the other two axes with you," Lonza said as he turned and headed for my kill.

"Looks like you got a yearling, Harris," Fishinghawk remarked as we walked up.

"I was more interested in turning the herd than picking out the best meat," I replied, and he laughed.

"I can understand that well! He should be tender enough and make some good roasting for supper."

"Yes, and those ribs will be extra good if there is enough meat on them," Lonza added. "The whole herd looked to be in good shape," Isaac said as we tied the hind legs together and started dragging him. After a few steps, Lonza said, "He's so light, I think we may be able to carry him." Without hesitation, he hoisted the carcass to his shoulder and started.

It must have weighed more than a deer, but he shrugged off offers to help and carried him to his kill. Fishinghawk's kill was big an' fat an' there was no way to carry her even by tyin' the legs together an' polin' her. Fish insisted that we not drag the carcass an' risk marrin' the hide, so we left it there. He pointed to the bluff we were camped under an' showed me how to get there without goin' down the creek an' climbin' back up out of the hollow. As I started off, they were about skinnin' and cuttin' up Fish's kill. I heard Lonza say, "Makes me wish we had brought along a woman or two."

Bluebird an' her mother were busy strippin' the hide off their kill where it lay and I heard Isaac chopping down sapling poles in the woods for a dryin' rack. There sure was a lot of work to do settin' up a new camp an' butcherin' all that meat. I hurried on my way.

It was a lot easier goin' along the shoulder

of the hill, but there was still a steep climb up to the bluff. I worked most of the afternoon gettin' camp ready to move an' it was really late when I started out, the two mules loaded an' extra horses tied head to tail b'hind. I took half the time back it had taken me to go an' rode into camp just at last light.

The others had sure been busy in my absence. The fire was long an' narrow an' surrounded by dryin' racks. Firewood was stacked nearby an' they had made the camp as comfortable as possible out there on the open flat. It wasn't until I smelled the roastin' ribs that I realized I was so hungry. It sure didn't take long t' hobble an' turn out the horses an' git to the fire.

The Tenkillers could git to their camp without goin' down the holler too, but there were two deep hollers they would have to cross or go around t' git there, so they had decided to postpone the trip until I got back with the mules. Instead, they had worked all day makin' camp an' dryin' meat, plannin' to move camp on the morrow. As soon as I unloaded the packs, there was a kettle on the fire renderin' fat. My kill had been light enough t' hoist up in a tree an' butcher an' we used it for our camp meat. It sure tasted good. Bluebird brought me water she had gotten from somewhere.

"Where did you find such good water up here?" I asked.

"It was in the bladder of our elk when we opened it," she replied with a toss of her head. The others laughed.

"I'm glad you didn't serve me any salad," I shot back, thinkin' about the contents of their bowels.

She kicked my shin b'fore I could dodge, then quickly moved out of reach.

"It looks like you need to hone your manners up some, Jerry, or learn to move faster." Lonza laughed. I just grinned.

Suddenly, Tenkiller threw a stick of firewood into the gloom. There was a thump and a yelp. "The wolves are out after our meat early," he observed. "We will have to keep a sharp eye out tonight."

"If we tie the horses close, they can warn us when they come," Fishinghawk offered. Soon they were tied at four places around the camp an' we got ready for bed. I rifled through the packs an' pulled out one of my blankets. "Here, Bluebird," I said, "the weather's warm an' my horse won't need this tonight. I don't think he will mind you using it."

She frowned, then brightened, "Oh, I thought it was *your* blanket and I *surely* wouldn't want to use it, but since it's your horse's I suppose it will be clean enough." She took the blanket an' wrapped it 'round her shoulders.

I could see it would be hard gettin' one up on her. We set the watches an' loaned the Tenkillers more blankets. They slept on one side of the fire an' we were on the other. My watch came at midnight so I went right to bed. I fell to sleep to the music of wolves an' coyotes quarrelin' in the dark over what little bones an' offal we had discarded. Watch was gonna be busy tonight.

It seemed I had just fallen asleep when Lonza shook my shoulder for the midnight watch. "Keep your eyes open, they are sure persistent," he whispered. I rubbed my eyes an' streched my legs afore gittin' up. The fire looked good, but I put a few more sticks on for good measure anyway. One of the horses stamped an' moved around on his rope. Lookin' over, I caught a glow from an' eye sneakin' around the outside of the circle. He wasn't payin' too much attention where he was goin' an' got too close to the heels of one of the mules. There was a thump, a grunt and the sound of a body hitting the ground several feet b'hind the mule an' another critter learned about the dynamite in a mule's hind feet. I grinned.

Stickin' Lonza's pistol in my waist, I wrapped my blanket around my shoulders an' circled around the outside of the camp. With snarls an' low growls, the scavengers moved ahead of me as I walked. Soon one of them got brave across the camp an' got too near. I cut across an' tossed a stick at him, missin', but close enough t' give him the message. This activity kept up for two hours or more, then with a low growl comin' from another animal, the wolves suddenly disappeared from the circle.

At first I thought the new creature might be a bear, but then I heard a kind of purring sound an' knew *that* wasn't so. It came from a cat an' not the kind you pet an' give milk. The best I could tell, it came from the opposite side of the fire from me an' the actions of the horses confirmed that, even the mule on that side was near panic.

Pullin' my pistol out, I ran around the fire an' racks to the other side of the camp. Tenkiller had jumped up an' was gatherin' up his gun. As I passed, I glimpsed Running Quail an' Bluebird sitting up. I tried t' calm the horses but they had the scent of the cat an' just then it screamed not fifteen feet away! My hair stood on end an' the horse went wild tryin' to break free. A faint gleam on a fawn coat showed me where the cat wus, an' holdin' on to the bridle with one hand, I fired at him blindly, missin' but the noise o' the shot was enough to make him think o' huntin' somewheres else.

It took a few minutes t' git the horses calmed down enough to realize the cat was gone. Still, they were awful skittish an' the rest o' the night they paid close attention to the slightest sound. When I looked around, everyone was up calmin' a horse, even the wimmin. At last, they were quiet an' all started back to their bedrolls.

"Next time you go cat hunting, take your bow, Jerry, they don't make as much noise and wake up the whole camp," Lonza called in jest as he pulled the blanket over his head.

"You would get more meat with a long gun instead of that pistol," Fishinghawk grunted.

It seemed the wolves came back more numerous an' more determined than b'fore. I was on the move constantly circlin' the camp an' throwin' chunks an' rocks at those scoundrels. It shore made me wish I had brought Sippie along. It wasn't until I saw Tenkiller up stokin' the fire that I knowed my watch was up.

"I don't think one man can keep them off," I said to him. "I'll take one side and if you take the other and maybe we can keep them away 'til sunup."

He didn't reply, but took up his gun an' started patrolin'. I went in the opposite direction an' began chunkin' rocks at ever critter I saw or heard. It seemed forever b'fore the sky began t' lighten. My tail wus draggin', I can tell you. Wolves began creepin' away, the lighter it got, but there were still one or two skulkin around whin the sun was full up. I felt like shootin' 'em but for the waste of good powder. It was a purty quiet breakfast after a night of poor rest. I drank about a gallon of strong hot coffee b'fore I finally got my eyes opened.

"We should have these carcasses stripped today, then we'll get rid of those pests for tonight," Isaac said.

"Won't be too soon for me," I mumbled, which made everyone smile.

"Let's see if we can track that cat, Jerry," Fishinghawk said. "Maybe we can keep him from coming around again." He rose an' reached his bow an' quivver an' I wasted no time gittin' my gear t'gether.

"Check your load, we don't want any misfires if we see him," Fishinghawk warned. He moved out about fifty feet from the camp an' started makin' a circle around the camp. "Looks like he's heading north," he called as he moved off. I hurried after him.

I learned a lot about trackin' that day and we spent the whole day at it. That cat did head north, then northeast, then around to the south on the east side of Red Hill. We lost the trail crossin' some rock outcropping an' it was quite a while b'fore we picked it back up.

He was headed west toward the bluff — either to den up or to lose his trail on the rocks there. Suddenly I realized we were about even with our old camp an' the cached things there.

"He's headed for our camp, Fishinghawk," I whispered.

"Looks like it, you put that meat up good and high, I hope."

"I did, but I don't think that's gonna hold up Mr. Cat much," I replied.

"Let's go see." Fish dropped the trail and headed straight for the bluff, me b'hind.

We came out on the edge of the bluff a few hundred feet north of the camp and walked quietly along the edge on solid rock an' pine needles. A soft growl brought us up an' Fishinghawk dropped to his knees. Slowly we crawled to the edge of the bluff an' looked over. We were still several feet north of the camp, but could make it out through the branches. The tree I had put our meat in stood away from the bluff a good distance an' I was very surprised to see the ground torn up all around it. Bark was skinned off'n it a good four or five feet above the ground, prob'ly enough so that it would die. A movement in the brush showed up a big gray wolf an' as I looked, there were several more layin' around.

Fish nudged me an' nodded toward the tree. There, layin' along the limb where I had stashed the meat was the cat. He had jumped from the bluff to a big tree, then through the treetops to the cached meat an' was quietly enjoyin' a meal of jerky.

"Do you think you can hit him through the limbs?" Fish asked.

"It would be a lucky shot if I could, but I can try," I replied.

"Go ahead, even if you miss, you might scare him away and save the meat."

Slowly I raised the rifle an' took careful aim at the only clear patch of hide I could see. It probably wouldn't be a killin' shot, but we had to act quick. Squeezin' the trigger slowly, I jumped in surprise when the gun went off. In spite of my care, the bullit clipped several twigs an' deflected away from the cat. Even so the sound gave him a scare an' with one leap he was on the ground runnin'. In the same instant all the wolves melted away.

"Too bad," Fish grunted. "Let's see what we can salvage out of that meat."

It was some distance around to the place where we could climb down the bluff, so I took the route the cat had taken, jumpin' into the tree closest to the bluff, but I couldn't go through the treetops like he had, so I slid down to the ground. I had stood on a mule's back t' reach the lowest limbs of the cache tree an' the way the trunk was torn up I knew I would never shinney up it. Lookin' around, I found a sapling pole long enough to reach the lowest limb. Leaning it against the crotch of the trunk, I began shinneyin' up it. About halfway up, it slipped an' the rotten top broke. I landed on my feet, an' threw the useless pole away. When Fish came up, we used his ax t' cut a better pole an' left stubs of the limbs on it to use for steps. It didn't take long t' git up the tree an' toss the cache down.

We had interrupted the cat's meal b'fore he got started good an' most of the meat was untouched. Dividin' the packs up, we both loaded down an' headed for the flat. The first leg was downhill an' we made it okay, but it was plain to us that we would not make the climb back up to the flat with these loads. Luckily, we met Lonza with one of the mules comin' to see what the shootin' was about an' we loaded everything on the mule.

The Tenkillers an' Lonza had been busy in our absence. They had taken the elk entrails down to the creek an' turning them inside out an' washin' them had made casings then filled them with the meat that was dried, tyin' knots between portions. I always liked meat preserved in this fashion. We would hang long strings of it above the fireplace an' when we ate it, it would have the best smoked flavor you could ever want. Later on, we built a smokehouse an' smoked hams an' jerky over hickory fires 'til they were preserved. Nothin' tastes better in my book. I enjoyed eatin' the fried casings. They were best when filled with pork sausage.

They had moved the meat on the outer sides closer to the dryin' fire an' it would be ready in another day. All four hides had been stretched on the ground an' mostly scraped.

"Now before it gets too dark, we're going to see that the wolves and cats won't bother our sleep tonight," Isaac said. "Mount up, Jerry, and tie this rope to the horn." Tyin' the other end to the biggest carcass, he trotted off up the flat. "Follow me."

444

We rode nearly a mile b'fore he stopped under a lone pine. "Toss your rope over that limb and we'll hoist that carcass up a little so it won't be too easy for them to get," he directed.

We tied the rope off on the trunk well out of reach and headed back to camp. "Now, let's see if we can get a good night's sleep," Isaac said, wiping his hands on the grass. The wimmin had cracked the legbones an' boiled the marrows out for a stew. It shore tasted good an' I had a big share of it b'fore retirin' for the night.

I can say right here that we *did* sleep better that night, though there were still some scamps hangin' 'round an' we still had to run 'em off. My watch was late an' purty quiet. Most of the time I sat at the end o' the fire, back a ways so my eyes were used t' the dark an' I could see if anything was creepin' up on us. Bluebird was sleepin' by her mother an' by an' by I saw her rise an' disappear into the dark. I had to chase a wolf away from our packs an' whin I returned t' my blanket, she was sittin' there. "I couldn't sleep," she said with a coy smile.

"I'll bet, after all that sleep you got last night," I said with a chuckle. When I sat down, she moved over against me an' wrapped her blanket around both of us. It was nice just sittin' there smellin' her fragrance an' feelin' her warmth agin me. We didn't talk much an' I might have been distracted from my duty a little.

Toward the end of my watch, she said, "I have to go before they miss me. We leave tomorrow, will you come and see me soon?"

"Shure will," I replied. She stood t' go, then suddenly stooped an' kissed me on the cheek. "There's more of those waiting for you at my house." And she was gone. I watched until she was back in her place, then made a circle of the camp just b'fore Lonza's watch.

Next mornin' was a busy one, packin the rest o' the meat an' gittin' ready t' move. We gave the Tenkillers half of the fat an' meat an' the hide from my yearlin' t' go with their hide. By noon, they were packed an' ready t' leave. I rode with them as far as the lone pine t' retrieve the rope. Bluebird teased me into lettin' her ride a ways. She shore cut a good figure on a horse.

All that was left o' that carcass was the bone the rope was tied to an' it had a lot of teeth marks on it. I marveled at how high a wolf could jump to reach it.

"Oh, they can't jump that high, one of them probably stood on the back of another to reach up there," Isaac chuckled.

Th' ground was tore up good all under the tree. There were tufts of hair an' a little blood here an' there where a controversy had arisen but there wasn't a bone to be seen. It was a clean sweep.

Bluebird rode up to the tree an' retrieved the rope. She coiled it up leavin' the bone on it an' tied it to the saddle. "There, you have your rope back and something for your dinner." She laughed, swinging a shapely leg over the saddle an' hoppin' down so close to me she fell against me an' I fell backwards with her on top.

"That wasn't an accident!" I was shore flustered. Isaac an' Runnin' Quail were laughing.

"Oh yes it was." She sat up on my stomach an' bounced a little. I grunted then rolled out from under her an' she sat hard on the ground.

"Ouch! I'll get you for that, Jerryharris!"

"You already have," I shot back. My face felt hot and Isaac and Runnin' Quail were still laughin' at us.

"We have had a good hunt, Jerry, and I have enjoyed hunting with you," Tenkiller said, slappin' my back. "You really should come to see us at the forks soon. I think we will see you later this winter when we come to visit Running Quail's family."

"We would be glad to see you there," I replied, "maybe we could get a winter hunt in then."

"We must get on, there is much to do and we will leave for home tomorrow. I may have to make two trips to get all our provisions home as it is." Without another word, he turned and led his packhorse down the ridge.

"Goodbye, Jerry," Runnin' Quail called back over her shoulder.

"Yes, goodbye Jerryharris," Bluebird said, bumpin' against me with her shoulder as she moved off. "I will find a way to even the score when I see you next."

"It's me that owe you something," I called. I watched them go a moment. She turned and waved just b'fore disappearing into the woods.

I mounted an' rode quickly back to camp. Lonza an' Fishinghawk had packed the two mules an' were workin' on loadin' more onto one of the horses, who was objectin' t' the whole process.

"Good, you're back," Lonza said, releasing the horse. "Unsaddle and we will load that horse with these packs, he is used to it and won't give us trouble."

The camp was cleaned up in a hurry an' I pulled the two carcasses out of camp, retrieved the other rope an' met them just as they were starting down the hill toward the bluff camp. That night, the Tenkillers' fire flickered through the trees an' we knew they had gotten back okay.

We spent the night there an' while we slept, a strong wind from the northwest blew in clouds spittin' snow. It was extra cold under that bluff with the wind hittin' it an' swirlin' down on us an' it didn't take long for us t' pack an' git under way. Out on the ridge, the wind was stronger an' it kept gittin' colder. We kept to the trees for shelter an' follered the ridge between Pee Dee and Weaver Creek until it dipped into the valley and we hit the trail b'tween Middle Fork Village and the Village at the Forks. I've always wondered how a creek in Arkansas got named after the rivers an' Pee Dee Injuns in South Carolina. It was a relief t' git down into the valley.

We pushed on without stoppin' for the noonin', hopin' to get home quicker. The snow got heavier an' began t' build up on the ground. It was dry an' blowin' so much it was sometimes hard t' see the trail. We got over the last pass b'fore dark an' discussed travelin' on down the mountainside in the dark, but decided agin it for fear of fallin' off the bluff. This portion of the trail followed an' old animal track that meandered around the mountainside with hairpin turns an' icy rock ledges on top of the bluffs.

We couldn't chance losin' a horse an' the provisions just for our own comfort, so we found a notch in the bluff an' made dry camp with no fire. The horses was restless all night an' we didn't git much rest ourselves watchin' them an' tryin' t' keep from freezin' t' death. They seemed t' appreciate the warmth of the packs when we loaded them an' started out in the gray light.

The wind had laid an' it was snowin' in earnest, big wet flakes that made a swishin' noise as they fell. We walked an' led the horses. Footing was good where the snow had built up over the icy solid rock trail but we still had to go careful an' slow. On some o' the downhill slopes, the horses almost sat down on their haunches as they slid. What little uphill runs we made were hard an' slippery. It was mid afternoon b'fore we hit the river bottoms. We had spent the whole day goin' no more than five miles down the mountainside.

Jesse an' Riley ran yellin' t' meet us when we came in sight, neither one wearin' more than shirt an' moccasins.

"Pa, Pa, Big Sam's here, Big Sam's here!"

Riley yelled as he ran.

We set them up on the horses an' they rode chatterin' to the house. The wimmin turned out t' meet us an' help with the packs. By the time we had the horses unsaddled an' fed in the corral, they had unpacked an' stored the meats. A big pot of venison stew was bubblin' on the fire an' the smell an' warmth of the house was mighty welcome.

"That was the only time Uncle Jerry hunted elk in what later became Arkansas," Zenas said at the end of his tale. "With Osage and Cherokee, Delaware, Kickapoo and a half dozen other tribes huntin' the Ozarks and disputin' with one another over the huntin' rights, the elk herds was decimated and run out. He had other encounters with the Tenkillers and the Village at the Forks I'll tell you about later, but next time we meet I will tell you Grandma Ruth's story about her life on the Middle Fork of the Little Red."

I made arrangements to meet with him the next week, said my goodbyes to Mrs. Meeker, and headed down the mountain toward the shining sands.

This is book one of four recounting the story of Zenas Meeker's family's migration west. Book II introduces Samuel Meeker and some of his adventures. Jerry spends time with the Osage, goes on his first buffalo hunt and rescues Sarah Kansas in a blizzard. We get a first-hand account of the Battle at Half Moon Mountain and Jerry and Kansas catch wild horses on the prairie.

ABOUT THE AUTHOR

Jim Crownover grew up in the woods and on the streams of Central Arkansas where much of this story takes place. He spent many hours walking fields picking up arrowheads and other artifacts possibly left by some of his ancestors. He has a keen interest in history, especially that of the west and southwest. Early, he became interested in the everyday activities of the pioneers and explorers and the oral histories of the day. This has led him to concentrate his attention in this book on the "minute historical accuracies . . . entirely devoid of importance" to historians such as Bernard DeVoto, but full of the drama of life of the time.

He resides in the small community of Elm Springs in Northwest Arkansas.

The employees of Thorndike Press hope you have enjoyed this Large Print book. All our Thorndike, Wheeler, and Kennebec Large Print titles are designed for easy reading, and all our books are made to last. Other Thorndike Press Large Print books are available at your library, through selected bookstores, or directly from us.

For information about titles, please call:
(800) 223-1244

or visit our Web site at:
http://gale.cengage.com/thorndike

To share your comments, please write:
Publisher
Thorndike Press
10 Water St., Suite 310
Waterville, ME 04901

2